Me Falling

A Cosmic Shores Novel

G. S. Jennsen

HYPERNOVA
PUBLISHING
2023

MEDUSA FALLING

Cover design by MetroShock.
Cover typography by G. S. Jennsen.

Hypernova Publishing
P.O. Box 1467
Libby, Montana 59923
www.hypernovapublishing.com

Publisher's Note: This is a work of fiction. Names, characters, places, and incidents are a product of the author's imagination. Locales and public names are sometimes used for atmospheric purposes. Any resemblance to actual people, living or dead, or to businesses, companies, events, institutions, or locales is completely coincidental.

The Hypernova Publishing name, colophon and logo are trademarks of Hypernova Publishing.

Ordering Information:
Hypernova Publishing books may be purchased for educational, business or sales promotional use. For details, contact the "Special Markets Department" at the address above.

Medusa Falling / G. S. Jennsen.—1st ed.

LCCN 2023911136
978-1-957352-18-3

CONTENTS

MEDUSA
FALLING

AN INCIDENCE
OF
MURDER

1

PLANET: BELARRIA
HOMEWORLD OF THE BELASCOCIANS

Blood the color of primroses at dawn pearled along the gleaming ebony metal of a hooked dagger. It lay askance upon a plush caramel rug, as if it had been carelessly tossed aside by its wielder.

The introductory speech she'd prepared ran on autopilot in her mind. *Good evening, Consul Thorkan. I'm Assistant Ambassador Marlee Marano of the Concord Consulate. It's an honor to set foot on the Belascocian homeworld, and to make your acquaintance.*

Her counterpart in the scheduled meeting had no response, however, for he was currently lying on said rug amid an expanding pool of blood.

Another Belascocian knelt on the floor beside him, cradling the consul's head and shoulders in their arms. The alien had been saying something when she entered the room. Her eVi replayed it in her mind, and the translator offered up a chilling interpretation: *Why did you make me do this, ahaide?*

Marlee struggled to absorb the unexpected and duly shocking scene in the 1.2 seconds it took for the alien to register her presence. Their gaze darted up to her, their wide, teardrop eyes shimmering seas of fuchsia and indigo. A ripple swept through their lamina-covered skin, and suddenly they were in motion.

So was she. She spun and dove for the wormhole that remained open behind her. On the other side of it, the safety of the Consulate awaited. Cool, crisp air displaced the warm humidity of the Belascocian embassy as her upper body breached the dimensional tear—

Something wrapped around her ankle and yanked her foot out from under her. She twisted sideways an instant before her chin bounced off the floor, kicking and flailing at her attacker as their prehensile tail dragged her closer to them. When long fingers snatched at her suit jacket, she cocked her leg and snapped it out with all her strength. The heel of her dress shoe connected with her attacker's flattened, slitted nose. They jerked away, hissing.

She clambered backward toward the wormhole in the brief pause, but the damnable tail had slithered endlessly around her ankle until there was no wiggling out of its grip.

Curse her lack of a weapon! Consulate etiquette for official diplomatic meetings forbid it—her eyes fell on the bloodied dagger lying off to her left.

Her attacker remembered it in the same instant. They both scrambled across the ornate rug toward the blade and each other. Damn but the Belascocian was fast. She'd started off closer, and her fingertips brushed over the dagger's hilt before the tail yanked her out of its reach.

The attacker's hand closed on the hilt, and they grabbed her by the hair and tugged her head up. The dagger pressed against her neck, its hooked end scraping menacingly along her throat. "What are you? Why are you here?"

The fact that they didn't kill her immediately was a promising development, considering the particulars of the situation. "Human. I'm a representative of the Concord Consulate, and I had a diplomatic meeting scheduled with the man you murdered."

"Don't pretend you understand what happened here. *Izorra!* What am I to do with you?"

She cautiously gestured at the shimmering oval cut into the fabric of spacetime across the room. "Just let me walk back through the wormhole and go home."

"So you can relay everything you think you saw here to the government, and they can send a full score of Kaldi to corner me like an arrato? No. I can't risk it." A long string of what sounded like curses purred out of their narrow lips. "You're coming with me. We must move, now."

"Wait!" Adrenaline coursed through her veins, driving her to *fightfightfight*. Cybernetic subroutines primed her every muscle for maximum efficiency. Still, she worked to keep her voice calm. "I'll give you a ten-minute head start before I report what happened. Please let me go."

"Everything will—no. That can't happen. You must not—you will accompany me."

'Accompany' was far too kind a translation to describe what she expected her kidnapping would involve, and she had zero desire to find out how accurate her imaginings might be.

Her elbow swung up to smash into the attacker's arm, dislodging the blade a touch. Enough. She slammed her head into their skull, *ouch*, and wrenched away to leap to her feet and surge toward the wormhole again.

But without a weapon to slice through the tail that still had her in its clutches, there was no escape. A blunt force impacted her back between her shoulder blades and sent her stumbling. She tripped over the lifeless arm of the body on the floor and crashed hard into the wall; her cheek stung hot where it smacked into cold marble. Hands dragged her along the wall toward a large rectangular station. A glass enclosure sat atop a matte black base; within the glass, two rows of elongated crystals lined the top and bottom.

When they were within reach of it, the attacker's body pressed against her back, holding her flush to the wall with shocking strength. One hand returned the dagger to her throat, while the other fanned fingertips onto a pad in front of the glass.

An alkaline-like material squirted up out of a receptacle in the bottom of the enclosure and writhed in the space between the crystals. In a few seconds, it had solidified into a muted-gray, flat cord of some kind, and her attacker hurriedly retrieved the cord.

In desperation, she risked the sting of the dagger and struggled anew to escape their grasp—

They flipped her around, wrangled one of her arms and snapped the cord hard against it. The material bound itself around her wrist as firmly as the tail gripped her ankle.

She pulled her other arm away, fighting with the zeal of a crazed animal against their attempts to grab hold of it. The dagger nicked her throat, and the sharp jab of pain distracted her for a split-second—long enough for her attacker to snap the other end of the material around her other wrist.

Just like that, she was in manacles.

"We move. Now."

The attacker—honestly, 'murderer' was a more apropos identifier—dragged her through a sliding door cut discreetly into the curving wall of Consul Thorkan's office and plunged them into a winding hallway. The walls arched into the ceiling in a smooth adobe texture akin to hard-baked sand. The floor was no longer the elaborate marble of the consul's office, but rather a rubbery material that absorbed the sound of their hurried, tumultuous footsteps.

How did this criminal know about the passage? Did they work here? Was this some sort of bizarre act of betrayal orchestrated from within the agency, or a personal act of vengeance? What maze of underworld intrigue had she stumbled into?

Focus, Marlee. Focus on staying alive, followed by escaping.

As they plowed through an intersection, she considered screaming, but there was the troublesome dagger in proximity to her jugular complicating the matter. She gave more fulsome consideration to messaging the Consulate to alert them of her peril. They would mount a full-scale rescue operation within minutes. But Concord's lack of deep knowledge about Belascocian...well, anything, meant such an operation would be a risky, messy endeavor. Other than the person holding her captive, Concord didn't know friend from foe. Perhaps the entire Belascocian government was a foe, and this meeting was a ruse on their part to try to…what? None of this made any sense.

Best case, if a bunch of Marines came barreling into the building to save her skin, this diplomatic overture on Concord's part would be wrecked before it had begun. It was her job to pursue positive, peaceful relations between Concord and the Belascocians, not cause an intergalactic scandal!

She couldn't study her kidnapper—truly, the descriptives were many, none of them flattering—as they were mostly behind her, propelling her onward, so she called up the visuals her enhanced virtual interface—eVi—had automatically captured and processed while she fought for her life. Their face was angular, with a chin drawing to a dramatic point. Coupled with the fact that she hadn't noticed any indication of a stomach pouch when they'd leapt around attacking her in those chaotic first seconds, she felt comfortable assuming this was a male Belascocian.

Her musings had distracted her from their course, and abruptly she was being herded into an opening in the wall and onto a circular pad. The next second they were plummeting down a shaft. Her stomach jolted up into her throat, and she had to check to confirm there remained a surface beneath their feet. Okay. So despite its dramatic nature, it was just a lift.

Her kidnapper muttered a fresh string of epithets; they slurred together too much for her translator or her ears to make sense of them, but the meanings were obvious enough.

Their death-defying plummet jerked to an unceremonious halt, and Marlee found her face once again smushed into the wall while her kidnapper peeked into the fresh hallway that waited.

"Bashi!"

The force of his hand at her skull abruptly lessened, and she shifted around in time to see him remove a weapon from a holster hidden in the folds of his pants then aim it out of the lift's alcove.

A *pop-pop-pop-pop* sounded, and in its wake they were fleeing the alcove.

She glanced behind them and caught a glimpse of a Belascocian staggering into a wall, multiple blooms of primrose spreading across their shirt.

Murderer, indeed.

Alarms began pealing through the air. She made a calculated stumble to slow them down. Now that security was in the game, her odds of rescue must be improving by some margin.

"Faster," the alien spat furiously under his breath.

"I can't run properly with you dragging me along with your fucking tail." She did not whisper.

"Quiet!"

"No."

"*Bashi de arima.*" The sound of light but hurried footsteps echoed behind them, and he hurtled her toward the door at the end of the hallway before spinning and raising his weapon. She got a better look at it now—a handgun with a wide, flattened metal body and two orb-shaped chambers.

Two Belascocians appeared from the left into an intersection just past the lift. They wielded handguns of a different make, with a single, large circular barrel.

Light flared, and her ocular implant rushed to filter away an overload of infrared radiation. Heat scalded her right arm where it wasn't shielded by her kidnapper's body. A force field surrounding him, invisible until now, rippled under an onslaught of whatever the other Belascocians were firing.

Pop-pop-pop-pop.

This time she enjoyed a clear view of the devastating effects of his weapon. Two clusters of projectiles impacted the chests of the security officers. Tiny hooks shot out from the projectiles to latch into their clothing then...spun up, shredding the skin as they burrowed into it. Barbaric.

Then the door was sliding open behind her and she was shoved out of it and into the humid, wet nighttime air of the capital city of Ausatan.

Rain drifted around them in a fine mist, the droplets so small they seemed to hang suspended in the air, daring gravity to claim them. Marlee's skin, clothes and hair were instantly damp.

They'd exited onto a sidewalk of clay hexagonal tiles bordering a city street. Small vehicles sped along it, elevated half a meter off a surface so smooth it resembled smoked glass. Pedestrians moved purposefully to and from intersecting streets in both directions.

Her kidnapper yanked her close to him. The dagger returned to her neck, and his breath was surprisingly cool at her ear. "If you try to run—if you try to attract any attention at all—I will kill you. Keep your head down. We'll stick to the shadows as much as possible to avoid surveillance cams. Do you understand?"

She didn't dare nod against the blade. After due consideration, she swallowed a dozen angry or snarky retorts and replied with a simple, "I do."

The blade lowered, and the vice-grip on her ankle vanished as the tail unwound. His hand, however, closed over her manacled right wrist. "Come with me."

With that, he set off, dragging her along with him into the cross-street.

The absence of the dagger gave her scant comfort, for she'd witnessed what violence his handgun could inflict. Would he shoot her in the back on a busy city street? What were the odds her defense shield would hold in the face of such a brutal munition? Did she dare find out?

Not until she had a solid escape plan.

They turned left at the intersection onto a much busier sidewalk. The mist hung like a fog, and the lights of the buildings on either side struggled to penetrate it more than a few meters. She tilted her chin down and slightly toward him. If passersby started shouting and pointing at her unusual appearance, he might panic, kill her and run for it.

"Where are you taking me?"

"I'm not letting you out of my sight until I determine what to do with you."

Not an answer. "Look." She stumbled as he abruptly swerved into a narrow alley to the right; curse her stupid dress heels! If she wore a pair of proper boots, she might actually be able to outrun him. Probably not, but maybe. "I don't know your name. I don't know what counts as distinguishing characteristics of Belascocians, so I'm certain to give the authorities a terrible description of you. Basically, all I can say is, 'I saw a male Belascocian of tallish Belascocian height and sort of blue-hued skin holding a dead Consul Thorkan in his arms.'"

A male Belascocian standing approximately one-hundred-sixty-eight centimeters in height, with indigo skin that turns scarlet when it catches the light. Matching eyes of indigo and fuchsia—not the plain, dark colors one usually finds. Long hair threads the color of flint, with disconcertingly sharp tips. Sentsores shorter on one side of his mouth than the other and ending bluntly on the shorter side, as if they'd been chopped off. A white marking on the left cheek showing three interlocking circles with a starburst at their center. Black pants of multiple layers hiding many pockets, and a charcoal vest wound through with silver filaments.

But she didn't voice those details. Let him think her a naive alien, ignorant about his species. "So I'm no threat to you. You're safe letting me go now."

" 'Safe'? None of us are safe. You think the Errigime will simply let you go home after what you've seen? After you've spent time in proximity to me?"

She'd seen a murder, or at least its immediate aftermath—then three more murders. She'd seen his use of a gruesome weapon that should be illegal. Also a secret hallway in a government building that meant nothing to her. "I don't intend on asking the permission of the 'Errigime,' whatever the hell it is. And I doubt your authorities believe your criminal mind and violent tendencies are going to infect me because we spent a few delightful minutes together."

"Your tongue is sharp, but you understand nothing."

"My point exactly. So let me go home."

Another turn deposited them in an even darker, more foreboding alley. She silently instructed the tiny Caeles Prism on her wrist to begin spinning up power. In her mind, she sifted through her options then picked the optimal location: the middle of security clearance at the primary docking wing of Concord HQ. Her kidnapper wouldn't dare murder her in full view of hundreds of people. Guards would promptly arrest him, and his return to Belascocian authorities could be negotiated between civilized officials. And if, against all sanity, he *did* shoot her in the back, she'd be seconds from the finest in medical care. If that failed, she'd die in her own world, where she'd undergo regenesis and reawaken in a new body. Not her preference, but it beat dying on an alien sidewalk forty megaparsecs from home.

She waited until they had regained a vigorous pace, as she couldn't leave enough time for him to divert their course.

When they were all-but-jogging toward a fog-laden street ahead, she sent the command to open a wormhole two meters in front of them and ran, now dragging him along behind her.

"Madari!" He lurched to the side in the alley, crashing into the nearest wall and yanking her with him. She scrambled to her knees and lunged for the opening that was but centimeters away—only to be forced hard into the ground by his full weight. Through the wormhole, multiple people started in surprise before taking several tentative steps toward the opening. Someone shouted for security.

"Shut it down." The dagger pressed harder against her neck, its tip digging into the delicate skin of her throat.

Dammit, she didn't want to get more innocent people killed. Or die herself. But freedom was *right there!* She drove an elbow into her kidnapper's torso and twisted her arm around in a move designed to pop her wrist out of his grip. She succeeded, but his hand closed over the rope connecting her manacles. Several strands of his hair honed into razored ends and darted at her face like Medusa's fucking snakes, slicing her cheek open in multiple places. The hell?

Then his gun was pointed at the open wormhole instead of her. "*Shut. It. Down.*"

Her brain glitched over the logistics involved. One of his hands held the dagger, and the other was all tangled up in her restraints. How...?

Holy shit, his tail wielded the gun. Could it press the trigger?

She didn't dare find out. A security officer approached the opening, his hand going to his own weapon, while bystanders crowded in behind him. This was shaping up to be a bloodbath.

She closed the wormhole, and misty darkness swept in to envelop them.

"Arima be merciful, you have surely killed us."

"Me?" She winced as he removed his knee from her spine and dragged her to her feet. "I think you've done far more to put us in danger than I could ever dream of."

"Ignorant bakara. How did you create it?" His tail tucked the gun into one of his omnipresent pockets. Agile appendage. Then he snatched her wrist and held it up to his face, studying the orb dangling from her bracelet as the golden aura faded from it. "Is this your tool?"

He was too observant by half. "No."

"I think it is." He enclosed the orb in his fist and yanked.

The gesture jerked her arm violently downward, but the chain connecting the orb to the bracelet didn't break. No amount of non-exotic force would cause the woven adiamene metal to do so.

He hissed at the orb, then let go of it to grab the rope between her restraints once more. "We have to move now. If you value your life, do not pull that kind of stunt again."

"Why did you say I've killed us?"

"Because they can *track* such emanations. Now move!"

Then he was hauling her forward once more. They slipped onto the street and danced along the edge of a crowd for a few meters, the mist and the shadows concealing from the pedestrians the fact that an alien walked among them, then quickly veered onto another side street.

Their pace again increased to a ragged jog; he really did act desperate, and desperate men were dangerous men. Another change of direction, back across a busy thoroughfare. A barrage of lights strobed out to struggle through the mist, and people strode defiantly against its lulling ministrations. A bridge rose ahead of them, a fog bank tickling at its ramparts.

"Halt!" The authoritative shout broke over the general din. Instinct caused her to peer behind them, but she couldn't discern the source of the order before her kidnapper took off at a full-out run.

The narrowest of alleys cut into a row of buildings, and he lunged into it—

White-hot heat seared across her lower back. She gasped and jerked to the side, instinctively trying to escape being burnt alive.

The heat resolved into a needle of agony as her defense shield failed; pain tore through her skin and ripped into vital places.

Her kidnapper flung her around behind him into the alley wall, his macabre handgun swinging up as he leaned out and fired. Shouts echoed and were swallowed up by the thick, moist air.

She blinked, an act that took a million years.

Again he was moving, and more shots *popped* into the night. Someone screamed.

She didn't see whether the volleys hit their marks; she didn't know who the targets were or even what they looked like. She noticed somewhat idly how she wasn't seeing much of anything, as her vision was blurring. Her eVi flashed warnings as cybernetics routines activated to rush resources to…it seemed she had a gaping wound in her abdomen. Well, that was never a good place to have one.…

She slid down the wall to land hard on the alley floor.

Sometime later, swirling pools of indigo and fuchsia stared at her from out of the mist. *"Madari.* You're injured. I've got to get you to a physician."

"No.…"

"You'll die if I don't, yes? I don't want any more deaths on my conscience this night."

But there were already so many. "No, mean…" her lips didn't want to form the proper syllables "…not a physician. An animal doctor."

"What? Are you mad?"

"Likely…but not the point." Pain overwhelmed the suppressors her cybernetics were pumping out, and a moan escaped her lips. "Physician knows only…Belascocians. Animal doctor knows many kinds of creatures. Different anatomies.…"

Her eyes closed. This time they refused to reopen, and a frigid darkness consumed her.

2

Owww. Her stomach hurt. What had she eaten? An alien dish of questionable origin? It wouldn't be the first time. Or was it….

Hazy memories struggled to the surface. The gleam of a bloody dagger in harsh interior light. A sprint across unfamiliar streets as the prisoner of an alien.

She'd been shot. It was the first time for that particular insult, though not the first time she'd had her internal organs scrambled by a weapon.

Keeping her eyes closed, Marlee prepared herself for what might await her when she signaled her return to the world of the conscious. The fact that she wasn't dead suggested her kidnapper had done as he'd threatened and sought medical aid for her. Awfully kind of him, vicious killer that he was. Curious, though; not the play she'd expected from him.

Under the circumstances, escape had to be her highest priority. But with no weapons to wield to protect herself, she was out of her depth here. She'd studied the Belascocian people for weeks in anticipation of her meeting with Consul Thorkan, but her information had been filtered through the bird's-eye view of fact-finding surveys, orbital surveillance scans and a few official communications. The view from the street, as it so often did, was proving to be altogether different. She spoke the language well enough and had an internal translator to fill in the gaps, but most people would get stuck on 'alien' and not immediately care that they could understand what the alien was saying.

She found herself in the company of a madman, for certain, but that might not be the worst of it. The murder she'd witnessed had clearly set off a manhunt for the culprit, and the authorities seemed willing to shoot first and ask questions later, as evidenced by the uncomfortable pain in her abdomen. It was possible her presence at the murder scene had cast suspicion in her direction. After all, a man was dead, and his meeting with her was on his calendar at the fateful time. Concord had behaved in only the most gentle, conciliatory and diplomatic fashion since initiating a dialogue, but first contact was always a touch-and-go affair. Though Belascocians were a sophisticated enough species, no one started off trusting entreaties from mysterious aliens wielding fantastical technology.

So it probably wasn't wise to seek protection from the first police officer she encountered.

As much as she hated to admit vulnerability and ask for help, it might be time to call in the cavalry. Salvaging the diplomatic situation here was likely beyond her capabilities at this point, at least from her current vantage. But she didn't want to set off an even bigger clusterfain and trigger active hostilities between Concord and the Belascocians. If she could escape on her own and return home, she could explain what had happened to her great-aunt, Commandant Solovy, and her boss, Dean Veshnael; they could then offer assistance to Belascocian authorities through official channels. If a special forces squad arrived here on Belarria to rescue her, though, events stood to spiral out of control in a violent and unpleasant way. The lessons imparted to her by Veshnael in the years she'd worked at the Consulate counseled to avoid such an outcome if at all possible. On the other hand, the lessons her uncle, Caleb, had drilled into her about the preciousness of her own life argued in favor of bringing in some guns to cover her six.

She decided to split the difference and assess the current state of her world first, then decide what course of action to take.

Marlee opened her eyes.

Soft light emanated in a beaded ring above her. The ceiling and walls were a drab beige and unadorned. She placed a hand on her hip and found a cushioned bandage with a webbed texture; the edges were tacky and melded to her skin. Her blouse, already torn to shreds by weapons fire, was cut away around the wound. On the upside, the restraints had been removed from her wrists while she was unconscious.

"You're awake."

The face of her kidnapper entered her field of vision from the left. His tone sounded neutral, but she didn't yet have enough of a bead on Belascocian mannerisms to judge his expression. The hooked dagger remained in his left hand, though it rested loosely at his side.

She pushed herself up to a sitting position and eased her legs over the side of the table. Several aches protested deep inside her abdomen, but nothing so acute as to prevent her from moving. "You treated me."

"Actually, Yethes here did. You can express your gratitude to him."

A second Belascocian male emerged from a doorway wearing a sage woven robe over sorrel skin. His step halted brief before he approached to study her. "Ah, yes. I, uh...forgive me, but you are my first alien patient. How are you feeling?"

"Sore, but...okay, I think. Thank you for helping me."

"I try never to turn away a creature in need—or a friend in a similar state, such as Galean presented when—"

"Don't tell her—" The kidnapper's long fingers flexed inward, sending light reflecting off the edge of the dagger.

Oh, fuck. Now she knew his name. He was never going to agree to let her go, was he?

Yethes dropped his narrow chin at a slight angle. "Did I do wrong?"

"Of course not." Her kidnapper—Galean—presented what Marlee recognized as the Belascocian version of a smile, lips widening across his face in a straight line, tugging at the split in the center, as his sentsores spread out in two fan shapes. "I am indebted to you, Yethes, friend of the Ozeal and the Tarazi, and this debt will be balanced."

"Of this I have no doubt. The honor of your odola is high."

The smile vanished. "All honor belongs to the Arbasoak, not to me."

"You sell yourself short, Galean."

"Don't speak of things your eyes are veiled from."

"As you say." Yethes shifted his attention to her. "I fear it would be too risky to send you away with medication, as your biological makeup is quite different from any life form on Belarria. You suffered significant damage to what I tentatively identified as a spleen and a liver analogue, but by the time I was able to look around inside, the damage was already healing itself. I noted the presence of extensive biosynthetic material—may I assume you have internal nanomachines tasked with nurturing your body?"

"I do."

"As I suspected. In that case, the nanomachines seem to have the situation well in hand, so I say your prognosis is good. Let me get you some additional bandages to take with you, and a bit of topical ointment." The man cast a sidelong glance at Galean as he departed the room.

Marlee sighed. Now that she knew her kidnapper's name, escape again vaulted to the top of the list as the only viable option. But she didn't want a repeat of the scene on the street, either, and it didn't appear he was going to let her out of his sight. She studied the floor below her dangling feet and reminded herself not to get stuck in simple directional thinking. She could open a wormhole beneath her feet as she shoved off the table and fall through it. Close it before this Galean had a chance to draw his fearsome handgun, and everyone back home was safe, including her.

She sent a command to begin spooling up power...and nothing happened. Her gaze darted to her wrist—her Caeles Prism was gone!

"Where is my bracelet?"

Galean rested against the wall, idly flipping the dagger hilt over edge in his hand. "I threw it away."

Panic overrode all diplomatic responses. "You *what?*"

"I said I disposed of it."

She willed herself calm. The nakedness of her wrist felt like a wound upon her soul, but now was not the time for hysteria. What argument stood a chance of convincing him of the extreme error of his action? "Do you have any idea what manner of technology is contained in that bracelet? If someone finds it and is able to make it work, it will disrupt the fabric of your society."

"Will someone be able to make it work?"

"I don't...I know little about what your people can do. I can't predict how it will react to them or what they'll be able to learn from it." His exclamation after she'd opened the wormhole echoed in her mind. *They can track such emanations.* Hell, if he meant quantum disruptions, she might be voicing a legitimate concern.

"Nonetheless, it's gone now. The risk is what it is."

"So you didn't throw it away here? At Yethes' place?"

"No. I disposed of it on the way."

Despair clawed at her thoughts. What now? She hated not being able to rescue herself; she always had. But she was going to have to comm in the cavalry, consequences be damned.

She readied an urgent message and sent it to her boss.

Belascocian Consul has been murdered, and I've been taken captive by his executioner. Am unable to evacuate via wormhole. Extraction from my location requested with due haste.

In her mind, she began preparing for the imminent incursion by a Marine squad. Though she usually enjoyed a good fight, at this point she was happy to play the innocent bystander and not get in the way when the shots started flying—

Error. Message unable to be delivered.

She worked to keep her expression blank as she tried to send a similar message to a coworker, then to her aunt. They all bounced.

Her eyes narrowed at Galean in accusation. "What have you done to me?"

"Whatever do you mean?" Another flip of the dagger.

"You're blocking some of my quantum capabilities."

"Am I?"

"Something is."

His tail swished languidly across the floor—the equivalent of a shrug.

She leapt off the exam table, ignoring the sudden sharp twinge in her abdomen, charged up to him and grabbed the upper arm whose hand held the dagger. His face drew close to hers in the challenge, but she stood her ground. "What did you *do* to me?"

His free hand rose between them until two fingers brushed lightly along the side of her neck, first on skin, then across…something else.

Her hand dropped from his arm to dart to her neck and found cool metal pressing flush against her skin. She felt around it…it was an oval shape, nearly three centimeters at its longest. She dug her fingernails under the edge and tried to pry it off.

Stabbing pain prickled her skin. "Fuck!" Undeterred, she tried again. The pain she could bear, but the plate simply would not budge.

"It's not coming off. You should stop inflicting agony on yourself."

"Why?"

"It has melded itself with your skin."

"I mean why did you put this on me!"

"You nearly killed us both with your portal stunt earlier. I can't risk you doing so a second time."

"How could me instantiating a wormhole possibly have…." She frowned. "You said they were able to track 'such emanations.' I admit our attackers, police or whoever they were, showed up rather fast. Are you saying they can track quantum activity some-how?"

"Is that difficult to imagine? Do you find us so provincial and backward?"

Yes. "No. But tracking changes in quantum fields requires highly advanced technology."

"Not for us. We have always sensed fluctuations in the quantum fabric. Even long before we developed the understanding to put a name to what we sensed. You do not?"

"Not natively. But why *this?*" She rapped a knuckle on the plate attached to her neck. "Detecting wormholes is one thing, as their creation requires a tremendous amount of power. But why prevent me from sending messages?"

"The principle is the same."

"No, it isn't. No one can detect quantum-entangled communication. That's kind of the point of it."

"As I said, we sense the fluctuations."

"From entanglement? Bullshit."

The sentsores around Galean's lips stiffened into rods. "You besmirch my honor so casually? I did not have to save your life."

Prickly murderer, wasn't he? "And I thank you for doing so. I…did not intend to insult you, merely to question the scientific basis behind your assertion. Look, it doesn't matter. Just take this thing off and let me go home."

"No. You know too much. You know my name."

Yeah, she'd figured that was going to be a problem. "I'll forget it."

"I don't think you will. Worse, you know Yethes' name. You'll bring a Kaldi squad down upon him for harboring a fugitive, when he is innocent of wrongdoing."

"I swear to you, I will not mention him, or any of this. I owe him my life and won't endanger his."

"Perhaps. But your words may be nothing more than sweet lies, for you will say anything to escape. I cannot sense you, thus I cannot trust you." He glanced toward the door. "You are mobile. We need to go. We have put Yethes in enough danger as it is."

She groaned in frustration. Without her bracelet, she couldn't get home. Without access to her eVi's messaging system, she couldn't comm for help. Her failure to return to the Consulate had surely been noted by now, and alarms had presumably been raised. But if this damnable metal plate was blocking all external quantum signals, then no one would be able to pinpoint her location. Concord had no formal relations with the Belascocian government yet, and its knowledge of the planet was limited to standard pre-contact evaluation scans. Finding her in order to rescue her was not going to be an easy task, even for Concord Intelligence.

Caleb could do it, if anyone could—as a former black-ops intelligence agent, he'd built a storied career out of finding people who didn't want to be found. But Caleb was beyond everyone's reach at the moment.

If she'd sucked up her pride and sent out a comm for help as soon as she'd been kidnapped, this would all be over now. But noooo, she'd insisted on proving she was capable of taking care of herself in the midst of even the most hazardous peril. Well, good job. Now she was trapped here, right and proper.

She shot her kidnapper a hot glare…but she had to admit, she was curious. About him, notably why he'd chosen to save her life, and about the story behind the spectacular crime she'd unwittingly waltzed into the middle of. The highest-ranking diplomatic official on Belarria had been murdered; horrifying as this was, it was also *interesting*. She'd give them this much—one evening in, the Belascocians were proving not to be dull.

"Can I ask where we're going?"

Galean went over to a table along the wall and retrieved a folded piece of gray fabric, then handed it to her. "Someplace safe…as safe as anywhere on this broken, fallen world can be."

3

They exited Yethes' place into a dark alley. Trash sat piled in a corner where the alley dead-ended, and an unusual odor made Marlee's nose wrinkle in distaste. All alien planets smelled peculiar, each in their own unique way. Thus far, when she'd randomly noticed, she'd found the odors of Belarria rather pleasant, but not this one. It occurred to her then that Yethes might not live in the nicest neighborhood.

How far were they from the scene of the shooting? It didn't feel like the same area. How had Galean gotten her here without drawing attention? Her interest in her captor was growing with every passing minute, which was a terrible inclination she should immediately quash.

She waved her hands in the air. "No handcuffs?" Wait, was she trying to provoke him into restraining her? Her injury had scrambled more than her liver.

"Lacking your quantum device, you will not escape."

"I can simply run."

"I will catch you."

It was true. Belascocians were capable of moving with remarkable speed for a bipedal species. It said so in the dossier, and she'd seen it firsthand. Galean had already bested her once, and she'd absorbed nothing from the experience that told her how she might beat him in a rematch. Not without a weapon.

"I can still make a scene."

"Unless you want more Kaldi to descend upon our location and fire with abandon in our direction, you will not. You will instead stay at my side at all times, one half-step back so you can follow my lead. If we encounter someone, you will stay silent; if necessary, I will explain away your silence. Do not entertain notions of appealing to a stranger for assistance. You will not receive it, and attempting such an appeal will only risk harm to them."

"Why? Will you hurt them? Kill them? Solely for seeing me?"

"Keep your hood pulled low over your face and your eyes averted. In the darkness, at a distance, hopefully no one will recognize you as alien. In all things, take your cues from me. If I say run, run. If I say hide, hide. If I say—"

"Do a little jig and stand on my hands, yes, I get it."

"Do your people frequently stand on their hands?"

"Only to confound other species."

His double eyelids blinked twice. "Then do not attempt any confounding, either."

She fiddled with the hooded cloak Galean had given her, drawing the fabric down over her forehead as instructed. Despite her outward bravado, she didn't want to provoke an incident, as it seemed apt to devolve into screaming and running and possibly stabbing and shooting. The Belascocians had never communicated with an alien species before, much less been visited by one. They searched the heavens for life, but Concord was the first to answer. Ergo, the average person on the street would not react calmly to seeing an alien up close and personal. Also, the disregard this 'Kaldi' had demonstrated for her safety or the safety of innocent bystanders during their previous encounter concerned her. She'd thought they were police, but what if instead she'd stumbled into some extrajudicial gang war, or worse?

"Why aren't you wearing a cloak as well? There's a manhunt on for you, I expect."

"The surveillance cams will not capture a clear image of me. Let's go." Galean strode toward the alley exit, motioning for her to follow.

She steeled herself for whatever waited around the corner and complied. "You aren't worried Yethes will turn you in?"

"He has helped us before. Also, he has no desire to bring the Kaldi to his door."

"Who's 'us'?"

"Quiet. Your voice risks drawing attention to us."

Attention from whom? The neighborhood wasn't exactly teeming with activity. As they crossed the first intersection, though, peculiar, off-tempo music wafted down the street, penetrating the mist and fog with a determined fervor. The melody dropped into abrupt silence at random intervals, and her brain automatically tried to fill in the missing notes. But they weren't missing; they simply fell in the infrasound range. An aural cybernetic function detected the notes and told her what they were, but she couldn't truly 'hear' them. For much the same reason, she'd installed a temporary larynx augment before traveling to Belarria to enable her to speak their language in full. She was finding it quite odd to voice syllables she could not hear.

Aside from the music, the neighborhood was far quieter than the crowded, overwhelming urban streets they'd fled across on leaving the State Affairs Building. To be fair, their initial sprint had mostly been a blur of panic and adrenaline and a constant battle of fight or flight waging itself within her. As such, she hadn't exactly had time to study the architecture or general vibe of the neighborhoods.

Nonetheless, this place felt different. It wasn't rural—buildings still abutted one another for entire blocks—but the structures were blander, sporting little ornamentation on muted façades that were more clay than marble. Shadows pushed in on the meager light at every opportunity. The sidewalks were deserted, and a pall seemed to hang in the air. Poverty, or fear? She couldn't fairly tell, but against the gloom, the music felt like an act of defiance.

The music turned out to originate from a space three blocks down from Yethes' clinic. She'd have called it a nightclub back home, but she wasn't certain the description fit. Through the open-air entrance, she made out three Belascocians playing instruments at the center of a three-quarters circle. The instruments were made of prismatic glass, full of whorls and holes, with glittering ribbons dangling off the ends that danced to the rhythm they emitted. The circle was comprised of perhaps a dozen Belascocians. Their bodies touched in so many intimate ways she was tempted to call it an orgy, though it didn't *look* sexual. Sensual, perhaps. Hands and tails and foreheads traded contact; hair strands wound together then spun apart—

Then they were past it, and she forced herself not to gape over her shoulder.

A maglev-powered conjoined set of vehicles raced by them on the road. At the next intersection, one car detached and took a left, and the rest continued on. She studied the mechanism of detachment, incorporating the knowledge into her meager understanding of Belascocian technology. At some point in the future, she was going to need to navigate these streets, or other streets similar to them, on her own, and her survival depended on her understanding how things worked.

Abruptly Galean turned left onto a side street. Ahead waited a lot full of vehicles. Not the detachable tram cars she'd just seen, but smaller units that resembled a cross between a small personal skycar and a covered levbike.

Galean strode up to a random vehicle and activated a panel on the side. Buttons with Scocian writing lit up, and he held a band encircling his wrist up to it. A door on each side slid open.

"Get in." He pointed to the other side of the vehicle.

She cast her gaze around the lot, but there wasn't a person in sight. Was he stealing it? Renting it? She highly doubted it belonged to him.

Where were they headed? She wasn't sure she cared for the idea of leaving the city. Despite his warnings, the city meant people who could potentially help her. Crowds she could hide in. Places she could seek shelter. Where they were going...she had no idea where they were going, or what fresh dangers it would hold.

She should have risked running, dammit. Back at the music club, she should have crashed the probably-not-an-orgy and pleaded for help. It would've been risky, but getting in this vehicle now struck her as infinitely more perilous. Intriguing, but perilous.

"I said get in."

"Do I have a choice?"

"Yes. But your other options are far worse."

She didn't believe him, but he did sound as if he believed it himself. "Yay." She sighed and climbed inside.

Anyone taller than her would find the interior cramped. The Belascocians were a petite species by humanesque standards, averaging around 155 centimeters in height; Galean was on the tall side for his people, which put him at eye-level with her. The inside consisted of two side-by-side seats, each one with a groove in the rear to accommodate a tail, and a small storage area behind them. A minimal dash was illuminated with a map, a menu and some indecipherable gauges. A control stick jutted out from the driver's side dash. All in all, not *so* different from a sky car, excepting its overall compactness. Manipulating controls with finger digits lent itself to a certain consistent design philosophy, no matter the species.

The doors slid closed, trapping her inside, and the interior suddenly felt much, much smaller.

Galean placed two fingers on the stick, and the vehicle lifted off the ground a few centimeters and backed out of its slot. Concord research had suggested the Belascocians used maglev technology for vehicles; the magnetics they'd assumed were embedded beneath the city streets appeared to extend throughout the urban grid.

In a few seconds, they were traveling along the nearest city street, and her attention drifted to the window. Outside, the buildings gradually grew more sparse. A minute went by without her catching sight of a pedestrian, then another.

The primary road split off to the left, and Galean veered right, onto a path that was barely more than leveled-out dirt.

Perhaps they'd been wrong about magnetics powering the vehicle's levitation.

Their speed increased markedly, and flora that started out tame but soon grew wild and overgrown flew by too rapidly for her to make out any details.

"You can relax now, for a time. Take a nap."

She arched an eyebrow. "Oh, can I?"

"If you wish. If we were being tracked, we would have been intercepted by now."

"Where are we going?"

"You should get some rest."

"I was unconscious for hours. I'm fine."

"It is your choice."

Damn straight, it was. She rested her head on the windshield and peered upward. They'd left the fog behind with the city, and now the gob smacking majesty of the Medusa Merger painted the night sky in a brilliant tapestry of raging starlight.

Concord had almost missed discovering the Belascocians. This was despite the fact that the Medusa Merger had long been a favorite research target of astronomers, with its double dose of cosmological activity. A violent collision of two small galaxies in the distant past sent arms full of stars flinging out in every direction until what remained was more a mare's nest of stellar activity than a proper galaxy. Its name came from how if you tilted your head just so and squinted one eye, the streams of stars and dust billowing out of one side resembled the writhing snakes atop Medusa's fabled head.

Far more interesting than the galaxy arms masquerading as snakes, however, was the Eye of Medusa, an enormous region of extreme, frenetic star formation surrounding the now solitary black hole at the center of the train wreck. The problem was, the Eye of Medusa was so loud across so much of the electromagnetic spectrum, it blocked most signals originating from behind it. When viewed from Concord territory, the Belascocian home-world was located four kiloparsecs beyond the dead center of the Eye, thus the region masked all evidence of an advanced civilization from their telescopes.

In the wake of their victory in the Rasu War, Concord and its member species began funding a vast expansion of their efforts to discover intelligent life across the Laniakea and Shapley super-clusters. The Rasu had very nearly wiped out over three trillion people belonging to twenty-two species spread across five thousand planets and sixty-two galaxies. That enemy was now gone, destroyed down to the last sliver of shapeshifting metal in a desperate act of genocidal self-preservation on Concord's part. But the universe was vast and untamed, and no one with any sense believed the Rasu were the last powerful enemy they would ever encounter.

They needed more allies. Good, stalwart allies with inventive technology and clever ideas on how to use it. After all, only by working together and utilizing each species' strengths—the nearly indestructible metal adiamene invented by humans, the Anadens' ability to literally resurrect the fallen using regenesis, the Asterions' skill in manipulating the data-transporting life form kyoseil, and the Katasketousya's ingenious dimension-bending rift bubbles—was Concord able to survive the Rasu onslaught and ultimately defeat them. The answer to defeating the next great enemy might well reside in the ingenuity of a species they hadn't yet met, so they'd set out to find and befriend as many species as possible.

And when a research mission had swung out around the Medusa Merger to catalogue a galaxy cluster some fifty megaparsecs from Concord HQ, the dulcet tones of an advanced civilization had broken through the noise.

The Belascocians were categorized as 0.8 on the Kardashev Scale. They'd escaped their planet's gravity well to build multiple space stations, as well as habitats on their two moons, and they were in the early stages of constructing permanent research outposts around the gas giants in the outer reaches of their system. They'd deployed four rings of solar arrays in orbit around their homeworld, Belarria, which they used to power activities both on- and off-world.

They had *not* discovered a method of faster-than-light travel, and thus were confined to their home system except for a couple of deep space probes. This had led to some minor debate among Concord Consulate and Command staff about the wisdom of reaching out to the Belascocians as equals. But they were a spacefaring species, if one only beginning to take their first tentative steps out into the cosmos. They listened for signals from aliens using powerful telescopes and cast their own messages out into the void, searching for those who could recognize them and respond. They were ready.

So after several months of studying the planet and its people from afar, the Consulate sent a message in the Belascocians' own language.

We are a multi-species alliance known as Concord. We follow an ethos of peace toward all living beings, while always standing ready to defend the innocent from aggression. We see you and recognize all you have achieved. If you wish it, we would like to begin a conversation. If you instead prefer to be left alone, we will respect that decision.

But no one ever turned down such an offer, and the Belascocians were no exception.

Marlee opened her eyes to crisp, silvery sunlight. Outside the vehicle, the entire landscape had transformed. Verdant land and boundless flora had been replaced with arid steppes of russet, adobe and straw. Ahead, two buttes ended in jagged cliffs, carving an uneven valley out of a bright, zinc-hued sky.

A wave of disorientation swept over her. Was this even the same planet? She peered down out of the window, but the ground raced by in a blur. At this speed they would have covered a lot of distance quickly, but....

"How long was I asleep?"

"About five and a half hours."

"So long? I'm sorry." What was she apologizing for? She was here against her will, and she didn't owe her kidnapper a damn thing.

"Don't be. I welcomed the quiet. I had much to ruminate on."

Like all the people you've killed in the last day? She stretched her arms out as best she could in the snug compartment. "Are you ready to tell me where we're going?"

Galean tilted his head toward the dash. "Lake Lasai is up ahead."

"That's not much of an answer."

"But it is our next destination."

She pinched the bridge of her nose in frustration. Her nap had eased the pain in her abdomen (or the passage of time had allowed her cybernetics to better patch things up) but had done little else to improve her situation. She remained at the mercy of a dangerous killer, on the run from authorities, trapped on an unfamiliar world and surrounded by a society and culture that was a mystery to her.

She was used to navigating alien cultures, but she preferred to do so on her own terms. Also with a ready escape hatch in the form of her Caeles Prism. Also, being shot was not up to par with the typical welcome she received when visiting new worlds. Even the Savrakaths hadn't shot at her until she'd given them good reason to.

The vehicle slowed as they approached the lake in question, then came to a stop a few meters from the shore. The doors opened, and Galean stepped out and strode to the water's edge. The lake stretched to the horizon, where it wrapped around the parallel cliffs of the buttes and out of sight. Despite its apparent size, the water was almost perfectly still, a muted slate gray that absorbed the sunlight rather than reflecting it.

Galean stared out across the lake for some time, then abruptly turned to the car. "You will exit the vehicle."

As trepidatious as she'd felt when entering the vehicle back in Ausatan, it didn't hold a candle to her reluctance now. They were in the middle of nowhere. No people, no streets, no buildings, no nothing. Her body would never be found.

But he wouldn't have gone to all the trouble of getting her wounds patched up, only to turn around and kill her the next day. Whatever was happening here, she simply didn't understand it yet.

She climbed out, shrugging off the cloak and laying it on the seat behind her. The door closed.

"Someone will find the vehicle. They'll wonder how it got here and where its owner ran off to."

"No, they will not." Galean went around to the driver's side and leaned in for a few seconds. When he stepped away, his door closed as well. The vehicle lifted up, banked into a turn and sped off to the southwest, taking with it her last hopes of salvation. "It'll crash into something eventually, but..." he gestured to the empty, bleak yet hauntingly beautiful landscape "...not until it's some distance from here."

"What now?"

He contemplated her silently for a beat. "Can you ura-ar-nasa?"

She didn't know the word, and her translator offered no help. "Can I what?"

"Breathe the…" a hand fluttered over the vestigial gills lining his neck "…you don't have these. Are you able to breathe the water?"

"No, I can't *breathe water*."

"A shame. Then you shall hold your breath." He spun and returned to the water's edge. "Come."

"You're not going to ask me how long I can hold my breath for?"

"It matters not. You cannot remain here alone, and I must descend beneath the lake. Therefore, you must accompany me. If you lose consciousness, a physician at our destination will likely be able to revive you."

"Likely?"

"There are no animal doctors where we are going. The physician will do the best they can."

Great. She gazed back in the direction the vehicle had sped off, but not so much as a plume of dust drifted in its wake. Then at the ominously still waters. She enjoyed swimming as much as anyone from Seneca, with its ubiquitous lakes and oceans, but considerably less so drowning. Also, what in the name of all ancient gods waited for them beneath the water?

"Well, you're going to have to hold on to me. Otherwise, when I fall unconscious then *die*, I'll lose my grip and float away."

"You speak truth." He held out a hand. "We should be on our way."

4

The dossier on the Belascocians had included a single paragraph noting the evolutionary adaptability of the species. For instance, the presence of narrow slits on the sides of their necks and a slight webbing at the separation of their limb digits could be traced to an ancestral aquatic life. The dossier had *not* speculated that those slits and webbing might not be entirely vestigial.

When she made it home, Marlee was going to have a conversation with the Consulate Research Director about the lack of thoroughness in his department's work. Because while the Belascocians were clearly a land-dwelling species, it turned out they were also able to breathe underwater, and this seemed like pertinent information to have had on hand before visiting their world.

With no fanfare, her captor plunged them into the steely depths of Lake Lasai. The warm water instantly soaked through Marlee's clothes, turning them into a clingy albatross. Her cybernetics slowed her body's functions to a crawl and dispensed the oxygen held precariously in her lungs with utmost stinginess. She hadn't volunteered that she should be able to hold her breath for a good while—far longer than an unenhanced human, assuming any of those still existed, especially since she wasn't being expected to propel herself forward. Her muscles and extremities sat neglected as her body worked to keep her nervous and cardiovascular systems functioning.

Galean kept a firm grip around her left wrist. Even with one arm occupied, he swam nimbly and swiftly, but lacking the desperation of one who was about to drown. He'd ditched his sandals on the lakeshore, and that minimal webbing between his toes sped them along into the depths with impressive efficiency.

Visibility was low, the water thick with tiny particulates, and she could discern no structures in the direction they were swimming. She had no idea how far or for how long they would be traveling; if it was longer than five minutes…well, she hoped the rumored physician at their destination was good at their job.

Yes, once her family and her employer gave up hope of retrieving her, she'd wake up in a cushy chamber back home with no memory of her Belarria misadventures. But this was the confounding thing about regenesis—about enjoying a kind of pseudo-immortality. *She* was alive now. Here, in this body, at this moment. And this version of her, which was all she knew and everything she was, would still cease to exist on death. Humans were finding that the promise of waking up again in a new body was, so far, unable to stamp out the most fundamental of impulses: the will to live. In time it might, for after hundreds of millennia of regenesis, many Anadens exhibited a callous disregard for staying alive. But that was for the future, if at all. Today, she wanted to live.

The urge to break away from Galean's hold and surge to the surface soon became overwhelming. Her lungs screamed at her to replenish them, and her legs spasmed ineffectually against the dead weight of her pants. Her cybernetics disabled her autonomous swallow function before she reflexively inhaled lungfuls of water.

If Galean noticed her convulsions, he gave no indication of it. He just dove ever onward into the creeping darkness. Because it *was* getting darker, though she couldn't say if this was due to their increasing depth or the increasing fogginess in her mind.

She forced herself to stop struggling, as every muscular contraction stole needed oxygen from her core functions. Every second became about staying conscious, staying alive for one more heartbeat. The initial warmth of the water proved deceptive, and shivers raced through her body as the cold seeped into her skin. She would never be warm or dry again. She'd never breathe again.

A wave of water displacement pushed against her right side, and she turned her head to see the faint outline of an enormous fish—half as long as she was tall—swoosh away. So something did live in these shadowy depths.

Galean launched into a steep, vertical dive, and the last meager light from the surface vanished. 'Up' and 'down' ceased to have meaning. Utter blackness closed in on her, and panic sped her struggling, oxygen-deprived heart.

Then light began to trickle back into the world. Not pervasively, though—it was coming from due ahead. And it was artificial.

The outlines of a towering structure took shape. Three parallel rings of lights illuminated a long edifice that curved in at the top and bottom and receded on the edges. She distracted herself from the few remaining drops of air her lungs possessed by doing a rough calculation of the size, based on where the edges disappeared into the water. A hundred-fifty meters wide, give or take? And sixty-ish meters high? A right proper underwater station.

When they were...she couldn't concentrate enough to guestimate the math on their distance...Galean dove beneath the structure, and a rough, unburnished olive metal hull raced by overhead. Then dark tendrils snaked in to overtake her sight from the edges inward. Her eVi screamed warnings in bright red, and her mind crept like molasses toward the realization that she was dying. Her eyes closed.

Suddenly they were surging in a new direction, and her arm was pulled hard above the rest of her body—

Her head broke through the surface.

Her eVi recognized the presence of air before what remained of her consciousness did, and her lungs spasmed. Air surged into her body, along with splashes of water as Galean dragged her forward through choppy waves. She coughed and nearly drowned here at the last moment of the journey as she struggled to gulp in more air. Her feet kicked against the water, her body determined never to sink into its depths again.

Then her feet found purchase beneath her, toes slipping over a slimy stone surface as Galean rose out of the water ahead of her.

Steps.

She stumbled up the stone after him, yanking her wrist out of his grasp and falling to all fours, where she crawled up the last step until a rough, tacky floor was beneath her hands and feet. A full-on coughing fit wracked her chest as water sputtered out of her lungs and onto the floor.

"Stay."

She half-glanced up enough to see Galean stride off toward the far end of the smooth-walled cavern they found themselves in. The walls, floor and ceiling appeared to be natural rock native to the environment, but they had been coated with a sealant of some kind. Off to the left, four vehicles sat in racks—they had fucking underwater vehicles!

Outrage flared but lost out to her cybernetics engaging in a wholesale shift of operations. Extreme survival mode gave way to recuperative measures as bursts of oxygen were directed to neglected organs before resuming a normal distribution pattern. Lungs were massaged back to full health. Her mind began to clear, and none too soon, because she needed to be paying attention to what happened next, dammit. Having somehow survived drowning—another first—she could at least try to solve the mystery of this infernal escapade.

She got her feet underneath her and stood. A little shakily, but she managed to stay upright.

Galean drew near two Belascocians who had materialized out of a tunnel at the opposite end of the cavern. When he reached them, he and the man on the right embraced one another. It was more involved than a human hug, involving the intricate movement of tails and fingertips and cheeks and hair.

When they separated, Galean took a half-step back and directed his attention to the man on the left. His tail swept up to rest its tip on his shoulder, and he lifted one hand to press flat just beneath where his tail lay while fisting his other hand at his hip. It looked like a salute, or the cultural equivalent of a bow.

Murmurs mixed with infrasound waves overlapped one another. She caught every few words, but the Scocian language was exceptionally complex. Body language, physical contact and pheromones communicated contextual meaning easily as much as the words uttered—and that was only what the Consulate Research Department had been able to determine through passive observation.

So she studied the body language. The man on the right swung wildly between excitement and dismay, while the one on the left acted tense and reserved. Galean appeared to be deferring to this man, though his tail repeatedly snapped in agitation against the rocky floor.

Abruptly all eyes diverted to her.

"You should not have brought it here," the man on the left said. His voice held an aura of authority that transcended species, and the severe tenor conveying the words sent a chill through her bones.

"Forgive me, Nedeni, but I ask you what my better options were? Let the Kaldi capture her, which would inevitably lead to her—willingly or otherwise—divulging everything she knows? Allow her to return to her homeworld, from where she would then do the same in the name of diplomatic relations? Murder her to keep her silent?"

The long, intense gaze this Nedeni leveled upon her led her to suspect he'd have chosen the last option, and she began to wonder if Galean was no longer the greatest threat to her safety.

Finally the man's coal-black eyes returned their focus to Galean. "It seems you have much to explain, starting with the abject failure of your mission and ending with the arrival of this alien into our midst."

"Yes, sir." Galean's tail lay flat as his fingertips met at his waist in supplication. No, she chastised herself, recalling the mantra Dean Veshnael had drilled into her on countless occasions: when you don't understand something in an alien culture, never ascribe your own societal traditions or motivations to it. Never assume they act as you do for the reasons you do.

So she continued to watch and absorb.

"May I visit Resamane first?" Galean asked.

"No. If we now find ourselves in imminent danger, I must know it forthwith." Nedeni turned to the third man. "Escort the alien to a secure room in Medical. See if we can provide her with suitable nourishment. And do take care to lock her room on your departure."

"It will be done, sir."

Nedeni cast a last ominous glance her way, then spun and retreated down the tunnel. Galean did not look back before trailing after him.

The third man approached her displaying apparent enthusiasm, hands and tail swaying freely. "I'm Deshka. What's your name? Oh, wait, I should start over. Can you understand me?"

"I can. My name is Marlee."

"You speak our language as well?" His lips spread wide in a smile. "Fascinating. Will you come with me?"

"Do I have a choice?"

"I'm afraid not." He held out a hand.

"I'll follow you without causing trouble."

"Be that as it may, we can't have you running wild through the Serba and frightening the residents. Shall we go?"

His hand closed over her wrist, but his grip remained loose. She could escape it if she chose, but then what? Dive back into the water and try to swim to the surface? Assuming she made it—a hefty assumption indeed—she'd then find herself in the middle of desolation nowhere, with no vehicle and no way to call for help. Her only realistic option was to see where this new madness led. And, hey, since she was already here....

She nodded, and he guided her toward the tunnel and out of the cavern.

Marlee's step hitched in surprise as they exited the tunnel. She stood on the threshold of a small city. A thriving underwater civilization filled with people and lights and technology lay hidden in the depths, and it was the last thing she'd expected.

Tall, wide archways lined an open area ahead of them, some open and others framing double doors. Above the rooms, horizontal, oval windows stretched across the length of the curving wall to look down upon the open space.

The widest archway, diagonally to the left, revealed a larger space that resembled some kind of bazaar, with food stalls along one wall. Several dozen Belascocians sat at circular tables, eating and engaging in conversation. Past the tables, a semi-transparent divider didn't entirely hide gatherings of couches and other types of seating.

The opposite archway exposed a series of glass-framed rooms containing printing modules similar to the one Galean had used in the Consul's office. The modules were flanked by holographic displays cycling through clothes, tools and other paraphernalia.

Deshka tugged her off to the right, where a set of opaque reinforced doors waited. "Come now. Let's be quick about it, before we draw attention."

Two Belascocians exited the doors as they approached and skidded to a stop, staring at her in obvious shock. Their hair threads danced outward, razored tips at the ready, and both tails swirled into tight loops in the air.

"What in the *izorra*?"

The exclamation drew more attention, and in a few seconds almost a dozen Belascocians were closing in on them.

"Have you never seen an alien before? Back to what you were doing!" Deshka tightened his grip on her wrist and plowed through the growing crowd with her in tow.

Long fingers reached out to touch her hair and skim across her soaked clothing amid a host of excited utterances; she withstood their probing with practiced composure. The doors opened ahead of them, and Deshka's pace increased to speed them through. On the other side, he turned to watch as the doors closed and ensure no one followed.

He gave her a little smile as he dropped his hold on her wrist. "Sorry about that. They haven't actually seen an alien before."

"I know." It wasn't the first time she'd been ogled like an attraction at a freak show. It came with the territory.

He gestured ahead, and they began traversing a brightly lit but unadorned hallway plastered in cornflower-painted adobe. "Forgive me, your presence here is a lot to take in. You've met species other than us?"

"Oh, yes. Quite a few."

"I'd love to hear about them. We've long speculated on what extraterrestrial life might involve. What we'd share, how we'd differ. You don't look so different—I mean, you *do,* obviously. You lack a tail and sentsores, your skin is squishy and horribly dull, and your nose sticks out for a fathom. But you're basically belascoid in form."

Marlee chuckled. This particular Belascocian did not strike her as the murdering type. She felt herself relaxing around him, though she really shouldn't do so. "Many aliens we've encountered are the same: two arms, two legs, a torso with a head on top. Eyes, ears, nose, mouth. It's nature's preferred assemblage. But not all aliens are so similar to one another. Some are distinctly odd in appearance."

Deshka's steps slowed, and he gestured to a door on the left. "We've arrived. Perhaps later, after you're settled in, you can tell me more about these aliens you've met. Especially the unusual ones."

"Sure." She peered inside as the door slid open. The small room contained a cot in the center, a workstation in one corner and an unfamiliar device in the other. No printer, alas. She was eager to try her hand with one. Out of curiosity, but mostly to attempt to print herself a means of escape.

"It's not much. This is a patient room in the Medical wing, so it isn't fancy."

"Why Medical?"

"I, uh, suspect because there's a lock on the door. To ensure patients don't start wandering around before they're healed."

This suggested they didn't have an onsite jail. Did no one here misbehave? She leaned lightly against the edge of the cot. "Thank you for being kind and friendly to me."

"Galean indicated you've had a difficult run of it. Said you almost died three times on the journey here. It sounded as though you could use a break."

She hadn't overhead Galean saying any of those things. Did Scocian span even more senses than they'd realized? "I appreciate it, but the break I truly want is to go home. I promise I will keep what I've seen to myself. This was not my mission, and I don't intend to get myself involved in domestic drama. My family, friends and coworkers will be very worried about me by now. At a minimum, I need to let them know I'm okay." She lifted her hair away from her neck to expose the attached plate. "I don't suppose you can remove this for me?"

The fine sentsores around Deshka's lips drooped listlessly. "I know what it's like to be cut off from family. I feel for you, I do. But if I were to remove the siliki, you would endanger us all, whether you intended to or not. Let Galean and Nedeni talk things out, and I'm confident they'll come up with a way to help you without jeopardizing our safety."

"I doubt Galean would have kidnapped me if he intended to help me."

"Kidnap? Eh, I imagine that is what it seems to you, isn't it? And maybe it was, but he didn't have much of a choice. Understand, you've met him in the worst possible circumstances. He's a good person. One of the best I've ever known. Everyone here is good and honorable, for that matter. We're simply trying to save those dear to us and right our world."

The plot thickened. "A noble sentiment, but murder can't be the way to achieve your goal."

"You mean Vasem. What you saw…it wasn't what you think."

"The Consul was stabbed to death. He was unarmed. If not murder, then what was it?"

"It's not my place to divulge."

"I see. So what now?"

Deshka made a sweeping gesture toward her. "Your attire is wet, yes? Do you want fresh clothes?"

"I'd *love* fresh clothes. But…" she glanced around "…there's no printer in here."

"An inprim? You would not be able to use one, in any event, as you lack the…the technology, but also the affinity. Worry not, though. I will create clothing for you. A match for what you currently wear?"

"God, no. This is a dress suit, which is my least favorite attire in the entire universe. Some, ah, pants? Like you're wearing, but not…you know what, yes. Pants like yours, in my size, would be wonderful. And…." She peered down at her cream blouse. It clung to her skin in sticky patches; where it didn't, the fabric had wilted into bedraggled folds. Then there was the shredded hole from where she'd been shot. "Just a basic shirt—material that covers my chest down to my waist and my upper arms. Can you create that?"

He studied her. "You have many strange curves. It's a wonder your body fits together as it does. But, yes. I've got the measure of you now. It won't be a problem."

"Thank you." Her stomach let out a roiling grumble to remind her how, on top of everything, she was absolutely famished. "Oh, and possibly some food? I haven't eaten in over a day."

"Can you consume our food?"

"I hope so. I'll be able to tell if it contains anything poisonous before I eat it. If it doesn't, my body is able to metabolize a wide variety of foods and extract the nutrients it requires. I definitely want to try, because…" she patted her stomach "…hungry."

"I understand. I will return in a while with food and clothes, and we can situate you in a more comfortable manner."

Real comfort was a long distance away, but dry clothes and some food would be a great start.

Deshka departed, and the door slid closed behind him.

Marlee waited ten seconds, then approached the door. It didn't react to her presence. She pressed on it, urging it sideways, but it didn't budge.

Despite his apparent kindness, Deshka had locked her inside. On Nedeni's order, so she'd try not to hold it against him. He might be her only ally on this planet.

Next, she went over to the workstation. This being the Medical wing suggested it was a medical device of some kind. A diagnostic tool, or a recording device, or a scan viewer. Its screen was blank, and the only visible entry tool was a long gray slate sitting below the screen. She ran her fingertips over it, then tapped a rhythm, but nothing responded.

The final object in the room was almost certainly a toilet…with an attached sink. The two basins, one low to the ground and the other waist-high, attached to piping that intersected the wall gave its function away.

This told her Belascocian anatomy was similar to her own in more ways than the basic bipedal structure. For all its messiness and annoyances, evolution again and again chose the same fundamental systems to manage bodily waste.

At the sight of a sink, her parched, raw throat let its state be known, and she rushed over. Two handles sat on either side of a spout, and she turned the left one. Clear water rushed out, and she eagerly cupped her hands beneath it, then brought them to her lips and swallowed the cool, soothing liquid. It held a faint aftertaste, but her eVi didn't let out a peep of warning, so she drank two more handfuls before moaning in delight and turning the faucet off.

Her tour of the room complete, she slid onto the cot and lay back to rest her head on the small pillow.

A wave of weariness swept over her, but she'd slept enough. Faced with quiet, solitude and relative safety for the first time since she'd stepped foot on Belarria, she needed to turn her mind toward everything that happened and try to make sense of it.

Alien societies rarely came to Concord perfect and pristine, with a one-world government ruling a peaceful planet of free peoples in a fully democratic manner. But the mere act of surviving to reach space travel did tend to wash out the worst tendencies of sapient life. Scientists posited that fewer than five percent of species in the universe who discovered fire survived to discover electricity, and the journey from electricity to rockets was even more fraught with danger. Navigating the gauntlet usually produced a people who were partial to peace and cooperation.

But not always.

So what was happening here? Had she simply had the terrible luck to stumble into the clutches of a rogue societal faction bent on violence and murder?

It would be par for the course for you.

She rolled her eyes. *There you are. I was wondering if you were ever going to come out and play.*

I was...collating data. Observing this rolling disaster and withholding judgment until all the facts were in.

And?

You haven't been this fucked since Namino. And at least there, the people who took you in were friendly.

Pretty much.

The Voice. Not a separate entity at all, but rather her subconscious given a megaphone and a snarky attitude. Its emergence had been triggered by her wholesale, revolutionary upgrade of her eVi and cybernetics systems to achieve Artificial-level functionality without the need for a genuine Artificial living inside her head. Instead she'd gotten something arguably worse—her own deepest fears and insecurities handed back to her, delivered by a voice that asked a question aloud she'd previously never considered: *Hey, is this a good idea?*

Their first months together had been rocky, to say the least. But in time, they'd reached a mutual understanding, and the results spoke for themselves. Since The Voice emerged, she'd not only not gotten arrested or imprisoned once, she'd advanced steadily up the ranks of the Consulate until she'd achieved her dream job: to be among the first to welcome new species into the intergalactic community. So in truth, she was relieved The Voice had finally piped up; maybe it could help her finagle her way out of this mess.

So what you do think? Was I in the wrong place at the wrong time and have gotten swept up in some fringe criminal group? Or does what Deshka said about trying to 'right their world' mean something else is going on here? Did the Consulate miss a serious warning sign about the Belascocians?

Perhaps not 'missed.' After all, this is one reason why Veshnael sent you, yes?

It was true enough. The Belascocians had been difficult to read from the outset. Their societal structure was full of contradictions that couldn't be understood without firsthand experience. Their communication system was enormously complex, stretching beyond the auditory to encompass sub-vocal emanations, pheromones and body mannerisms to a far greater extent than with humans.

Marlee, however, intuitively comprehended language in a manner few did. She'd learned her first alien language when she was six years old; by the time she was twelve, she spoke five. She'd helped decipher the Galenai's sonar-based language and the Rasu's machine one, so she wasn't new to extra-auditory forms of communication.

So the Consulate had sent her along to get a feel for the Belascocians. Her true mission was, aside from the usual diplomatic song-and-dance, to observe the aliens as they interacted with one another. To get a bead on what the Consulate was missing in how they communicated, then hopefully begin to decipher it. Because they'd never become true allies if they didn't understand one another.

Instead, she was lying here on a cot in a locked room in a hidden underwater base run by some manner of insurrectionists, if not outright terrorists.

Which didn't mean she couldn't complete her mission. All she had to do was find a way out of the locked room, and she'd be positively surrounded by Belascocians. When Veshnael had taught her that immersion was the fastest way to learn about a society, though, she didn't think this was what he'd had in mind.

5

The food Deshka brought taxed Marlee's digestive system's ability to extract nutrients and neutralize toxins to the limit. Her eVi confirmed nothing about it was poisonous; the Consulate had given its provisional sign-off on the non-lethality of Belascocian food before she'd traveled here, but it was always good to double-check these things. The taste was pleasant enough, tart and heavy on the spices. But it left her stomach crampy and unsettled. Still, it was nourishment.

The clothes, on the other hand, were exceptionally well made. Deshka had the eye of a tailor, so perfect were the measurements he'd captured from sight alone. The pants were a charcoal gray and hung low on her hips, with voluminous folds that hid more pockets than she could have imagined possible. The shirt was a little baggy in the middle…because Belascocians didn't have breasts, so the pattern to accommodate them didn't exist in the printer's database? But it sat well on her shoulders, with three-quarters sleeves tapering off at her elbows, and was a deep sapphire blue that matched her irises. There was no underwear, because she hadn't specified, and she had no idea if these aliens wore undergarments.

"You have new attire."

She spun around to find Galean standing in the doorway of her cell. The man who was responsible for her predicament now gazed at her expectantly. What did he want from her? A response, she supposed.

"Yes. Deshka printed some clothes for me." The clothes he wore looked identical to what he'd worn for as long as she'd known him—black pants and a charcoal vest over a mesh shirt—but they were free of bloodstains and other wear and tear their journey had inflicted. Did his closet contain a wall of matching outfits? "Are you here to remove this infernal contraption from my neck and let me go home?"

"Against my better judgment, I'm taking you to meet someone. Nedeni's orders." Galean held out a hand to her.

She glared at it in distaste.

"I can put restraints on you for the walk over."

"Fine." She grabbed his hand and allowed herself to be led out of the room and back down the hall. "Who am I going to meet?"

"Someone who can provide answers."

"Great, because boy do I have questions."

"As do we."

When the door to the main thoroughfare opened, every head in the space pivoted to stare. Word of her presence had obviously spread like wildfire through the community.

Galean's quick, determined pace toward another set of doors warded off anyone from approaching them, however, and she conceded that his demeanor was considerably more threatening than Deshka's had been. Did he strike fear in the hearts of even his compatriots?

Then they were through the gaping onlookers and the doors were closing behind them.

The ceiling opened up to stretch several stories high. Three stacked rows of balconies meandered along in waves, occasionally dipping out of sight before returning a few meters later. The walls and balconies were made of the same textured adobe substance she'd seen at the State Affairs Building, though here it was painted in bright pastels. Smoked glass ornamented the railings and, every so often, covered a wall in an elaborate pattern. Each one was different. Art, or something more meaningful?

The overall motif was bright, airy and cheerful, suggesting spaciousness where space was in limited supply. She'd never have believed they were at least three hundred meters underwater.

Narrow spiral staircases spun upward every twenty or so meters. Galean led her past three of them before turning to ascend one on the left. They continued up to the third floor and exited into a wide hallway with curving walls interrupted by four doors, then approached the second one on the right.

Abruptly Galean drew her close, his grip on her hand tightening painfully. "Before we go inside, know this: if you hurt her, I will kill you. If you make any attempt to injure her or cause her physical or emotional pain, I will kill you."

"I've been expecting you to kill me every minute since we met. As far as I'm concerned, this changes nothing."

"You were mistaken before. Understand, you should take me at my word now."

Danger radiated off him in a way it hadn't since the altercation in the Consul's office. On the whole, she was inclined to believe him. She nodded mutely.

He stared at her for a long moment, seemingly hesitant to proceed. Finally he swept his free hand horizontally across a square piece of metal affixed beside the door and gave her a bit of space. A second later, the door slid open.

Inside was a casual living area. Three chairs framed a circular glass table, and two screens adorned the left wall. The far wall held a viewport looking out on the waters surrounding them, with a couch beneath it. Fish she'd been too distracted to notice during their harrowing dive into the depths darted about in small schools, and an orange coral analogue arranged itself in a series of arches and swells. Beside the couch, the dramatic strokes of a mural painted the same three-circle-and-starburst pattern that Galean displayed on his cheek in lavender and teal. Off to the left of the main room, a narrow space was lined with gadgets and cabinets. A kitchen?

This was an apartment. Her refined deductive skills told her this entire wing of the structure was apartments. Smart as a whip, she was.

"Resa, we've arrived. Where are you?"

"I'm here." A stunningly beautiful Belascocian—one of the most beautiful beings of any species Marlee had ever seen in her life—glided in from a hallway on the right.

Her skin was the color of dendrobium orchid petals dipped in stardust. A rounded chin softened the typically harsh lines of Belascocian facial features, and her hair threads were pure silver ice down to their tips. A small bump across her abdomen, coupled with the chin, marked her as female. She wore a soft, flowing robe of amethyst woven through with silver and princess sleeves that rippled as she walked.

Most arresting of all, though, were her eyes. They were every color at once—a rainbow spectrum spinning around tiny pupils in a mesmerizing dance. Belascocians weren't supposed to have eyes like this; Galean's were somewhat unusual, but hers were utterly hypnotic.

Galean dropped Marlee's hand and strode forward to embrace the woman. Their interaction made the earlier greeting between Deshka and Galean seem like a formal handshake in comparison. This was intimate on multiple levels; every part of their bodies touched, their limbs caressing one another with languid affection. It felt like a violation to watch them.

Perhaps twenty seconds passed before they separated. Galean indicated her with a swoosh of his tail. "This is Marlee. She's a 'Human' and is, for now, my charge. Marlee, this is Resamane. My twin sister."

Oh.

The Belascocian woman swept toward her, and Marlee was overcome by a dizzying sensation of warmth and welcome. It was as if everything was suddenly right in the world. An absurd notion, given her circumstances, yet she felt her worries floating away and her stress abating. Here, in the presence of this woman, nothing could possibly harm her.

A hand rose toward Marlee's face, then paused.

May I? A voice asked in her head.

It was not the first time an alien had spoken directly into her mind, but it was the first she'd heard of the Belascocians possessing such a rarefied skill.

"Um, yes, of course."

The woman's hand alighted gently on her cheek. It felt cool and surprisingly soft, given the textured nature of the skin. Prismatic eyes stared through her, straight into her soul. Whispers echoed in her mind like eddies in a pond, and everywhere they traveled, they left a sense of peace in their wake.

Do not be afraid, newcomer to us. All is not as you have imagined. We are not your enemy. My brother is not your enemy. He wishes only to protect me, as I wish to protect him. I am sorry for the travails you have suffered in arriving here.

"It's okay, really." What? It wasn't okay at all!

A fluttering trill passed through the woman's throat. *Politeness is accepted with honor, but it is not required. You suffered, as did Galean. The world is a hard, brittle place at this moment. But not here. Here you are safe.*

Everything she was feeling reinforced the statement—she struggled against the calming aura cocooning her mind. She had to retain control of her own thoughts. "Am I, though?"

"Resa, what tales are you spinning for her? Kindly include me in the conversation."

The woman's gaze flitted over to her brother, and a smile broke across her lips. "Galean never did care to be excluded. I merely told her she was safe here among us."

"As safe as anywhere can be. This much is true."

How safe was that? And what else was true that he wasn't revealing? But Marlee didn't ask, for she was too transfixed by this stunning creature before her. In Resamane's presence, everything was soft and gentle and loving and always would be.

She blinked hard. "What are you doing to me?"

"Only surfing your essence. I'm sorry if I disturb. I cannot prevent it. If you wish to leave, I understand, and I will not take offense."

Leave? The thought of leaving was abhorrent. "No. I'd like to...know more about you."

"And I you. Shall we sit?" Resamane gestured to the couch with her tail and to Galean with one arm. "Galean, won't you give us some privacy to get acquainted?"

"What? No. She is a stranger to us and our ways. I will not put you in danger."

"I'm not a danger to her!"

"She speaks truth," Resamane replied. "All will be well. Return in, oh, twenty minutes. And bring a meal for us."

He stood there staring at Marlee, a deadly warning oozing out from his every pore.

"I am not a child, brother. I said go."

He seemed to wilt beneath the order. "Fine. Marlee, what I said when we arrived still stands."

"I'm sure it does."

He spun on a heel, tail whooshing violently around, and strode out the door.

"Forgive Galean his stubbornness. He wants to protect me, and for that I am grateful. But not all evils of the world can be guarded against. He is…turbulent, thrashed to and fro by violent emotions and clashing loyalties. Today, he is also heartbroken."

"Heartbroken? Why?"

Resamane sat on the couch beneath the viewport, and Marlee joined her. "The man whose death you witnessed—the Consul?" The woman's posture faltered, and an aching sorrow overtook the aura of peace and warmth to drown Marlee in anguish. "He was our brother."

"What?" Marlee jerked back, aghast. She hadn't imagined that the horror of the scene she'd walked in on could get any worse, but it was worse. To kill a stranger, or an enemy, was one thing, but to kill family? Such an act was surely unforgivable on any world, in any culture. And yet she detected no rage from Resamane, only quiet grief.

"Why are you not angry at Galean? Why do you not hate him for what he did?"

"You feel my sorrow, yes?"

She nodded.

"It is as wide as the great Ketsua Mountains and as deep as the Zerule Ocean. Galean went to Vasem to enlist his aid. But instead, he learned our brother had renounced odola and arima and bonded himself to the Errigime. In doing so, he chose to forfeit the lives of my kind. If Vasem had his way, he would have stripped me of my soul in the service of his ambition. See, Galean acted as he did to protect me. To slay one's ahaide in order to save another is the most calamitous act one can be forced into, don't you think? So, yes, my heart is broken, but not for Vasem, as his free choice determined his fate. My heart is broken for Galean, to have to carry the burden of such an act upon his soul."

Questions spun chaotically through Marlee's mind. She didn't even understand what she didn't understand. Was this nothing more than a convoluted family drama? Or was it all entwined in some greater theater? There were hundreds, if not a thousand or more Belascocians here in this base, and they appeared to be devoted to some cause or other. What role did Galean, Resamane and their murdered brother play in that cause?

"I sense your confusion. There is no proper place to begin, so ask your questions as you see fit, and I will convey what I can."

"Okay, let's start with that. With you. Are you reading my mind? How?"

"It is not so explicit, not for you. Your mind is foreign, so what I sense are only your strongest emotions. But with my own people, my perception is much greater, for I am desbida."

"Desbida?" Marlee asked. "What does that mean?"

A long breath escaped the woman's lips, and a weight settled onto the aura enveloping Marlee. "Belascocians enjoy heightened connectivity among those we value. Family, both of blood and by choice. We do so through our eamonals—a sort of…the scientists say it is a pheromone-driven aura. Our sentiments are laid bare to those in our circle, and nothing is hidden. Perhaps because of this, we are always seeking to improve ourselves, as a people. Thirty-two years ago, the government initiated a campaign of genetic enhancement targeted at refining how our eamonals communicate and our ability to control it.

"In a tiny percentage of the population, the genetic manipulation triggered a radical mutation that amplified the power of the eamonal tenfold. What was once a sense of mood, of inclination, became, as you put it, 'mind reading'—the irakurri. Not solely of odola, but of strangers we pass on the street. Those who were affected by the mutation came to be known as 'desbida.'

"For those people, the mutation did not emerge until puberty, at which point it often overwhelmed us. Confusion followed. Odolas fell into crisis; victims were hospitalized and many committed suicide. For myself…it was not a pleasant experience. I believed myself to be going mad, for a time. Gradually, however, I regained control of my mind and discovered the thoughts of everyone were open to me.

"The government could have led in this crisis, providing aid and guidance. Instead, they lied. They told the world the mutation rendered the desbida insane, and that what we insisted was mind reading was actually the psychotic ramblings of the deranged. They brought us into medical facilities for treatment—a cure, they said."

Resamane shifted around and placed a hand, palm open, upon the viewport. "The 'cure' wreaked havoc upon those treated with it. Some truly did go mad. Others developed cancers and terminal illnesses. As for me? It left me blind and, for a time, mute. I count my blessings that the strengthened irakurri means I can still sense the world around me through my eamonal, for to be walled off in my own mind would be…." A shudder rippled through her limbs.

Empathy welled up in Marlee, and she was fairly certain the sentiment was her own. "And it didn't cure you, did it?"

"No. To my knowledge, not a single desbida lost the use of the irakurri following the treatments. The government—likely at the urging of the Errigime—used this colossal failure to argue the desbida must be permanently segregated from society. Confined, for their own good and the good of all people. The therapeutics camps were formed, the desbida rounded up en masse, torn from their mothers' arms and their odolas' homes to be locked in cages masquerading as dormitory rooms."

"That's horrible! Thank goodness you were able to escape their dragnet."

"Escape? No. I lived in such a camp for five years, until one day Galean rescued me."

"Oh." Marlee frowned. Noble of him, she supposed; it was already obvious he loved his twin sister. Love made people do stupid things, but fratricide? "Can you leave here whenever you wish? Or are you simply a prisoner of a different kind? Plusher accommodations, I imagine, but just because you can't see the bars on the windows doesn't mean they aren't there."

"You misunderstand. I dare not leave, but not because anyone keeps me here. We desbida cannot hide our nature from others. Were I to walk the streets of Ausatan, everyone would know me for what I am. The government has told them to fear me, so they would report me. Capture me, try to strike me down. Ignorance drives them, and they know not what they do. But they do it all the same."

Shame flushed Marlee's skin, for her knee-jerk reaction was to...kind of sympathize with the response. Resamane's *otherness* went beyond the woman's status as an alien. The intrusion into the inner sanctum of her mind made her deeply uncomfortable. At the same time, she felt all sorts of warm fuzzies toward the woman...but could she trust these feelings? Was Resamane projecting them onto her?

I feel your discomfort. Part of you understands why they would want to seal us away.

"No! I mean...maybe a little." She cringed. "I'm sorry. For my people, privacy is extremely important. It's one of our most foundational values, that our minds are sacrosanct."

The woman's sentsores lifted a touch. "I wish to respect your ways. You may leave my quarters at any time, and you will not give offense."

"That's not what I...I don't want to leave. I'm just not sure I trust my feelings right now. Resamane, are you manipulating me?"

"Honesty in all things, yes? I confess I projected an elevated sense of calm upon you when you arrived, but only because I imagine this is unsettling, even frightening, and I wanted you to stay and listen with an open mind. I withdraw the projection now, and I vow to not manipulate your emotions again. What we are left with is simply...who I am."

Marlee wanted to say that the aura of comfort, of warmth and safety bordering on bliss, ebbed away, but the truth was it didn't much at all. This woman's magic was powerful stuff.

"Thank you. It's important to me to be able to trust my feelings. My instincts, if I want to survive. Your people—the public, everyone out there. Can't someone tell them? Explain how the government has been lying to them about the nature of the desbida? Expose whatever nefarious schemes are behind their actions?"

Resamane smiled gently. "What do you think this place is?"

"I honestly have no idea."

"We are the Tarazi, and we are dedicated to freeing the desbida and exposing the rotten heart that has overtaken the government and the Errigime, and thus our world."

6

"I'm sorry—I forgot to grab food. Resa, Deshka needs your help in the library."

Marlee turned to see Galean standing in the doorway looking, if she judged him correctly, profoundly uncomfortable. His gaze scoured his sister for any outward sign of harm; finding none, it remained wary as it settled on her.

"I did promise him I would assist him, and look at how the time has flown by." Resamane offered her hands to Marlee. Giving her the choice of physical contact.

After a second of hesitation, she took Resamane's hands in hers. The woman was like a drug. Dangerous to be certain, but Marlee couldn't detect an ounce of malice or ill intent in her.

"I realize your circumstances are not what you wished, but I am glad you have come to us. I am happy to have met you. We will speak again soon, yes?"

"I'd like that."

"As would I." Resamane stood and glided toward the door. "You both may stay as long as you wish. My home is your home." Her tail reached out to stroke Galean's as she passed. Then she was gone.

"For someone who's blind, she gets around very well. She can make her way to wherever she's going on her own?"

"Yes. Though she has been robbed of visual sight, her mind's sight is more expansive than any of us can imagine. Even the walls speak to her, in their way."

Marlee sighed and, given what she'd learned, tried to consider Galean with new eyes. Still a murderer; worse, a committer of fratricide. If everything Resamane had said was true, he might have done so for noble reasons, but was it enough?

Where before she'd seen only hostility, now she saw conflict. Frustration that explained his unnerving outbursts. Above all, a war between grief and seething anger churning beneath his skin. At his brother? At the world for forcing him into this situation? Likely not at her, so long as she didn't step too far out of line.

She accepted how the last day had been a nightmare for him. But could she trust a man who'd acted as he did? It wasn't the mere fact that he'd killed another person that bothered her. Caleb had killed...she couldn't say how many people exactly, but definitely more than a few dozen, and he was one of the most honorable, moral, loving people she knew. But to kill family? Resa's explanation suggested it was justified, but a nauseating revulsion nonetheless churned in her gut at the notion.

"The man you killed was your brother."

Galean gazed at her evenly. "He was."

"But you did it to protect Resamane."

"Yes!" He strode forward into the room with sudden energy. "So now you understand. Now you see why I had to act as I did."

"I don't understand anything."

"But...Resa said she explained matters to you, as I asked of her."

Again, she hadn't heard Resamane say any such thing. For all her augments and facility with language, there were aspects of Belascocian communication that remained closed off to her. "Oh, she explained about the mutation and the treatments and the therapeutics camps, but now I'm more confused than ever. Why would Vasem want to hurt his sister? Why is the government lying to its people, when the truth isn't so terrible? How could they get away with wholesale internment of the desbida? Those are people's sons and daughters, brothers and sisters. Does no one question the camps?"

"Every person here at the Serba questions the camps—no, *rejects* them."

"But no one else? Are your people so easily led as to willingly send family members off to be imprisoned for life? Does family mean nothing to Belascocians?"

"Family means *everything* to Belascocians." Galean dropped onto the cushion where his sister had sat. He brought one hand to his face, fingertips absently caressing the marking on his cheek.

"Galean, what happened in Vasem's office before I arrived?"

"You want to make me relive it through words?"

She winced. "I need to know."

"As you say." His eyes fell to study the beige texture of the couch. "I believed the bonds forged by our arima—the spirits of our deceased odola—still held sway in Vasem's heart. I went there to convince him of the dark, festering corruption writhing at the heart of the Aterpe Project—the program that imprisons and experiments on the desbida—and enlist his aid in our cause. Only I discovered he was not blind to the corruption. He was complicit in it. In my horror upon learning this terrible truth, I exposed too much. Of myself, of the Tarazi. Vasem...he transformed before my eyes into someone I have never known. He threatened to have me arrested on the spot—to send a complement of Kaldi squads out to locate and capture Resamane and the other free desbida and put them first in line for the new Soldad program."

"What's that?"

"An experimental treatment designed to rob a desbida of free will and turn them into a slaved weapon. Spies, infiltrators, assassins, working on behalf of whomever controls them."

"That sounds lovely."

He stared at her. "How can you say such a thing?"

"Sorry, I was being sarcastic. It sounds suitably horrible. So he threatened Resamane, and you killed him for it."

"He would have lobotomized her soul! I would be less than the dirt beneath my feet if I allowed this to happen."

His fervor nearly sent her scrambling away from him. Obviously guilt over his actions was tearing him apart, and she had to wonder at the state of his sanity, or lack thereof. 'Unhinged' came to mind.

But as she sat there and watched, he visibly put himself back together. His long throat worked, and his eyes pressed closed several times before he allowed his gaze to again settle on her. "Apologies. My ari is...not as it should be. I ask you to not judge the Tarazi by my failings. They are honorable people, and their cause is a just one."

"It sounds as though it is. Thank you for explaining." She offered him an encouraging smile. "So back to my original question: why do people willingly allow their own family members to be imprisoned for life?"

"How to explain a broken world in a few sentences? How our history as a people wove the tale that brought us to this fraught moment? How the slow, creeping fascism of a rotted government and its allies who serve the Errigime has sapped the life-blood of Belarria from its arteries? Crushed our vitality and dynamism beneath the hammer of control and authority? Not with a thud, but with a thousand whispers weaving through every facet of life?"

"You can start at the beginning."

"The beginning? In the beginning, Ama, Aita, Arreba and Anaia—together, the Arbasoak—created the web of souls that enfolds us all. They endowed the first Belascocians with the power of thought and—"

"Whoa. Not that far back, please."

His lips parted in a tiny smile; he was fucking with her. Good gods, did Galean actually have a sense of humor beneath all his brooding?

"Very well. It is difficult to know where to begin to provide the context you need. But perhaps this story began with Josune Kartean. She was desbida, though the term didn't yet exist when her role in these events occurred. More importantly, she was the daughter of the Business Advisory Council Director, Bihar Kartean."

"What's so special about this Council?"

"We call it by another name—the Errigime."

"Oh, yes. Resamane mentioned it, but we didn't delve into it. What is the Errigime?"

"A shadow government run by the wealthiest and most powerful business leaders on the planet. Now allow me to tell the story my way, yes?"

She sat on her hands—figuratively, but also somewhat literally. "Fine. Continue."

"Thank you. By all accounts, Josune was the light of Bihar Kartean's life—until her irakurri abilities manifested, and she saw the many sins he'd committed as head of the Errigime. In her despair, she flung herself off the balcony of their home, to her death—that is how the news reported the event. In reality, she was presumably pushed, or else murdered by her father, who then tossed her body to the street below to cover up his crime."

"Do you know any of this for certain?"

"I know it well enough. At the time, people had begun to suspect something had gone wrong with the genetic enhancements. Too many children were suddenly troubled. Violent at times, lashing out. Fits of hyper-emotionality. The emergence of a desbida's abilities does not happen overnight; like the puberty it accompanies, it is a disruptive process for the mind and body."

"What about you? You're not desbida, but Resamane implied everyone received the enhancements for a while."

"They did. I did. The irakurri mutation only manifested in a small fraction of those treated. We estimate 0.5%. For me, the sole mutation was my eyes."

This explained why his eyes blended through indigo into fuchsia, when those of most Belascocians were single-hued and dark. "Okay, got it. Keep going."

"We don't know what happened behind the scenes in the government, but the result was that the president declared a public health emergency for these poor, troubled youth. Families were encouraged to bring their children in for testing and treatment with new, 'innovative' therapies. When—"

"Resamane talked about that. The treatments, then the camps. What I don't understand is why everyone just went along with it."

"We *believed* them, Marlee. Everyone who knew a desbida had seen the torment the condition caused them. It was an easy leap to make us believe they were a danger to themselves and others. The story the government weaved was ingenious, because it felt right. Yes, sending our most beloved away was heart-wrenching, but we thought it was the best choice."

"When did you realize it was all a lie?"

"Me, personally? Not until several years later. My parents told me Resamane was where she needed to be. That she was being cared for. And I accepted it. I continued on with my life—went out into the world, served in the military, then started a career as an architect and construction manager. And when troubling rumors began circulating, I ignored them at first. Though my soul was gutted from the loss of my sister, I trusted my odola. I trusted the government. Until I met Nedeni. He—his story is his own to tell, but he gently sowed the seeds of doubt in my mind. Then, when I was ready, he exposed the full scope of the web of lies to me. And my world was overthrown."

"So you rescued Resamane from her camp."

"Eventually."

"And brought her here?"

"Ah, no. That came later. We didn't build the Serba, though we have made significant modifications since taking it over. This structure was a mining facility for manganese extraction. The veins ran dry fifty years ago, and it was abandoned.

"In time, our rebellion grew. People discovered the truth, or simply refused to believe the lie. We rescued more desbida from the camps. Nedeni transformed us into a fighting force. He gave us structure and purpose beyond flailing out in anger at the injustice inflicted upon our people."

She leaned forward and rested her chin on a fist. "And what is your purpose, precisely?"

"To reveal the truth about the desbida and the camps to the world. To expose the criminals in the government and the Errigime who spread the lies and abet the torture of the desbida, and ensure they are brought to justice. To enable the desbida to rejoin society, and to have the people not fear them, but welcome them."

"It's a noble goal. But mind reading...when the truth comes out, many will still fear the desbida. It's such an intrusion."

"Not for us, it isn't. The bonds we share with our odolas are open and honest and true. Nothing is hidden. The disruptive nature of the desbida is that for them, those connections transcend odola. They can discern a stranger's thoughts as easily as they can their brother's."

"You've spoken of 'odola' several times. You mean your family, right? Resamane, your parents...."

"The Ozeal odola stretches across many dozens of people." Galean spread his arms wide. "Deshka, for instance. He is my cousin, from Lilura's pod, though the bond we share now goes well beyond blood relation. Most of the Ozeal odola disowned me when I tried to convince them of the truth about the desbida. They labeled me a blasphemer and shut themselves off from me. So now, the Tarazi is my hartua odola—a sort of adopted family, if you will."

"And when you adopt someone into your family, you each open your eamonal up to the other?"

"Correct."

"Everyone here at the Serba has bonded so closely?"

"It is our way. Is it not yours?"

She snorted a laugh. "Um...not exactly, no. Humans are very independent. We hold our true thoughts and emotions close, only revealing them to people we care deeply about. Sometimes not even them."

"I feel great sorrow for you, to be so alone in the world."

"Don't. I'm not alone. I have many friends and colleagues, and a great family. But I am also myself—independent, forging my own path—and I wouldn't have it any other way."

Galean's lips twitched. "Well, you are quite strange."

"Hey! As are you."

"I acknowledge your perception. So, now, after many more excruciating words, do you understand?"

She sighed. "A little, yes." In some ways, though, she was more confused than when the conversation had started.

She felt enormous empathy for Resamane, as well as horror at the cruelty inflicted on both the desbida and the families they'd been stripped from, and she recognized Galean's actions were all dedicated to protecting his sister. But the fact remained that he had kidnapped her, cut her off from her home, and silenced her in a far more devastating manner than sticking tape over her mouth. Then he'd brought her to his den of insurrection, and now she knew far too much for the Tarazi to allow her to leave.

Unless she could gain their trust. Convince them that when she returned home, she wouldn't reveal their secrets. Given all the conflicting emotions churning through her mind, it might even be true.

TARAZI

7

Marlee studied the excruciatingly blank slab beneath the screen in the corner of her pseudo-prison cell. The problem with the technology was that it was designed to respond to Belascocian touch. Possibly not even touch so much as presence. Perhaps they sent out one of their eamonal waves to activate it. Trapped in this room except when she was brusquely escorted to a destination and back again, she hadn't been able to observe others interacting with their technology enough to pinpoint the method of operation.

Regardless of the details, however, she possessed neither Belascocian biology nor an eamonal. As a result, the interface and the information it might provide remained silent and dark.

Objectively, little about her situation had improved since arriving. She spent ninety percent of her time in this room, and she was never going to earn these people's trust from here. She needed to get to know the Tarazi. Nedeni above all, for he was clearly the ultimate authority around here. She needed to involve herself in their daily lives. Ingratiate herself toward them so they felt at ease around her, since people feared most what they didn't understand. She needed to make herself useful.

And how the hell was she supposed to do that? She was skilled at languages and cultures, but these people walked around with their hearts and minds wide open for anyone who wished to take a peek inside. Her eVi could analyze a host of information in nanoseconds and identify connections and sometimes generate creative solutions to problems. She was quick on her feet, figuratively and literally. But none of it mattered if she wasn't on the inside. Before she could devise a plan, she needed observations. Interactions. Data.

A sense of well-being crept into her thoughts. She shouldn't worry. It was all going to be fine—

The door to her room slid open, and Resamane leaned in. "Is it permissible for me to enter?"

"Of course." Marlee waved her in, belatedly realizing the woman couldn't see it. Unless she could? In some perception of air being displaced by the motion of her hand, causing a vibration in the emanations of the universe? Or something like that.

"You are well?"

"I'm...yeah. My stomach is adjusting to the food, and the clothes are great. I got a decent night's sleep." A slight exaggeration.

"Then why are you in a Medical exam room?"

"Deshka said it was because the door locked from the outside."

"This is a prison, then." Revulsion radiated off the woman.

"Well, sort of. I've been in worse prisons, though—or one, anyway. But it *would* be great if I had ready access to food without having to call for it. Also a somewhat cushier bed. And...I admit, it would be nice if the door wasn't locked. I'm starting to go stir-crazy in here."

"Unacceptable!" Resamane held her hand out to Marlee. "Come with me."

Her impression had been that Nedeni or Galean had to pre-approve her movements outside of the room, but she wasn't going to argue. Anything to get out of here, even for a few minutes. She took the woman's hand, then almost stumbled beneath the wave of emotions that surged through her skin. She should start preparing herself for such encounters.

"Are you certain you are well?"

"Yep. Where are we going?"

Resamane swept out into the hallway with Marlee in tow. "To resolve this travesty."

Holograms of two Belascocians vanished as Resamane led the way into Nedeni's office. The man offered a pleased countenance to her escort. "It is good to be in your presence, Resamane." He bestowed a decidedly chillier glance upon Marlee. "And our guest, I see."

The office was oval-shaped—the Belascocians never used straight lines or sharp angles when a curve was possible—and adorned with inset glass in a variety of colors and patterns. Marlee added to her impossibly long list of questions lacking answers whether the frequent patterns were art, symbolic or another aspect of their language. Nedeni's desk was similarly sculpted in the shape of a gentle wave and crafted of wood so dark it was nearly black. A screen with a slab surface similar to the one in her room occupied half of it. On the opposite side, a motion photo of a smiling Belascocian woman and child hovered. An inprim sat on a small table in the back corner of the office, next to a cabinet.

"You are keeping Marlee in a locked cell, with no access to food, exercise or companionship. This is unacceptable."

Nedeni's sentsores fluttered. "She need only ask for such things, and they are granted her. But while this Human is our guest, we must take precautions. She is a stranger to us and our ways."

"I have seen her heart, and I vouch for her."

"And your word carries tremendous weight among us. But not everyone is as welcoming as you. None here have seen an alien before, much less interacted with one. Many are afraid. If she is allowed to freely wander our halls, she might put herself in danger. The way Galean spoke of her fighting skills, perhaps others as well."

Marlee fisted her hands at her side to keep from gesturing too wildly. "I'm not going to *attack* anyone."

"Nedeni." Resamane glided around the desk to draw near to him, her tail wafting up to stroke his arm. It seemed a shocking invasion to Marlee's eyes…but if what Galean had said was true, then the two of them were 'hartua odola' and thus shared much. "You proffer such a weak justification. Simply tell everyone she is not to be harmed—unless she initiates harm, of course, which she will not—and they will obey your directive. Better yet, hold a convocation and introduce her to everyone. Give her presence your blessing. I realize Galean brought her here on his own initiative, and you would have made a different choice. But this is where we all are now, and we need to construct a way forward. She is here through no fault of her own, and I will not see her treated like a desbida in a therapeutics camp."

Marlee got the impression Resamane was speaking aloud for her benefit—that all these sentiments, if not the precise words, were also being conveyed through touch and sense.

Nedeni's narrow jaw flexed noticeably. "You know that is not my intent. But I must protect the Tarazi above all. She cannot be given free rein of the Serba—for her safety and ours."

"Reasonable restrictions can be maintained. But going forward, she will stay with me in my residence." Resamane abruptly shifted her head toward Marlee. "If this is amenable to you?"

Fear gnawed at Marlee's instincts. If she spent all her time in proximity to this woman, would she end up a brainwashed thrall, content to be in her presence and bask in her warm glow forever?

But this was the way outside of the locked room. She'd work on methods to temper the intoxicating effects of Resamane's presence, but she could not let this opportunity slip away. "Yes. I'd be honored to stay with you."

"There." Resamane knelt before Nedeni, draping her hands over one knee. In Marlee's world, it would be viewed as an act of submission, but here, she couldn't say. "Thank you for trusting my irakurri and deciding to act on the side of kindness and decency toward a fellow soul."

Had Nedeni silently assented, or was Resamane leaving him zero wiggle room and charging ahead? For someone with such a gentle spirit, the woman displayed a shocking amount of fire.

Nedeni placed four fingertips on Resamane's forehead, and she continued. "Tell everyone about her, and state she is to be treated with respect. Have someone show her around and explain to her where the necessities are located. As for everything else—" another turn toward Marlee "—our interfaces do not respond to you, do they?"

"No, they don't."

"Locked spaces will be inaccessible to her. Your concern is therefore resolved."

"And what if something happens to her? Or because of her?"

Marlee cleared her throat. "I absolve you of blame in advance. I take responsibility for my own safety."

"You don't get to decide such things, Human."

"Actually, humans prefer to decide exactly that."

"Hmm." Nedeni ran the back of a hand down Resamane's cheek. "You are certain of this? Do not let your history and the injustices you suffered cloud your judgment."

"I am certain, aliatua."

"Very well." He shifted to face Marlee, steeliness returning to his expression. "Do not betray the trust we are placing in you, Human."

"I won't."

"This area is the food bazaar." Deshka gestured grandly to the row of food stalls, then faltered. "Obviously. I know you've been having a few issues with the food and are being polite about it, but hopefully you can find something that sits well with you."

Marlee eyed the offerings as they strolled by the stalls. A couple of fried treats looked appealing, but what she required right now was nutrients. She offered Deshka a confident smile. "I'm sure I will. Do I need money to buy food?" The dossier had indicated Belarria operated under a capitalist economy, at least in the formalities.

"No. Not here. Most of us gave up our jobs and careers to join the Tarazi, and there's not much money to be made in working to overthrow the government."

This was the most honest, unapologetic explanation of what they were trying to do that she'd heard so far. Deshka didn't seem to have much in the way of guile, which was going to make him her go-to source of information.

She endured the gaping stares of a group of men as they got up from their table, empty plates in hand. Word had gone out about her presence, and she recognized the reactions were not going to be uniformly positive. "But food still costs something to acquire. Where is the money to buy it coming from?"

"Nedeni, for the most part. He hails from one of the wealthiest odolas in Ausatan."

"And this is how he's choosing to spend his fortune?"

"You should probably ask him about it."

Alas, there were limits to the information she could squeeze out of Deshka.

He caught notice of the stares from the men off to the left and turned toward them. "Raisan, Sikel, Txeru, it's good to see you. This is Marlee. As Nedeni announced, she's visiting us on a diplomatic mission and is our special guest."

She nodded at an angle, in the manner Belascocians did, but didn't receive much of a warm greeting from the group.

"What do they call your people, alien?"

"Human. Though where I come from, many different species live in peace together."

The one in the middle—Sikel?—snapped his tail. A show of assertiveness, if not quite aggression. "Must be nice. What do you imagine alien diplomacy is going to do for us?"

"You'd be surprised how often diplomacy reveals a solution that violence does not." The Consulate Handbook said so.

"Do us a favor and don't try to make nice with the Errigime in search of a 'solution.' The blood they've spilled overflows our rivers and lakes and stains our land. They don't deserve peace."

Deshka moved subtly into a protective stance. "Now, Sikel, that's enough with the fire-breathing for today." He offered her his hand. "Come on. We've got a lot more things to see."

She made it a point not to glance over her shoulder at Sikel, though the waves of his piercing stare tickled at her back. She'd witnessed the bloodlust of revolutionaries before. Under strong leadership, such emotions could be honed into a force for good, as Corradeo Praesidis had done with the anarchs' revolt against the Anaden Directorate. But in its absence, or if the leader themself was overtaken by rage, such fiery bloodlust risked destroying the people seeking justice, and they often took their society down with them. It had happened to the Savrakaths, an aggressive, war-hungry species who now found themselves forever exiled on their own homeworld, cut off from the civilizations of the universe. The Ch'mshak, too, for that matter.

Once they'd moved past the food court, Deshka leaned in closer. "We don't really have a lot more things to see. But when Sikel gets spun up, he'll go on for hours. Best to vacate while you can."

"Thank you. I don't want to get into a fight on my first day of freedom."

"Nedeni wouldn't care for it, I think." They returned to the atrium then entered the next archway, where a row of glass-walled rooms waited. "Here's where the shopping happens. I know you can't use the inprims on your own. But please, whatever you need, ask, and I'll make it happen."

They stepped inside one of the rooms, and she considered the row of rotating holograms. One showed off a series of clothing items that matched the attire most people were wearing. Practical gear suitable for utilitarian living and missions of insurrection. The second one cycled through objects, from plates and cups to hanging racks, light fixtures and several mystery items. The third hologram displayed furniture—chairs, beds, tables.

She motioned to the glass-encased chamber in the center of the room. "It looks a little small to fab a couch."

Deshka chuckled. "It is. If you ask for furniture, the order gets routed to a big machine in the back. We've only got one of those."

"Hmm." She studied the undulating goo in the chamber. Programmable nanomaterial, it had to be. "How does it work?"

"You're asking the wrong person if you want details. It just..." he shrugged "...works."

She doubted he was being evasive. People spent their lives using technology they didn't understand. "But you put your hand on the pad and...what? Think in your mind what you want it to make?"

"Not exactly. The pad is registering you as an authorized user." He tapped the metal of the slender cuff he, like everyone she'd seen, wore on his wrist. "The information is transmitted from the aldra to the device."

"So, you mentally tell your band—your aldra—what you want, and it relays the information?"

"Sort of." He touch a fingertip to his cheek, close to one of the narrow slits that served as ears. "The aldra is tuned to our individual eamonals. When in contact with our skin, it can translate directed thoughts and requests, yes. Most of our tech interfaces with it."

She'd seen several instances of this occurring during her and Galean's mad dash across the city, and again since she'd been here. The auras—eamonals—presented as magic, but they were just biology. Much like her cybernetics, the Belascocians had developed the means to enhance their bodies with complementary, symbiotic tech. It was a relief to be able to quantify this aspect of their culture in a meaningful, non-mystical way.

"Got it. That's a handy invention."

"I guess. The aldras have been around for centuries. The inprims...sixty or so years?" He gestured toward the door. "Shall we continue?"

"Sure." She studied the rotating holograms for another beat. "And the inprims can print anything at all? Even if it's something the computer doesn't have in its database?"

"Anything you can be precise enough in your description of."

She suspected Deshka simply suffered from a lack of imagination, for she highly doubted the device could print something with special requirements. Like a new Caeles Prism, for instance.... Regardless, she needed to be able to use the device. She didn't ask whether it was able to fab weapons, but she assumed the answer was yes.

Then she reminded herself how her mission was no longer to escape, but rather to earn their trust to the point where they would freely release her.

Still, a weapon couldn't hurt.

For a second there, I thought you were seriously considering shooting this place up in order to escape.

She growled at The Voice. *No! Do you know me at all?*

All too well. Never forget that I am you.

Whatever. There was a larger issue here. So long as she couldn't interact with their technology, she was effectively helpless. Dependent on the kindness of others for the necessities. Trapped in any dangerous situation. She *needed* to devise a way to use their tech. She set a sub-process in her eVi to work the problem until she was again alone and able to turn her full attention to it.

Which reminded her. She tilted her head to expose the piece of metal attached to her neck. "Can you tell me why I have to wear this? I mean, I understand the authorities can track quantum disruptions—however they do it—but why are they tracking them?"

"It's the desbida. It turns out their irakurri power uses quantum fluctuations to work. Which I guess means our eamonals do, too, since the irakurri is a supercharged eamonal. Anyway, the heightened fluctuations are detectable and so...."

"That's how they locate desbida who are hiding or on the run."

"Correct."

"But Resamane is using her irakurri here. She used it on me. I assume the other desbida here do as well."

"True. We—by which I mean Mattin, our resident tech genius—developed a way for an aldra to dampen the fluctuations to a localized area. A few hundred meters or so. Someone would have to use a tracker inside the Serba to detect the desbida within its walls."

Frustration gnawed at her gut. They had the technology to counter the tracking, but it was bound up in their aldra, which was tied to their unique biology, making it inaccessible to her. She buried a sigh. "I see. Thanks for explaining it."

"Come on." They exited the print shop, and Deshka pointed up, where a single winding staircase led to a door. "Through there are weapons storage and the combat training and staging area. Nedeni would have my tail if I took you in there."

She brushed this off with a smile as well. "Not a problem."

"You can use the gym, though. Second door on the left."

"And I definitely will."

They returned to the atrium, where Deshka indicated the remaining archways and doors with a sweeping gesture. "You're already familiar with the Medical and Residential wings. The third entry leads to all manner of maintenance and storage. Keeping an underwater station of this size running is no small feat. Fully a third of the people here devote their efforts to making sure the Serba keeps us alive. But it's pretty boring in there, so we'll skip it for now."

"Okay." She pointed to the final archway. "What's this way?"

He shot her a devious expression, eyes curving up and lips parting. "The Docks."

She frowned and glanced behind her. "You mean the pool? I could have sworn we came in from back that way."

"I don't mean the pool. I mean the Docks. Where we store and launch our ships."

"Aircraft?"

"They do fly through the air. But I'm speaking of spaceships."

She'd give the Belascocians this much; they continually surprised her. "You have spaceships? Down here?"

"Naturally. Want to see?"

"Do I ever. Nedeni won't mind?"

"We don't have to mention it to him."

In retrospect, she should have realized that, even when accounting for the expansive residential space, sufficient to house over five thousand people, the visible area of the Serba only occupied maybe a third of the width and breadth of the station. Geothermal power generation wasn't a compact process, so the power station likely took up another fifth of the space. The maintenance functions Deshka referred to, such as water purification and recycling, waste management and so on, another fifth.

But this left over a quarter of the structure unaccounted for…until now.

Through a door at the end of the hallway lay a hangar bay. In two long rows flanking a wide thoroughfare, twenty ships sat in docking clamps. They were small, somewhere between a typical fighter craft and a larger, Artificial-flown Eidolon, and no two looked precisely the same.

Marlee could pilot a ship—the basics, anyway—but unlike many members of her family, she didn't 'know' ships. They were a tool. Sometimes an indispensable tool, but still a tool. All of which was to say, she had no idea what she was looking at.

The only things each vessel had in common were their segmented nature and the bronze hue of their hulls. Two had a tall center module with blocky appendages; another was nearly flat in design, with sweeping segmented wings, while a third was a long, thin, model of aerodynamics.

"Why are they all different?"

"It depends on what their last mission was. They're reconfigurable in most gross respects. These here can act as weapons delivery systems, stealth reconnaissance vehicles, small cargo ships or personal transports."

They strolled down the thoroughfare as they talked, and past the docked ships, the space widened into a circular platform with a mammoth frame. Embedded into the floor was a series of circular interlocking mechanisms surrounding two large, heavy clamps.

Her gaze rose to the ceiling far overhead. At the center, an iris lens sat closed. A launch tube.

"So the ships are able to fly in water, air and space?"

"Not quite. Water plays havoc with the mechanisms, so it's not a great idea to do so regularly. On the other side of the iris is a sonic displacement system. It forcibly displaces the water in a funnel around a ship that's launching vertically to the surface."

"Oh. We use something similar to make planetary atmospheric traversals easier."

"Sounds like a great idea, as things do get bumpy on the way to space, but we don't have that kind of technology. Now back here..." Deshka pointed toward the other side of the platform, where two much larger ships sat "...these guys are suited mainly to transport groups of people. Though I suppose they could be outfitted to drop some big bombs if need be."

"Is there a need?"

"Not yet. But it's not really my area."

That reminded her of something she'd been wanting to ask. "And what is your area? What do you do here, when you're not babysitting strange alien visitors?"

"Mostly, I try to keep Galean sane. Failing that, I try to keep him alive."

8

"This is a mistake, Resa. I know you have a giving heart, but you can't risk your safety so foolishly—"

Galean cut himself off as Marlee entered the apartment with Deshka. His turbulent gaze landed on her, and she willed herself not to shrink beneath its force.

"Welcome! How did the tour go?" Resamane approached them, reaching out to brush a hand across Marlee's shoulder before engaging in a brief exchange of limb-touching with Deshka.

"Good. You have an incredible place here. It's practically a city unto itself. I'm impressed."

"Thank you. It's home for us, and so much more."

Galean glared at Deshka. "You took too long. We were due at a mission briefing five minutes ago."

"Sorry, we got carried away. Let us go now." Deshka stepped toward the door and made to depart.

Galean started to follow him out, but pulled up short when he was even with Marlee. "I trust I don't need to repeat my warning from earlier?"

"I won't hurt her."

"See that you don't." He strode brusquely out the door.

Marlee frowned as she turned back to Resamane. "I don't think he likes me."

"Want to know a secret? He actually likes you quite a bit. More relevantly, he respects you—and that's what worries him. He's merely being overprotective of me, as always. I try to dissuade him from it, but I wouldn't be here if not for his fierce desire to defend me. I owe him everything."

The waves of adoration swirling out from Resamane gave truth to the woman's words. "Enough of my brother, boor that he can on occasion be. I emptied out the small storage room and had a bed fabbed. There's not room for much else in there, I'm afraid, but at least you can sleep comfortably."

Marlee followed the woman down the short hallway out of the living area. A glance into the room on the left suggested it was Resamane's bedroom. A door on the right was open. "Is this acceptable?"

The room *was* tiny. A twin bed sat against one wall, and the opposite sported a small dresser. The bed was covered in a soft-looking, poufy comforter and two pillows.

"This is wonderful. Such a huge improvement from the Medical exam room. Thank you so much for extending your hospitality to me. And for vouching for me to Nedeni."

"Nedeni is a good man. Life has beaten into him the need to be too suspicious and slow to trust. I cannot fault him for it, but he at times struggles to distinguish friend from foe."

"He trusts you, though. This much is clear."

"And I try never to abuse his trust. But I am not above wielding it for a good cause from time to time." Resamane smiled. "You've had such a stressful couple of days. You must be exhausted. Why don't I let you get settled in? I want you to be at ease here. I won't try to entertain you every minute, for I know the immeasurable value of solitude. But anything you require, simply ask."

"I will. I think I'm going to shower. It's been days, and I'm feeling pretty ripe."

"Do you need instruction in its operation?"

"I'll shout if I have a question, but you'd be shocked to learn how many alien showers I've had to figure out on my own. I should be good."

When Marlee exited the lavatory and returned to her new room, she found four sets of clothes waiting for her on the dresser. Three of them were variations on what she wore, but the fourth was a soft, flowing gown of ivory and mint. When she slipped into it, a moan escaped her lips; the fabric drifted across her skin like the finest silk.

She hoped it wasn't supposed to be a ball gown, because she was going to treat it as pajamas. She curled up under the covers in her new bed and sighed with the first bout of contentment she'd experienced since arriving on Belarria. She hadn't expected it, but the Belascocians did physical comfort right.

Her gaze went to the closed door. She sensed the tendrils of Resamane's presence through the door, but only faintly. Her mind felt like her own.

She'd worked out that the full effect of the woman's presence didn't kick in until she was around three meters away. Yet even now, part of her mind begged her to get out of bed and walk to the door, solely to be more fulsomely enveloped in the aura of warmth the woman projected.

She shook her head against the urge. This was addict behavior, and she couldn't let it take hold. Resamane was wonderful. Kind and giving and intelligent and quietly formidable. But Marlee had to retain her own identity. Few things were more important to her; it was why, three years ago, she'd spent months writing her own upgrades for her eVi rather than joining with an Artificial and becoming a Prevo. She didn't *want* to share mindspace with anyone else. So she needed to work out a solution to Resamane's undue level of influence over her.

The Novoloume, who were one of the most influential species in Concord, had a biological quirk where the natural pheromones they emanated acted as a powerful aphrodisiac for most organic species. They didn't use it on purpose, but they had long taken advantage of its effects to their benefit. Many Novoloume were diplomats, and the ability to distract one's counterpart with lascivious thoughts during negotiations was only one of many reasons why they were excellent conciliators. Her career choice meant her boss and many of her coworkers were Novoloume, so she was intimately familiar with the pheromones and their effects.

But humans had addressed this issue almost immediately upon first encountering the species, for understandable reasons. A little program loaded into one's eVi acted to nullify the biological response to the pheromones. Problem solved. Even better, the program was able to be toggled on and off, so when one *wanted* to be swayed by their ardor, one could shut it off and enjoy the luxurious, sensual passion of a Novoloume partner. There were few experiences more heady.

Except maybe sex with someone you genuinely loved...but it had been a while since that had happened for her.

Anyway. Back to her problem, before she got distracted by self-pity. In theory, there ought to be no reason why she couldn't modify the Novoloume-targeted nullification program to work on Resamane's eamonal. She spent a little while running through the code. She'd never needed to understand how it worked before, but the logic was straightforward. Once the nature of the specific pheromones was identified and linked to the receptors in the human autonomic nervous system that responded to them, it was a simple matter of directing her cybernetics to cap those receptors.

She wrote a new script for her eVi to analyze the chemical makeup of Resamane's eamonal, assuming it functioned on a physical basis and wasn't...spiritual or something. The next time she spent a few minutes in proximity to the woman, she should be able to collect enough data to counter the effect.

She acknowledged the welling sadness the notion invoked, then snuggled deeper into the covers and closed her eyes.

Marlee awoke with a start. Confusion scrambled her thoughts as shadows lurched out of the corners to grasp for her—

Belarria. Kidnapped. Galean. Resamane. Serba.

She breathed in and imposed a measure of calm. This was her new bedroom in Resamane's apartment. The mattress, covers and pillow all felt strange, but she'd been too exhausted the night before to care.

She took a minute to evaluate her state. Her conditions had now improved considerably. She had a proper bed, for one. She was no longer trapped behind a locked door and had been given somewhat free rein of the Serba, albeit with a few caveats. She'd gained an advocate in Resamane and a chum in Deshka.

But she was still a prisoner here, still cut off from home. She couldn't relax and get comfortable, not when she needed to find a way to get back to Concord space. To contact someone, as a start. God, what sort of diplomatic crisis was astir due to her disappearance? Her aunt would be holding meetings and strategizing how best to do whatever was necessary to pluck her out of the Belascocians' clutches, while firmly urging Dean Veshnael to put a defined edge on his normally soft, conciliatory diplomacy. Had matters escalated yet further by now? Dozens of people on Concord HQ had seen her violent, armed struggle with Galean before she'd closed the wormhole; everyone would assume the worst.

Ugh, she would kill to talk to someone for even a minute! For all their preparations ahead of her meeting, the Consulate had no real understanding of the political and social complexities of this place, nor how she'd been yanked straight into the volatile eye of a raging domestic storm.

A wave of helplessness threatened to overwhelm her, and she kicked back against it. Maranos did not do helpless. So with a burst of righteous energy, she climbed out of bed and changed into one of the outfits her host had provided, then left the bedroom.

The apartment was quiet. "Resamane?"

No response. She felt not even the faintest tendrils of soothing comfort in her mind, which meant the woman wasn't home.

Great. An opportunity to investigate.

In an alcove off the living area sat an inprim. It struck her as odd for one to be here. Why have the stores downstairs if everyone could print most of what they needed in the privacy of their apartments? She'd bet not everyone had a personal one. Maybe it was due to Resamane's blindness—a concession so she didn't have to navigate half the Serba every time she wanted to print a napkin. Or maybe Resamane occupied an elevated status among the Tarazi? She'd only seen this one apartment, but a bit of quick spatial math suggested most of the living quarters weren't this large. Galean seemed to operate within Nedeni's inner circle, so it would be safe to assume the Ozeals were not the hoi polloi of the rebels.

Lucky break for her. She grabbed a glass of water from the kitchen and made to return to the inprim, when a prismatic reflection caught her eye. Embedded in the wall to the left of the kitchen was a transparent enclosure, almost like an aquarium. It was decorated with miniature rocks and desert plants.

Inside, a serpent seemingly crafted of spun glass floated languidly. Its body, some thirty centimeters long, undulated through the...it didn't look as if the aquarium was filled with water, but rather with air.

As she approached it, two eyes resembling faceted sapphires locked onto her. A ripple passed over its 'skin'—transparent, yet reflecting the light that fell on it and transforming it into subtle hues of pink and yellow.

She held out her hands, palms up. "Hi, little snake. I'm Marlee."

It considered her for another moment, then drifted down to settle upon a stretch of rocks.

Okay, then. She gave the serpent a nod and went over to the inprim.

There were two necessary pieces to this puzzle: a Belascocian handprint and a way to communicate with the inprim's control software. If she could snag a high-quality image of a Belascocian palm and acquire a DNA sample from Resamane or Galean, she'd be able to fool the system into believing she was an authorized Belascocian.

The bigger problem was how to talk to the control software. She needed to get hold of one of their aldra bands and break it down, but she doubted they left them lying around. In fact, she'd never seen a Belascocian without one. Did they take them off while sleeping? Probably too much to hope for.

She should come at it from the other end. What type of communication was the inprim expecting? The door lock? A random comm system? The answer should be the same for all of them. Perhaps she could reverse engineer what the bands transmitted by studying the receivers on any of those devices.

She'd hacked alien technology before, with the caveat that said technology was created by aliens biologically similar to humans. It wasn't the biology that mattered, though, so much as the brain structure. Species that were bipedal and humanoid, with brains stored in a protective braincase held atop a torso and attached to eyes and ears, tended to approach the world in a fundamentally similar fashion. Though the details of their history and development might vary wildly, they inevitably built the same tools. Constructed buildings and roads and cities in analogous ways. Discovered electricity and devised circuits that became gadgets that became computers. Unlocked quantum mechanics and advanced their technology to use it in the most logical ways—ways which were inescapably similar due to the nature of quantum mechanics.

The further one strayed from the humanoid type, the more the similarities began to break down. She'd never been able to hack Savrakath security, for instance, because the lizards' brains (it wasn't an insult—they literally were lizards) were wired too differently. Efkam technology was completely off the table.

But the Belascocians were humanoid. They drove vehicles and built skyscrapers and used handheld weapons that fired projectiles or lasers. They slept in beds and ate at tables and watched visual screens.

This meant if she gained direct access to the programming driving their devices, she could understand it. If she could understand it, she could devise a way to interact with it, then control it.

She studied the inprim again, then glanced back at the door. She wished she knew how long Resamane was going to be gone, but she had no way to contact the woman and find out. The Belascocians used a remote comm system, one she assumed was not quantum in nature, but she hadn't been given access to it…oh. Was this her way in?

Maybe. If the comm system used discrete hardware and she was able to convince them to grant her such a device for clearly practical reasons…it might be enough. It would definitely be a solid first step.

9

Marlee danced around one of the training dummies in an erratic staccato motion. She kept her movements deliberately unpredictable, designed to keep her opponent off guard. Three quick punches jabbed out, all hitting center mass—then abruptly she spun and delivered a roundhouse kick. The top of her foot impacted the neck of the dummy, and she let the spin carry her around full circle to return her foot to the floor, which was when she discovered Galean glaring at her from the corner of the mat.

She offered him a blasé smile. "I didn't see you there."

"Deshka said you were exercising. But this isn't exercise—it's combat training."

"Double the benefit?" She held out her hands. "No weapons, see?"

"It appears to me as if your fists and feet are serving as the weapons."

He was in a fine mood today. Again. "Non-lethal only." She wiped her brow. "What do you need?"

"Nedeni wants to talk to you."

"Okay. Just let me take a shower and change—"

"No. He wants to see you now."

"Then I hope neither of you minds the smell of human sweat."

"I don't know what you mean. You smell...as you smell. Strange. Like a bandero after too long in the sun."

"Is that good or bad?"

"It simply is. Come. We're already late."

A news feed was running on the screen on Nedeni's desk when they walked in. "Sir, you wanted to—"

Galean cut off his inquiry, for a video looping on the screen to the left of a reporter showed Marlee being guided down a sidewalk by a man hidden in shadows. *"The video we're sharing with you now is of an individual who fled the scene of Consul Vasem Ozeal Thorkan's office following his tragic murder. As you can make out in the video, this person is severely disfigured, we believe as a result of unauthorized genetic experimentation performed by an illegal lab in Emankor. They are wanted by authorities for questioning in connection with the consul's death. If you believe you have seen this individual or the unidentified male accompanying them, alert the Bureau of Security immediately. If you are harboring this fugitive, you will be subject to criminal charges unless you turn them over to authorities."*

"Oh, fuck!" Marlee collapsed into one of the chairs and brought her hands to her face. "They're trying to pin the murder on me?"

"Unknown." Nedeni silenced the screen, though he left the segment running. "One possibility is, they believe it will be easiest to track down and capture you, someone who will instantly stand out on any street corner."

"About that. Is this 'severely disfigured' cover story going to pass muster? The video quality isn't great, but I don't look Belascocian in it."

"You must understand. The desbida crisis turned genetic manipulation from a social good to a boogeyman almost overnight. Now, the scourge of experiments gone wrong populate the frightening stories parents tell their children before bed."

Marlee arched a dubious eyebrow.

"Perhaps not literally, but you take my point. Yes, people will believe the cover story, because they have been taught to fear what was once celebrated. Disfigurement from genetic meddling will ring true in a way that 'aliens are among us' will not."

"So the government hasn't told the public about Concord…which makes some sense." First contact with aliens was a civilization-altering event; each government handled it in its own way, but always with delicate care. "And the other possibility?"

"They truly do believe you committed the murder. After all, we don't know your species. The diplomatic mission could have been the opening salvo in your plan to conquer us."

Marlee groaned. "Conquer you? Don't be ridiculous!"

"Hmm." Nedeni pressed his hands together. "How large is the Concord military?"

"Um...large."

"This tells me nothing. How large?"

"Fifty-five million ships, roundabouts."

"I fear there is an error in your translation. You said fifty-five million."

"No error. That's right."

"*Arimaka*," Nedeni cursed. "You do mean to conquer us."

"No, we *don't.*"

"What other purpose could a fleet of such size serve but to conquer?"

"Defense, obviously. There are over three trillion people living under the Concord banner. The military is responsible for protecting fifty-one galaxies. You haven't been out there in the black yet, but trust me. There are plenty of evils in the void, waiting to not merely conquer, but destroy. We just barely survived a war against one of the greatest of them—a species of shapeshifting metal called the Rasu. Before that, we had to defeat an oppressive, totalitarian regime led by a bunch of cracked, power-mad immortals who enjoyed using planet-buster weapons against anyone who displeased them. So, yes, we have a lot of warships. We need them simply to survive."

Nedeni's alarm appeared to ease. "Your words sound fanciful, like something out of the absurd films the kharant theaters show...but I shall take them at face value for now. Tell me, if our government does formally accuse you of the murder of a high-ranking official, how will your Concord react?"

"Well, my great-aunt probably won't be too happy."

"How is a member of your odola's feelings relevant to the question?"

"Oh, I guess that little detail might be important. Commandant Miriam Solovy, my great-aunt, is in charge of those fifty-five million warships."

"I see. Then President Lormain may well kill us all with this course of action. Panic is making our leaders stupid."

Marlee clasped her hands together at her chin. "Listen. Concord isn't going to raze your planet. Their response will be targeted and judicious. But you have to look at this from their perspective. They can't reach me, which either means I'm dead or am being detained behind some sort of quantum block. If it's the former, they'll insist the government hand over my body—which it can't do, because it doesn't possess it, because I'm not dead. If it's the latter, Concord will view this as evidence I'm being held against my will. They won't stand for it."

"The government will tell Concord you're on the run."

"And Concord will think your government is lying." She tapped the siliki on her neck. "Remember, they don't know about this."

Nedeni stroked his sentsores as one would a mustache. "Will Concord not even consider the possibility that you *did* commit the crime? That you are on the run and aren't returning home because you're guilty?"

"Um...I hope no one would suspect I'd committed cold-blooded murder, but killing someone if I was attacked or in an otherwise fucked-up situation? Maybe. But it doesn't matter. Without this blasted device attached to my neck, an enterprising Prevo could find me within a couple of hours of searching. The fact they can't has got to be raising red flags back home."

"Your government knows where you are at all times?" Galean asked in challenge. "I thought you said Concord was a free society."

"It is. Look, I don't want to waste time trying to explain to you about Prevos and the Noesis and the quantum traces we leave behind in sidespace. The point is, Concord knows something is deeply wrong. They won't trust your government's word about anything, and they will try to come for me."

"What will this entail?" Nedeni asked.

"For starters, they'll do reconnaissance to determine where the government keeps prisoners, then conduct a visual search of every square meter. That's likely already happened."

"How? If Concord agents infiltrate a facility, they will meet resistance."

"No boots on the ground. So, some of us can project our consciousness out into...." She waved a hand in the air. "We can send it literally anywhere in the universe. We can't interact with the physical world while doing it—usually—but we can observe the world unseen. Honestly, as adept as you all are at sensing quantum fluctuations, I'm a little surprised you can't do this yourselves."

Nedeni's sentsores fluttered. "I daresay we've never tried."

"Fair enough. It's not exactly intuitive. Anyway, they'll search for me—and they won't find me. I don't know what will happen then. They'll make more fervent demands for the government to produce me, which it can't. The situation will escalate. How far and how quickly, I can't say."

Her gaze settled on Galean. "Please take this blasted thing off of me. Let me comm home and tell them I'm okay."

But she'd appealed to the wrong authority, and Nedeni was shaking his head. "And in the two seconds it took you to send your message, you could also provide our location and all of our names. I'm sorry, but no. We cannot risk allowing you to communicate with the outside world."

Marlee leapt up from her chair. "Even if not allowing it causes a war between our people? Concord tries never to cause unnecessary death, but make no mistake, people will die. Your people, not mine."

"We have made a fine mess of this." Nedeni didn't glance at Galean when he spoke, but Galean shrank into his seat nonetheless. "If we had another contact within the government, we could give them enough information to let them talk their way out of this crisis. President Lormain would be able to tell Concord their diplomat was kidnapped by a group of radical extremists who are blocking her access to quantum communications. Hopefully this true information would prevent, or at least forestall, bloodshed."

"But then Concord would insist on helping the government track us down," Galean protested. "With their superior technology, they'd likely accomplish it. We do not win in this scenario, Nedeni."

"No, I suppose we don't. A friendship between Concord and the government, and thus unknowingly with the Errigime, will mean our end."

Marlee tried again. "So let me contact my people. Short-circuit all those machinations—"

"I have rendered my judgment, Human. We will solve this problem without your assistance. You are dismissed."

Marlee's jaw fell open. She stared at Nedeni for a moment, then turned on a heel and marched out.

10

Marlee wore treads in the flooring of Resamane's living room. Miriam would never believe she'd murdered Vasem. Surely. Granted, she'd pulled some foolish, short-sighted stunts in her younger days—deeply, epically foolish—but only to help people. Her aunt knew this. Dean Veshnael knew this. Her boss sometimes took issue with her methods, but never her goals.

She spun on a heel to reverse course—and found Galean standing in the doorway staring at her. He kept doing that!

"Sorry. I'll come back later."

"Stay. I want to talk to you."

Galean shook his head slowly. "Any new insights you have to contribute should be vetted through Nedeni."

"Why?"

"Because I no longer trust myself."

"With me?"

His lips twitched. "You are a symptom, not a cause."

Okay.... The mystery of Galean Ozeal was a long way from being solved. Time to retrench. "What were you and Nedeni discussing? Before my face got splashed all over your news feeds, I mean."

"We've received actionable intel from one of our contacts inside the Aterpe Project that a group of six desbida is being moved from the Northeast Lorsal Regional Camp to the new research facility outside Ausatan tomorrow—the one where the Soldad trials are being conducted."

"So you plan to intercept them and bring the desbida here?"

"Yes. It will not be the first time we've done so—" He jerked in surprise as the glass-like serpent undulated past him, circled his head once, and flew off toward Marlee. She stretched her hand out and ran her fingers softly along the ingari's body, and he curled up in her palm.

"I see you've met Bibine."

"Resamane introduced us. He's sweet. Granted, he bit me the first time I touched him, but we've since reached an understanding."

"Curious."

"You're surprised he likes me? Maybe he's a good judge of character."

Galean simply stared at her, sentsores wavering in a nonexistent breeze.

She smiled lightly. "According to Resamane, some people believe the Belascocians are descended from the ingari. Not these little guys—I guess there are larger ones out in the wilderness?"

"There are. Quite a bit larger. However, it's a legend designed to inspire pride in our ancestry, nothing more."

He watched with a perplexed expression as she made cooing noises and funny faces at Bibine while stroking him. "Do you, ah, have pets back home?"

Small talk? This was new. "Not really. I mean, I have a dragon."

"A...?" He lifted his hands in question.

"Oh, you don't have a word for them. Interesting. Almost every species I've met has myths surrounding dragons. But perhaps the ingari took on this role for your people." She gave Bibine a friendly pat, and the serpent wandered off to his habitat. "Dragons are enormous creatures, taller than you or me. Four legs, stout body, tremendous tail—nothing like yours, their tails mean business—and a long snout that breathes fire."

"They sound monstrous."

"Oh, they are. Definitely not to be trifled with. But I've known Cupcake since he was a wee baby dragon, and we're friends now. He doesn't live with me, obviously, as he'd never fit in my apartment, but I visit him on Vrachnas often. I'd show you a visual of him, but…" she tapped the siliki on her neck while shooting him a pointed glare.

He tried to hold her gaze with defiance and disdain. But the next thing she knew, he was collapsing onto the couch in a flail of limbs. "This is all my fault. I should have let you depart through your portal in Vasem's office. Everything has followed from that one mistake. I am sorry. I have endangered your life. I have endangered the lives of everyone in the Tarazi, and now everyone on the planet. All because in my overwhelming grief and shame, I panicked.

"My brother's blood soaked my hands, and you were standing there, alien and unknowable except for a look of profound horror in your eyes that transcended species. Your gaze proclaimed me a murderer, and I did not want the world to know. So I stole you away in a desperate attempt to conceal my shame. And it will be our ruin."

Here, at last, was the truth of what had happened that night…and in the face of it, she found that her heart ached for him. Resamane and Deshka were both right about him; he was a broken man.

She sat on the cushions next to him. "Look, Galean. I think you're being a *little* hard on yourself. Yes, you should've let me go in Vasem's office. But everything about the circumstances you've been operating under is crazy. The government is hunting you and everyone here because you would dare to tell the truth and protect the innocent—and listen, that is totally my gig. I get it! And you're making me wear this siliki in order to protect the people here, Resamane most of all. I *understand*. I want to protect her, too. I just wish you would trust me, and I don't know how to bring you around to doing so."

"My ability to trust in most things was dealt a grievous blow when I discovered the truth about the desbida. I'm afraid it suffered a fatality when Vasem revealed his true nature to me. I do not have any trust left to give."

"Then what do we do? How do we fix this so no one dies—or so only the bad guys die?"

Galean brought his hands to his mouth and sighed into them. "I told Nedeni the solution lies in us succeeding in our mission. All of it—exposing the truth, bringing the perpetrators to justice, freeing the desbida from the camps. He rightly shot me down. We can help a few desbida here and there and provide them a safe place to live. But when it comes to exposing the crimes of our leaders, with Vasem's betrayal and death we find ourselves returned to the beginning."

"No, you're right! That is the solution." She leapt up, returning to her vehement treading. "What is your ideal end goal? Be specific, if you can."

He considered her frenetic pacing with an odd stillness about him. "We've come to understand that the conspiracy winds through the upper echelon of the government in spidery tendrils, infecting virtually every agency and initiative. It's had years to take hold and grow, encouraged by the influence of money from the Errigime. We'd hoped to root the conspiracy out, and Vasem was the key to this plan. But now…that's no longer possible. Not by that route.

"We want to reveal to the world the truth about the desbida— that they are not insane. They are, in many ways, our future. The bearers of an evolutionary mutation scientists merely sped along with their gene therapy. The natural conclusion to our eamonals, extending them beyond odola to all Belascocians. We want to ensure they are never held prisoner in camps or subjected to barbarous medical experiments against their will. To do this, we must expose the cover-up that led to the lies in the first place, to the camps and treatments. Charges must be brought against those who implemented those policies with full knowledge of what they were doing, as well as against those who have continued them in the years since. But doing so will require allies in law enforcement and the judicial system, and we enjoy none."

"It might not. Do you have the proof in hand you need to expose them?"

"No. We have testimonials—desbida who can recount what was done to them—but this is simply their word against that of the government. And in our current political situation, the government always wins such a contest. See, the corruption and rot now extends far beyond the Aterpe Project. Powerful officials in government and business used the opportunity the desbida crisis caused to expand their control, bit by bit, into every facet of society. We blinked, and when we reopened our eyes we found ourselves no longer living in a free world."

"Never let a good crisis go to waste."

"Excuse me?"

Marlee shrugged. "Something an old politician back home once said. Yours is not the first government to take advantage of a crisis to grab for greater power. I assume you're not in a position to overthrow the entire government and start over fresh. Not with the man- and firepower you have here. Wait, is this everyone? Is this the only Tarazi base?"

"The only one of any real size. We employ safe houses and meeting spots around the world, but they are minuscule in comparison. We possess a few fighter ships and a stockpile of small arms. We cannot win a war against those in power. Their snuffing out of us would be as a meteorite crashing into the desert."

She winced, as he wasn't even close to wrong. "But the good news is, all you need is proof of the truth and the ability to broadcast it to the world in a way the authorities can't silence. So, where does one find this proof?"

His gaze unfocused, as if his mind had drifted off to someplace far away—then his head jerked, and he was again present. "The medical information—the studies on the desbida, the details of the different treatments tested and their true effects, the notes on the Soldad program—will likely be stored at one of the research facilities. Possibly at more than one."

"Do you have people, or technology, that can break into the databases there and retrieve this information?"

"If our people were onsite, yes. But getting onsite is—"

"A solvable problem for later."

"Yes, fine. The real difficulty is, it will not be enough. We need to expose the bad actors, and those types of people tend to be smart enough to cover their tracks. Nothing will have been left in writing."

"Not true." Marlee's lips curled up in a smile. "It won't be in the official government databases, sure. But it does exist in writing. I guarantee it."

"Where?"

"In someone's home, locked away in a safe. When we—you—obtain the medical data, you need to search through it for the naysayers. Find the names of the people who protested, who put up a fight, even if, or maybe especially if, they eventually relented. Those people will have kept the receipts for the day when they need them to save their own lives."

His swirling eyes lit up with what might be a tiny kernel of hope. "Then once we know who they are, we break into their homes and acquire these receipts."

"Or, you could try convincing them to help you."

He leaned back to consider her anew. "What about you? You act as if you are interested in helping. Why?"

She slowed her steps and returned to the couch. "I want to go home. Unfortunately, I'm also now emotionally invested in protecting the desbida. It's a character flaw I never outgrew—a bleeding heart for underdogs and downtrodden souls. So I would feel horribly guilty if I went home without helping the desbida...unless I could help them *from* home. Which I can. I will. When I get home, I'll tell Concord leadership the truth about what's happening here. But the thing is, they're going to require proof, too. Probably not as exhaustive of proof as you need to convince the public, but proof nonetheless. So I'm going to help you get it."

He stared at her oddly. "You are a most unusual person."

"You're not the first person to say that. Thank you, I think."

"We'll see—oh!" He reached into one of his pockets and removed a small, dark object, which he held out to her. "I managed to fab you a comm device. Deshka mentioned you'd asked for one."

She took it, studied it for a second, then glanced up at him in question.

"If you hold it to the skin in front of one of your ears, it'll pick up your tonal vibrations and send auditory signals. But I assumed you didn't want it permanently affixed to your skin like the siliki, so I added a hook to go over your..." he reached out and flicked a finger at her ear lobe "...oversized, misshapen ear."

She chuckled mildly as she tried it on, adjusting the seating of the hook. "This is perfect. How do I work it?"

"The way we identify people to contact them...there's no way for you to do it. So I programmed in the addresses for myself, Resamane, Deshka and Nedeni. Word of advice: don't contact Nedeni unless you have a good reason for doing so. Speak the person's name, say 'Send,' speak your message, then say 'End.' If there is anyone else you want added to the list, inform me."

"Like who?"

"I don't know. I thought maybe you'd made some friends here."

"Friends? I...not yet." She removed the device and cradled it in her palm. "Thank you so much. I won't feel so isolated now."

"Good." He sighed. "I've got to concentrate on this desbida rescue mission right now, but once it's done, I'll give some serious thought to how we can acquire the proof we need. It seems impossible, but...you're right. It's why we're here."

After Galean left, Marlee sat at the dining table and tried to figure out what had just happened. Yes, her assertion that she'd help the Tarazi get the information they needed would, if she followed through on it, increase their trust in her, which increased her chances of getting home. So in this respect, her statements were all in accord with her stated goals.

But she hadn't been lying when she said she wanted to help the desbida. Or at least wanted to help Resamane. The woman had introduced her to a few other desbida, and they seemed as kind and open as Resamane was, but she hardly knew them well enough to judge their character. Also, she'd found being in the presence of multiple desbida at once to be a heady, dizzying experience that clouded her thoughts and confused her emotions.

Luckily, her rewrite of the Novoloume pheromone damper was ready, and she'd already turned it on. The next time she saw Resamane, or any desbida, their eamonal shouldn't affect her as much. She had to make certain her mind remained her own; she couldn't become a thrall.

Anyway, back to the issue. She felt confident in saying the desbida as a rule weren't insane, and the only extraordinary danger they posed to others was in the secrets they were able to reveal. Ergo, the Tarazi were correct in their assertion that the government was lying about the desbida—to their families and to the public. Ergo, the lies should be exposed. This much was straightforward.

Now, how was she going to help exactly?

Acting as an ambassador meant being a jack of all trades. She studied not merely a wide array of alien cultures, but also their governmental framework, social structures and the historical reasons for their traditions. While certain fundamentals were nearly always found in a civilization that survived to escape the gravity well of its planet, there was much devilry in the details. Navigating alien societies was about more than using a translator and memorizing a few social formalities. It was about understanding not only what they did, but why, and how those practices had come to be.

Admittedly, she'd scarcely begun her study of the Belascocians when she arrived for her meeting with Consul Thorkan, as there was only so much one was able to discern about a society from afar. She'd learned a lot in the four days she'd unwillingly been trapped here, but was it enough to be able to play detective and root out the patterns underlying their secrets, lies and conspiracies?

She wished like hell she could ask Caleb for advice. But he and his wife, Alex, had warned everyone they would drop out of contact when they entered an unusual star system they'd gone to investigate, with no firm return date, so they were off the grid until further notice. And it was a moot point anyway, as she remained cut off from talking to *anyone*.

Enough chasing the tail you don't have with agonizing philosophical musings. Time to focus.

The Voice often surfaced thoughts she didn't want to hear, but this time, it was spot-on. She had work to do.

She retreated to her room and closed the door, then sat crosslegged on the bed and turned the comm device over in her hand. It was a flat oval shape, about a centimeter thick, with the rubbery hook addition extruding from one side. She'd need to take it apart to discern how it worked, but she also wanted to keep it functional, as she genuinely needed to be able to use it.

There was no obvious seam, so she retrieved a knife from the kitchen then returned to the bed. It was painstaking work, but after ten minutes she'd cut a seam around the width of the device, hopefully not deeply enough to damage the electronics inside.

She slipped a fingernail into the gap and wiggled it around as she ran it down the length. The top grudgingly dislodged, leaving the interior exposed, and she set the top to the side.

The design was primitive by Concord standards, but recognizable as circuitry constructed with photal fibers and a conducting metal.

She placed a fingertip on the core circuitry and held the device up to her ear. "Resamane. Send. Hi, it's Marlee. Galean fabbed me a comm device. I hope it works. I wanted to see when you were getting back to the apartment. No rush or anything. I was thinking of going down to get something to eat. If you'll be back soon and want to eat together, though, I can wait. End."

She kept her fingertip in place while she waited.

Marlee, this is wonderful. I should have thought of requesting such a device for you myself. I will return in twenty minutes, and I would love to share a meal with you.

"Resamane. Send. Terrific. I'll wait for you. End."

She set the device down on the covers and replayed everything her eVi had recorded. She wasn't an engineer by any means, but her Artificial-level eVi pretty much was. While many Artificials, solo and Prevo, specialized in fields they found interesting, they were all polymaths, because they could be. It was trivial to store the sum total of all knowledge in multidimensional quantum orbs.

So though she'd never taken an engineering course, she understood what she was seeing.

She spent the next fifteen minutes identifying the structure of the signals the device accepted as inputs, then how it translated both her spoken words and the transmitted ones into signals and vice versa. The most confounding part was the manner in which it delivered the signals to the ID designated 'Resamane'...until she realized it was using a form of encrypted infrasound. It made sense, as the Belascocians were able to both intonate and hear infrasound waves. Still, she'd never seen it used in comm tech before.

Infrasound was able to travel great distances, as well as easily propagate through solid matter that defeated normal auditory waves. Back on Earth, whales famously used it to talk to one another across the oceans; with technological enhancement, such waves could theoretically travel intact for thousands of kilometers.

So this was how the Tarazi were able to communicate without using quantum entanglement. Good to know.

Signals deciphered, she dove into the code driving them...and shook her head wryly. They used old-school binary code. No wonder they didn't have sentient machines. It seemed an anachronism, as she'd never met a species with ubiquitous fab machines driven by programmable nanomaterial that didn't also use ternary-level computing. But technological advancement could be weird that way, often driven forward unevenly by societal and historical quirks.

But the lines of code the device used provided enough details for her to decipher the structure of their programming language, which meant she ought to be able to write commands for inprims, interfaces and more. Now to solve the palm print problem....

Muffled sounds emerged from beyond the door as Resamane arrived home. It would have to wait.

"Welcome back. How are you?"

Resamane went into the kitchen to retrieve a bottled drink from the refrigeration unit. "Well enough. We're preparing for the arrival of a new group of desbida."

The woman brought her drink to the dining table, and Marlee joined her. Relief followed, but also a touch of sadness. No warm, dreamy feelings brimmed up to overwhelm her. The damper worked.

"That's Galean and Deshka's mission, right?"

"Yes. They departed a few moments ago. The desbida they bring in will have resided in a therapeutics camp for many years. It's a jarring experience, to be removed from your surroundings, however horrible they are, and transplanted to a new home populated with thousands of strangers. You have your freedom, but you don't necessarily remember what to do with it. Not at first."

"And this is where you come in, I'll bet."

"Mmm." Resamane took a long sip from her bottle. As she did, one hand moved around animatedly, and her body language became pronounced. It conveyed a lack of distress, yet increased energy, as if the woman was a touch fired up about something.

Crap. The woman was talking inside Marlee's head, and she couldn't hear it. Warily, she dialed the damper down to 70 percent.

—and I warned Deshka that if the desbida were being transferred from the Northeast Lorsal Regional Camp, we must expect them to need extra care on their arrival—is something wrong?

"Um...." She didn't want to lie, but she also didn't want to hurt the woman's feelings. Resamane had been her fiercest defender here and, selfishly, she couldn't afford to lose an advocate. "Sorry, I was just distracted. My mind ran off on a tangent, and I didn't catch all of what you said."

"Oh. Forgive me. I tend to slip freely between spoken and transmitted thought. Half the time, I'm not aware of which one I'm using."

"No, it's fine." She swallowed a sigh. With the damper at 70-percent strength, the eamonal did affect her a little—like the slight lift in mood after having drank a single glass of wine. But, hey, she did that all the time, right?

11

Vasem's final breath wafted through the space between them to imprint Galean's skin with its memory. Frustration, dismay and genuine confusion screamed out from his brother's eamonal. Despite the bond of odola, their souls spoke different languages until the end. Then pain overwhelmed all, until it, too, leaked away, following Vasem's spirit to the arima, where Galean's sin would now be known to all his ancestors, his shame inescapable for eternity.

Guilt and grief eddied in the shadows of Galean's mind, dark and viscous and seductive in their whispers...he shook his head and tried to clear his thoughts. Now was not the time to wallow in the mire of his sins. He had a mission to complete, and it required all his attention.

Deshka: "In position at Lookout Point Alpha."

Galean: "Confirmation received of transport departure from Northeast Lorsal Regional Camp twelve minutes ago. Expect acquisition in the next six minutes."

Deshka: "Acknowledged."

Fremen: "In position at Staging Point. Waiting for your signal."

Galean: "Acknowledged. Strike team?"

Raisan: "In position and awaiting your signal."

Galean performed the second field check of his rifle in as many minutes, then set it on the wide fronds layering the ground around him. He crawled forward a few centimeters, the hot noonday sun warming his back as he let his gaze fall on the small copse of palmon trees to the north. Nothing stirred to give away Deshka's location amid their branches. His gaze shifted to the road, where a single vehicle sped away toward the Ausatan skyline in the distance.

There wasn't much infrastructure in the vicinity of the camp. The prisons were built in dead zones for a reason, and their presence did not inspire businesses to move into the area. The government worked to maintain a fever pitch of fear and anxiety over the existence of the desbida, the better to use them as an excuse for one power grab after another. But in truth, most people simply wanted to forget they existed, and the camps went a long way toward accomplishing this. Out of sight, out of mind.

The new research lab these prisoners were being transferred to was closer to the city, in an industrial exurb on the eastern outskirts, but it was small enough to thus far go unnoticed and unrecognized by the local populace. He imagined the Aterpe Project kept the number of patients in residence low at any given time, in case one of their brutal treatments actually did drive the subjects violently insane.

The intel indicated that the Soldad program was focused primarily on creating infiltrators—desbida who could get close to targets, pluck their every harbored secret out from the recesses of their minds, then report back to their handlers. But once one had gone that far, why not keep going? Why not create assassins who could read their targets' every move before they made it? If such a program wasn't already being tested, it would be soon, for the Errigime would be unable to resist the temptation of creating their own personal assassination squads to eliminate threats in business and government.

Galean couldn't do much to stop any of this. But what he'd told Marlee was true. Today, he intended to deny them a couple of test subjects and save these desbida from a terrifying future.

Deshka: "Transport spotted traveling southwest on Laidak Road. Speed is one-hundred-twenty-two kph."

Galean: "Acknowledged. Keep eyes on it. Fremen, move to alert status."

He reached for his rifle and slid it silently forward. The tripod extended and snapped into place, legs digging into the dirt for stability. Next, he flipped out the viewscreen and linked his vision to it, then returned his attention to the road.

Hitting the underside of a vehicle traveling over a hundred kph was no easy feat. But the rifle did most of the work, with a dynamic target lock and tracking system built into its hardware. He simply needed to provide it with a target to lock on to and make the call as to when to fire.

And, of course, choose a vantage that provided the best possible angle of firing, considering the spot he needed to hit was snuggled up underneath the carriage of the transport. This had put him flat on the ground thirty meters back from Laidak Road, in the dip of a flora-saturated ditch. It was the lowest accessible point on the entire road, which was surrounded by stretches of grasslands except for the occasional cluster of palmon trees. He didn't feel overly exposed once prone; it should do.

The vehicle came into sight, and he focused all his senses on the gap of air between its chassis and the road. Tilted his head just so.

The image on the viewscreen tilted with him, and the spinning core of the levitation engine flitted across the screen. His vision raced back, past it, then locked on. Targeting engaged. The distance until the optimal firing range arrived flew toward zero in microseconds.

He fired.

The transport slammed into the ground and skidded off the road. The front bumper bucked downward, the rear flew up into the air, and for a horrifying second he thought it was going to flip. But the levitation engine made the vehicle bottom-heavy, and gravity righted it off its precipitous edge. It bounced through thick foliage and came to a rough stop by a palmon tree forty meters off the road.

Galean: "Strike team, move in!"

Raisan: "Moving."

Galean leapt to his feet, rifle in one hand, and took off running for the wreck. The driver was climbing out of the transport, which had settled at a twenty-degree angle against the tree. A weapon came up, likely a dialed infragun so the guards could subdue the prisoners without killing them. A second person emerged around the rear of the vehicle, similarly armed. The doors to the passenger cabin remained closed.

Galean: "Be advised. We've got a minimum of two armed guards taking up defensive positions outside the transport."

No acknowledgment followed, but two seconds later, the driver jerked violently, grappled by an unseen force. His weapon went off, the shot heading off into the jungle as he collapsed to the ground.

A louder scuffle erupted on the other side of the transport, but Galean didn't have a proper view of it.

The strike team could handle a couple of guards, but he'd feel much better once he was on the scene. Fifty meters to go—

Deshka: "Alert! Vehicle approaching from the northeast. Looks civilian."

Galean spun around and dropped to his stomach beside the road, sweeping the rifle up in front of him. They couldn't have someone happening upon the scene and complicating everything. He wouldn't harm innocents, but those innocents could certainly harm them, even if unwittingly.

His vision and target laser locked on the vehicle at maximum range, for optimal range was far too close to the transport. He fired.

The projectile landed a glancing blow off the engine. Its rotations stuttered and slowed, and the vehicle bounced lightly off the road before coming to a stop half a kilometer away.

Good enough.

Galean: "Neutralized. I'm coming in."

The next instant he was back on his feet and again racing toward the transport.

By the time he arrived, Raisan and his people had the two guards in restraints and secured to nearby trees.

He walked up to the closest one. "Only two guards? The Errigime is getting overconfident."

The driver sneered at him. "Tarazi scum. They will come for you."

"They'll have to find us first." Galean moved to the rear of the vehicle, unlocked the double doors and swung them open.

Six people sat strapped into full jump seats on each side of the passenger cabin. All were struggling to unfasten their restraints, with no luck, because the restraints weren't for their safety.

Panicked eyes locked on him. Confusion radiated out from them in a tidal wave, and he focused on meeting it with projected calm. "We're here to help you. We're going to get you out of here and somewhere safe."

The man closest to the door continued to fight with the webbing holding him stationary. "You're Tarazi, aren't you?"

"The Tarazi are a myth!" This came from a woman in the back.

"I assure you, we are real. I'm coming in to unfasten your restraints."

Galean: "Fremen, proceed to the Extraction Point. We'll be ready to move in two minutes."

Fremen: "On our way."

He laid his rifle on the ground beneath the rear bumper and climbed in, moving first to the man who had spoken. He studied the intricate combination of webbing and straps, looking for the origin point. "What's your name?"

"Taephan."

"It's good to meet you, Taephan. Ah, here we go." He reached up high, almost to the ceiling of the cabin, and depressed a button.

The restraints loosened and retracted into the wall.

"Arbasoak be blessed." Taephan leapt out of the seat and clasped Galean's shoulder. "I see the truth of you. Thank you." Then he stumbled out of the vehicle.

Galean reminded himself not to take offense at the bodily contact from a non-odola. The desbida weren't like everyone else, and they'd been imprisoned for months or even years. Also, when one lived with the irakurri, one knew no secrets and no barriers. "Don't go anywhere. We'll have a transport here in thirty seconds to get you all to safety."

Now that he'd figured out the system, he freed the other five prisoners in a matter of seconds. One of the women hugged him, her tail caressing up and down his back as she trembled against him. His skin crawled at the copious physical contact...but if it were Resamane who was so terrified, he wouldn't want anyone to reject her. So he stroked her arm and told her everything was all right now, then helped her out of the cabin.

Three women, three men. None were blind or mute—because of course a good Soldad drone needed both sight and speech in order to infiltrate their targets.

Resentment surged through him at the unfairness of Resamane's fate. The early treatment programs were blunt instruments, brutal in their attempts to stamp out the mutation at all costs, and there were consequences. Resamane hadn't even suffered the worst of it. Patients died, were rendered catatonic, immobile, out of their minds.

But his sister would never gaze upon his face again, or the faces of all whom she loved, and this had left a mark that could not be erased.

Their evacuation transport banked in from the road to hover a few meters away, and Galean urged the desbida toward it. "This is our ride. Let's move quickly."

"Where are we going?" Taephan asked.

"Someplace safe. Where you'll be free."

"Are there other desbida there?"

"Yes, many. You'll be welcomed."

Five of the desbida scrambled into the passenger cabin of the transport like their lives depended on it, which they arguably did. "You'll find only standard safety harnesses on the seats. No restraints here."

The last man stared up into the cabin. Hesitation and distrust swirled through the air around him.

"What's bothering you?"

"Merely wondering if I am trading one prison for another."

"You aren't. The Tarazi are dedicated to freeing the desbida and protecting you from harm."

"I understand that," the man snapped. "But you're not truly free, are you? You have to hide. When you walk the streets, you conceal your identity. You live in constant fear of the Kaldi squads."

"Only for now. Things *will* change. We will change them."

"I suppose that is something to hang hope on." With a sigh, the man climbed into the cabin.

Raisan confirmed the government vehicle was empty, then approached Galean. "We're ready to move."

"Past ready. We've lingered too long." The strike team members joined the desbida in the passenger cabin. If the transport was attacked before it reached the Serba, they would defend their charges with their lives.

Galean went up to the driver's door. "Fremen, everyone is secure. Time to head home. The long way. Once you're clear, Deshka will pick me up, and we'll meet you at the Serba."

"Yes, sir." The transport's engine had never stopped running, and now it rose in the air and carefully avoided the palmon trees as it pivoted, ran parallel to the road for fifty meters, then headed to the northwest—

Deshka: "Galean, look out!"

The warning sent him moving without consciously deciding to do so, and the blow glanced off his shoulder instead of landing on his skull. He let the momentum carry him around to find a man in Kaldi combat gear swinging a baton for his head.

He ducked and charged forward, grappling the man at the waist, and they both tumbled into the verdant groundcover.

The next second, cold metal pressed into the base of his spine. "Our orders are to take any prisoners alive—if possible. If not? Don't force us to find out."

Fremen: "I'm turning around. The strike team can take the Kaldi down."

Deshka: "I'm on my way, too."

Galean: "No! Fremen, you get the desbida safely to the Serba. That's an order. Deshka, you don't have the weapons needed to neutralize Kaldi. Stay put."

A rumbling sound grew in the air, and he twisted his head to spot a vehicle speeding in from the southwest. The lone vehicle that had been on the road ahead of the transport—the one they'd assumed was occupied by innocent civilians. It came to a stop, and three more Kaldi officers climbed out to encircle him.

Deshka: "Bashi! Galean, tell me what I can do."

His hands were wrenched behind him and restraints slapped on. Someone hauled him up by his arms. The officer he'd tackled scrambled to his feet, then immediately pressed the barrel of an infragun to his forehead. "Tell us where that transport is headed, and we'll treat you gently."

The Tarazi transport had stealth capabilities; odds were, they'd already lost any satellite tracking over the grasslands. Another half-minute, and they'd be safe.

So he spat in the face of the Kaldi officer.

Galean: "Go home. Tell Nedeni what happened. Tell...tell Resamane I'm so sorry, and I love her. Tell her she'll be well. She's always been stronger than me. All of you, keep fighting for the cause."

Deshka: "We'll come for you."

Galean: "No. It's too risky. Focus on finding a way to get proof of the Aterpe Project's crimes and share the truth with the world. Nothing else matters. Certainly not me."

The baton swung again, and this time he had no way to avoid it. A sharp crack connected with his skull, and everything went black.

12

Resamane leaned in close to Marlee. "What's happening now? What do you see?"

They were gathered amidst a sizeable crowd, all watching a feed from the Docks. The cam pointed straight upward, where sonic waves had created a wide funnel of air carved into the lake. The water swirled furiously around the funnel like a whirlpool fighting to drain, but the sonic pulses held it at bay.

Suddenly a ship darkened the funnel as it fell in a controlled plummet, growing rapidly larger as it neared the cam and the launch platform.

"The transport ship is descending now. This funnel technology is impressive!"

"It is." Resamane straightened up and patted down a few wrinkles in her shirt. "Pardon me, as I need to go now. I'm expected to help greet the new desbida and...orient them, as it were."

"Can I come?" Marlee asked.

"Ah, my dear. I would love for you to accompany me, but they are apt to be overwhelmed by the events of the day. Arriving at an unfamiliar place and instantly seeing their first alien might be too much for them."

She'd grown up in a world of multiple species constantly intermingling; sometimes she forgot her presence here was strange and often disconcerting for the Belascocians. "Right. Go take care of them."

"Perhaps I can introduce you to them later, after they've settled in."

"Whenever you think they're ready. I'll try to catch up to Galean and find out how the mission went."

"Be forewarned. He is usually grumpy after missions."

When was he not grumpy? "I'll keep that in mind."

Resamane headed off for the Docks entrance, weaving nimbly through the crowd as it started to dissipate. Marlee had observed that the woman seemed most at ease when moving around people; their eamonals must shine so brightly in her altered vision.

A few suspicious or curious glances fell her way as she sought a vantage where she could keep an eye out for the returning crew, but no one approached her. Most of the people here didn't know what to think of her or what to do with her. When it doubt, they tended to give her a wide berth.

The excitement level of the morning suggested such rescue missions weren't common occurrences, whether because it was difficult to get intel on prisoner movements, or because they were dangerous to execute, or both. Many of the desbida here had arrived alongside family members who had hidden them from the government roundups until they learned of the Tarazi. As the story went, a full twenty percent of those here had been prisoners at a newly formed camp three years earlier. With a bit of outside help from the Tarazi, the prisoners had overwhelmed the guards and the still-being-implemented security and executed their own jailbreak.

Desbida who hadn't been mentally or physically crippled by one treatment program or another tended to be rather spirited. They, more than anything else, gave credence to the Tarazi's professed mission. Marlee may not have trusted Nedeni or Galean, but the desbida were competent, whole people. People with hopes and dreams and souls. The earnest desire of the desbida to be free—and the horror stories they recounted about their time in the camps—gave truth to the group's purpose.

A rush of movement caught her attention, and she turned to see Nedeni storming out of the Administration wing toward the Docks entrance. He acted agitated, to say the least. Had something gone wrong on the mission?

Resamane emerged a minute later, she and a friend of hers flanking six new arrivals. They did indeed appear shell-shocked, and Marlee resisted the strong urge to go up to them and introduce herself. They had far bigger concerns at the moment than meeting the Serba's newest attraction.

Resamane led them into the Medical wing, and Marlee's gaze returned to the entrance. For security purposes, the atrium door was the only access to the Docks. Everyone would have to come out through here. So with a sigh she leaned against the wall and settled in to wait.

Almost twenty minutes passed before the door opened again. Nedeni led a procession out of the Docks. To a one they were grim-faced, sentsores drooping and tails dragging behind them. Nedeni diverted toward his office, while most of the others trudged off toward the armory.

Deshka brought up the rear...and there was no one else. She hurried over, intercepting him on his way to the armory. "Where's Galean?"

Deshka's chin dropped to his chest. "They took him."

"What do you mean?"

"We missed a Kaldi team that was scouting ahead for the transport. The transport driver must have gotten off a distress call to them. They circled back and ambushed Galean as we were leaving."

"And you didn't try to rescue him?"

Deshka's shoulders drooped even farther, his head hanging listlessly.

"I'm sorry. That was rude of me. I'm sure you tried."

"But we didn't. He ordered the strike team to stay with the transport and bring the desbida safely here. And I...they had him in restraints and stowed in their vehicle before I could reach him. I'm no match for five Kaldi—I'm hardly a match for one." His gaze finally rose to meet hers, dark eyes gleaming with tears. "There was nothing I could do. I failed him."

"I'm...I'm confident he doesn't think so. He'd want to protect you."

"He always has. Our whole lives. Just once, I'd like to do the same for him, but...look, I need to, uh, tell Resamane."

Oh, no. "She's in Medical with the new arrivals."

"Yes, of course. We'll talk later." He wandered off in the vague direction of Medical.

She pivoted and made a beeline for Nedeni's office.

"Not now, Human."

"Yes, now, sir." Marlee planted herself in front of Nedeni's desk and crossed her arms over her chest. "I want to help on the mission to rescue Galean."

"Help? How do you imagine you would do so? You're not one of us. You can't go out on our streets or present yourself at the front desk of the local police station. You can't work our technology."

"I can work your guns."

"Which I'm sure would only make things worse."

"What went wrong with the mission?"

Nedeni sighed, leaning into his hands atop his desk. "We were overconfident. We thought because they weren't moving the prisoners in a full armored convoy that they weren't concerned about security. Or we thought we'd have time to get in and get out before security arrived—and we very nearly did."

"Even if I can't go on the rescue mission itself, I can still help. I have experience in this area. I've been privy to multiple rescue missions back home. I can point out flaws in the plan and alternative strategies to consider."

"You think you know enough about how our security works? Our prisons?"

"No. But I know people. Please, let me do what I can."

Nedeni pushed off his desk to rub circles around the skin in front of his ear slits. "Your request is irrelevant. There won't be a rescue operation."

"There…*what?*"

"I said there won't be a rescue operation. The Kaldi know this was a Tarazi mission, and now they have their prize. They will take Galean to the most secure confinement facility on the planet and plumb his mind for all our secrets. Which they won't learn."

"I've no doubt Galean is quite resilient at resisting torture— he strikes me as the type—but does your government not have pharmaceuticals that can force him to talk?"

"Worse. They have desbida on their roster. The irakurri is simpler to employ and far more accurate than any drug."

Mind-readers…the ultimate lie detector. No wonder the government was trying to level them up with the Soldad program. "Shit. Do you need to evacuate this place before it gets raided?"

"To where?"

"I don't know." She scowled, starting to doubt the praise Galean had heaped on Nedeni's leadership skills. "You do have contingency plans, don't you?"

"We do. None of them are good. But we don't need to evacuate."

God, he was infuriating. "Why not?"

"Because Galean will do what he must before they're able to extract any information."

Dread pooled in her gut. "What he must? What does that mean?"

"It means he will sacrifice himself for the cause he has devoted his life to pursuing."

"He...are you saying he will suicide?"

Nedeni activated one of the screens on his desk and punched in a command, as if this disaster was somehow *perfectly normal.* "All operatives are prepared to do so, should they be captured. Keeping the location of the Serba secret is our highest directive. Everything falls to the wayside before the necessity of it." His long throat worked, betraying the merest hint of emotion. "Make no mistake, Human. This is a great tragedy. Galean was one of our best men, and we will honor his sacrifice. He was hartua odola, and I will miss him greatly. But I have a responsibility to everyone here, not any single individual. So there is no rescue operation. Instead, we will redouble our efforts toward achieving the higher mission he championed: protecting every desbida we can."

"I...see." It came out as a whisper. Part of her was stunned into a loss for words. Mostly, though, she recognized that Nedeni was an immovable object. She could not change his mind. "I'm going to go spend some time with Resamane. She will be devastated."

"Yes. She will be. She likes you. Provide what comfort you can."

"Oh, I will."

Resamane and Deshka sat intertwined on the couch, every limb wound together, foreheads pressed close.

It felt as if she was violating their every intimacy to enter their space, but she didn't have a choice. Time was ticking.

She didn't trust Galean. She didn't *like* Galean. But she did rather like the two people suffering before her eyes right now, and she'd never stood by when injustice was being wrought, anyway. Even to her own detriment. This was probably going to royally trash her plan to finagle her way into Nedeni's good graces so he would grant her freedom, but...fuck it. Some things were more important.

They both shifted slightly toward her as she entered the apartment and approached them, though they kept their foreheads touching. Glistening tears carved streaks of prismatic brilliance down their cheeks.

Resamane stretched out a hand. "Come. Share in our sorrow."

"I already do." She knelt in front of them and reached up to press a palm to each of their jaws. Their anguish radiated off of them in real, tangible waves, all vivid color and love and pain. Even with the damper on, Resamane's grief threatened to overwhelm her.

Deshka's face contorted. "He is the reason both of us are alive. And now we have lost him forever."

So they both knew how this was seemingly fated to play out. "I say you haven't. Not yet. We're going to rescue him. Aren't we, Deshka?"

"Right. Of course we are—" Deshka jerked out of Resamane's embrace. "Wait. Are you mad? How do you expect to do that?"

"With your help. Nedeni said they would take him to 'the most secure confinement facility on the planet.' Do you know to where he was referring?"

Deshka frowned and looked away—Resamane cupped his cheek and turned his face back to her. "If there's a chance...?"

"Oh, prezia. I don't see how there can be."

Marlee rolled her eyes, hoping they didn't comprehend the mannerism. "Then let me tell you how. Answer my question—where would they take him?"

"The Seguru Instal. It's on the military base outside Buruja. But, Marlee, the entire base is impregnable. We'll never get two meters inside before being shredded into a thousand pieces by a hailstorm of auto-fired atzapars."

The notion of being torn apart by a volley of those awful hook bullets evoked an involuntary shudder. "You're exaggerating."

"I am not. It is a fortress, and it is protected like one."

She pressed a palm to her forehead. "Dammit, why did Galean have to trash my Caeles Prism? If I had it, we could skip right past the firing squad and waltz directly into his cell."

"Your what?"

"The device I use to open wormholes—portals between two locations. I wore it on a bracelet. But Galean removed it while I was unconscious and threw it in the trash."

Resamane sat up straighter and wiped tears off her cheeks. "No, he didn't."

"What do you mean?"

"When Galean first returned here after...after Vasem, his emotions were flowing so wildly, everything that had happened leaked freely out from his mind. I saw it all." A fresh tear escaped one rainbow eye. "Marlee, he misled you. He kept the bracelet. Nedeni instructed him to store it under lock in the armory."

"Yes!" She leaned over and hugged Resamane. "This is wonderful news. With the Caeles Prism, we can rescue Galean."

Deshka sniffed back lingering tears. "How?"

Her hand came up to touch the metal plate on her neck. "I'll explain my plan." *Just as soon as I finish making it.* "But in order for it to work, I'm going to need you to deactivate the siliki."

"I don't know...."

"Can you do it? Are you physically capable of removing it, or at least turning it off?"

"I can acquire and operate a tool to do so, yes. But..." if it was possible for Deshka to look more stricken, he did "...when he learns what I've done, Nedeni will turn me out into the desert."

"We'll make certain he doesn't." She renewed her hold on their hands. "I swear to you—to both of you, with my heart and mind open—that I will not use any form of quantum excitation while I'm at the Serba. I won't use it until I'm far away from here.

I will not endanger the Tarazi. You have my soul-word. But there's only one way we stand a chance of reaching Galean and bringing him back, and that's by gaining direct, point-to-point access to where he's being held. I can make it happen, but only if you retrieve my Caeles Prism and remove the siliki."

Resamane's eamonal radiated with a burst of hope. "I trust you, Marlee my friend. Deshka, I feel her truth, do you not?"

"I do. I...*madari*. Will you tell me your plan first? It might be so insane that...but I suppose I will try anything. Galean would do no less for me. He's done more."

"Right. The plan." Her brain had been racing in circles ever since she left Nedeni's office, patching together a plan, then tearing it up with each new kernel of intel and starting over in successive loops. "It's pretty simple, really. Deshka, you and I take a comp-craft to the middle of nowhere. Then I open a wormhole to Galean's cell. We free him and return to the craft, then the Serba."

"That's it? Your plan is a little light on details."

She shrugged. "I tend to improvise on the fly. Now, I need you to gather up every tool and weapon we can use. Do you have something that can hack or override security protocols? Such as on doors? If everything goes according to plan, we shouldn't need it, but I don't want to be caught empty-handed."

"Yes. We're always struggling to keep up with the newest military-grade tech, but we do have tools. And weapons, you said?"

"Yes. Blades for both of us, as well as infraguns. Also something to break through the restraints they'll presumably have Galean tied down in. Back home we would use a gamma blade, but I don't know what you have."

"A karbur knife."

"Great. Grab a pack of emergency first aid supplies, too, in case...well, in case. Also two of those personal stealth devices Galean was wearing when he kidnapped me."

Deshka was nodding steadily now, so she hadn't asked for anything unattainable.

"I'll let you know if I think of anything else. Go start acquiring everything, as we don't have much time. But be discreet."

"Right. I can—should we meet back here?"

"Yes, please." She shifted toward Resamane. "Now, my friend. I need you to make me look like a Belascocian."

13

"I make a terrible Belascocian, don't I?"

"You are striking. But…perhaps it is a rather poor impersonation. Still, I think it will suffice for anything other than a close-range encounter."

Marlee considered herself in the mirror and wasn't so sure.

You look positively ridiculous.

Thanks, Voice!

Resamane, with considerable help from two of her sighted desbida friends, had divided her always unruly hair into over a hundred individual locks, then straightened them and wound them into thick strands using a goopy gel. Makeup created the illusion of widening her eyes toward her temples, and contact lenses darkened her irises to black; they had also used makeup to both thin and widen her lips. A binder flattened her chest; her breasts weren't particularly noteworthy to begin with, but now they were invisible beneath clothes. A fabbed tail hung droopily down from her coccyx, secured with tacky glue. She couldn't control it, unfortunately, because that would be fun to play with.

But the most dramatic change was her skin. Full-body paint shifted its hue to a deep, dusky burgundy and added an impression of the lamina scales that gave texture to Belascocian skin.

Resamane frowned and reached out to touch her nose. "I wish I could do more to reduce your nasal cavity, as Jauri says the protrusion remains extreme. I hope the makeup will suffice to draw attention away from it."

Marlee had never considered noses to be the most obnoxious feature of human beings, but she conceded hers did stick out far more than Belascocian noses. Resamane's friends had utilized shading to de-emphasize her nostrils and soften away the tip, but there was nothing else to be done.

"Well, it looks hardly there to me. I'll try to keep my chin down."

"Fine, but if you are actively engaged in combat, do not worry about your nose."

"Right." She chuckled with forced levity. She wanted Resamane to sense how appreciative she was, while also *not* sensing how terrified she was. The last time she'd tried to rescue someone being held prisoner by evil, reprehensible and also armed government forces, she'd ended up in prison herself. Though she *had* succeeded in the rescue.... Regardless, it was pointless for her to try to hide her feelings from the woman's irakurri.

Resamane touched the top of her hand. "You and Deshka can bring him home, if anyone can."

See? "Thank you for the vote of confidence. I am going to try my best." She took a few steps back and spun around, confirming the tail remained firmly attached. The clothes were more purely Belascocian in style than what she'd been wearing since arriving. As a bonus, they were padded in crucial areas with a material resistant—though not completely impervious—to puncture wounds and the intrusion of those atzapar hooked bullets.

In a crucial moment, if she was under direct fire, she could also activate her internal defense shielding. It would paint a bullseye on her location, but if people were shooting at her, they already knew where she was.

She strode around the room, trying to get used to the feel of the sandals. Due to the webbing between their toes and how much they used those toes for grappling, Belascocians never seemed to cover their feet. They sported a hundred varieties of sandals, but always sandals.

But fighting in sandals was better than trying to fight in dress heels, as she'd done such a poor job of in the consul's office.

The door to the apartment slid open, and Deshka hurried in. "I've got—whoa. This is...a pretty remarkable transformation."

"Resamane is a wizard."

They both stared at her oddly, and she realized 'wizard' translated to something entirely different in Scocian. "Sorry. She is a master of transformation."

"That she is."

"It wasn't me. Apala and Jauri did all the work. I merely projected an image of what I wanted done upon their minds."

Deshka dropped a duffel bag on the floor and approached them. "Still. I mean, she doesn't look like one of us, but now she doesn't *not* look like one of us."

"Close enough for the mission, then." Marlee's expression sobered. "Did you bring the tool?"

"I did." His whole body sighed, and he stepped close to her, his hands lightly touching her arms, as he would a member of his odola. "Understand, we are placing nothing less than our continued survival in your hands. You can kill every person living in the Serba with a simple thought."

"I won't. I would rather die myself first." In truth, she was so nervous she'd accidentally use her eVi or cybernetics in a way that would send off quantum waves—because back home, she did so a thousand times a day without conscious thought—that she'd written a program in her eVi to block everything the siliki blocked. She'd need to consciously toggle off the program in order to send a message, open a wormhole, access the Noesis or execute a myriad of other actions.

She activated the program, then tilted her head to the side to expose her neck. "Please, Deshka."

He nodded grimly, then retrieved a rectangular claw device from the bag. He pressed it against the siliki, and the little claws latched onto the edges. Warmth spread across the metal to the point of pain—then the fibers embedded in her neck withdrew, and the metal plate came away in the clutches of the device.

She breathed out. "It was that simple all along, huh?"

"With the right tool." He reached back into the bag and produced an identical metal plate. "Now I'm going to attach this one.

It's inert, but this way no one here will know you're no longer inhibited."

She didn't want him to attach it; the plate and its tendrils irritated her skin and hurt her neck when she slept. But she supposed it was necessary. "Go ahead."

She flinched as the fibers burrowed their way under her skin. When Deshka removed the tool and stepped away, she scratched absently at the new plate. It hurt all the more for her skin having been momentarily free of it.

Let it go. This is a monumental act of trust on their part, so stop whining.

I know. Fine.

She turned to Resamane and grasped her hands. "Thank you for your help. If it is within my power to bring Galean back to you, I swear to you I will do it."

"As will I." Deshka joined them, his tail gently intertwining with Resamane's.

"I believe in you, both of you. My soul goes with you on this journey, for my heart waits at your destination."

All right. Each second they spent standing around being sentimental was another second in which Galean could be faced with interrogation and forced into committing suicide. She stepped back and indicated the bags Deshka had brought. "What about my Caeles Prism?"

"When we're ready to use it."

She flinched at the realization that kind, open, friendly Deshka didn't fully trust her. She told herself it was the technology he didn't trust, but didn't quite believe it. "But it is in the bag?"

"It is. Now, we need to move." Deshka picked up the bag and secured it over his shoulder. It held all their weapons and other devices, as she couldn't exactly walk through the atrium armed to the teeth. "Nedeni thinks I'm going on a reconnaissance mission in Emankor, so no alarms will be raised when I check out a compcraft. We'll take the maintenance passages to the pool so your presence doesn't draw attention. Hopefully we won't bump into anyone on the way."

Consciousness invaded Galean's mind by way of a throbbing ache near the base of his skull. His thoughts meandered through a fog, and he had to concentrate to focus them.

The mission. The Kaldi. *Bashi*, had the team succeeded in escaping with the desbida? He had no recollection of events after he'd ordered everyone to leave him behind, and the possibility that his comrades and six innocent souls had been captured clawed rakes of despair through his mind.

The first thing he did was try to send a directed message to Nedeni. The waves bounced right back at him. Soundwave block around the room, then; disappointing, but not a surprise.

He worked to calm himself. The transport had already been well on its way when the Kaldi struck. If Fremen had followed his orders, they should have been able to elude detection and reach the Serba. He had to trust in this.

The tip of his tongue carefully poked at the device seated in a left upper molar. A precise flick, followed by a long press of his tongue to activate it, then a shift of his jaw and a firm clampdown, and his life would end by his own hand.

No secrets could be kept from a desbida. Resa had taught him some techniques to muddy and confuse a probing by one, but they weren't apt to present much of an obstacle for someone trained in using their irakurri for interrogation. They'd likely use one of the new Soldad to make certain; he'd provide an excellent test of their skills.

His mind held many secrets that, were the enemy to discover them, would be devastating for the Tarazi. The name of their leader. The identities of their informants scattered throughout the government, powerful corporations and the Aterpe Project who fed them information. The technology and methods they used to evade detection while traveling out in the world.

But all this paled beneath one crucial fact etched in his mind: the location of the Serba. If they learned this, it was all over. Resa was dead. Deshka and Nedeni were dead. The hundreds of desbida they'd taken in and thousands of people dedicated to their cause were all dead.

He didn't want to die, but in comparison, his sacrifice was nothing against all the lives saved. He'd do it willingly and without regret.

But he also wasn't the type to give up without a fight, so he returned his tongue to its resting location and prepared his mind for escape the instant an opportunity arose.

He opened his eyes and looked around. The cold, featureless walls of an interrogation cell greeted him. A terminal sat in one corner. Beside it was a cart laden with what had to be instruments of torture. Restraints tugged lightly at his wrists, ankles and tail. They weren't so tight as to impede circulation, but he wasn't going to succeed in wiggling out of them, either. Not quickly, in any event.

The door slid open, and a man wearing a white lab coat walked in—and immediately scrambled backward. "I'll let them know you're awake." He spun and disappeared down the hall, starting the clock of Galean's life accelerating toward zero.

14

Their comp-craft cruised beneath the hull of the Serba until they cleared the structure, at which point Deshka pointed it toward the surface.

Marlee splayed a hand on the elongated glass bubble that covered the top half of the vehicle and peered outside. But the water was murky and dark, revealing only the occasional ripple of a passing fish disturbing the stillness.

"This is *so* much better than drowning."

"Drowning?" Deshka asked.

"Galean and I swam to the Serba. No vehicle."

"And?"

"And...I can't breathe water."

"Oh!" He glanced over, horror flashing across his features. "You did look to be in some distress when I first saw you. And Galean knew about your inability to ura-arnasa before you entered Lake Lasai?"

She snorted. "He sure did."

"Oh, my. You must forgive him, though. His ari was not in a proper state when he returned."

"Because he'd just killed his brother."

"Yes."

"Still, he could have commed someone to bring up a vehicle."

Deshka contemplated this for a moment, then shook his head. "Nedeni would never have allowed you entry into the Serba, had he been given advance warning."

"That, I believe. I'm surprised he didn't immediately throw me back in the water and let the drowning complete its work."

"Nedeni is called upon to make many difficult and often morally gray decisions, but he would not knowingly condemn an innocent person to die. Galean knew once he got you inside the

Serba, you'd be safe. So though it was most uncomfortable for you, he made the right choice."

"I suppose so." The *right* choice would've been to simply allow her to return home in those fateful first seconds of their meeting. But he'd explained why he hadn't, and she understood, after a fashion.

The vehicle slowed as light began to filter down through the water in particle-clouded rays. They breached the surface with scarcely a ripple and eased to the shore. Deshka pressed two buttons on the dash, and a low rumble from below the seats preceded the vehicle rising fully out of the water until it hovered above the ground. Another button, and a new engine engaged, sending them cruising off to the east with some haste. The comp-craft was a useful convertible if one made one's home beneath the waves.

Marlee tried to focus her mind on the coming mission, but there were too many unknowns to do much detailed mental preparation. Until she got a look at the prison, she couldn't predict how she would need to proceed, and she couldn't slip into sidespace and do reconnaissance until they were some distance away from the Serba. No, this would be a 'make it up as she went' mission, which to be honest was where she did her best work.

So, time to get to know her partner a little better. "Galean said you and he are cousins?"

"It's a close enough description of the relation, yes. We grew up together at the Ozeal enclave in Maistel."

"With Resamane, too?"

"For a while. Before she was taken away."

"Were you always close?"

"We were always friends. But there were a lot of kids in the enclave." Deshka made a course correction, veering toward a cloud-strewn horizon decorated with increasing foliage. "When I was eight years old, and Galean nine, we were out playing a good stretch from home—five of us. We stumbled upon the fresh kill of a cypone."

"What's that?"

"It's a beast of the marshes in the southwest region of Estapa. It has a thick hide that's difficult to penetrate and sharp ridges down its spine. Long legs to give it speed and razored teeth that will rip you to shreds in seconds. But the worst part is, it has two detachable...stalks, I guess you'd call them. They can scramble across the ground and send sensory data to the creature: limited sight and sound, but especially smells."

"That's freaky."

"Yes. So we were poking at the carcass of the kill, as kids do, when Galean spotted one of the stalks in the weeds. He shouted for everyone to run, and we did. Except the cypone had been hunting us the entire time. It charged out from the opposite direction and grabbed my ankle in its jaw. Snapped it in two with a single bite.

"The next thing I knew, Galean was wrestling the damn creature. He'd leapt onto its back and was stabbing at its eyes with his puny steel blade. He managed to get the blade into one of the eyes, and the cypone started thrashing about like a fiend. Galean dropped the blade and grabbed its jaws with both hands and yanked them open. I was about to pass out from the pain, but I managed to scoot back and pull what was left of my foot out of the cypone's mouth.

"Galean's hands were shredded to bloody bits by its teeth. As he let go, the creature bit one of his fingers off. But he just kept going. He pinned it under him as he climbed to his feet, then stomped on its head. This stunned the creature, made it sluggish. He grabbed the blade off the ground and stabbed it in the one place where a cypone is vulnerable—where the stalks detach along its neck. The hide of necessity thins and becomes flexible there.

"I'll never forget, this putrid black blood gushed out all over Galean's hands and into the bog. Caused third-degree chemical burns on his skin. See, one of the cypone's defense mechanisms is acidic blood."

"They sound lovely."

"They are not. Now it's dying, or close enough. Galean helps me to my feet—one of them anyway—and, though he's bleeding and has to be in agonizing pain himself, supports me as we start hobbling toward home. We were almost halfway there before a group of adults found us. The other kids with us had run when Galean shouted and hadn't stopped until they got back to the enclave."

Deshka reached down and tapped his right ankle. "The tendons in my ankle and two bones in my foot are synthetic. The doctor barely managed to save the rest of the foot. But Galean had it worse. They had to grow skin grafts for his hands and attach an entire synthetic finger. He suffered through tremendous pain for weeks.

"He saved my life, without a thought for his own. And somehow, he never held it against me, never used it as leverage or to invoke guilt or shame in me. I owe him nothing less than my continued existence in the world. So since then, I've followed wherever he leads. I try to pay him back, every day of my life."

She recalled what Deshka had said when he'd taken her on her tour of the Serba. *Mostly, I try to keep Galean sane. Failing that, I try to keep him alive.* The comment made a bit more sense now.

"Well, I think if we succeed in our mission today, you can consider the debt repaid in full."

Deshka huffed a laugh. "Galean will probably say the same, but this is a debt that can never be erased. And I wouldn't want it to be, anyway. Thanks to Galean, my life has purpose."

Deshka brought the vehicle to a stop on the edge of a chaparral, amidst some tangled foliage beneath the overhang of a small copse of trees.

"Don't do anything yet." The doors swung up and open, and Deshka climbed out.

Marlee sat there with her hands in her lap. *Now* it was time to psyche herself up for the mission—

Deshka bent down and stuck his head in the cab. "Sorry. Poorly phrased. You can and should get out of the vehicle. Just don't do anything to compromise our location."

"Ah." She stepped out and gazed around, considering their surroundings. They'd reached the edge of the jungle that stretched from here to Ausatan and beyond. It wasn't exactly camouflage, but the trees and groundcover made the vehicle difficult to spot from the sky.

"Will you be able to open a portal to here once we free Galean?"

Her gaze went to the night sky. If she could access sidespace, even for a second, it would be so much easier. But she possessed enough data for her eVi to pinpoint their location. She had a map of the Estapa continent—of the whole planet—stored, and she'd nailed down where Lake Lasai was. She'd tracked their course and approximate speed since leaving. Coupled with a quick survey of the landmarks in sight and the stars overhead, she managed to mark this location within a few dozen meters.

She nodded. "I will."

"Wonderful." Deshka stretched his arms and legs, then dropped down onto all fours. "Secure the pack with our weapons and tools on your shoulders, then hop onto my back."

"Excuse me?"

"My back. Climb on."

"I...don't understand."

He sighed and stood. "We can't portal directly into the prison from here, as the quantum activity will bring the authorities right to the vehicle, possibly before we have time to reach Galean, free him and return. So we need to move some distance away before you perform your magic. The best way to do that is to run. And, respectfully, I can run at least three times faster than you. So you will ride me."

The situations you get yourself into....

I know, I know.

Her brow furrowed at the absurd notion. "Won't I be too heavy?"

"I've carried heavier. And, as we've covered, I'm willing to do quite a lot to save Galean's life. I will manage." His hands landed on the ground once more. "Time is wasting."

She slid her arms into the pack and secured the clasp at her waist. Then she tightened the hood of her cloak around her neck to protect her specially crafted hair before throwing one leg over Deshka's back, cringing as she did. His hips were narrow, his frame lithe, and he wasn't any taller than her. No way could this work.

"Squeeze your thighs against my waist and wrap your arms around my neck. I don't want you to be thrown off."

She gingerly leaned down until her chest was pressed against him and draped her arms over his shoulders, then lifted her feet off the ground, letting him support her entire weight.

"Am I too heavy?"

"No." The word came out in a hiss, though. She definitely was.

Without further commentary, he took off running.

Instantly her grip tightened. His loping gait was surprisingly smooth, but there were no restraints or handholds or inertial dampers or anything except her own muscles and limbs to keep her secure on top of him.

The Consulate briefing files had talked about how the Belascocians retained notable adaptability from their evolutionary past. She'd seen it already in their ability to breathe underwater and their freakishly dexterous tail. But this was above and beyond what she might have imagined possible. Deshka ran like a hyena. No, a larger cat. Not a lion—his body was too lean—but perhaps a panther. His arms and legs flowed in perfect sync with one another, with his shoulders, back and hips fluidly absorbing the motion, as if traveling on four limbs was his natural state.

The Belascocians were a truly remarkable species.

Wind whipped past her face and chilled her arms; they must be traveling over sixty kilometers per hour. They ran parallel to the increasingly dense jungle, keeping away from the open flat-lands while avoiding the uneven roots and grasping plants to their left. Deshka seemed to have an innate sense of the terrain, easily shifting to avoid obstacles long before she spotted them.

After a few minutes, she allowed herself to relax a little, open-ing herself up to the wind and the trees speeding by. There was a...wildness to their travel. No technology, no devices, merely muscle and limb working in perfect harmony to propel them across the land. It reminded her of flying on Cupcake. The dragon's body and muscles were much larger and stronger, but the sensation was oddly similar.

The realization provoked a profound longing. For home, for freedom, for her dragon. Her actions now weren't likely to get her home any faster—the opposite, in fact. But she was who she was.

Deshka finally slowed to a stop. She shook herself out of her reverie and hurriedly climbed off of him. He stood a mite creakily, pressing his hands into the small of his back as he twisted from side to side.

"I was too heavy, wasn't I?"

"More like I haven't run for that distance, that fast, in a long time." He gave her an easy smile; no longer animal but man. "Let me see the pack. I'll distribute our gear."

She unfastened it and handed it to him. He set it on the ground and crouched in front of it, then began removing items. "How will you find Galean?"

"Sidespace. You showed me where the facility is on the map, so it's merely a matter of locating the wing where prisoners are held, then searching the rooms until I find his."

"With your mind."

"I project my consciousness to the location, so...yeah. With my mind."

"Incredible. How long will it take?"

"Hopefully, only a few seconds. No more than thirty, as you said the prison itself was only one floor. And the instant I find him, I'll open a wormhole into his room. We'll be gone from here long before anyone can reach this location."

He handed her the infragun and karbur knife...then, hesitantly, her Caeles Prism.

Fastening the bracelet on her wrist was like reattaching a severed limb. She exhaled in relief as the cool metal tickled her skin. She could go home now.

She'd be lying to herself if she said the urge to simply open a wormhole to Concord HQ, depart, and leave Galean to his fate didn't flare in her mind. She'd been attacked, kidnapped and imprisoned by these people; she didn't owe them anything.

But Resamane was a beautiful soul who had helped her at every turn. Deshka was earnest and kind and thoughtful. Galean was...well, she still wasn't certain of the quality of his character, but she had a sneaking suspicion he might be a better man than he'd first let on. Regardless, she'd be a horrible person if she walked away from them now, and she couldn't leave Galean to die for the crime of freeing innocents.

She flashed Deshka a brilliant smile. "Thank you."

"You're welcome, but I didn't so much do it for you. Now, they'll detect the perturbation caused by a wormhole opening inside the facility. We'll need to move with the speed of the wind."

"You concentrate on getting him out of whatever restraints they've locked him in, since you know the tech. I'll act as lookout and shoot anyone who shows up."

"It's a plan."

Not much of one, but any plan at all was better than most of the situations in which she'd found herself under fire.

15

The door to his cell slid open, and a man in a nondescript navy business suit walked in. Galean detected no eamonal from the man at all. He was blank, a void in the world. The mirror opposite of the desbida, who saw and touched every thought and emotion.

"Galean Ozeal of Maistel. Son to Otsoko and Nahia Ozeal of the Nekane pod, brother to Vasem Thorkan and Resamane. Served your two years in the military and earned an honorable discharge. Became a carpenter, then an architect of some good reputation—until one day six years ago, when you quit your job and vanished without a trace. Until now."

Galean kept his expression blank, but inwardly he felt a surge of relief—then buried his thoughts using the techniques Resa had taught him. They didn't know he'd killed his brother, hadn't identified him as the man who fled through the city amidst a sea of surveillance cams with a strange alien in tow. The Tarazi utilized sophisticated anti-surveillance tools, but they had limits. A pity he'd never be able to tell Nedeni how well they'd performed.

"We know you are Tarazi. We can surmise that you kidnapped your sister from her therapeutics camp and harbor her now, just as you assisted in the kidnapping of those poor desbida before you were captured."

Galean stared silently at the man.

"You know we can extract the information we require from you. There is no escaping it. But I'm not a callous or unfeeling man, and I see no need to take by force that which can be given freely. So here's my offer. Tell us the locations of all Tarazi bases, as well as the names of those in leadership positions within the organization. Do this, and I will allow you to live. Through living, you can perhaps perform enough penance that, when you die, your ari will be admitted into the Ozeal arima.

"Refuse, and we will acquire the information anyway. Then you will die a damned man."

Galean kept his mind and expression blank atop a storm of raging emotions. Turmoil tore at his soul. Not turmoil over whether to take the man's offer—he'd never willingly give up the secrets of the Tarazi—but over the sins he'd committed in this life. Nothing could wash away his brother's blood on his hands, and no matter what he did here and now, in all likelihood his ari would be cast adrift on his death, condemned to wander the lands alone. But he'd also done what good he could. He'd rescued his sister from torment and brutality and protected her ever since. He'd rescued others as well. He'd tried to be a good comrade to his fellow Tarazi, his hartua odola. He didn't dare hope the arima would grant him a mercy for those actions, but the knowledge provided him a bit of comfort, even peace, here at the end.

He said a silent goodbye to Resa, and hoped she felt it in her heart.

"No."

"Alas. How disappointing." The man turned toward the door as it slid open again and a woman walked in. She wore the loose-fitting beige jumper of captivity, and her eyes were hard and cold. Soldad.

She gazed at the man expectantly. "Your orders, sir?"

"Take it all."

Galean flicked the spot on his tooth, pressed hard, then slammed his jaw shut.

If putting on the bracelet was like reattaching a limb, diving into sidespace was like returning to her childhood home after a long trip and finding it lit up in Christmas decorations, with a roaring fire and hot cider waiting. She'd been rendered half dumb and blind when her access to this realm was cut off, and she only now realized how much.

Don't dawdle! Already your actions have registered as a blip on a screen somewhere. They are coming.

Marlee sent off a pre-prepared message home while her consciousness raced to the location of the Seguru Instal. It was a maze on the inside, and it took her two seconds longer than it should have to locate the prisoner floor. Twenty rooms spread across four hallways on the third floor of the east wing of the second-largest building. Twelve of them were occupied. Two of them housed captives currently in obvious physical agony, but dammit, she couldn't save everyone. She checked the next room, then the next, then the—

Galean lay in an exam chair, convulsing against the restraints holding him down. A man ransacked two drawers in a cabinet, hunting for something, while a woman stood in front of the door. Were they too late?

She yanked herself out of sidespace and back into her body. Her arm extended, energy building up in the Caeles Prism. "I found him, but it's not good. There are two people in the room. I'll take the woman, you take the man."

"What about—?"

A wormhole opened in front of her; on the other side waited the chaotic scene. "Go now!"

She didn't wait for Deshka before charging through the opening, infragun in hand.

The woman was turning and lunging for the door, intent on escape. Marlee shot her in the shoulder, sending her sprawling out into the hallway. Was the woman armed? She didn't want to kill her unless necessary, but—

A loud crash clanged behind her, and she spun to see Deshka driving the man into the cabinets along the wall. Equipment scattered to the floor in a racket.

Marlee leveled her gun at the man's head, but he and Deshka were fighting with arms and tails and hair, and she didn't dare shoot for fear of hitting her partner.

Out of the corner of her eye, she noted the woman struggling to reach her feet. Marlee shot her in the leg, and the woman collapsed to the floor with a mournful howl.

A loud *pop* rang out to her right. The man slid down the wall to the floor, leaving a winding streak of blood in his wake.

Deshka's chest heaved. His eyes were wide teardrops of coal, his hair fanned out around him, tips razor sharp in alert. "Spirits...."

"Galean. We have to help him."

For a long nanosecond, Deshka stared at her incomprehensibly...then his gaze darted to his cousin. "Oh, no. He's already taken the etenail. Use the karbur knife to disable his restraints while I—" Then he was digging in the pack for something. After two agonizing, slow-motion seconds, he produced an injector and climbed half on top of Galean's convulsing body. "Come on, prezia. Don't die on me now."

Marlee fumbled with the karbur knife's hilt, searching for how to activate it. Her thumb slid over an indentation, and a narrow, curved implement—more screwdriver than blade—popped out and began spinning. She pressed the tip against one of the ankle restraints. Not so easy a maneuver when Galean's legs were thrashing against them, and she immediately sliced a gash into his left ankle. But this was fixable later.

The knife vibrated against her tight grip as its head ground into the metal of the restraint, until it split apart and flopped loose. She scurried around to the other side. Deshka remained on top of Galean; the convulsions had not stopped.

The second ankle restraint fell apart without her inflicting further bloodshed—

Loud footsteps thudded down the hallway. She dropped the karbur knife, brought up her gun and leaned out into the hallway. Four angry-looking Belascocians in black tactical gear raced toward them.

She fired, then fired again. One of the men stumbled, but that was it. Shields. She fired again, lower. The beam splashed across the lead man's thigh, and he collapsed to the floor. "Deshka, we have to hurry!"

"Almost...done. Hopefully that will stabilize him."

"The knife's on the floor. Get his wrist and tail manacles."

She leaned her upper body out to fire again, dragging the weapon diagonally for maximum coverage. The first man was struggling to his feet, but her fire sent a second stumbling into the wall—an atzapar hook swarm whizzed by a fraction from her head, and she ducked back inside. Stupid of her to leave herself exposed. "Now, Deshka."

"He's free. Help me get him up."

She blew out a breath, sprayed the hallway with a sustained round of gunfire that stopped the pursuers in their tracks, then moved to the chair. Deshka had Galean's arm draped over his shoulder and one leg dangling off the chair. She squeezed in on the other side and struggled to maneuver Galean's flopping limbs up with one arm, while the other arm held out the Caeles Prism. The air at the foot of the chair tore apart in a golden ripple, and she forcibly dragged them all through the opening as it was still forming.

Gunfire whizzed over their heads as they all fell to the dirt near the comp-craft. *Close!*

Silence fell across the jungle.

Deshka rolled Galean over and leaned in to his chest. "He's breathing, but it's shallow and halting."

Marlee leapt to her feet. "We can't treat him here. We need to move. If what your people have said is true, this location is lit up like a spotlight."

"Yes. Help me get him into the vehicle."

She and Deshka again wrangled Galean up between them and dragged him the few meters to the comp-craft.

"Let's lay him down in the back."

The backseat was one long bench covered by a cushion of marginal softness, but Galean was in no condition to be complaining about comfort. As soon as all his limbs were crammed inside, she sprinted around to the passenger side and climbed in. "Go."

Deshka engaged the engine; the vehicle lifted off the ground and sped toward the brightening horizon. "Stealth activated. It's far from foolproof, but so long as they're not scanning exactly where we are, we should escape notice."

She peered behind them, searching for lights that signified approaching police vehicles as she belatedly remembered to reactivate the block on her eVi's quantum capabilities. When she survived her current predicament and was safely home and diplomatic relations with Belarria were developing in a proper manner, the Belascocians were going to disclose how they were able to detect and track the tiniest quantum perturbations.

Of course, once they had it, Concord deploying such technology was certain to be a thorny issue. While she wasn't overly thrilled at the notion of unleashing a surveillance tool that could be abused, this wasn't about catching criminals. It was about defending all of civilization against vastly powerful enemies. Defeating the Rasu had taken everything Concord had to give, and the next enemy stood to be even more formidable. They had to be ready. So they'd use every capability at their disposal to ensure they were, and this incredible skill possessed by the Belascocians just might be a game-changer.

Thudding sounded from behind her, and she peered over the seat. "Crap, he's convulsing again!"

"Grab the pack. There's one more injector in there."

She rummaged through the pack, fingers fumbling over various items until they felt a small cylinder. She unfastened her harness and climbed through the narrow gap between the seats into the back.

Her right knee landed hard on a spot that, were he conscious, Galean surely would not appreciate. Ugh, there really was no space at all back here.

"You need to inject it into his neck, about one centimeter in front of the gill slits. And up almost to his jaw."

She balanced herself over Galean as best she could, what with all the convulsing. Her left foot braced against the rear of the passenger seat and her right on the door as she leaned down over him. His skin felt clammy and damp, a dull, lifeless gray in the faint light.

She positioned the injector against his neck—his head ricocheted off the bench, knocking it away. "Shit!"

"What's wrong?"

"He's jerking around too much. How long until we reach the Serba?"

"Longer than he has."

"Right. I'll do my best." She dug the injector out of the crease in the cushion, then squeezed her thighs against Galean's sides so he didn't buck her off. She placed her left hand along his jaw and shoved it firmly to the side, then brought the injector up with her right, pushing it into his neck as close as possible to where Deshka had instructed, and pressed the button.

Galean's back arched in a spasm, and she slammed her skull against the roof. *Ow....*

The spasm released, and his whole body went slack. She put a hand on his chest and felt the shallow but reassuring rise and fall of his chest. "The convulsions have stopped, and he's still breathing."

"Great job."

She exhaled and let her chin drop to her chest. Were they all going to live through this?

After another breath, she wiggled into the front and collapsed into the seat. "Good thinking on your part, bringing the medication."

"I knew he'd suicide rather than give up any intel. I'm just glad we got there in time." Deshka glanced over his shoulder. "Probably."

The adrenaline had started to dissipate by the time they dove beneath the waters of Lake Lasai. She considered ramping it up again, but the truth was, medical personnel would take over as soon as they reached the Serba, and her part in this escapade would be over.

Well, except for the fallout. She couldn't predict Nedeni's reaction to their mission with any certainty. She thought he'd be relieved Galean was alive and back in the bosom of the Tarazi, but would his relief be eclipsed by his anger at having his orders flagrantly disobeyed? Very possibly.

"Listen, when Nedeni finds out my siliki has been deactivated, and about the Caeles Prism, too, I'm going to take full responsibility. You had nothing to do with it, okay?"

Deshka looked over at her in surprise. "What? No. I'm not sorry I did whatever was necessary to save Galean."

"I know you're not. But it'll be easy enough to say I figured out how to deactivate the siliki, then broke into the armory database and discovered where my Caeles Prism was located. Only after I did all that did I come to you with a plan for rescuing Galean. You realized you couldn't put me back in chains, and you wanted to save your cousin, so you went along with it."

"Marlee, I don't think—"

"It'll work. You all don't really understand my abilities, which means it's easy to make them seem larger than life. He'll buy it."

"But you can't interact with most of our technology."

"I can, actually."

"What?"

"I've been able to for a little while now. I haven't abused it, because I haven't needed to. But I can work your inprims. Your door locks. Your screens. I think I could drive this vehicle in a pinch."

"Then why haven't you simply left?"

She sighed. "Because I made Resamane and Galean a promise. Also, I have a terrible weakness for oppressed peoples, one that has gotten me into heaps of trouble more than once. And now again here on Belarria." She chuckled wryly. "It's either my worst failing or my greatest strength, depending on if I survive."

"I for one am glad we appealed to your weakness—or your strength. Also, thank you for trying to protect me, but I'm not going to lie to Nedeni. I doubt I could if I wanted to, but I don't."

"Oh. I suppose not. So the 'hartua odola' is a real thing, then? When you adopt someone into your family, or vice versa, you gain the ability for your eamonals to interact? To convey sentiment and intentions, even thoughts?"

"It's real. It's a choice each of us can make."

The lights from the Serba began to shine through the murky waters ahead, and Deshka's fingers flexed over the controls. "I've alerted Medical to meet us at the pool. I'll stay with Galean. You should go retrieve Resamane."

"Can't you send her a message as well?"

"I can, but I don't want to worry her unnecessarily. Let her sense the truth of our mission from you in its fullness. Then she can come to Medical knowing what to expect."

"Okay." Marlee exhaled as they surfaced in the pool and eased onto the platform. The next hour was apt to be fraught with conflict. Possibly a bit of yelling, but hopefully no more restraints or jail cells.

16

Holographic representations of eleven individuals encircled President Hasane Lormain. Their faces were shrouded in shadow, and the projections designated them only as Member #1, #2 and so on.

One could speculate as to their identities, of course, and Hasane often did, simply by noting the most powerful corporations and wealthiest businesspeople. But it was only speculation, and at the end of the day, it didn't matter. They were the Errigime. The puppeteers of his world.

"You've spoken with the Concord official today?" Member #1 asked.

"Yes. They are most concerned about the welfare and location of their ambassador—understandably so. They grow more insistent with their 'offers' of assistance in each conversation, and I suspect they are using technology we cannot detect to conduct their own remote scans and searches of our planet. I fear if we do not report concrete progress soon, we will have aliens in our midst whether we wish it or not."

"We do not wish it," Member #1 replied, imbuing his voice with an unmistakable firmness.

Hasane swallowed the biting retort he wanted to snap back with. "I realize that is your position, and accordingly I am doing everything I can to prevent their arrival. But when Concord finds out we are implicating one of their own as a murderer, they will not be pleased, to say the least. Respectfully, we are balanced upon the head of a pin here; provoking them in this manner may well bring about war. A war, I will remind everyone, we cannot win."

"I highly doubt Concord is watching our news broadcasts, Mr. President. They will be none the wiser."

"Don't be so certain. One of their people is lost on our world. We have their full attention now, for good or ill. Surely everyone here recognizes that we must ensure it is for good."

"Matters might already have escalated," Member #3 stated with a hint of frustration. "I have reason to believe the aliens are here, on the ground, as we speak. The Sare network has surfaced multiple reports of sightings of strangely dressed, tail-less individuals moving deliberately within urban shadows. We've done what we can to explain away the sightings."

Hasane nodded. "I too have seen evidence that Concord has sent people to the surface, though their representative, Dean Veshnael, denies it. He states they will request our permission before deploying any forces."

"Diplomatic posturing on their part—a game of carrots and sticks. Meanwhile they do as they wish, because they can. It is only a matter of dwindling time until their warships arrive in our skies."

"All the more reason why we must take every step available to us to remain in Concord's good graces." Member #2 leaned forward in their chair, until Hasane could *almost* make out a few facial features. "We must not wreck the greatest opportunity our world has even been granted over one individual. Everyone, we need to abandon this foolish stonewalling and open our arms to Concord. If we play things very astutely and are very lucky, we might be able to undo the self-inflicted damage we've caused and emerge a winner in this negotiation.

"I propose we announce to the media that we have been contacted by Concord. We speak glowingly of our new alien friends and invite them here in full view of the public. We allow them to search our lands for their lost ambassador, while aiding them at every turn. Perhaps they will find her, perhaps not. But the choice is a simple and stark one. Continue down the path of rejection and obfuscation against an objectively superior counterparty, and we risk losing everything, including our lives. Or extend a hand in friendship, and see the riches of the universe open up to us. Are we in agreement—"

Member #1 interrupted #2. "There is no vote on the floor. The greater weight of the table strongly disagrees with such a na-ïve statement by Member #2. If we supplicate ourselves to these aliens, we will never again be masters of our own fate." Member #1 shifted to speak directly to Hasane. "Continue the course. Express all the platitudes and assurances you wish to the Concord representative, but keep the aliens at a firm arm's length. Our domestic affairs are none of Concord's concern, and we will keep it this way. In fact, if their disapproval of our policies leads them to reconsider diplomatic relations, all the better.

"I say again: we do not need them. We do not need their wealth, their technology or their help. That is our formal position. Have we made ourselves clear?"

Hasane kept his outward composure, but he made a mental note of the heated tempers on display tonight. Emotions rarely ran so high among the Errigime members. Was there trouble brewing at the table? "Yes, sir. However, recognize that if we do not soon produce their ambassador, we will find ourselves facing a collection of poor options."

"We've shifted one hundred percent of the Sare's cycles to the problem," Member #8 replied. "If the alien pokes her head out of a door in any of the cities, we will know it."

Member #1 let out an audible sigh. "Given the thoroughness of our searches, we must conclude she is not being held in a city at all. I believe the Consul's murderer was Tarazi, and we know they operate primarily from the wildlands."

"Your obsession with the Tarazi blinds you to every other manner of crime." This from Member #6. "They are your monsters in the shadows. The Consul had only the most minor of connections to the Aterpe Project. The Tarazi would have no reason to target him, when there are many far richer targets for their rage."

"The Consul's sister is desbida."

"*My* sister is desbida," Member #6 retorted. "That doesn't make me Tarazi."

"True, but your sister remains safely and, one presumes, contentedly secure in one of the therapeutics camps. Consul Thorkan's sister was extracted from her camp by a team of Tarazi six years ago."

"Oh?" Member #2 replied. "What do we know of the rest of the family?"

Hasane tried to wrangle back control of the discussion. Vasem had been...not a friend, but certainly a colleague. "The Ozeal odola is unremarkable in most respects. Consul Thorkan was the first of its members to achieve any notable level of success. His sister was identified as desbida and removed from the home eleven years ago without incident. The parents and aitona, by all accounts, accepted this necessity and have not expressed concerns in the years since. Thorkan's younger brother—twin to the desbida—disappeared from public life eight months prior to his sister's extraction from the camp, however. He quit his job, canceled his apartment lease and vanished without a trace."

"Recruited by the Tarazi," Member #2 replied.

"A reasonable conclusion to draw from the facts."

"Mr. President, are you suggesting Consul Thorkan had gotten himself mixed up with the movement?"

Member #1 jumped in before he managed to reply. "They are not a movement—they are terrorists bent on destroying a carefully crafted system that has worked to keep our society stable and ourselves well-protected for a decade now. As for Consul Thorkan's interests, we don't yet know enough to say. He appeared to be estranged from his odola, and this was not his only personal failing. Still, we ignore coincidences in such affairs at our peril."

"Indeed," Hasane replied. "I ensured the appropriate investigation teams were made aware of these facts and their import."

"Oh, *izorra*...."

Everyone directed their attention to Member #8.

"As you all know, earlier today we captured a Tarazi member during their interception and kidnapping of a group of desbida. I've received word that unknown persons infiltrated the Seguru Instal and absconded with him before he could be interrogated."

Hasane scowled—only in part because in a just world, such news would have reached his ears first. "Seguru is impenetrable. It should have been impossible for anyone to gain access to the grounds, never mind the prison wing."

"And yet," Member #1 replied sardonically. "Concord possesses portal technology, as does their ambassador. Given this news, we have to consider the possibility that not only do the Tarazi possess her, but she is now willingly working with them as well."

Dread pooled in Hasane's gut. How had the situation spun so far out of control, and so swiftly? "If the Tarazi have managed to persuade her of the rightness of their cause...when she returns home, she will poison the minds of Concord against us with wild tales of persecution and tyranny."

Member #8 clasped their hands on the circular table. "Then we might need to do more than find her."

The dread turned to ice, chilling Hasane's soul to its core. *Please do not make me do this, I beg you.* But in truth, it wasn't up to him. If the Errigime wanted the ambassador dead, he could do nothing to prevent it.

WRECKING
BALL

17

Sensory waves always came first upon awakening. Galean knew immediately that Resa and Deshka were close by. Their worry intermingled with hope, his identity at the center of it. While his thoughts fought through an unnatural fogginess to collate and link together, he basked in the warmth of his most beloved prezia...until his last memory solidified into a semblance of clarity and confusion and uncertainty overtook him. The Soldad's bottomless eyes searing into him as he did the unthinkable, sacrificing himself to keep his sister and the Tarazi safe.

Yet he was somehow alive, and Resa and Deshka were here. Unless he was delusional in his final breaths, or his ari was hallucinating as it wandered the desolate steppes....

He opened his eyes. Much to his shock, he was in a patient room in the Medical wing of the Serba, which was a dramatic change of scenery from his previous location.

Resa vaulted across the room to clasp his face in her hands, a tidal wave of love and relief pouring out of her to cleanse his soul. "You're awake. Can you speak?"

"Of course I can speak." His throat burned fiercely with the act, though, and the words came out hoarse and halting.

A nurse arrived beside Resa to offer him strawed water. "Here. Sip carefully."

He nursed the straw for a moment, welcoming the cool liquid as it coated his abrased throat, then let her withdraw the cup.

Deshka appeared at his other side to clasp their arms together at the elbow. "It is good you remain with us."

"But how? The Soldad interrogator was there. I had no choice but to activate the etenail. I felt myself slip into unconsciousness, so I know it worked. Now I am here, and I'm not certain if this is a dream overtaking me in the instant of death."

"It's no dream. You're really here." Resa smiled so magnificently, all the way to her eyes that could not see, yet saw everything. "Deshka and Marlee rescued you."

"Truthfully, Marlee did most of the rescuing. I just drove."

"Not true, Deshka. You were amazing."

Marlee? Deshka shifted a little to the side, and only now did Galean see the Human leaning against the far wall, arms and ankles crossed. "You came for me?"

She lifted her shoulders. "It seemed the thing to do."

"I have no words sufficient to thank you." He didn't understand. Surely she would not perform such a tremendous act out of love for him, as he had done nothing to earn even feelings of mild goodwill from her. Out of love for Resa, perhaps? "Dare I inquire as to how you accomplished such a feat?"

Her normally full lips formed a line so thin they almost disappeared. "Hmm. There have been a few developments while you were gone."

The door slid open, and Nedeni walked in. "It seems there have been." He strode directly to the bed, and Deshka backed away to allow him access. "It is welcome tidings, to see you returned to us."

"I told them nothing, sir. There was a Soldad, but she did not gain access to my thoughts. I activated the etenail, as I swore to do. Deshka and Marlee must have arrived just then...I confess I have no memory of what happened after that point."

"We'll sort the details, but you needn't concern yourself with them right now."

"The desbida from the mission. Did they make it here safely?"

"Yes, and they are being integrated into our world without too much difficulty. Your sacrifice held great value."

"Good. I worried. The Kaldi were clever in their tactics. We will need to be more clever as well on future missions."

Nedeni's tail reached up to stroke his shoulder in a calming gesture. "We'll talk of such matters at a later time. You need to concentrate on regaining your strength. The doctor tells me that while there should be no permanent neurological or physical damage, the etenail took a heavy toll on your body. So do as the staff says and rest. Body and spirit."

"Yes, sir."

Nedeni raised his gaze to meet his sister's. "Resamane, my heart sings with the knowledge you have been made whole once more."

"We all have been." She smiled and caressed Galean's arm.

Nedeni stepped away to level a much harsher gaze upon Deshka, then Marlee. "You two, with me."

Galean struggled to sit up in the bed, but only made it to his elbows before exhaustion crippled him. "Sir. They saved my life."

"And this will be taken into due account." Nedeni strode out, assuming they would follow.

Deshka shot him a confident expression. "It'll be fine. How angry can he be?" Then he placed a hand on Marlee's shoulder to nudge her along as he walked past her, ushering her out of the room.

Galean sighed and leaned into Resa's hand, worry dampening his relief, for the answer was quite angry indeed.

My brother, my world. I thought I lost you.

He struggled against the painful emotions. "I had to protect you, even at the cost of my own life."

"I know I cannot convince you to do otherwise. But in your absence, the world is a cold and lonely place. I do not know how to live in it without you."

"Don't be ridiculous. You have Deshka, and Nedeni, and all the desbida here who look to you for guidance. They need you to show them the way. You're strong, and you will be fine without me."

"No, I will not. Oh, brother, where do you think I draw my strength from?"

"You disobeyed a direct order. Went behind my back, stole Serba weapons and equipment. Pursued an unconscionably dangerous course of action that risked the lives of everyone here."

Deshka stood front and center of Nedeni's desk, feet planted wide and hands clasped at his stomach. "I did."

"After everything you've learned, everything I've taught you...why act so recklessly?"

"I couldn't let him die, sir."

Nedeni stared at Deshka, silently to Marlee's ears, for a solid five seconds before delivering his edict aloud. "You're suspended from missions until further notice. Your travel and inprim privileges are revoked. Report to Grade One Maintenance for your new work detail. Dismissed."

Deshka bowed in diffidence and exited the room without protest.

"Sir, Deshka never would've acted as he did if I hadn't bullied him into it."

Nedeni glanced over at her, as if he'd forgotten she too was present in the room. "He is responsible for his own actions."

"Fine, but they don't exist in a vacuum. I convinced him I could reach Galean and bring him home. And, respectfully, I *did*." Pride and anger flared in equal measure. "You know, I thought you cared about Galean. I thought you were his aliatua."

"You know nothing, Human, least of all the true import of that word." Annoyed she was still here, too.

"When I first got here, it's true I didn't know much. But now? I'm starting to figure some things out, including you. I think you're scared. I think every decision you make about the Tarazi is driven by fear, and it's no way to run a revolution."

A bitter laugh rippled up through his throat. "Is that what you imagine I'm doing here? Running a revolution?"

"Um, yes?"

"Tell me, Human. Have you ever had 4,126 people depend upon you for their safety? For their food and shelter? For their lives?"

Her mind leapt to the Godjans, slaves on their own world until she'd stepped in. "Not myself alone, but yes. I have."

"Well this burden falls on me alone."

"No, it doesn't. You don't think it was the same burden that caused Galean to try to commit suicide? Caused him to murder his own brother? He feels the weight of protecting the Tarazi every bit as much as you do."

"And I would have honored Galean for his sacrifice—every Tarazi would have—had you and Deshka not stolen his agency from him."

"We shouldn't have had to. That was your job. You're no leader at all if you abandon your people the instant they get into trouble on your behalf."

Nedeni's hair strands danced—not quite a threat, but the rising possibility of one. "Do you speak to your superiors in this manner back home?"

"Honestly? Sometimes, yes."

"And how does that work out for you?"

"It depends. Sometimes I get rebuked pretty hard, I admit. But more often, I win them over to my side."

"And you believe your rudeness and arrogance will win me over to your side now?"

God, he truly was a brick wall. Why was she even trying? "Galean thinks so highly of you. I want to believe his admiration isn't misplaced, but damn are you making it difficult. You can't genuinely be this callous and unfeeling."

"Unfeeling? Is that what you think?"

"I don't know what to think. If not fear, then I don't understand what drives you."

Nedeni pressed his palms together in a prayer position, which she'd learned was more akin to a human clasping their hands behind their back. "Very well, Human. In the hope doing so will remove your thorn from my side, I will tell you.

"My son was a desbida." He gestured to the visual on his desk. "That's him, along with my wife. In his case, the mutation manifested suddenly, in an explosion of mania that destroyed two rooms of my family's home and sent him into a catatonic state. But unlike many odola who reacted to such transformations with horror, we chose to continue loving our son. We worked gently with him, and in time he began to speak again.

"He'd nearly returned to normal—as normal as a desbida can be—when the authorities came for him. Confinement was for his own good, they said. The good of everyone. I was away on business, but my odola, they fought for him. Refused to hand him over. The situation grew violent, and my wife was killed, as well as my son."

"I'm so sorry. That's beyond horrible."

"Yes, it is, though ask around in the common area, and you'll find similar stories told many times over. The forced internment of the desbida has wrecked our world." His throat worked, and he stared at the visual of his family for a moment before turning away. "I was devastated—a weak word conveying but a fraction of the pain their deaths inflicted upon my soul. But more than this, I was angry. So passionately, wildly angry. But explosions of emotion are not my way, so I strove to harness my rage into purpose. I moved my considerable wealth into a variety of secret accounts, then I faked my own death. The news reported how the loss of my wife and son had driven me to suicide, and they weren't far from wrong.

"I walked away from my life and began a new one devoted to protecting desbida—to protecting the people who had their lives shattered due to the horrific policies of our government and the Errigime that manipulates it. To saving as many people as possible from the fate my family suffered."

Abruptly he dropped his hands to the desk and leaned in, tail curling up to rest its tip upon the surface. "I love Galean like the son I lost. Know that if he had died, I would have suffered that devastation all over again. But the Tarazi isn't about my personal feelings or ensuring my ari is comfortable and happy. This is bigger than me, and it's bigger than Galean. It's bigger than any one person, even the best of us."

She winced. She hadn't expected his story, and dammit but it did explain a great deal. "I understand, I do."

"Self-evidently, you do not."

"I *do*. There are people close to me who have carried the weight of entire civilizations on their shoulders. I've seen the toll it takes on them, the agony of making impossible decisions and living with the consequences. But once you start sacrificing one life for another, how long until every life is expendable?"

"I assure you, I struggle with the calculus every single day."

"Fine. I accept that you do. I don't agree with this choice, but I appreciate why you thought you had to make it." Proper sense counseled her to make a tactical retreat now, but when had she ever listened to sense?

Never.

"But Deshka isn't sitting in your chair. Don't punish him for acting to save someone he loves."

"I have to, or else before I know it, everyone will be running around acting as *they* see fit, without regard for the larger purpose we serve here. Someone will fail, a mistake will be made, and we will lose everything. It's called discipline, and it is the only thing that keeps a group such as this one together and alive."

"No, belief in the rightness of your cause keeps it together. Love for one another and a desire to protect their hartua odola keeps it together."

"But not alive."

"Ugh!" She grabbed at her hair in frustration, and Nedeni jerked back in surprise. Oops, it might have resembled an aggressive action to him. She returned her hands to her side and tried to keep them from clenching into fists. Hell, while she had his undivided attention, she might as well go for broke.

"I get that you worry you can't keep everyone safe. And you know what? You probably can't. So bring an end to this. Expose the sins of the Aterpe Project. Drag their secrets into the light and free not merely a few desbida, but all of them."

He huffed a breath so sharp it whistled through his sentsores. "You think you can waltz into our world, blithely make such grand pronouncements, and expect to conjure their success out of the winds? We are not ready, not even close. We don't have the resources or the connections or the proof required. Vasem was supposed to be our way forward...but that opportunity is gone now. No. I must think first and always of protecting everyone here."

"Don't cower in fear, Nedeni. You want to protect them? Then fight for them! This place can't remain secret forever. You're right—someone, somewhere, will make a mistake, and the Kaldi will swarm in and end this dream. Don't huddle up in here like a turtle and wait for the hammer to fall. If you do, this place will either wither away from the loss of hope or be cut down by government fire. Go on offense while you still can. Make your stand."

"Ah, to be young and idealistic. I assume you are young—you must be, to remain so naive."

"I'll have you know I've retained my idealism through three wars and multiple near-death experiences."

"That you've experienced the latter does not surprise me, but in this case allow me to add foolishness to my assessment. You have experienced the harsh truth of life, and still you refuse to acknowledge reality."

"Yep, and my stubbornness has served me damn well. Let it serve you. I can help you expose the Aterpe Project. If you can obtain some proof of their crimes, Concord can help you. Please, you must try."

Nedeni chuckled softly, and his demeanor finally began to lighten. "You arrived among us with a whimper, a bedraggled confluence of fragile limbs and confused desperation. Now you threaten to become a nuclear bomb in our midst, upending everything we have built for the tantalizing promise of sunlight and freedom. I wonder. Will you be the one who brings it all crashing down around us, Human?"

"Well, for starters, you can try calling me 'Marlee.' It might help you see me as an individual rather than an abstract you can afford to ignore. Also, this is not the first time I've been likened to some sort of wrecking ball or other. But sometimes you can't build something new without tearing down the old. Look, I want to protect the people here, too. More than that, I respect your overriding desire to protect them, and I'm trying to honor it. During our mission to rescue Galean, I went to herculean lengths to ensure my brief uses of quantum tech did not expose the location of the Serba. *Herculean*—which I just realized doesn't mean anything to you as an adjective. Anyway, it was a pain in the ass, but I did it.

"So trust that I will do everything in my power to continue to protect the Tarazi and the Serba. But there comes a point when you have to take a few risks if you want to ever achieve your goal."

He stared at her for a moment, then waved a hand at her neck. "I assume the siliki you're wearing is nothing but a useless scrap of metal now?"

She nodded.

"And your bracelet? I don't suppose you would consent to return it to storage?"

Crap. In all the commotion, she'd forgotten to take it off and pocket it. "This is my lifeline, sir. And it can be yours, too. Use me—use my skills and my technology and my resources. Use me to achieve what you've long dreamed of."

"You are incredibly persistent. You wear me down like a belt sander upon a wood plank floor."

That was possibly the worst compliment she'd ever received. "So you'll let me help you find the proof you need?"

"I will...consider your arguments. For now, let us ensure Galean is nursed back to health, and that we catch our breaths. The events of the last day have been as a tornado whipping through our souls, and we must recenter upon the stillness before moving forward."

The Belascocians were nothing if not poetic. "And Deshka?"

"Deshka must learn there are consequences for disobeying my orders. But I will not be too harsh with him."

"Thank you, sir."

His order of 'dismissed' trailed off as the door closed behind her.

18

Marlee set her fork down with a smile. "Dinner was good, Resamane. Thank you." And it was, in a way. Her palette had begun to adapt to the sharp, pungent tastes of Belascocian food.

"You are kind. Perhaps one day, you can make me one of your native dishes."

"Eh, the truth is, I'm not much of a cook. Never had the patience for it. I usually throw a couple of ingredients together and let the stove make of them what it can. But I do know where to buy the best scones in three galaxies. I'll bring you some."

"I look forward to it."

The door to the apartment slid open to allow Galean entry. Vigor had returned to his gait, which was practically bouncy. A full recovery, then?

"Good evening, my dear sister." He paused to pet Bibine, who glided over to circle his head, then continued on to the table, where he placed a hand on Resamane's cheek for a moment before taking a seat. "Marlee."

"Good evening. You seem well-mended."

"Among other things." He glanced at the plate of vegetables at the center of the table. "Are you all done? May I?"

"Help yourself." Resamane stood. "I must depart to meet with the recent desbida arrivals. Having overcome their initial disturbance at a dramatic change in circumstances, most of them are now eager to learn about their new home."

"You're a wonderful mentor, Resa. They'll be comfortable here in no time."

"I hope so." She returned Galean's touch, then gave Marlee an odd, almost devious look before departing. Interesting.

Galean's hands came up to intertwine his fingers, then twist them around. "I haven't properly thanked you for saving my life."

"There's no need. I'm not one to stand by when someone is in trouble."

"Still. It took a great deal of initiative and determination to defy Nedeni, construct your own plan, acquire the necessary means and execute on it."

"Nedeni is not my boss."

"No, I suppose he isn't. Though he does exercise some control over your movements...or so we all thought." A clouded expression overtook Galean's features. He picked at the beans on his plate.

"For what it's worth, Nedeni was very relieved to have you back and alive. He didn't want to leave you to your fate, but he didn't feel as if he had a choice. He was wrong, of course."

"The burden of leading us all is a heavy one. I don't begrudge him his decision. In fact, I would have been shocked had he made any other. We know the risks when we go out into the world." His gaze settled on her, eyes suddenly sharp and piercing and rather beautiful, what with their endless swirls of fuchsia and indigo. "But you have changed all this, haven't you?"

"Changed what?"

"Your arrival here has been like a spark that lights a flame. If we dare nurture it, the flame can become an inferno. Your fresh perspective on everything demands we reexamine our premises, our old assumptions that have become dogma through habit and repetition. You say we can expose the government's lies and end the subjugation of the desbida. You believe it, and this makes me want to believe it."

This was an interesting development. Had Nedeni shared the details of their argument with him? "What are you saying, Galean?"

"I have an...idea. Not a plan, yet, but perhaps the beginnings of one. These wormholes of yours—how long do you need to create one? Do you require time to recharge before you can create a new one? How do you determine the destination? Need you have visited there in the past?"

"That's a lot of questions."

"Apologies. I only wish to understand how this technology works."

"For your 'idea.'"

"Perhaps."

"Not long, a little bit, and no, but I do need to know where it is on a map."

He stared at her. Belascocians didn't have eyebrows, but the skin above his eyes twitched.

"I need a few seconds of preparation for the power in the Caeles Prism to charge up. Call it two and a half seconds. Once it has, I can maintain it at full power for around ten seconds before it starts to get unruly."

"Unruly?"

"Um, the power wants to go somewhere. If it isn't used or discharged, it'll keep building. Eventually, it gets explosive. But don't worry, I can manage it. To your second question, no, there's not a cool-down period, only the charge-up time. To choose a destination, I need its coordinates, which my eVi typically handles with no problem."

"E-V-I?"

She pulled a knee up to her chest and got comfortable. Luckily, this wasn't the first time she'd had to explain their technology to a foreigner. "Enhanced virtual interface. It's basically a synthetic intelligence that acts as the control system for my cybernetics and as my gateway to the exanet—to everything really—as well as performing a whole host of other functions. It's my second brain, and it happens to be a lot more powerful than my first one in most respects."

His face screwed up. "You have two brains?"

"Sort of. Inside my physical brain—" she tapped her skull "—resides hardware that houses a bucketload of quantum programming. The hardware is integrated into my brain via bio-synth cybernetics, though, so it's not separate as such."

"I see." His expression suggested he did not, in fact, see. "And it can determine coordinates which your, ah, Caeles Prism uses to open a portal?"

"Right. A detailed map is typically sufficient to give it the data it requires, though if I have to be precise in my choice of locations, it helps if I can visit it in sidespace first."

"Sidespace? You have said that word several times without explanation."

She sighed; she probably shouldn't have mentioned it. Too much tech hurtled at him at once, and he'd tune it all out. "It's a sort of quantum dimension that overlays the physical ones. I can project my consciousness to any location in sidespace, regardless of distance. You know, I suspect you—all Belascocians—are using sidespace when you communicate using your eamonals. It's possibly how you can detect quantum perturbations as well, and I'm intensely curious to learn if it's a capability we haven't stumbled upon yet."

"We know not of this 'sidespace.'"

"Doesn't mean you're not using it."

He shook his head. "I don't understand."

"Sidespace is how I found where you were being held. Your specific cell. I went to the Seguru Instal with my mind and searched until I found you. Then I was able to open a wormhole directly to your location."

"Ah!" He nodded eagerly. "This is good."

"For your idea."

"Correct."

"Are you going to tell me what this idea is?"

"Not yet. You told Deshka you've learned how to interact with our technology. Will you show me?"

She eyed him suspiciously as she stood. His behavior was bordering on aberrant; she'd never seen him so enthusiastic. New lease on life triggered by almost forfeiting it? He wouldn't be the first.

She went to the inprim and placed her palm on the input pad, then sent it instructions. The nanomaterial billowed up into the chamber and began to resolve. In a few seconds, a teacup emerged from the drawer. In a perfect world, she'd like to take it back home with her and gift it to Miriam. Her aunt would enjoy adding the unusual, alien design to her collection.

"Impressive."

"I guess. It's easy enough to get it to create things you all use. Belascocian things. If I try to instruct it to build something it has never seen before, it struggles. I'm trying to refine the translation program I wrote to improve the results."

"And terminals? You can use them as well?"

"That's easier." She moved to Resamane's terminal beside the inprim and touched the surface. The screen above it lit up. She opened a news broadcast channel for a moment, but on finding another government propaganda story about a new habitat orbiting one of the inner planets, she returned to the menu and opened one of the internal Tarazi databases. She typed in a search for Deshka.

"Oh, he got promoted from maintenance to armory duty. Nedeni actually kept his word."

"He always does. How much information do you have access to?"

She noted the tone of warning in his voice. "Anything Resamane does from this terminal, I assume." In truth, she was close to deciphering their encryption system, at which point she'd theoretically have access to everything. She did not share this tidbit.

"Resamane has access to a lot."

She turned to face him. "I'm not stealing Tarazi secrets to turn them over to the Errigime, Galean. How many times must I demonstrate my trustworthiness before someone other than Resamane starts to believe me?"

"I…" his posture dipped into a posture of supplication "…forgive me. I am notoriously slow to trust, I am told. You saved my life when you could have simply departed. You *have* earned my trust." His eyes rose to meet hers, and her breath caught in her throat from their power.

She wished she could sense his emotions, the way she could with Resamane. His expression conveyed forthrightness and sincerity. Yet she'd mistrusted *him* since the moment she'd met him. Doubted and feared and projected all manner of ill intent. She couldn't fairly blame him for having done the same.

After consideration, she decided he meant what he said…up to a point. Should the limits of that trust be tested, though, she wondered where his breaking point would emerge.

She smiled. "Thank you."

"You are…Resamane can doubtless read your every facial tic and discover your deepest sentiments from them, but I have not…been paying the attention I should. Your arrangement of features means this pleases you, yes?"

Who was this person standing here, and what had they done with Galean Ozeal? "Are you okay?"

"What? Yes, I am fine. Why do you ask? Did I get it wrong?"

"No, you got it right. This is what it looks like when I smile." She flashed one briefly to emphasize the point. "But you're not acting the way I've come to expect from you."

"Oh." His chin dipped in an arc, and he wandered away, tail swooshing softly across the floor. "You met me at the second worst moment of my life, the first being when I learned the truth about the torture being inflicted on Resamane. I have not been as I should be since that night in Ausatan. But I suppose I have found some small measure of redemption in my willingness to sacrifice myself, without hesitation, to protect everyone here. Resamane says it is time to move forward from Vasem's death, and so I will try. You understand, yes?"

"I do."

"Good. Show me you can unlock the door."

She absorbed the whiplash coming from his rapid shift in topic with an arched eyebrow and went to the door. She placed her palm on the pad and sent the signal, and the door slid open.

"You have done something to your skin. On your palm, or your fingertips."

"Yes. I wrote an interpreter to match the natural language of my cybernetics to the inputs your tech is expecting."

"Interesting." He placed his own palm on the pad for several seconds. "Try it now."

Her hand replaced his, and she again sent the signal to unlock the door…nothing happened. "What did you change?"

He leaned against the wall beside the door, looking thoughtful. Unlike him, she'd spent a great deal of time studying her counterparts' body language and had gotten quite adept at reading it. "Before, the lock solely required a passcode to be provided. Given what you've said about your second brain, I imagine you can brute force this manner of security without much trouble. But the kind of security you'll find protecting more sensitive materials—in places such as high-security government labs—is of a different nature. It's based on…'affinity' might be an approximation.

"This—" he held up an arm to indicate his aldra band "—provides a kaleidoscope of information to the lock that, in sum, identifies me as someone worthy of opening the door. Any Tarazi can unlock most doors and access most files here, because their band communicates that they are Tarazi. Any member of the Ozeal odola can access an Ozeal vault, because they are Ozeal. Now, such an identity *can* be spoofed by one skilled in such things. But the spoofing is not done via clever coding. It involves a manipulation of one's eamonal and…" he frowned "…I struggle to find words to convey my meaning with any specificity."

"It's okay. I think I've got the gist." She gestured to his band. "Can you get me one of those? I tried to convince the inprim to print me one, but it balked at the request."

"Of course it did. You would not have known the information it required in order to create one for you, as each one is unique to the individual. I think together we can craft the information, but it matters not. The band links intimately with our biochemistry on many levels. You are not Belascocian. It will not understand you."

"You let me worry about that after we've succeeded in printing one." She crossed her arms over her chest. "But first, it's time you told me your idea."

"Is it?" His tone was almost teasing, and it gave her pause; she was having a difficult time adjusting to this new Galean. She kept expecting him to shut down, scowl and tersely depart any second.

"Yes, it is. I've jumped through your hoops. I've earned my prize."

He blinked. "Yes. I believe you have." He pushed off the wall to pace purposefully around the room. "I spoke to Mattin this morning. Before he joined the Tarazi, he worked at the Aubera Facility—the research center where they are running the Soldad program. What he saw while employed there led to him joining us, but that's not relevant. Mattin says they maintain a massive database at Aubera. It's where they track the results of a decade of failed experiments—and successes, from their point of view—as well as store the genetic imprints and treatment history of every desbida who has come through the camps. The database is siloed from any larger network, so it can only be accessed onsite.

"But if I can reach an appropriate terminal inside, I can retrieve the data. In part because of my brother—his affinity will be recognized by the system. Access to the facility will be highly restricted, so like with the Seguru Instal, I will need the use of one of your portals to gain entry. But I fear this will not be enough. Security will be tight, and my mission will require time. So I had the thought you might serve as a distraction—if you are willing."

A flutter of excitement danced through her. *This* was what she had signed up for when she'd told him she'd help uncover the proof they longed for, wasn't it?

Most people would feel trepidation at the notion. But no, not you. Nope.

"I am willing. But what do you have in mind? Me dancing a jig and shouting, 'hey, look at me, I'm an alien'?"

"You are not far off. You will in fact make your presence and identity known. Then you will leap through your portals all throughout the facility, setting off every security alarm in the building. Sowing chaos and confusion. You will make them chase you, until they end up chasing themselves. Then, when I have completed my task, you will return to me and we will depart through another of your portals."

"That's a brilliant plan! I love it."

"You do?"

"I do." She grinned broadly. "I am a terrific sower of chaos."

"This I do not doubt. You believe you can perform your role in the plan?"

"Absolutely. I'll want to scout the location ahead of time from sidespace, as I talked about, so I can pick out places to portal to. And I'd love the best defense shielding you guys have got. My cybernetics can generate a field to repel incidental strikes, but something tells me I'm going to need more robust defenses."

"You will have it."

"Great." She chewed on her bottom lip as an uncomfortable thought occurred to her. "I assume we'll take a vehicle far from the Serba before infiltrating the facility, the way Deshka and I did?"

"Yes. We must ensure your portal does not lead them back here."

"Right." She frowned. "Does that mean…after we leave the vehicle behind, will I have to…ride you?"

"I expect so, yes. We'll want to protect the location of our vehicle, as we will be gone for some minutes. Is that a problem?"

"No. It's just…weird."

"How is it weird?"

Dare she explain how the act was both strangely intimate and horrifyingly demeaning? It felt analogous to a beast-and-master act in so many ways. When she rode Cupcake, it was done with mutual affection and enjoyment and served to deepen their bond, but no one would deny that Cupcake was a beast, and while astride him, she was his master. Yet Deshka had not been—Galean would not be—her beast. They were fully sapient beings, equal to her in every way. The dichotomy was deeply uncomfortable.

"Marlee? You grow silent."

"Sorry. It's just not something we do back home is all. If that's what we need to do, it's fine. Let's talk about getting me an aldra band."

"Yes. We will have to—" His head jerked, and in an instant his entire bearing had transformed to radiate tension and darkness. "I must go."

He spun and headed for the door. She, obviously, chased after him.

Galean pushed his way through the small throng of people that had gathered in Recreation. Someone laid a hand on his arm, impeding his progress.

"She screams if anyone gets near her. We tried."

He acknowledged Txeru's statement with a grunt and broke through the front of the crowd.

Resamane was curled up against the wall, her knees drawn in, tail coiled up in a knot. Her hands clutched her head as she rocked back and forth.

He crossed the open space and dropped to his knees in front of her. He brought his hands up to rest over hers while letting his tail gently stroke her back. "I'm here, Resa."

Loudloudloudloudloudloud—

"Let me make it quiet. Sense only me. Feel my eamonal enveloping you. I'll protect you from the noise. Here, together, we are safe."

So loudloud...loud...I can't make it stop. Everyone wants in...the talking the crying the loving the anger...it's too much I can't bear it.

In her distress, she'd reverted to speaking wholly through thought. After the 'treatments,' when he'd brought her to the Tarazi, she'd had to learn to vocalize again. Though she now did so fluidly, he knew it continued to take conscious effort on her part.

"You don't have to. Let me bear it for you. You and I are all that exist in the world. Together we have peace, and calm. Take my calm into you. I give it to you freely, sister." It took all of his strength to project an aura of peace and tranquility when he wanted to explode with anger and impotent frustration. But he managed it, because it was the only thing that could rescue her from this madness.

I can't...can't...so loudloudloud....

But her breathing started to slow and regulate. He stayed there on the floor, stroking her and holding her, until her shaking abated to a soft tremble. Then he whispered, "Come, Resa. Let's steal away from the world."

At her halting nod, he gathered her up in his arms and carefully stood. He cradled her against his chest, protecting as much of her body as he was able.

The crowd parted, creating a path for him to traverse to Residential. They'd seen this before, and none tried to interfere.

He continued whispering calming words as they climbed the stairs and he walked the steps to her apartment door. He had to brace her a little to reach the pad, then the door slid open.

Her racing heart had slowed considerably by the time they reached her bed, and he laid her down on top of the covers. "I'm going to get you some water. I'll only be steps away, and I'll return anon."

Her only answer was a soft but keening moan.

He hurried back out into the main room—only to find Marlee standing there, looking...well, he hadn't figured that part out yet.

"What's wrong with her?"

"Now is not the time, and this is not the place for you." He strode brusquely past her on his way to the kitchen. "I need to stay with her, but your presence will only bring harm. You...you can sleep in my apartment tonight. The code is 4381." He filled a glass with water and made to return to the bedroom.

"But I want to help."

He spun on her, hair threads standing on end and tail snapping in the air. "*Go.*"

Her eyes widened, and she backed toward the door.

He resumed his course, fearful of every second he was not at Resa's side, and rushed back to the bedroom.

Her limbs had curled up on themselves once more, and she shook against the bed covers.

He set the water down—for later, when things were better—and crawled onto the bed next to her, taking her in his arms.

So loudloudloud...why can't they stop...why can't I...?

Tears stung his eyes as stroked her agitated hair and down her back, then reversed course, over and over. "I'll quiet them for you. Simply listen to my voice, and only my voice. Nothing else exists. Only you and I. And we are at peace."

Peace...don't leave me, please.

"I will never do so." He'd left her once, by allowing them to take her away to the camp, by in his ignorance abandoning her to suffer in that hellish place for years. He'd nearly done so again mere days ago, if in an earnest attempt to protect her. But never again.

I love you, brother.

"And I love you, sister. You are my heart-home, my ari, my most beloved prezia."

19

The sound of muffled movement woke Marlee from a troubled half-sleep. Unfamiliar shadows greeted her, and she tensed, all her senses expanding in a search for exigent threats. "Who's there?"

A light came on in an adjacent room, and a form leaned around the corner. "Sorry. I was trying not to wake you."

Galean. Because she was in his apartment. Because last night, Resamane had...she didn't exactly know.

"It's okay. You can turn on the lights." She pushed the rest of the way up to a sitting position. She'd grabbed a blanket and curled up on the couch the night before, and the blanket was now twisted around her legs.

The rest of the lights illuminated as she was extracting herself from her blanket prison; she swung her feet to the floor and stretched out the kinks, eyeing Galean warily as the scene in Resamane's apartment returned to her mind. He'd been...like he was when he kidnapped her from Vasem's office. Harsh, cold, vaguely terrifying. He didn't look so now, but she stepped carefully nonetheless.

"How is Resamane?" she asked quietly.

"Much better. She asked for some time to herself to regain the trappings of normalcy, so I returned here." He hesitated, then came over and sat on the couch next to her—which was when she remembered she was wearing only a long shirt. It didn't matter; he wasn't interested in her legs. "I was abrupt with you last night. I apologize, and I feel I owe you an explanation."

She relaxed a little. This was closer to the Galean who had begun to reveal himself yesterday. "I want to understand what happened to her."

He nodded, but was silent for another moment before he began. "Not every drawback of being a desbida comes from the cruel treatments the Aterpe Project subjected them to. Some are a result of the genetic mutation itself. To be a desbida is to sense the whole world, and every soul in it, without respite. I cannot imagine such an assault upon one's mind. Can you?"

She thought of the Noesis, of how one could drown in an ocean of Prevos' thoughts and schemes and calculations. But that was simple enough to tune out and lock away when you didn't need it. "No, I can't."

"Resa is the strongest person I know. She is resilient and as stalwart as a seawall. But sometimes, the noise overwhelms even her. To hear her describe it, it is like an endless wailing on every frequency. A ceaseless discordant clashing of soul-tones."

"That sounds horrible. What sets it off?"

"We don't know. Stress would be an obvious answer, in which case it was my fault this time, for I do not doubt my capture strained her deeply. But sometimes there is no identifiable cause. Life can be normal and quiet—as quiet as is possible here in the Serba—and she will be struck down without warning. But it happens less frequently now. When I first rescued her from the camp, it was a weekly occurrence. Now she can go many months without an episode. I credit this entirely to her determination to control her own mind and body."

"Your presence soothes her. That's what happened yesterday. When you reached her, you were able to calm her down."

He nodded. "She says because we are twins, my ari is always in harmony with her own, and so I am able to tamp down and muffle the noise. I stayed at her side through the night, doing what I could to ease her anguish. It felt..." he blew out a breath, his wide eyes narrowing at the corners "...like such a pitiful gesture. Stroking her arms, whispering calming nothings in an endless mantra. But it is what I can do to help. What only I can do."

"It seems to me it makes all the difference for her. You're her savior."

"I try to be." He smiled a little.

"Do all the desbida suffer from such breakdowns?"

"Yes and no. The effects manifest differently in everyone. Some fly into violent rages of self-harm and have to be put in restraints until the storm passes. Some go catatonic, sitting with their hands in their laps staring at a wall for days." Abruptly he exploded off the couch in a fit of motion. "This is what the Aterpe Project should have been focused on. They should have worked to treat the side effects of the mutation they created, to ease the suffering of everyone afflicted with it. Instead they made everything infinitely worse by working only to suppress the cause. Curse them and their arimas!"

Marlee simply watched him, for she had no answers beyond the grand one: if the Aterpe Project was exposed and the truth revealed, doctors and scientists might finally be allowed to turn their attention to helping the desbida instead of harming them. But he understood this. Knowing what she now knew, she'd daresay it was one of the primary drivers propelling him so relentlessly forward in advancing the Tarazi's cause.

After several fervent circles around the living area, his agitation calmed, and he returned to kneel in front of her. "Apologies. Experiencing one of her episodes is not so easy on me, either, though my discomfort is a pittance compared to her own."

"And you didn't get any sleep."

"Sleep is for the idle. We have work to do. Our conversation was interrupted yesterday, but let us resume it now. You wish to print an aldra, so that you might attempt to use it."

"I do. But…can I go visit Resamane first? Will that be okay? Is she well enough to see me?"

"Yes. Yes, of course. She would welcome it, I think. You stop in to see her, then let us meet at the Tier 1 inprim in twenty minutes."

"And take a shower while I'm there?"

"Forty minutes, then."

Galean squinted at the readout from the inprim. The advanced model had cost Nedeni a fortune to acquire, and in theory it was capable of constructing anything Belascocians had ever designed, all the way up to a starship, if given access to a large enough chamber and enough nanomaterial.

He didn't need anything so gargantuan or complex. In fact, all he needed was a simple aldra, if a unique one.

He altered a parameter on the screen. "Place your palm on the reader again."

Marlee did as instructed while pulling on her bottom lip with her teeth. It must be a tic, but he did not know what it signified.

She was such a strange creature, full of odd mannerisms and frenetic energy and fervent opinions, willful of action and lacking any respect for authority. Because he could not sense her eamonal, he had only her words and deeds to judge her character by. For a long time, this had left him feeling off-kilter, unbalanced, when he was around her. But the deed of her fighting to rescue him against all odds was like a thundershout across the heavens. It told the tale of her soul more purely than any eamonal could. And now that he perceived her truth, much else about her was beginning to fall into place.

And so he thought the lip-chewing must signify restrained impatience. A curtailing of her innate desire to do, to act. This, he understood, for it reflected his own compulsions.

"Any luck?"

He checked the screen. "I'm afraid not. The problem is, it doesn't comprehend your inputs. As I said, the aldra is attuned to each individual on a level that goes beyond DNA or fingerprints.

You are not Belascocian, so you do not possess the markers it requires."

She yanked her hand away and darted in a quick circle, then another one. "Will it print a blank band? One not attuned to anyone, but capable of becoming so?"

"Yes, I believe so, but the band will be inert. Useless."

"Do it anyway. Please."

"As you wish." He executed the order, and in a few seconds a pristine aldra arrived, a narrow strip of curving metal sitting in the receptacle of the chamber. He handed it to her.

"Great." She slipped it on her wrist above her bracelet, frowned, then switched it to the other arm. She held both arms up at an angle. "I'm really sporting the bangles now, huh?"

"Um...."

"Never mind. Can one of these screens show me the inputs the band is looking for? In code form?"

"I think so. Give me a minute." They were dancing on the edge of his understanding; his forte had always been building things. Solid, real things that existed in the firmament. He comprehended the esoteric world of coding only as much as he'd ever needed to.

The screen beside the reader populated with line after line of code, empty input receptacles marked in garish orange.

Marlee scooted up close to the screen, nudging against him until he gave up his position. Her skin was notably warm against his, like a hot-blooded mammal that...he supposed she was.

"Does it make any sense to you?"

Now the lips pursed tightly, her brow forcing her eyes into narrow slits. Concentration? "Fascinating. This is ingenious. I know someone who would have an absolute field day with it."

"Oh?"

"The doctor who helped me with my eVi upgrades. If we get through this alive and free...well, let's focus on that part for now." She flashed him a smile. "Give me thirty seconds."

He gestured acquiescence, and she closed her eyes. Her body fell perfectly still, and only then did he recognize how much she was always moving, every limb animated by coiled energy, even when she was sitting in apparent relaxation. Now, only the slow rise and fall of her chest gave any indication she inhabited her body.

After twenty-six seconds, she reopened her eyes. "Got it."

"What is it you have?"

"I wrote an interpreter that takes the program I created to be able to interact with your usual tech and translates the inputs into—" she pointed to the screen "—that. Hopefully. I'm going to try to print it on a film, okay?"

He gestured to the reader and stepped away. It appeared she was running the show.

She placed her palm on the reader. "I'm sending the code and the schematic for a film. I hope it understands what I'm asking for."

The chamber lit up as the nanomaterial stretched and flattened, then tiny lasers burned light upon it.

The receptacle opened to reveal a thin film decorated in the minuscule lines of circuitry. The dimensions matched those of an aldra.

She slipped her new band off her wrist, then lifted the film up by one corner. "Help me out? Hold the band for me?"

He took it from her and held it out with both hands.

She pressed the film along the inside of the aldra, sliding a fingertip along centimeter by centimeter until the printed circuitry all but disappeared against the alkaline metal. Then she took the aldra from him. "Moment of truth." She slipped it back on.

Her eyes darted back and forth without focusing on anything.

"Well?" he asked, her inherent impatience bleeding into his voice.

"I think…I can't tell for certain if it worked. I need to test it on something. Can you do the thing you did with the lock on this door?"

"I don't have to. This door is encrypted. Let's step outside."

They exited the room, and the door closed behind them. She immediately spun back around and placed her palm on the access pad.

"Wait. It's not going to work. Functional aldra or no, you're not on the list of authorized—"

The door slid open.

"How did you do that?"

She shot him a wide smile over her shoulder, oddly bright eyes dancing with an inner light. "I already hacked your security system. The only missing piece was the biochemical keys."

"H-how?" he stammered.

"It wasn't so difficult. You all rely on your affinities too much. Your coding is, frankly, sloppy, because it can be."

"I believe I should be offended."

"Not you personally. You didn't write the security algorithms. I mean, I assume you didn't."

"I definitely did not. Are you saying we are vulnerable to attack?"

She shrugged. "If a bunch of Prevos invade and want to take over the place, yes. In the absence of that, which isn't likely to happen…" she seemed to stutter over the thought "…no, your security is robust enough. It works for you. Still, if we get out of this alive—again, let's focus on that part for now." She fondled the aldra with her other hand, twisting it back and forth across her skin. "What's next?"

A weighty breath escaped his chest. Everything up until now had been toying with a 'what if' scenario. It was about to become real—or not, depending. "Now we present our plan to Nedeni."

Her posture instantly tensed. "Are you sure that's a good idea?"

"Marlee, I appreciate beyond words how you and Deshka dared to go behind Nedeni's back to rescue me. But he is still our leader. You going rogue is…honestly, to be expected. You are alien and not a part of us. But if *I* go rogue, my actions will explicitly call his leadership into question. Morale will suffer. Nedeni holds this entire place together with his strength and vision and, yes, authority. Disrupt that, and everything falls apart."

"I see." Her gaze met his with stridentness. "And if he says no?"

"Let's worry about it if it comes to pass."

Nedeni glared at Marlee, waves of discontent flowing out from him. "Once again, you have concocted a plan so reckless, it is nigh-on suicidal."

Galean cleared his throat. "Actually, sir, I came up with the plan."

Nedeni's stare bore into him with equal intensity. "Did the etenail adle your brain after all?"

"No, sir. I don't believe so. The plan makes the best use of Marlee's unique capabilities to provide a necessary distraction for long enough for me to extract the information we need. I know it's not our usual type of mission, but her ability to portal to any location changes the equation in fundamental ways. You simply need to bend your mind to the possibilities."

Nedeni's hair strands flared out, and Galean considered whether he had pushed too far into insult. He started to offer amelioration, but stopped himself. His words were true. Nedeni would see this.

After a beat, the hair settled back down. "You've never broken into any database half so secure as the one at Aubera."

"No. But we have the tools needed to do so. We spent years and many dangerous missions acquiring the equipment so we would have the capability. This is the time to use it. Sir, I believe the information stored at Aubera is what we need to break the conspiracy wide open. It's what we've professed to want from the day we came together in common cause. Marlee gives us the best chance we've ever had of obtaining it."

"And what if the information you find isn't enough? We don't have any real idea what's stored in their mysterious database. Those in power will have covered their tracks. Erased crucial data, put a veneer of legality around their actions."

"Then it will still get us closer than we've ever achieved before. And I believe the breadcrumbs to get us the rest of the way will be found in the data." He gestured beside him. "Marlee, this is your theory. Why don't you explain it?"

"Of course." She'd been sitting there vibrating as he talked, but had restrained herself from jumping in until asked. "There will have been dissenters, I guarantee it. Doctors or researchers with an honorable conscience who could not abide by what their superiors were ordering them to do."

"And the evidence of their protestations will have been erased from the records long ago."

"Yes, but all we need are some names. A single name, perhaps. Because while those in charge will have deleted the evidence of dissent from the official databanks, those individuals will have made copies. Taken their protestations with them. As insurance, or maybe to wait for the day when someone came along who was strong enough to topple the whole conspiracy."

"And if these dissenters are dead? You should not underestimate the lengths to which the Errigime will go to maintain their power. Legalities do not concern them."

Marlee's chin dropped to her chest, and she nodded. "It's possible. But you have to believe you can find the answers. I mean, without hope, why are you here, giving so much of yourselves? One name—it's all you need. Believe it's there."

"This is madness." Nedeni spun around to stare at the filigree artwork adorning one wall.

Marlee leaned forward in evident frustration, hands coming up in preparation for an outburst.

Galean reached out and placed a hand on her arm. When her gaze darted to him, he shook his head silently. All her features squinted together, but after a beat, she nodded.

The silence stretched on for some ten seconds before Nedeni slowly, gravely, turned back to them. "You'll need protection while you're in the server room. Marlee's antics will draw most of the security away, but they will not forget to protect that which is most valuable. Take Raisan and Txeru with you."

Galean let out the breath he'd been holding, gratitude welling up and out across his eamonal. His faith in this man who was like a father to him had been rewarded once more. "Thank you, sir. You don't want me to take Deshka?"

"Deshka has had enough excitement for one week. Galean, he accompanies you on your missions because he loves you and wants to be of help to you. He is not a warrior in the way you are."

"I know he isn't. But he performs well in the roles he's given."

"True. But the roles he is capable of performing will not be sufficient for infiltrating the Aubera and returning safely. You will need the best at your side if you hope to survive and...I thought you lost once already. I would not have you lost again."

The multitude of strains their relationship had suffered since he'd returned from that fateful night with Vasem had burdened Galean's every idle moment and fitful dream, but he felt the fractures healing now. A bond as strong as any blood odola bound them together, and it would not be easily severed.

A wisp of a smile crossed Nedeni's lips, in time with an acknowledgment of the same from his eamonal. "Now. I have a couple of suggestions for ways to improve your plan."

20

Marlee eyed the two Belascocians Nedeni had assigned to the mission. She'd conversed with both Raisan and Txeru a few times, always when accompanied by Deshka and usually in the gym. They seemed serious men, as dedicated to the Tarazi's cause as anyone else, and quite proficient in their use of weapons. Not particularly talkative, though, so it was difficult to say how they felt about her.

She finished strapping on her infragun and diamond knife. She'd still prefer a Concord-made Daemon and plasma blade, but the weapons were effective at their jobs, sometimes scarily so. Satisfied, she found herself fondling the Caeles Prism on her wrist. She'd felt adrift and helpless without it, which she recognized wasn't especially resilient of her. Caleb had lectured her any number of times about how she should never depend on any weapon or tool, only on herself. And she'd done a damn good job of it since getting stuck here. But she'd fought a constant war against her inner doubts and simmering panic at being cut off and stranded.

But now she could again use this astounding piece of technology—not to escape, but to help her new friends.

Preparations looked to be wrapping up, so she stepped toward the center of the armory and cleared her throat. "Before we depart, I want to walk through the initial phase of our infiltration. I've been thinking a lot about how the Kaldi track quantum perturbations, and how we can use it to our advantage. I want to do a series of quick wormhole jumps in rapid succession. First, out on the plains. This mission is going to put us inside the Aubera for some time—it's not a fast in-and-out—which means they'll have time to reach our initial departure point."

"But there won't be anything there," Raisan protested. "We'll put some distance between us and our vehicle before we begin the infiltration."

"I know. But why not split their forces from the start for good measure? I propose we wormhole to two additional deserted locations before traveling to the Aubera. And when we infiltrate the facility, I don't want to immediately drop you all off at the server room. If that's the first location to light up, they'll know what we're doing. So all of us will first appear on the second floor, far from the servers. We'll then move across the building, to the executive level, worryingly close to the director's office. Only then will I drop you off at the server room and set off the chase for real."

"Won't that take too long? It'll give them time to bring in a horde of security."

"Ten seconds at most once we're onsite. And I fear security is coming no matter what."

Galean stepped up beside her and gave his assent. "Good idea. You're thinking tactically. The more confusion we can sow, the better."

"That's the idea."

"All right. Everyone meet at the pool in ten minutes."

Raisan and Txeru acknowledged Galean's instructions and departed. Galean started to follow, but Marlee laid a hand on his arm. "I want to talk to you for a minute alone."

"You have concerns you didn't want to express in front of the others."

"I have so many concerns, but none that can be alleviated. Well, perhaps *one* that can be alleviated." She hesitated; their relationship had improved markedly in the last few days, but the nuances of Belascocian interactions remained a thorny morass, and none more so than where Galean was involved. She needed to choose her words carefully. "The last time we were out in the world, away from the Serba, I was your prisoner."

"I am acutely aware of this. I have expressed how I—"

"No, I don't want to rehash everything. You had your reasons, and I accept them. But this time, we're going out there as equals. As teammates. I simply want to make certain you...of course you understand it. I know you do. I guess what I mean is, I need to know you trust me. Trust me to do everything in my power to help the mission succeed. With this trust in place, I hope you won't...."

He smiled a little. "Try to control your actions. Order you around. Interfere with your decisions, even if I don't understand what you're doing. You need to know that I will let you run wild in a government facility with deadly weapons and mysterious and fearsome capabilities I comprehend nothing of, all while trusting that you are on our side."

"And trusting that I will come for you when you call for me."

His sentsores danced around his lips. "You refused to leave me in the Seguru Instal. Why would you leave me behind now?"

Warmth flooded her chest. "Exactly. I won't." She frowned. "Unless I get captured. Or shot and grievously wounded. If this happens, I guess...try to shoot your way out and make your way back to the vehicle. You did it in Ausatan, you can do it again."

"What about you? I do not wish to leave you stranded and captured, but it will be considerably more difficult for us to mount a rescue operation without possession of that tiny miracle on your wrist."

"Don't worry about me. If I get captured, I'll comm home for help with a screaming fury, and a legion of Marines will descend upon my location to retrieve me. Though this might trigger a war between Belarria and Concord, so let's do everything we can to avoid such an outcome, okay?"

"Yes, let's do try."

She squeezed his hand; his head jerked in surprise at the very human gesture, but he didn't pull away. "On that note, does the armory have any grenades we can take along?"

Galean talked for most of the drive. He reviewed what he expected to find in the server room and how he planned to circumvent the security measures. He counseled Raisan and Txeru on how best to guard him, what to react to and when to stand their ground. He seemed to have a good rapport with the men, and they responded to his instructions without complaint. Marlee got the sense this was not their first mission together.

She listened to everything he was saying, because she needed to know his plans if she was to make her own moves with maximum effectiveness—not that she expected anything to go as planned. When did it ever?

But mostly she stared out the windshield. It was a clear, moonless night, and the sky was afire with the four hundred billion stars of the Medusa Merger. Even planets situated close to the Milky Way galactic core didn't have skies like this. More stars, perhaps, but they lay in an orderly if glutted blanket from horizon to horizon. No, this was chaos made manifest—the strewn wreckage of a galactic collision that had wrent two galaxies apart and smashed them together in an act of supreme cosmic power. To stand beneath its aftermath tens of millions of years later was to gaze upon the majestic and terrifying wonder of the universe.

She made a note to look up and snap a visual when she exited the vehicle. Alex would love it, and she didn't want to forget the glorious spectacle.

Finally the vehicle slowed, and Galean brought it to a stop beneath a rocky outcropping hundreds of kilometers from where she and Deshka had traveled. She climbed out and peered up, breathless for a beat at the sight.

After a few seconds, she realized Galean had come over and was staring at her. "What?"

"You make a terrible Belascocian. Your skin tone is atrocious, and your eyes remain far too round. You would not be welcomed into any proper gizartea."

She winced, her shoulders dropping, and he passed a quick hand down her face. "I am joking. Well, I am not, but Resa did a remarkable job, all things considered."

She forced a closed-mouth smile.

"I have hurt your feelings. Accept my apologies, please."

"No, no. You're right. I do make a terrible Belascocian. But hopefully the disguise will pass muster from a distance, which is all we need."

"It will, I'm sure."

She'd considered going au natural for the mission as Galean had initially suggested, but decided it would be better if the government couldn't definitively link her and the Tarazi. Better that they not be able to comm up Dean Veshnael and report how she was consorting with terrorists. Let them instead wonder if the Tarazi had invented a wormhole device and other marvels.

"So how is this part going to work?"

Galean looked relieved at the change of subject. "You will ride on me, and Txeru and Raisan will run alongside."

"You don't want me to…." She trailed off weakly.

"Ride one of them? Why would I?"

"No reason." Again she failed at articulating why the notion made her so uncomfortable. Riding on the back of any Belascocian seemed like an affront, but Galean especially. Maybe because the power dynamics between them had fluctuated so wildly in the time they'd known one another.

But this was something the Belascocians simply *did*. She should not try to impose her own alien sensibilities upon an act that wasn't fraught with complications to them.

Everyone double-checked the secureness of their packs, and Galean and the others dropped to all fours. She took a deep breath and threw a leg over Galean's back, then leaned down to press her chest against his spine. She wound her arms over his shoulders, careful to not squeeze his neck, and pressed her thighs into his hips.

...and now she realized why it made her so uncomfortable. It wasn't the power dynamics, though those were certainly present in spades. It was the fact that, though it absolutely was *not*, this felt like a sexual act. Bodies pressed close together, and in some intimate places. If he were to flip over, they would be well on their way to making love.

Oblivious to her mental perturbations, Galean took off across the land alongside Raisan and Txeru, and she hurriedly adjusted her positioning so she wasn't flung off.

The notion itself did not repel her. The Belascocians were a beautiful species, and Galean was far from the first alien she'd found attractive. When one grew up surrounded by a multitude of aliens, the lines of what constituted 'strange' and 'off-putting' got pushed pretty far out. Or maybe she was just wired that way.

But it was neither here nor there. She was a grown woman who had learned (eventually) how to put aside every random hormonal flare, so she did her best to ignore the tingly feeling spreading wherever she touched his cool skin. And clothes, for she was mostly touching his clothes with her clothes. In other words, it was all in her head.

They ran for much longer than Deshka had. But Deshka had been driven by urgency, when every second could be the second Galean died. This time, thoroughness and caution were more important than speed—at least until they reached the Aubera. If Galean tired, he gave no indication of it, and his pace never let up.

Once her initial discomfort eased—a little—she took the time to admire the cleverness of evolution. While many bipedal species evolved from four-legged ancestors, they typically left such movement behind when they began to walk upright. But to be able to function completely as a bipedal species, with full use of the dexterity of hands and finger digits, while also retaining the speed and agility of four-legged movement, was noteworthy. Much like with the gills and tails, something about Belascocian genetics held onto useful traits even as evolution created new ones. The biologists back home were going to have a field day with them—respectfully and from a distance, of course.

They came to a stop upon an arid steppe free of distinguishing features. Marlee swiftly climbed off Galean's back, and he straightened up with nary a wince.

"We will begin here. A supply check, please, as things could have come loose during the journey."

Everyone complied; Marlee adjusted the belt on her hips to redistribute the weight evenly. She carried the lightest load, as her job was not to get into a shootout with security but rather to escape them, over and over again.

Once the belt felt right, she undid the clasps and drew the gun and the knife in turn, then returned them to their places and confirmed the grenades hadn't fallen out of their pouch.

"If I may ask, how did an ambassador become so skilled with weapons?"

She flashed Galean a breezy grin. "By repeatedly insisting on going where I shouldn't and promptly getting into trouble I had to fight my own way out of. When I was younger, I mean. Before the ambassadorial job."

"Are you old now? I know nothing of the Human aging process."

"No, not really. I guess I got an early start." She patted her belt. "All ready."

"Yes." He went over and spoke briefly to Raisan and Txeru, then motioned for everyone to come close. "We will move as one unit through the portals until we arrive at the server room. Do not wander off, even a meter."

"Um…what is it like? To traverse one of these…portals?" Txeru asked.

Marlee adopted a reassuring tone. "Just like stepping through a doorway from one room into another. There are no strange sensations, no queasiness or disorientation. Promise."

"Right. Fine then."

He was a brave soldier; they all were. Marlee nodded at Galean. "Whenever you're ready."

21

Golden ripples of power churned inside the tiny orb, waiting on her command.

She'd called upon the Caeles Prism on an immediate, emergency basis before, but never multiple times in a row. The logic was sound, though. The well of power it drew upon was effectively infinite, and its circuits wouldn't tire from reuse. All she had to do was pay proper attention to its status throughout the mission, and the device would give her what she needed to pull this stunt off.

"Two jumps to other locations hundreds of kilometers from here, then we go to Aubera, where we leap around a few times before I drop you off at the server room. I leave you to do your work, and I go play hide-and-seek with security." They simply stared at her expectantly, so with a deep breath she opened a wormhole. On the other side waited dense undergrowth and sprawling trees. "Go."

She ended up leading the way, though, as everyone had first-time jitters. The instant all were on the other side, she closed the wormhole and counted down the seconds while the power spun back up—an insect bit her, and she swatted the side of her neck.

Galean frowned in concern, and she winced. "Poisonous?"

"Not to us."

"Okay." She opened a new wormhole, and this time their strides weren't so hesitant as they stepped through to a frost-laced expanse of tundra. Close the wormhole, restart the power.

Her gaze found Galean's once more. "Good luck. Comm when you're ready to get the fuck out of there."

"I assuredly will."

The next wormhole opened to a clean, sterile environment with cool, dry air. Raisan and Txeru drew their weapons, and everyone stepped through.

Again. Faster this time, as she tuned to the rhythm of the Caeles Prism's power flow. Blank walls of beige adobe flashed by as they moved again, then once more. The server room.

All the secrets of the desbida, from their creation to their repression to their attempted transformation, hopefully sat stored on the data banks in this room. Galean moved to the terminal situated in front of racks stacked with computer equipment.

A shrill alarm rang through the air. Security cams in the room, one presumed. Time to go.

She created a wormhole that opened just down the hallway from the main security office and hurried through it. Her chaos plan wasn't going to work unless they noticed her, after all.

"Hey! Stop right there!"

Well, that didn't take long. The wormhole vanished as she sprinted down a side hall, gripping her gun and tossing haphazard fire over her shoulder to make extra certain they fixated on her.

Return weapons fire whizzed past her arm, way too close for comfort. She skidded around a corner and opened a new wormhole, rushing through it and closing it before any security officers reached the hallway. They'd have no idea where she'd gone.

Where she'd gone was back to the executive level, where a series of luxurious offices lined a wide hallway floor of soft oyster marble and decorated with the elaborate murals Belascocians seemed to love.

She pulled up in front of a door and tried to open it, but wasn't overly surprised to find it quite locked. With a functioning aldra and a host of Belascocian-friendly programs she'd written, she could probably hack it, but that wasn't her mission. Instead she started banging on the door, then shooting ineffectually at the lock. More alarms rang out. They were pitched on the high precipice of human hearing, and gods, they were going to give her the mother of all headaches.

Three security officers appeared at the end of the hallway. Damn, they had an impressive response time.

Wormhole. Quickly now. Through it and closed. She was on the lab level now. She didn't think any live-person experiments were being conducted in this area. Computer simulations, data analysis and hypotheses formulated for testing, most likely.

A long window afforded a full view into a room lined with small, transparent enclosures. Robotic arms hovered over dark rubber seals used for entry. It reminded her of the type of lab her mother had worked in before going all-in on teaching. A biochemical lab. Those enclosures safeguarded biological material. Organic compounds.

She shielded her face and fired point-blank into the window. Glass shattered in chunky fragments.

The shrieking this new alarm emitted sent her fleeing through another wormhole—one that exited behind two security officers sprinting down a hallway.

"Hey! You're looking for me, aren't you?"

They spun toward her as a new wormhole formed, and she pivoted and dashed—

Pain lanced through her shoulder, and she landed in a mockery of a braced roll. *Close!*

The room she'd traveled to was quiet for the moment, so she wrenched her head around to inspect her shoulder. A glancing blow from one of the atzapar bullets had partially penetrated her defense shield to shred the skin near her rotator cuff. It didn't look deep, though it did look ugly.

On your feet!

Her cybernetics were already delivering a dose of painkillers and closing off the blood flow to the area, so she took The Voice's suggestion. This was no time to sit around whimpering in pain.

Before departing, she checked to confirm her current location held no strategic value. She should take a second pass at the executive level, creating the impression she was after one of the bosses. Better yet, tap a toe *inside* one of the offices, suggesting she could in fact break the encryption on the door locks.

Her next wormhole led to a shockingly ostentatious spread more penthouse apartment than office. Bronze and silver statues adorned every wall that wasn't painted in elaborate murals. Plush couches were framed by verdant ferns, and by the window sat a natural wood desk some three meters long.

Righteous indignation boiled at the thought of these people getting wealthy off the horrors they inflicted on the desbida. Her anger bonded with the painkillers to wash away any lingering aches from her injury, and she attacked the map with renewed vigor.

The server plates were stacked high in three racks. Clusters of yellow operational lights blinked out of the shadows like an approaching pack of cypones.

But Galean was not their prey tonight. Cognizant of Txeru and Raisan standing guard in the entryway, he wasted no time in slotting the spike into the input port, followed by an empty data storage plate.

He wasn't much of a security hacker, but he didn't need to be. The spike acted faster and with greater deviousness than any belascocian could, impersonating a new data load until it crossed the threshold into the file directory, then letting loose an army of coded serpents to crawl through the data banks and siphon off their contents onto the plate.

A soft beep let him know the first plate was full, and he swiftly exchanged it for a second one.

In order to capture all the information stored here, he'd need as many plates as there were storage devices in the server room, which wasn't practical. So the spike's programming also contained a search algorithm that prioritized the terms 'desbida,' 'camp,' 'genetic,' 'treatment' and a list of other relevant terms in proximity to one another. It pulled the oldest data first, because the greatest lies had been perpetrated in the earliest days, when the true nature of the genetic mutations had first made themselves known. One exception was 'Soldad,' for any information gleaned about the infernal program would only strengthen their hand.

Another plate switch out. Due to the space limitations of a pack he was able to wear, he only had six, and now he began to worry over the algorithm's choices. He was like a blind man fumbling about for the glass of water he'd been told was on the table; what if it filled up the space with obscure statistical tables, blood test results and other errata, and as a result left something crucial behind? Something that alone revealed the truth about the Aterpe Project's sins? But there was nothing to be done for it now.

The *pop-pop* of gunfire echoed behind him, and he tamped down the primal urge to spin and leap into the hall, firing upon the men who would deny him his prize. Txeru and Raisan could handle it, until they couldn't any longer. When that moment came, Marlee would evacuate them.

Marlee. When he'd kidnapped the alien in a fit of shame-induced panic, he'd never imagined she would hold the key to finally achieving their goals. The fact that taking her captive had turned out to be one of the wisest decisions he'd ever made did little to temper the guilt he felt for having done so, however, as his motivations had been anything but noble.

Yet she forgave him, dared to call him friend, and now risked her life to aid them. To aid Resamane, if not him personally, and this was more than enough.

"*Madari!*" Txeru growled amid a staccato of crossing fire. "We've got incoming from both sides!"

It was too soon. He wasn't done.

Galean: "Too many security units are bearing down on our location. Marlee, can you take some of the heat off?"

Marlee: "With pleasure."

She altered her destination to right outside the server room, and arrived to find five officers exchanging fire with Raisan and Txeru.

She shot the closest one square in the chest. A force field rippled into existence to absorb the brunt of the blow, but the impact knocked him into his comrade.

And now five weapons were trained on her.

She sprinted back through the still-open wormhole amid a rain of gunfire, immediately spinning to the left and running down a hallway while leaving the wormhole open. After all, the whole point was to get the officers away from the server room.

The always surprisingly lightweight gait of multiple Belascocians rushing after her was muffled by the spongy floor, but not so much that she didn't know they were coming. She closed the wormhole and began spinning up power once more.

Three followed her route to the left. She made sure they saw her as she barreled through a new wormhole leading to the atrium of an uninteresting administrative wing. Again she left it open so they'd continue the chase.

This time she slipped around behind the wormhole, where they couldn't see her thanks to the mind-bending characteristics of a portal between two points on the spacetime manifold.

Once they were through, she closed it and tossed a grenade into their midst. Shrapnel exploded out, sending blood splattering across two walls.

Not waiting to see if any of them recovered, she opened a new wormhole behind her and hopped through.

But she'd gotten too clever by half and lost track of the other two officers. White-hot fire ripped into her hip, and she fell face-first through the opening. *Close....*

She curled in on herself on the floor, instinctively trying to protect her injury. After another second an eVi routine forced a modicum of clear-headedness on her, and she gingerly felt along her hip. Her fingers came back doused in blood, but at least there wasn't gushing. This wound was on the opposite side from the one she'd suffered while trying to escape from Galean, so she'd torn up all new muscles and possibly organs.

She grunted out a command. "Mission's not done. Get your ass up, Marlee Rosa Arrigucci Marano!"

As she climbed to her feet, she discovered she was in a dark, shadowy room. Empty, as far as she was able to make out in the nonexistent lighting.

She swayed unevenly and reached out for the closest wall to brace herself. Her mad sprinting days were behind her on this mission. What could she still do to attract attention, while not getting further shot? Toss some more grenades, because that had been rather effective.

She opened a succession of wormholes until she located security reinforcements heading toward the server room, lobbed a grenade through, and closed it without waiting on the results. How many security officers did they have in this building?

Galean: "We're ready to go. And do please hurry."

Her vision swam. But this was the end, and not a moment too soon. So she authorized a wholesale dump of pain suppression mechanisms by her cybernetics, followed by a wallop of a dose of adrenaline to keep her on her feet.

Then she opened a wormhole back to where they'd begun, inside the server room.

Galean, Raisan and Txeru were exchanging gunfire through the open door. An explosion rocked the hallway just outside, and the blast knocked them all to the floor.

Oh, boy did that hurt. She clenched her jaw and struggled to her feet while switching out the wormhole for one leading to the steppes. "Get up! Let's go now!"

Galean should have been the first through, as he presumably now held the key to salvation in his hands, but instead he helped Raisan to his feet, then urged him through the opening. Txeru moved through next, and Galean turned around and extended an arm out to her.

She grabbed for his outstretched hand and stumbled through. Ominous clouds of smoke billowed into the server room as she left it behind. *Close.*

A few wisps of smoke wafted into the crisp night air where the wormhole had been.

Galean drew up short as he looked around and spotted the vehicle nestled under the rocky outcropping. "You brought us directly back to the vehicle?"

"Yeah." She nodded unevenly. "Because this is, I'm afraid, our last stop."

Her legs buckled, and darkness claimed her.

22

Galean paced ineffectually while Mattin sat at the workstation processing the data. Identifying it, tagging it, and sorting it before letting loose crawlers to distill it into meaningful information.

Nedeni, on the other hand, was the picture of calm patience. He sat in a chair near the door, studying a portable screen resting on his lap while his tail swiped lazily across the floor.

Galean supposed the ability to impose a veneer of patience upon oneself in the most difficult of situations was one of the requirements of Nedeni's position. He'd witnessed the man do it innumerable times over the years. Another reason why Nedeni was the leader, and he was not.

His thoughts continued to ricochet off the jagged crevices of his mind. They bounced to Medical, where Marlee remained unconscious. Dr. Osane had staunched the bleeding and sutured the wounds, then pronounced the rest would be up to the alien's cybernetics. Resa was holding vigil at her bedside and had promised to alert him the instant Marlee woke up. So there was nothing he could do on this front, either.

Days like today made him question what skills he brought to the Tarazi. He was good in a fight, but Raisan, Txeru, Fremen and half a dozen others were better. His analytical abilities were also above average, but he was no genius. He'd already covered his failings at breaking electronic security—Mattin's tools had retrieved the data, not any skill of his. He wasn't a poet or deliverer of inspiring speeches, nor a great organizer of men.

Once upon a time, he'd been a builder. Molding material into a form that performed its highest purpose while pleasing its users had brought him satisfaction; on occasion, even joy. In the early days of the Tarazi, he'd spearheaded the transformation of the

Serba from gutted-out industrial rig to a livable base for thousands of people, but that was years gone.

Now, what he did was protect his sister. Every day, in his every action. Today, perhaps, he'd played a small role in protecting her forever.

"What's taking so long?" The question slipped out unbidden.

"It's a gargantuan amount of data," Mattin murmured distractedly.

"Can you tell if it contains anything useful? Did we get what we were looking for?"

"Probably. Much of it, anyway."

"What does that mean?"

"The sooner you stop bothering me, the sooner I can tell you." The annoyance rippling off Mattin's eamonal was mild, however, easing the sting of his words.

Galean checked on Nedeni and found him unaltered. Still reading, tail still conveying an air of absolute tranquility.

Nedeni had once said the most crucial skill Galean brought to the Tarazi was passion. A selfless insistence on safeguarding the desbida under their care and a righteous zeal for exposing the crimes of the Aterpe Project and the men and women who had spearheaded it.

It was true enough. But passion was nothing without execution, and he'd been whiffing on this one of late. The devastating failure of his mission to recruit Vasem, getting captured on the desbida rescue mission.... But maybe today would change things.

"Now." Mattin spun his chair around, arms spreading wide. "Do you want the good news or the bad news?"

The fact there was bad news to be had pierced his ari. He needed a win, so he replied before Nedeni. "The good news, please."

"I'm still collating everything, but we now possess a treasure trove of information on the early treatment attempts and how they went wrong. How the research shifted once the camps were instituted. Compilations of the worst side effects, and how little was done to ameliorate them. We also grabbed a fair bit on the Soldad program—mostly scientific in nature. What traits they're trying to bring out, the markers for good candidates, and so on."

"That all sounds terrific. What's the bad news?"

"I'll keep looking, but I can't find a smoking gun. Nowhere does it say in writing, 'the desbida aren't crazy or a danger to others, but since they do pose a danger to us, the powerful, we need to lock them up anyway.' There's a lot in these files worthy of criticism. Information that deserves a public accounting. But what's lacking is…malice aforethought. You can make a case that it's implied in what's missing, but…" Mattin glanced at Nedeni "…I'm told we need a clear, unequivocal argument that resonates with the public, not a labyrinthine legal debate."

"Correct." Nedeni stood, set aside his screen on the chair, and approached the workstation. "We always knew this was a risk. So let's find the name."

"Sir?"

"The name of the dissident. The person who objected to the direction things were taking and, as a result, disappeared from the Project."

"Hmm." Mattin stroked his neck. "I can run a time-lapse analysis of the appearance of names in the files. Are we looking for one of the researchers or an administrator?"

"It could be either. It could even be a nurse or other desbida caregiver, though it's less likely someone in such a position would possess the necessary incriminating data."

"All right. Any and all names of people employed by the project, starting from its inception. It's a lot of names."

Nedeni returned to his chair and resumed studying his screen, and Galean suppressed some uncharitable emotions before they manifested too clearly in his eamonal. Nedeni couldn't afford to be overly emotional, and he should try to emulate the man.

His thoughts went to the day the government arrived to take Resamane away from their home in Maistel. She was desbida, they said, and thus represented a danger to herself and their odola. In a therapeutics camp she would be cared for, and maybe one day there would be a cure.

His parents and aitona had been sad, but also relieved. No question, Resa had struggled as her mutation manifested, brought on by the onset of puberty. Wild mood swings, acting out in rebellion. Days spent in utter withdrawal, refusing food and companionship. In retrospect, this had simply been the process by which her body and mind adjusted to its new capabilities. The most extreme behaviors were already fading away when the officers arrived. But the family had been worn down by the difficulties, and they handed her over without much of a fight.

He'd been fifteen years old, little more than a child. And so he'd stood meekly by and allowed them to put her in restraints— because she *had* put up a fight—and march her out of the Nekane pod forever. He should have fought, should have rescued her that very day. They could have run away, naught but the clothes on their back between them, and found a way to make a life. If he'd acted then, his sister would still be able to see the beauty of the world around her.

He could never go back in time and undo this fateful mistake, but he'd taken what recompense he could. Eventually.

"And here we go. We've got three names who were active in the first few years of the Project, then vanished from the files in an unnaturally abrupt manner."

Galean noted that Nedeni removed himself from his chair with a touch more energy this time, and they crowded around the big screen in front of Mattin.

"Danel Eskuin. Deputy Director of Research and Development, until he resigned in 4838. Was killed three weeks later in a hunting accident."

"Murdered to keep him silent," Galean replied.

Nedeni's head tilted in agreement. "Likely so."

"Tere Usoa. Head nurse on the treatment recuperation floor. Resigned for medical reasons and died six months later of acute gaixot."

This one was a tougher call. Medical records could be faked, but gaixot had been a scourge at the time.

"Lastly, Dr. Ctaro Melar. Director of Emergent Therapies, until he applied for and received a transfer."

"He's still alive?" Galean asked.

"According to the public records, he's running a research facility on Veuna Atoll."

Nedeni took two steps back, hair strands stiffening. "*Madari….*"

Galean considered him in surprise. "Why? This is terrific news—exactly what we were hoping for."

"It is." Nedeni coaxed his hair strands back into relaxation.

"Then what's the problem?"

"I know Melar. Or once knew him."

"Yet more good news. We have a route through which to reach him."

"The problem is, he's not going to be happy to see me."

Galean poked his head into the Medical exam room to find Marlee sitting up in bed, laughing softly as Resa stroked her arm.

His heart flooded with warmth and relief. Many things about their guest continued to confound him, but he did not doubt that she'd come to care deeply about Resa. His sister often had such an effect on people, though he'd never imagined it might extend to aliens as well. But why shouldn't it? Possibly some things were universal across all sapient species. The desire for connection, for companionship. The desire to understand another being, and for them to understand you in turn.

"Galean, come in." Marlee motioned him forward.

He stepped up to the other side of the bed. "How are you?"

"I'm *fine*. Or I will be in a few more hours. It's not the first or the second time I've been injured in a melee."

"And how many times have you been shot twice in one day?"

"Oh. Good point." Her hand rose to rub at the bandage taped over her shoulder. "This one hardly counts, though."

"I will let you be the judge of how well your body can weather its wounds." Perhaps responding to the waves of compassion and tenderness emanating from Resa, he took Marlee's hand in his, placed his other atop it, and curled in toward her. "Thank you for risking your life yet again on our behalf. We'd never have achieved success in our mission without you, but I pray to the arima that you need not do so again. You have given enough."

Her gaze flickered between their hands and his face, though she did not pull away. Her full lips parted, then closed again, and he wished he could sense the tumult of her emotions, for they would provide a guidepost upon which to anchor his own.

After a moment, her lips parted again. "Well, that depends. Did we get what we needed?"

Her use of 'we' did not escape his attention. He didn't dare hope she had fully internalized their cause as her own, but he conceded she seemed to do everything wholeheartedly, holding nothing back.

He squeezed her hand; it felt an unnatural and awkward act, but she'd done so to him once before, which suggested it was a Human act signifying comradery. Then he removed his grip and stood up straighter. "We retrieved a lot of information. Arguably more than we had any right to hope for. As we'd worried, the data doesn't contain outright evidence of high crimes—quite a few lesser ones, but nothing strong enough to bring down the entire conspiracy. But we do have a name, one that might hold the key to breaking everything wide open."

Marlee smiled, flashing her too-white and strangely flat teeth. "What great news. Who are they? How are you going to reach out to them?"

Galean sighed. "That part is a touch problematic."

23

Resamane entertained Marlee until the doctor cleared her to be discharged. She loved the woman's company, but she also desperately needed some privacy...but then Resamane insisted on getting a proper lunch, during which Marlee obliged her by recounting the most exciting details of the mission to the Aubera Facility.

Finally Resamane had to depart for an appointment, and Marlee made a beeline for the temporary privacy of the apartment.

Once there, she settled onto her bed and at last opened the message from Miriam. It had been sitting out there in the void, waiting for the next time she was able to access the quantum network of her messaging system. Six days, damn. But she'd grabbed it while dashing around Aubera, as well as sending out some additional messages.

> *Marlee,*
> *Words cannot express the relief we all feel to learn you are alive and in good health.*

Ha! But at least she was all patched up now, for the second time.

> *David has been urging me to declare war on the Belascocians in order to rescue you, so deep has his concern been. I have not done so, of course, but the situation is rather tense. I would be lying if I said the possibility of armed action was not actively on the table. The information you've shared only complicates matters further, but I vastly prefer the truth to diplomatic lies.*

On that front, Dean Veshnael is quite displeased to learn the Belascocian government has been 'spewing falsehoods in our direction.'

Marlee giggled at the image of serene, stately, always gracious Veshnael being spitting mad. She wished she could have seen it.

Rest assured, we will be using your information to take a different tack in our future conversations with the Belascocians. Our highest priority, however, is seeing you return safely home.

I understand your desire to protect those who have sheltered you, and I will take you at your word that you're unable to wormhole home at this time without exposing them to discovery. Knowing the Belascocian government is not hiding you—instead, you are hiding from them—introduces some new opportunities to our diplomatic 'negotiations,' and we will endeavor to make it safe for you to reveal yourself and come home as quickly as possible.

If you find yourself with the freedom to travel, don't wait to deliver a reply before acting. I look forward to you appearing unannounced in my office, safe and sound. David will get some gelato, and you can regale us with your harrowing tale.

All our love,

Miriam Solovy

Marlee sighed blissfully. It was so goddamn good to hear from family, even if only in the bare words of a written message. As much as she'd come to care for the people here at the Serba, it was torture to be utterly cut off from her world and everyone in it. But they were still real, and they missed her.

With the significant lag time in the correspondence, Miriam had no idea exactly how involved Marlee now was in the Tarazi's crusade. And though her heart ached with the desire to do so, she couldn't go home yet. She'd promised Resamane and Galean she would see this through, but even if she hadn't promised, she *had* to see it through. It was her cause now.

Marlee found Galean waiting outside the tech lab. "Has Nedeni left?"

"He took off a few minutes ago." He sighed and leaned against the wall. "I'm worried. This is a high-stakes play he's making, and if it goes wrong…but the time has come to make our move."

"Life is nothing without risk."

"As you have reminded us." He offered her a pensive expression and fell into silence.

"Um, your message said you wanted to talk to me?"

"Yes! No. I mean, Mattin wants to talk to us both."

"Oh?" She hadn't met Mattin, though she'd heard plenty about him. "Is it about the data we snatched from Aubera?"

"I don't think so, no." He gestured to the door with his tail. "Shall we find out?"

"Absolutely." She followed Galean into the lab. It resembled every mad scientist's workspace the universe over. Servers stacked precariously in every corner, terminals attached to screens displaying reams of code scattered here and there, multiple worktables strewn with tools.

At the center of the lab, a man sent his chair flying over to one of the terminals. The long legs adroitly maneuvering the chair suggested he was tall for a Belascocian, with dullish sage lamina-skin but dancing gray eyes that landed on her as he spun around.

"The Human. The whispers about you have reached even my den of seclusion. Most notably, your magical theatrics at Aubera."

She performed the Belascocian equivalent of extending her hand. "Hi, I'm Marlee."

"Yes, you are. My name is Mattin Erlantz." He checked with Galean. "She's cleared for all this?"

"You didn't tell me what you wanted to discuss."

"Oh, right. The kabanat."

"Truly? You've been working on the kabanat for two years now. You said it was just a pet project of yours that was unlikely to go anywhere."

"And it was—until it wasn't. Tales of all the quantum manipulation our alien friend here can perform encouraged me to refocus on it. Yesterday, while I was letting the system organize all the Aubera data, I had a eureka moment of sorts."

Galean's posture shifted forward in apparent excitement. "You've made it work?"

"A little. I think. I still need to conduct some tests."

"If you have...this could change everything for us."

"Yes, yes." Mattin waved a hand in the air. "Some things."

Marlee blew out a breath. "Can someone tell me what a 'kabanat' is?"

"Sorry." Galean smiled a touch sheepishly...she thought, because she'd never seen *that* mannerism from him. "It's a sort of...quantum diffuser. It creates a field around something, or someone, and resonates their quantum disruptions with the natural fluctuations in the area, thereby dissipating any spikes they create." He glanced at Mattin. "Did I explain it correctly?"

"Poorly, but correctly I suppose."

"Good. Such a device would, in theory, allow the desbida to go out into the world without being detected and allow us to resume normal quantum communications with one another and third parties. It would..." a corner of Galean's mouth twitched "...allow you to talk to your people whenever you like."

Mattin straightened out of his slouch. "Slow down. I never said it would work for her. It's designed for Belascocians."

Marlee frowned. "Why should that matter? Quantum mechanics doesn't care about species."

"Perhaps not. A moment." Mattin held up a finger and kicked the chair over to another terminal. A series of hums and hisses emerged from the man's throat as he studied a schematic on the terminal's screen. After ten seconds or so, his tail went rigid along the length of his leg, and he got quiet.

A minute passed, then two. Marlee started fidgeting; patience had never been her highest quality, and Mattin's quirky genius routine was a bit much. How fantastic would it have been if the man had managed to complete this kabanat device a few weeks earlier? It would have saved her *so* much trouble...but then she might never have gotten the chance to get to know Resamane or Deshka...or Galean.

He was watching her fidgeting in seeming amusement, and she rolled her eyes at him in response. He'd gotten much better at reading her mannerisms lately (or maybe Resamane had taught them to him), and that earned her a genuine smile.

Were they friends now? Not colleagues of necessity given their circumstances, but actual friends? If so, she thought she'd like that very much.

Abruptly Mattin spun around again, interrupting their silent banter. "It will work for her, if it will work for anyone. Obviously."

Galean clapped his palms together. "Can we help you test it?"

"Yes! But not yet. It's not ready."

"Then why did you ask us here?"

"So someone would know it was almost ready."

Galean's sentsores snapped out horizontally. Annoyance, definitely. "How long until we can test it?"

"Six hours. Possibly eight. Unless someone brings me some food along the way. I'll ask Halona." Mattin resumed typing.

Galean extended a hand to her, and they left the lab.

"He was interesting."

"We have other words for men such as him. But if he succeeds in making the kabanat work, it will be a transformative event for us."

"Ironic, though, don't you think? If Nedeni's meeting goes well, you might not need to hide quantum spikes for much longer."

"True. Irony is well appreciated by the Arbasoak, I suspect."

He was apt to invoke his gods from time to time, though she hadn't decided if it was simply a cultural reflex or a sincere belief that they both existed and exerted power over the world. And since religion was a third rail even among close friends, she elected not to ask.

He was still holding her hand, somewhat to her surprise, and now he tugged her off to the left. "Come. Resamane and Deshka are expecting us for dinner. I believe you'll find Deshka is an excellent cook."

24

The aircraft accelerated to hypersonic speeds as it neared the apex of its parabolic flight path, and for a moment, Nedeni could almost see the stars. Hints of light danced through the thin, wispy atmosphere, and if you narrowed your eyes enough, they started to resolve....

Then the craft flipped its nose and began descending, and they were gone. Nedeni forced his mind to the mission at hand; if he was successful, he'd likely be seeing the stars soon enough.

But that was an enormous 'if.'

Dr. Ctaro Melar was one of the most preeminent genetics researchers in the world, but this hadn't stopped Nedeni from firing him fourteen years ago. Of course, the event hadn't been so stark and ugly in the formalities. Rather, as head of the Proml Foundation, Nedeni had simply elected not to renew its funding of Dr. Melar's research project on using post-natal gene therapy to eradicate several debilitating childhood deformities. Not because the research didn't hold the promise of delivering a tremendous good for the lives of children afflicted with the deformities, but because he had discovered that Melar was flagrantly disregarding crucial safety protocols during the therapy trials, resulting in the deaths of three participants.

If the black mark on Melar's resume had harmed the man's career in any way, it had been of passing, ephemeral impact. But this would not have stopped Melar from nursing a grudge, as the man's pride knew no bounds.

The thing Nedeni couldn't figure was, given Melar's demonstrated lack of respect for safety and his patients' well-being, why he had walked away from the Aterpe Project. Had an attack of conscience finally manifested in the man's soul, or was there another reason? The fact that he remained alive many years later suggested the latter, in which case this was a futile endeavor. But he had to try.

The autopilot eased its angle of descent and speed as Veuna Atoll came into view. Stretching for six kilometers of opalescent beaches and verdant flora, it was the largest island in a chain of pearls some hundred kilometers in length. Resorts dotted the beaches in sweeps of marble and stone, but the center of the island was dominated by a vast complex of more utilitarian buildings, though they were accented by a smattering of pools and leisure parks.

The New Horizons Institute was the crown jewel of Veuna and one of the most prestigious centers of scientific inquiry on Estapa. Graduating students competed fiercely to win externships in its labs, to sit at the feet of the masters of science and absorb their knowledge like sponges. Patients paid tens of thousands of credits to earn a place on waiting lists for research studies.

Given the prodigious money flowing into the New Horizons Institute, he wondered if anyone had ever bothered to review the safety protocols in use here. Something told him it had been a while.

Local Flight Control interfaced with the ship's computer to direct it to a clear runway, and after a few seconds of jittering bumps he was on the ground almost halfway around the globe from where he'd begun.

Fifteen minutes later, his turn arrived at customs, and he stepped up to the security station. He placed his palm on the reader while giving the officer an ingratiating smile.

"Estebe Gero. Reason for visiting Veuna Atoll?"

"I'm a real estate investor. I'm here to meet with several developers about a potential new resort property."

The officer gave a bored nod. "Have a nice visit."

There had never been much risk of his false identity being discovered by a simple customs check, but Nedeni nevertheless untensed several muscles as he strode toward the airport exit.

The Gero cover had served him well for many years now. The man practically existed, so extensive were his background and confirmatory legal records. As founder, leader and financier of the Tarazi, he needed to be able to operate out in the real world. Materials and products needed to be commissioned or purchased; potential converts needed to be approached by an actual person to either assuage or stoke their fears, depending. In short, while the Serba was his home, matters needed to be attended to across Belarria, and so he'd spent a small fortune establishing an airtight identity.

The humid air washed over him as he stepped outside, and his skin soaked in the heat to warm his body. Veuna had much to commend it, and in another life, the life he'd once had, he'd spent a good bit of time here enjoying its offerings. Time with Kemina and Arnas and as many of their joined odola as they were able to fit in the largest rental home.

But that path was closed to him now, so he ignored the siren call of patio seafood restaurants and musical amphitheaters and caught a tram car for the New Horizons Institute.

Sweeping white arches framed the entrance in a cascade that narrowed into an awning for wide glass doors etched with floral motifs. The doors slid open as Nedeni approached, revealing a pristine lobby with whorl-marbled floors, ubiquitous diffuse light and trellises of ivy.

An elegant woman with open features and a convivial public eamonal greeted him at the counter. "Welcome to the New Horizons Institute, sir. How can we be of service to you today?"

"Estebe Gero. I have an appointment to see Dr. Melar."

Her eyes flickered to the screen residing below the counter. "I see you do. I'll let the doctor know you've arrived."

"Thank you." He went over and sat in one of the cushioned, wing-backed chairs arranged with studied randomness in the lobby. To Dr. Melar, Estebe Gero was not a real estate investor but a representative of an investment fund that managed the superfluous money of an interlinked batu-odola of several wealthy families.

By the look of it, the Institute was not hurting for financing, but one should never underestimate the greed of men such as Melar.

"Mr. Gero? Dr. Melar is ready to see you now. You can take the lift on the right to the top floor."

"Thank you." He followed the directions, and the lift deposited him on a floor awash in marble and glass.

A second receptionist confirmed his identity then escorted him to a conference room with a wall of windows looking out over the island. Teal waters glittered in the midday sun, and the beaches were dotted with frolickers like seeds upon a loaf of bread.

"Mr. Gero, is it? Welcome to the New Horizons Institute."

Nedeni turned from the window, his hands arranged in a casual, friendly fold at his waist. "Hello, Ctaro."

The man blinked twice, his spine stiffening. "Nedeni Proml. You're dead."

"To the world, yes."

"No, I mean you are literally dead. There was an obituary and a funeral—it was all over the media at the time. You committed suicide after—"

"There's no need to recount the nightmares of my past to me. I am familiar enough with them."

Ctaro shook his head, as if clearing a fog. "But is any of it true? You stand here today, hearty and hale. Am I to surmise that your lovely wife still lives as well? Your son...I suppose I know the truth of that. But little else, it seems."

Pain and anger bristled against Nedeni's restraint, and he was swiftly reminded of how he detested this man. But in war, one did not always get to choose one's allies. "Arnas and Kemina are well and truly dead. In the wake of the...crimes against my family, I found I needed to remove myself from the world and begin a new life, with a new purpose dedicated to their memory."

"I take it said purpose is not investing the excess coins of the Proml Foundation."

"It is not. It is so much more important."

"Oh, I do so love a good crusade. Pray tell me of it."

Nedeni did not. "You were the Director of Emergent Therapies for the Aterpe Project for four years. In 4837, you abruptly resigned from your position and, shortly thereafter, opened this Institute. Why?"

Ctaro gestured around the conference room, the sweep of his arms drawing in the rest of the building and the grounds beyond. "The government was generous with its seed money for the Institute's founding. At last I had a place where I was able to set the course of my own research, free of the stifling requirements of government projects and their narrow restrictions. How could I refuse such an opportunity?"

Nedeni hesitated. It sounded so close to truth that he wondered if it might be, in which case this trip had been a waste of time and him revealing his identity a mistake that would prove costly. But his gut screamed otherwise...that or desperation.

A smile hinted across his features. "They bought you off, then. Endowed you with millions and your own personal fiefdom to buy your silence. A better option than what Dr. Eskuin suffered, no doubt."

"I know not to what you refer."

"They murdered him. But you do know this. See, I remember what things were like back then. The desbida 'problem' was the only thing that existed in our world. Every resource was being thrown at it. The scientist who solved the problem would have been heralded as a new savior, his name uttered in prayerful thanks at dinner tables for years to come. You would not have willingly given up the glory. Not even for this monument to scientific hubris you've constructed here.

"Not unless you witnessed something so horrifying, it tweaked your starved and meager conscience."

"Your barbs are not endearing yourself to me, Nedeni." Ctaro gestured meaningfully to the door. "One more, and I shall ask you to leave."

But he didn't need to be able to read the man's eamonal to know it was an empty threat. Ctaro had already deduced that Nedeni knew his dark secret but hadn't yet discerned what this meant for him. The doctor wasn't leaving the room until he determined the nature of the danger Nedeni represented.

"Forgive me. Because you *did* follow your conscience when it mattered most, and that's why I'm here." The first was a half-truth at best. Ctaro could have gone public with the atrocities. At a time when the desbida crisis was still in flux and the Errigime hadn't solidified its total control over Aterpe, the public outcry could have torn it all down. But Nedeni needed Ctaro's cooperation the way a dying man needed water, so he ground his jaw and appealed to the man's vanity.

"Again, I know not to what you refer."

"Cast your mind back to 4837. Thousands of young people we would come to label 'desbida' have begun to exhibit a variety of abnormal behaviors. Research links these abnormalities to gene therapy administered to wide swaths of children beginning seventeen years earlier. Obviously, not all who received the therapy developed such symptoms. But for those who did, behavioral issues were the least of the problems caused by the genetic manipulation.

"One day, a breathless report reaches your desk—or more likely, is delivered by a breathless researcher in person. The desbida's eamonals have been supercharged. No longer limited to interacting with odola and chosen hartua odola, they can read any person, anywhere. And not just vague senses of emotions, mood or inclination. They can read thoughts."

Ctaro's body stiffened. "I would interject that this is a lie, but you've never been a liar. An insufferable truth-teller, in fact. How do you know?"

"I'll get to it in a bit. So you confirm this shocking finding, then report it to the Project Director. At this point, you're probably jubilant. The gene therapy program has succeeded beyond your wildest dreams. It has kickstarted an evolutionary leap in our people. Imagine the possibilities!

"But it isn't long before the order comes down from on high: this emergent ability must be suppressed. Develop treatments to tamp down the desbida's hyperactive eamonals by any means necessary.

"You're disappointed. Maybe you argue with a few government officials or mysterious corporate executives who've been granted outsized influence over the Project. You get nowhere, and the order is delivered more sternly. Since you value your position, you comply. But in your heart, bitterness takes root.

"The new treatments are a disaster. Not only do they fail at their primary purpose of suppressing the desbida's eamonal abilities, they also cause a plethora of negative side effects. Blindness, muteness, physical deformities, cancers, sometimes a descent into insanity. Patients commit suicide in droves. You want to stop the treatment trials, but the higher-ups insist you continue. No matter the cost, they say.

"Then the news starts reporting on how the desbida are a danger to themselves and others. How many turn violent, even against their own odolas. You know any such behaviors aren't due to their desbida nature, but instead a reaction to experimental therapies. Maybe you push back, privately, and are told that the desbida do in fact represent a threat to others—to society as a whole. Until they can be cured, they must be segregated from society. But the reasons are too nuanced and complex to be explained to the general public, so a simpler story is required. A lie. Tell me, have I gotten this right so far?"

Ctaro stared at him silently.

"Close enough, then. Now, maybe you felt a rousing empathy for your patients and wanted to protect them, or maybe you were morally offended at the wreckage the government was making of your valuable scientific research. Regardless of the reason, you threatened to go public with the truth. Luckily for you, Bihar Kartean knew you too well, and he recognized that you could be more easily dealt with via a bribe than a hit squad. He expressed regret and sorrow over how matters had turned out, and offered you all this..." Nedeni gestured toward the window and the grounds beyond "...in exchange for you quietly stepping away from the Aterpe Project and never speaking of its secrets. And you took the deal."

Ctaro snorted derisively. "What is it you want, Nedeni? Extortion money? Have you burned through your family's entire fortune and need to take mine now?"

"Living as a ghost has proved somewhat expensive, especially given my chosen hobby, but no. I'm going public with all of this, Ctaro, in a way the government and the Errigime will not be able to suppress. I'm here to give you the chance—one chance—to be on the right side of this story. To see your research vindicated and your principles win out. To be a hero to the desbida you abandoned to torture."

The man dropped hard into a chair. "You're Tarazi."

Nedeni forced an appearance of ease into his expression. Ctaro could bolt from the room and report his resurrection and job title to the authorities...but how much would it change? "Sorry, did I forget to mention that part?"

"You did. And not just Tarazi...their leader, or at least their financial benefactor. You know much of this because you have under your protection desbida who were there in the labs in those early days. The rest I assume you've deduced. I never doubted your intellect, merely your prudish judgment."

"I'll take that as a compliment."

"It wasn't intended as such. They will kill you, Nedeni. They will kill you and everyone you hold dear. They will take the desbida you shelter from you, and they won't even transfer them to the therapeutics camps. They'll simply execute them, lest they try to foment revolution from inside the camps."

"We've managed to avoid such a fate so far."

"Barely, I imagine. You try to go public, and they will spare no resource to track you down and smashing you like a baco bug."

"This is why I want you on my side." Nedeni worked to keep the desperation he felt out of his voice. "You bring evidence to our fight—irrefutable proof of their crimes."

"All the more reason for it to be stamped out. I would be mad to join your cause, as I will be the first one they kill."

"Not if we expose the conspiracy. The public, the media and the law will come down on them. The worm will turn."

"Not fast enough."

"I'll protect you. I've protected thousands for eight years now."

"Ha!" Ctaro stood and strode to the windows. "Give up all this splendor to sleep in a bunk in some overcrowded, grimy fortress and eat prefabbed, rationed food? I think not."

"Our home is rather nicer than you assume. You'll be quite comfortable. But that's beside the point. This is all coming crashing down, whether you wish it or not. We *are* going public. You will be named for your involvement in the original experiments and the treatment research. The ravenous hounds will swarm at your door, and that will only be the start—there's no escaping it now. I'm giving you a chance to get in front of this and craft matters more to your liking. A chance to be the hero of this story."

Ctaro's eyes cut over to him, a speculative glint lighting them, and Nedeni thought he'd snared the man now. An overabundance of vanity had always been the key.

"What role do you imagine I will play in your mad scheme?"

"Ready for distribution all the incriminating files you secretly made copies of before Kartean ordered you to erase them. Construct a story around them that persuades and scintillates, the way you've done for all your scientific breakthroughs. I don't care if you play up your role or embellish either your moral outrage or the extent to which you feared for your life. You do as you are wont to do—so long as the blinding core of your story shows the world that the desbida were victims here. Victims of a corrupt, power-hungry government-corporate cabal who were terrified the desbida could destroy them. Our story—your story—will expose the crimes of this cabal and the shining light of the desbida in equal measure."

"I am not a playwright, Nedeni. I'm a scientist, and science is not always romantic."

"Then simply hand over your files and swear under oath to their authenticity, and we'll do the rest. I merely wanted to give you the opportunity to be the star."

"Hmm. You make a good point. The world won't understand much of what is in those files, not without someone knowledgeable to explain it to them. But why should I believe you can protect me?"

"Because I've protected hundreds of desbida and thousands of individuals who believe in their right to live free. Because the government has hunted us for years and has never found us. Which would you prefer?" He gestured to the windows and the beaches below. "A clear shot for a Kaldi sniper, or a fortress and trained fighters ensconcing you?"

"You want me to come with you, then. Right now?"

"We will be moving very soon—in a matter of days. There might not be another opportunity for you to seek refuge before then. Go to your office and gather your files, and we will depart together, as if for a seaside lunch meeting."

Ctaro stared down at the table. "To walk away from all this...."

"If we succeed, it will all be waiting for you upon your triumphant return. Please, Ctaro. Come with me, and let's change the world. For the better this time."

The man nodded slowly in acceptance.

"Your office, then?"

Ctaro reached into his pocket and removed a case holding a tiny data storage plate. "For the last seven years, I've never let these files out of my sight."

25

Nedeni emerged from the Docks accompanied by an older man in an expensively tailored business suit. The man's eyes flickered over every corner of the atrium, taking in its design, decor and occupants with an air of disdain.

Nedeni whisked the man away to Mattin's lab without stopping to talk to anyone.

"I guess that's Dr. Melar," Galean remarked.

Deshka made a face at the closing door behind them. "One can assume. He looked friendly."

To say the least. "It doesn't matter if he's an asshole. The important thing is, Nedeni convinced him to help us."

"Or forced him at gunpoint."

Galean didn't doubt for a minute that, if it were required, Nedeni would have done exactly so. "The doctor didn't act happy to be here, for certain. But he is not the first or thousandth person here to be ripped away from the life they'd built in order to hide from powerful forces that will kill them on sight. And unlike everyone else, his inconvenience should be rather temporary."

Deshka's eamonal radiated a rare edginess. "So we're really going to do this then? Go public and expose the Aterpe Project? Call out the government and Errigime leaders who have fueled its barbarous acts?"

Nedeni re-emerged from the lab alone and began crossing the atrium in the direction of Administration. As he did, his gaze passed across then landed on Galean and Deshka. His chin dipped to the side, toward his office.

"Let's go find out."

"The operation will consist of three independent missions. The most critical phase, requiring most of our forces, will involve boarding Inarska II and taking over the studio of Belarria First News. Only from the space station can we reach the entire planet simultaneously—which is of course why all the major news corporations have studios there. Once we're in control of Belarria First's facilities, we'll broadcast a pre-prepared message, and the world will finally learn the truth."

"Are we going to shoot our way onto the station?" Fremen asked.

Nedeni shook his head firmly. "No. A team will take one of the transport ships and dock at Inarska II using their preexisting false identities. However, they will need to be prepared to shoot their way into the studio, or possibly the broadcast booth itself."

Fremen nodded. "I assumed there would be shooting at some point."

"Do try to keep it to a minimum. The CEO of Belarria First News may well be a member of the Errigime, but the employees working at the studio are innocent bystanders. The judicious use of temporary restraints on them will go a long way.

"At the same time as the team is infiltrating the studio, a number of couriers will be delivering packages to these government and corporate officials."

A list of names and affiliations displayed on Nedeni's screen, some recognizable to everyone, others more obscure. The list went on for some length, and Galean felt definable stirrings of excitement. No way could the authorities suppress information from so many disparate sources.

"The number of deliveries is going to strain our vehicle resources, so as soon as the first packages are ready, we will begin sending people out in waves. The earliest departees will need to linger near their target until the appointed time arrives. These delivery missions should not be especially dangerous, as the packages will be labeled as ordinary correspondence originating from sources known to the recipients."

"What's the third mission?" Deshka asked.

"It will be mine alone," Nedeni replied. "The Errigime has no head, only limbs—but the government does. I am going to deliver my own package, directly into President Lormain's hands. I will make certain he watches our broadcast. Then I am going to offer him a way forward."

"You're planning to make a deal with him?" Galean exclaimed. "After all our hard work? After everything we've endured at the hands of his police?"

"I am planning to ensure that all of you have a future."

"But you can't let him off cleanly."

"I won't. But a cornered rat will tear its attackers apart with its claws, even when there is no hope of escape or survival. Lormain needs to believe there is a path by which our society can be brought back from the brink of madness, violence and death. If he shows reason, we will work together. If he does not...the government will find itself in need of a new president, and perhaps they will show reason."

Galean sank back in his chair, forcing his instinctual rage to simmer down. He'd prefer to see Lormain swing from the rafters, but as usual, Nedeni saw the bigger picture. Their highest purpose was to free the desbida still suffering in the camps, and bloodlust had to bow in submission to this goal.

Nedeni gestured to Marlee. "I may require your assistance, if you are willing."

Galean sat up in interest; he'd wondered why Nedeni had asked for her to attend the meeting.

"You need me to deliver you to President Lormain's office and, if he doesn't take your deal, get you back out in a hurry. Not a problem."

"I can get myself in front of the president, but I concede I might require your assistance to depart, should the conversation not fall in my favor. Therefore, I want you to be on standby."

"I can do that, but I was kind of hoping to participate in the Inarska II phase of the operation."

"No. The presence of an alien in a public space risks sparking confusion and the kind of chaos we don't want."

"And what if I didn't look like an alien?"

Nedeni scoffed. "I've seen the disguise you and Resamane generated. It's passable from a distance, but there is no 'from a distance' on a space station."

"I know. I actually had something else in mind—"

"I said no. The issue is closed."

Marlee opened her mouth to retort again, and Galean set a hand on her thigh to ward it off. She shot him an odd glance, but clamped her mouth shut and settled back into her seat.

Nedeni pivoted back to the briefing. "The Inarska II mission is far and away the most complicated part of this plan. We need to get our people onto the station with weapons. Mattin says he can fab a shielding material that will allow our weapons to pass undetected through a security scan, but it's never been tested. We also need to gain entry to the internal offices of Belarria First News all the way to their broadcast booth, again with as little bloodshed as possible. This goal will be greatly aided if we can prevent the employees from alerting security."

Galean had been about to suggest they portal directly into the studio, thus bypassing security altogether, but with his last statement Nedeni gave voice to why this was a bad idea. A portal would attract the immediate attention of every security officer on the station, and they would find themselves mired in a firefight from the start. But if instead they could evade detection until the message broadcast was well underway, they might actually survive until its completion.

"We must maintain control of the broadcast long enough to send out our message in its entirety," Nedeni continued. "The message will be clear, direct and forceful, but it will not be short. Once it has transmitted, we need to get our people out safely. I hope in the days and weeks to come, we will no longer need to hide, but that time will not arrive in the first hour after our broadcast."

Marlee leaned forward. "I can also—"

"I realize you can. In theory, the timing of the various elements will coincide such that you can evacuate the team from the studio."

"It'll be easier if I'm already on the station."

"Marlee, I said no. Do not challenge me again."

Marlee's body language was so expressive, Galean had to suppress a laugh. Once he'd started to pay attention to it, started to understand it—with Resa's help—he'd come to appreciate the endless variety of ways in which all her parts moved and morphed. It wasn't an eamonal, but at times like this, her mannerisms told the story of her emotions well enough.

"An additional complication is this: as soon as we hijack the Belarria First broadcast, the military will presumably launch electronic-warfare craft to jam the signal. Now, we have three combat-capable aircraft, and they will be in place near Inarska II. But the military will send far more than three EW craft. Mattin is working on software countermeasures to evade the jamming, but if they deploy full-spectrum suppression, we cannot get around it. I am, frankly, open to suggestions on alternative ways to solve this problem. "

An uncomfortable silence descended upon the room. Five seconds ticked by.

Marlee raised her hand in the air.

"Human, I do not care to repeat myself repetitively—"

"This isn't about me being on the station. I can maybe help with the jammers. Possibly."

Nedeni leaned forward in interest. "How do you intend to do that?"

"I don't want to overpromise right now. But Mattin finished testing his kabanat quantum diffuser shortly before this meeting started—and now I'm wondering if the guy ever sleeps. Anyway, I think this is an excellent opportunity to test it out. Safely, of course." She shot Galean a little smile. "Care to go for a ride with me?"

26

Marlee listened with half an ear as Galean worried over the details of the operation. She tried repeatedly to give him her full attention, but nervousness and second-guessing kept drawing her back to what she was about to do. For so many reasons.

She ought to contact Miriam instead. Respect the chain of command, the way a proper official of Concord should do. But her aunt was almost certainly doing everything in her power to avoid kicking off a war with the Belascocians (a war Concord would win handily, but the organization wasn't in the habit of shooting the aliens it met into submission). An authorized military action, if it were discovered, risked doing exactly this. Also, while Miriam respected Marlee's analyses of diplomatic situations, she wasn't apt to throw all in with the Tarazi based solely on Marlee's word.

Morgan Lekkas, on the other hand, would do it for shits and giggles, chain of command be damned. The woman had always played fast and loose with the rules; this was now her third time climbing up the military ranks, because she was also too damn skilled at combat piloting to be kept on the sidelines.

But this was the other reason to be nervous. She hadn't seen Morgan in eight months…and was startled by how she knew instantly how long it had been, almost down to the day. She went about her life *not* thinking about Morgan, but apparently the same couldn't be said about her subconscious.

True enough.

In that case, thanks for not blabbering on about her all the time.

I do actually try to protect you when I can.

I know you do.

"What do you think?"

She hurriedly had her eVi replay the last thing Galean had said. "Nedeni's from a wealthy, well-connected family, right? If anyone can peacefully get the president's attention, he can."

"You're right." Galean peered out the window. "This should be far enough." He brought the vehicle to a stop in the midst of a vast plain leading to stair-step plateaus in the distance, and they climbed out.

He left the driver's side door open and rested against the front of the vehicle. "Moment of truth, yes?"

"We're not going to run as well?"

"I know how you hate it, which is why I drove for such a distance. If your wormhole is detected, we can be on our way in seconds and use the vehicle's stealth capabilities to elude any pursuers."

"Thank you. And it's not that I hate it. It's just..." her cheeks flushed at the notion of explaining to him why it made her so uncomfortable "...it's not something humans do in normal...non-intimate situations."

He stared at her for a moment, his sentsores twitching erratically. "*Oh.* Forgive me for causing you discomfort."

"No! It was crucial for our missions. I totally get that. And if we need to run again in the future for the same reason, I'll happily do so. The problem is with me, not you."

His chin dipped in concession. "Even so. I never anticipated the many ways in which the differences in our cultures would clash and clang. Least of all...intimate ways."

She chewed on her bottom lip. Ugh.... "Hey, how about we go ahead and do this thing?"

He reached into his pocket and withdrew the small device Mattin had crafted to hold his diffuser, then depressed a small button. "It is yours to perform."

Yes, it was. She removed the blocking software in her eVi and sent a message.

Morgan, hi. I hope you're not too busy this instant, as I need to meet with you in person for a quick second. It's important, or I wouldn't ask.

She waited. Wound her fingers together, popped her knuckles, yanked her hands down to her sides. Shot Galean a confident smile.

Marlee! This is a surprise. Let me duck out of this insufferable meeting.

Whew. And now she was somehow more nervous, which was just absurd. Any awkwardness between them was ancient history. They were both adults and professionals.

Okay, I'm free. Thank you for that, by the way.
Huh?
Getting me out of the meeting before I fried the speaker with my mind and lost my commission. Again.
Oh. No problem.

She pulled down the location information Morgan broadcasted and opened a wormhole to the Presidio.

The woman spun at the spatial disruption. "Should I come over, or...?"

"Yes, please. If you don't mind."

"Not at all." Morgan sauntered into the opening and stepped onto the soil of Belarria. As soon as she was through, Marlee closed the wormhole; no reason to tempt fate by allowing it to continue agitating the quantum space.

The woman had grown her chestnut hair out a bit, until it brushed her shoulders, though it still hung razor-straight to half obscure one glittering iris. She wore AEGIS navy BDUs, likely under protest, and a casual swagger that belied her elevated rank.

Morgan glanced around. "So, this is Belarria." Her attention settled over Marlee's shoulder. "And this is a Belascocian."

"What? Oh, yes!" She turned and gestured to Galean. "This is Galean Ozeal. My friend. Galean, this is Morgan Lekkas. Also my friend."

"How interesting. It's a pleasure to meet you, Galean Ozeal. Have you been keeping Marlee out of trouble?" Morgan used a translator, but it perfectly recreated her voice and speaking style.

"Assuredly not. My honor to meet you as well."

"Hmm. No one ever succeeds in keeping her out of trouble for long, so don't feel too bad."

Marlee jumped in before their interchange reached mortification levels. "I'd love for you two to get to know each other, but we can't linger. Morgan, I have a huge, tremendous favor to ask. Before I do, know that you should absolutely say no. And when you do, I'll understand, and my feelings won't be hurt." Not that she expected Morgan to care about such a thing.

"Sounds intriguing. Miriam told me a little about what you've gotten mixed up in here. She didn't volunteer it, but when I was tasked with drawing up battle plans for a potential hostile encounter with the Belascocians, I used my renowned skills of persuasion to squeeze a few details out of her."

God, she'd missed Morgan. "I wish I could have been witness to that discussion."

"Oh, it went about how all our conversations go. So, what are you really up to here? Fomenting revolution?"

"No. No, no, no. Not at all." Marlee grimaced. "I might be abetting one, though."

"Uh-huh. Sounds about right. So, framed for murder and now *abetting* some revolutionaries who want to upend an oppressive government. How can I help?"

"Don't commit until you've heard the ask."

Morgan spread her arms wide, one eyebrow raised. "And the ask is?"

"The Tarazi—the revolutionaries—intend to take over a transmission station on the Inarska II space station, so they can broadcast to the world their evidence of the crimes the government and the Errigime—a corporatist shadow government—have committed against a segment of the population known as desbida. But as soon as they start broadcasting, they expect the military—well, they expect the military to do a lot of things, but one thing in particular they expect them to do is send a squad of electronic-warfare craft to jam the signal. If they do, the mission fails, and they won't get another chance.

"This mission is everything to the Tarazi. It's what they've been working toward for years. It's make or break, all or nothing, et cetera, et cetera. So I thought you might be willing to quietly send a specialty craft or two over here to jam the government's jamming."

Morgan studied her, and she forced herself not to flinch away from the intensity of the woman's bright amethyst Prevo eyes. "And you believe in the rightness of this cause, I'm assuming?"

"I do. Don't tell Miriam, but I could have come home a week ago. Instead, I chose to stay and help the Tarazi win the desbida's freedom."

Something that resembled respect, or possibly amused dismay, flitted across Morgan's expression. Her gaze darted to Galean, then back to Marlee. "I'd need the frequencies they'll target and whatever details are available on the tech the EW craft will use for the jamming. Granted, not *need* as such, but it will make things easier."

"We can get you those details," Galean said matter-of-factly.

"Fantastic. In that case, a couple of Ghosts could do it with no problem, and without being detected—probably. I understand the Belascocians have some quirky quantum detection capabilities. In theory, nothing can detect a Ghost at greater than a hundred meters, but the theory hasn't been tested against Belascocian tech."

Galean stepped in again. "It's conceivable they'll be able to detect that *something* is in the area, if the quantum fluctuations are strong enough. But they won't be able to determine what."

"That's better. And they're going to know they're being jammed either way. So long as they can't see us, it should be kosher." Morgan rubbed at her temple. "In the aftermath, any chance these Tarazi can claim they developed some secret jamming technology? It would be great if the Belascocian government believes it was homegrown."

"We have no qualms about lying on that point. Whether we are believed…hopefully it won't matter, as those who would argue otherwise will find themselves locked behind prison walls."

"Ambitious revolutionaries, then." Morgan returned her attention to Marlee, this time sternly and not in the slightest bit amused. "If we are discovered, it will kick off a war. Miriam deeply, fervently does not want this to occur. We're all about making new allies and working together to advance to ever greater heights and all that bullshit, so we can maybe stand a snowball's chance in Hell whenever—well, you know."

She did. "Which is why I started off saying you should refuse my request. I don't want a war. And if this were to come back on you and hurt your career, I would never forgive myself."

"Eh, it wouldn't be the first time I've had to start over from scratch. I'm not worried about me. I just had to give voice to the risks involved." Morgan sighed. "We're in, quiet as mice, we jam for a minute or two—"

"Five or ten," Galean interjected.

Morgan huffed a laugh. "We jam for five or ten minutes while dancing around to evade detection, and we're out. No one ever knows we were there. I can make it work."

"Are you saying you'll do it?" Marlee asked.

"I definitely shouldn't. But I appreciate a good revolution, having once been an architect of one, in my own way. And it's important to you, so…why the hell not."

Later, Marlee was going to spend hours noodling over the possibility that something being important to her held some sway over Morgan. But she couldn't afford to gush now.

So she beamed instead. "Thank you. Thank you so, so much. This means everything to me—to the Tarazi."

"Mm-hmm. Shoot the details of this operation to me as soon as you can. I'll need a few hours to requisition a Ghost team and some pilots."

Marlee glanced over her shoulder at Galean. "Tomorrow?"

"Tomorrow."

"Got it—oh! Hang on one. Be right back." Morgan opened a wormhole with a flick of the Caeles Prism on her belt, and walked through it to...Concord Special Projects? She disappeared off to the left and was gone for around twelve seconds, then returned to Belarrian soil.

She offered a small bag to Marlee. "From Devon. He picked up in the Noesis that I was with you, because he is a sneaky, meddling S.O.B., and asked me to deliver this. Said you asked for some things in your last communication."

"I did. It works?"

Morgan shrugged. "You should have a message from him rambling on about how only his genius enabled it to be crafted and talking you through how to use it."

"Wonderful. Thank you, again."

Morgan bestowed a beguiling smile on Marlee. "After this whole revolutionizing gig is over and done, and you finally consent to come home, give me a comm. We should have lunch, and you can tell me about..." Morgan's eyes flickered to Galean "...your adventures here."

Marlee worked to keep her voice casual. "I look forward to it."

"Then I'll let you get back to planning your mission. Galean Ozeal, good luck in your revolution. And in trying to keep up with her."

"Your blessings and your assistance are appreciated."

Morgan reopened a wormhole and, with an amused twitch of her lips, walked through it and closed it behind her.

Galean's eyes went to the sky. "Still no incoming. I'm inclined to believe Mattin's device works."

Her whole body relaxed in relief at the news. She could talk to her people again, without having to climb out of the murky depths of Lake Lasai and drive for an hour, then elude Kaldi squads. It felt as though a significant piece of her life had been handed back to her. Caleb's advice about not letting technology define her murmured in the recesses of her mind, but she'd worry about healthy priorities when she was warm and cozy in front of a fire in her apartment on Seneca. "This is great news."

"Yes. We've operated under significant restrictions for so long...before the Tarazi even had a name. The greater freedom this gives us comes at a most opportune time. And for you as well."

"True." She climbed into the comp-craft, feeling all warm and fuzzy inside from seeing Morgan. Not that the relationship was ever going to amount to anything more than a casual friendship; she'd accepted this long ago. But it was so good to see another human again! And one she enjoyed the company of, to boot.

Galean started the ignition, and they set off on a roundabout course for the Serba, as they still needed to be cautious.

"Thank you for taking me out here."

"It was not a burden. Also not necessary, I suspect. I assume you've determined how to drive our vehicles."

"I think so. The basics, anyway. But...I don't mind the company."

"Oh." His browless forehead compressed. "Good. Neither do I. But now I am wondering. Are all Humans female?"

"No, not at all."

"Forgive me. You've spoken of your aunt, and now I've met this Morgan Lekkas, and of course you. It's a small sample size, but enough for me to ask. I know you, Marlee, but your species remains a mystery to me."

"And I hope one day soon this will change. But for now, you can take my word that there are many, many male humans. More or less fifty percent, in fact."

"Ah. At least this one thing is not so strange about your people." His fingers touched the steering mechanism, and they arced a touch to the north. "May I ask you something else? Something personal?"

"Um, sure."

"The woman—Morgan. She is your lover, yes?"

"Why would you think that?"

"I do not need to be able to sense Human eamonals to know when there are pheromones in the air."

"Oh, god." She stared at her hands in her lap to hide the heat on her cheeks. "No. I mean, we sort of almost...but no. She's not."

"Perhaps she should be."

"Ha! That's not up to me."

"I see. In that case, my apologies." His sentsores twitched; he was emoting so hard she swore she could almost feel his eamonal in the air, though not what sentiments it conveyed. "I confess, I did not realize you were zafikoa. Is it common in Human society?"

The word was a rather colorful term for lesbian. "Common? I mean, most people aren't, some people are. Also, I'm not—zafikoa, that is."

"And now, I confess to being confused. But I am sure there is much I don't understand about Human sexuality."

"How could you?" She blew out a breath and gazed out the window. They were far off the reservation now, and she didn't mean the drive. "I guess the term for what I am is 'pansexual.' I'm capable of being physically attracted to someone irrespective of their gender or, within some bounds of reasonableness, their species."

"Oh, my."

"Yeah, that's what my mother said, too."

"She doesn't approve?"

"It's pretty far down the list of things about my life she doesn't approve of. I guess she's come to be okay with it. Probably doesn't love it, though."

"So, if I can ask—merely out of curiosity and because we have a long drive ahead of us to fill—what does 'some bounds of reasonableness' mean?"

She studied him uncertainly...but he wasn't teasing her, nor did he appear offended. Genuinely curious, maybe. And something else running a layer beneath it.

"Um...humanoid, more or less. But it's more nuanced than that. The Ourankeli, for instance, have this gelatinous, semi-transparent skin, and they're always altering the shape of their bodies, including adding and subtracting limbs. Sometimes they look like octopi, which does nothing whatsoever for me. Then there's the Khokteh. They qualify as 'humanoid,' but they have four eyes and these ridiculously long snouts with a whole bunch of teeth, and I just can't bring myself to find them sexy. I mean, some of my close friends are Khokteh, but it's platonic all the way. Also, they're huge and would crush me in bed." She laughed lightly, and he joined her.

"But for the species that are closer to the human norm, it's..." she sighed "...I see beauty where beauty is there to be seen. When I'm in the company of an alien I find attractive, my body and my *pheromones* respond the same as if I were admiring a strapping, muscular lifeguard with a great tan."

"A what?"

"Never mind."

Galean was silent for a long moment. When he did speak, his voice was quiet. "And...do Belascocians fall within those 'bounds of reasonableness'?"

She stared at him, mouth agape. Words utterly failed her, but the tingling sensation spreading to indecent places did not.

He drew in on himself, hair strands lying flat against his skull as he discovered a sudden intense interest in the dash. "That was in no way an appropriate question. Please accept my apologies."

Her expression must have frightened him, and she worked to soften it. "Yes, they do."

His head whipped back to her. "I...see."

She gave him a blasé smile and shrugged.

He breathed out and appeared to relax a little. "The tail isn't too much?"

"The tail raises some interesting possibilities—" Oh, this was definitely more than she'd intended to share. "I only mean...no, it isn't too much."

"Good to know." With that declaration, he refocused on the road, leaving her to sit there sifting through all sorts of conflicting emotions she hadn't expected to need to address. This was Morgan's fault. Seeing the woman had lit up the prurient areas of her brain, as it always did. And when Morgan had departed, those areas had promptly leapt for the next attractive person in the vicinity.

But Galean wasn't like her, and she had no right to expect him to be. Even back home, most people weren't attracted to other species, and she wasn't merely of a different species—she was *alien* to him. He had no frame of reference for sexual attraction to someone not of his kind; how could he? He was being polite, or indulging in a bit of morbid curiosity. Nothing more.

So she occupied herself with the horizon, counting down the seconds until they reached the Serba.

Full dark had fallen by the time they arrived at Lake Lasai, or what passed for it on Belarria. As Galean slowed the vehicle to prepare for the transition to watercraft, Marlee realized this might be the last time she'd get to see the night sky here.

She reached out and touched Galean's arm. "Hang on. Let's take a minute before we go down."

"Oh?" He stopped the vehicle. "What do you have in mind?"

She opened the door and stepped out, motioning to him. "Come on."

The air was warm, with no hint of wind to carry a cool breeze off the lake. She plopped down on the hard ground of the steppes near the shore and leaned back on her hands to look up at the explosively star-strewn sky. "Most planets don't have views like this, you know."

"I did not know." He settled onto the dirt beside her and tilted his head to match her perspective. "What do the heavens of other worlds look like?"

"Fewer stars, for one thing. And they tend to be more...orderly. This is chaos."

"For us, it simply is, and always has been."

"Sure." She eased the rest of the way down until she was stretched out on the ground and sighed contentedly. "Here's the thing. All this—" she waved her hand in the air "—it's nothing but your own double galaxy. The Medusa Merger, and especially the Eye, is so glutted with activity, it overwhelms the light from the billions of galaxies and trillions of stars on the other side. Everything you see, it's all *right here*. But there's so much else beyond it."

He gazed at her a little oddly, then lay down beside her— snugly enough beside her for her to notice. "So you can't see your home from here?"

"Goodness, no. It's forty megaparsecs away, so it would be a challenge to spot under ideal conditions. And we can't see yours from Seneca, thanks to that blazing Eye of yours." She frowned as a realization occurred to her. "You know, it's dangerous for you to live here."

"Underwater? In the Serba? We've taken gargantuan steps to increase its safety—"

She punched him softly on the shoulder. "Stop pretending to be dense. I mean Belarria. The collision has rendered your galaxy enormously active. The threat of asteroid and comet impacts has to be much higher here than it is for most planets where life has arisen."

"What do you think Lake Lasai is?"

"Hmm? You mean it formed in an impact crater?"

"Indeed. And this isn't even the largest crater on the planet. We are aware of the threat, which is why we deployed an advanced 'close-approach' tracking system as soon as our technology enabled us to do so."

"Good." How elitist of her, to assume them backward in this respect. She shifted position to dislodge a tiny rock at her back, and her hand brushed across Galean's. He didn't snatch it away, instead letting his fingers gently caress her palm. She breathed in deeply, savoring the moment and his touch.

"Still, I fear you all will need to move one day. This isn't a proper, organized galaxy. Stellar systems and their planets are careening wildly all around out there, and sooner or later, one is going to barrel into your path and disrupt Belarria's orbit."

"Yes." His hand settled in to rest comfortably atop hers. "Astronomers tell us the Jasane System is headed directly our way. It will begin to exert detrimental effects on the planet in around eight hundred thousand years." He shifted his head to gaze at her, a faint smile teasing his lips. "So we have some time."

And though their own time together was rapidly drawing to a close, they stayed there for as long as they could, gazing up at the stars of the Medusa Merger falling endlessly upon them.

(YOU SAY YOU WANT A)
REVOLUTION

27

Marlee paced around Resamane's apartment, pent-up energy driving her through ragged circles and figure-eights. The team assigned to the Inarska II mission was meeting right now to hash out the final details of their infiltration—and she was sidelined. Relegated to standby retrieval girl.

They needed every centimeter of help they could get, and Nedeni was being blockheaded in his refusal of her earnest and justified pleas to be allowed in the game. Yes, yes, she'd be on standby for emergency extractions and all. And this stood to matter a great deal. But she could pull off an extraction from anywhere, to anywhere, at virtually any time.

Bibine landed on her shoulder, and she ran a hand down his long, glass-like body. "You don't have any idea your world may be about to change, do you?"

The ingari gazed at her, gemstone eyes refracting endlessly into the depths.

"I didn't think so." She urged him on his way and resumed pacing. Was it pride on Nedeni's part? A desire for the Tarazi to win the day on their own?

No. Her fingerprints were all over this mission. They'd never have arrived *at* this mission if not for her.

Perhaps some part of him still didn't trust her. That, at least, would be fair, for she'd been rather cavalier about disobeying his edicts.

Have you ever considered the possibility that you should welcome the order to stay here and keep your skin safe? You've given these people the means to achieve their goals. You don't have to continue throwing yourself in front of weapons fire, for them or anyone else.

Of course I've considered it. Considered and rejected it.

Adrenaline junkie.

It was true. She'd gotten good at acting responsible and professional in her job. Putting away childish things and all. And doing so had earned her promotions and the increasing respect of her peers and superiors. All of which had led to her being sent to Belarria as the Concord representative, and thus led to her being here, at this moment, in which she was in a position to help these people win justice and their freedom. If only they would let her.

She'd delivered all the intel the Tarazi had on the Belascocian military's electronic warfare craft to Morgan, who had confirmed that she'd managed to requisition a couple of Ghosts and recruit some pilots loyal to her to fly them. So one part of the plan was on track—

The door slid open. She spun around, expecting to see Resamane. Instead, it was Galean.

"How long until you depart?"

"Twenty minutes. Nedeni just left for Ausatan."

"I guess there's no going back now."

"No, there isn't." He crossed the room to draw close to her, stopping less than a meter away. "In case this goes badly, I want to say thank you. I should apologize again for bringing you here, but I can't rightly do so. You coming into our midst has been like an ocean wave that cleansed us and revealed new truths previously hidden beneath the sand. Because of you, today we can make our every dream fulfilled. Thank you for this chance."

"When I believe in a cause, there's nothing I won't do to support it."

"Even at the risk of your life?"

"Especially at the risk of my life. It's a character flaw, as friends, family and my overly vocal conscience are always telling me. But it's mine to own."

"You are an incredible person, Marlee. I am honored to have known you. And now, I'm going to take advantage of your foolish disregard for your own life. Did you mean what you said in the meeting? Do you want to be on the Inarska II team?"

"Yes! Desperately so."

"Good, as I will feel much better with you at my side. Not that I don't trust my comrades. I do. But you bring a level of…chaos and unpredictable energy to every fight you engage in. This has already made the difference between life and death for me twice now. So, can Resamane get you in your makeup in twenty minutes?"

Marlee grinned. "She doesn't have to. This is what I was trying to tell Nedeni, but he wouldn't listen. The device Morgan brought me? It projects a field immediately around my body that alters my appearance to the perception of anyone who sees me. It combines our Veil technology with the Asterions' morph tech, modified of course because the morph is designed to work specifically on other Asterions' unique eyesight…and you have no idea what I'm saying. That's fine. Anyway, it's called a Shroud. Its use is highly restricted, since the opportunity for criminal mischief is through the roof. But I appealed to a friend, and he was able to customize one for me, pretty much on the fly."

"I still don't have any idea what you're saying."

"Right. I should just demonstrate it." She reached around and depressed the button on the small device she'd attached to her belt.

Galean stumbled back two steps. "You…you look like a Belascocian. In every detail."

"Nifty, isn't it?"

"I…." His expression morphed about in a tumult of emotionality, but most of all confusion.

"Is there something wrong with it? I gave Devon several visuals of Belascocian women to work off of, but this is definitely an ad-hoc job."

"No. Nothing is wrong with it. It's merely…you are beautiful. I don't mean to say you weren't before, as the truth is, I have no idea. Something tells me you are what Humans consider beautiful, but I don't know. But now? To my eyes, you are…quite beautiful."

"Oh." She swallowed past a lump in her throat. The images she'd given Devon as references were of women *she* found attractive. If it turned out so did other Belascocians, well, perhaps certain determinations of beauty were universal. It wouldn't be the first trait where evolution had found a configuration it fancied and stuck with it.

Galean stepped closer, his demeanor hesitant yet deliberate. "Is it real?"

"No. I'm afraid I haven't actually been transformed into a Belascocian, even temporarily." She took his hand, then brought his fingertips up to her lips. "See here? Behind the projection of Belascocian lips—split at the center and a bit on the thin side—my lips are the same as they were."

His fingertips traced over her lips. "Full and soft. So it is an illusion."

"I'm sorry."

"No, don't be. I would not have you change for me." His throat worked, and he took another half-step until they were all but touching. The starburst marking on his cheek gleamed bright white in the light. "I am ashamed, for this transformation has exposed a shallowness in me I wish was not true. Your appearance...it gives me permission to enjoy feelings I dared not allow myself before now."

"Because I looked alien."

"I regret to say yes. Forgive me my immaturity."

Her heart fluttered around in her chest. His fingertips still hovered along her face, sending jolts of electricity wherever they touched. "I'm your first alien. I forgive you."

"Good, good." His eyes drew even wider than normal. "Ah...some bounds of reasonableness?"

"Yes. Definitely."

He nodded minutely, then leaned in and kissed her. His lips were cool and expressive, his sentsores tickling her cheeks in a delightful surprise. One of his hands rested above her waist, and she brought her own up to his neck, where his pulse raced beneath his skin.

The realization she was having such an effect on him sent her own pulse skyrocketing, and she renewed the kiss with more vigor.

In her experience, kissing worked much the same across humanoid species. Lips, teeth and tongues danced the waltz they were fated to perform. He seemed to agree, as his hand on her at the small of her back fisted and pressed her against him.

But finally and too soon he drew back, smiling unevenly and a touch out of breath. "My eyes and my lips are having a small disagreement. But I find I no longer care. That was nice, yes?"

"Nice? Yes, that was very nice indeed."

"Ahem." He took a step away, and his hands fell to his side. "I'm afraid our timing is less than optimal, however. Come, let us get you armed."

28

Akain Hibai tried not to gawk at the obscenely ostentatious gardens lining the central boulevard of downtown Emankor.

He'd grown up on the urban streets of Ausatan, his odola a diminished, poor family barely making the rent on an overcrowded apartment floor in the Saishan District. He was raised on bustling thoroughfares and knock-off inprim shops and, later, xabola bars and pastixa shows.

Then Ipar, his odola-kin, was named desbida and taken away by armed officers, and everything he thought he knew was exposed as a lie. He'd found the Tarazi shortly thereafter, for by then their name was whispered in the shadowy corners of the xabola bars and darkened alleys of Saishan. They'd brought him to the Serba, and he'd rarely left the sanctuary in the years since. But today, he'd been entrusted with a sacred duty: playing a tiny role in spreading the truth of the Aterpe Project to the world.

Winding trellises of giant ivy decorated wide, sprawling buildings constructed of arabesca marble. Ausatan was a vertical city; when he was a kid, he'd thought its towers yawned into the very stars. Emankor, though, claimed the land as its own. It was not afraid to spread its arms and stretch. From afar, one had the sense that wild jungle had overtaken the ruins of an ancient city. But here among its streets, he realized it was a façade, a glamour. Every leaf and stem was immaculately tended. No weeds emerged through cracks in the sidewalks; no soil littered the stone pathways.

For all the glitz and panache of Ausatan, this was the most flamboyant display of wealth he had ever seen.

Akain stopped at the sweeping archway entrance of one of its greatest hoarders, Estapa Renewal. Owned by the joined

Laurendi and Kemer odolas, it had led the flowering of Emankor when it moved the company headquarters here fifty years ago, along with the sprawling pods of both odolas.

His delivery service uniform marked him as suitable to be allowed to sully the company's fine marble floors, so he opened the door and walked directly up to the reception counter.

"Can I help you?" A woman in a colorful silk robe asked.

He set the package on the counter. "Special delivery for Chairman Laurendi."

"Thank you." She took the package and placed it next to her screen.

"It's, uh, marked urgent, so you might want to get it up to him straightaway."

"I can perform my job without your commentary." She glanced at the package, though, and her eyes widened a little. "From Mr. Todor. Hmm. Well, I need to take another package upstairs anyway." She glanced back at him. "I'll see the Chairman receives it. You may go."

He turned on a heel and strode back outside, where a deluge of flowering aromas greeted him anew.

He took the next left onto a cross-boulevard lined with evenly spaced and manicured palmon trees. He carried one additional package for delivery in Emankor, to the foremost entertainment company on the continent. Then his role in this mission was complete. For many of his comrades, however, the work was just beginning.

29

Marlee trailed Galean and Deshka into the crew cabin of the transport. It was a spartan affair, with a row of jump seats on each curved wall. Handles lined both walls above the seats, with more along the ceiling. A small station in one corner held a tank of water with a nipple and two drawers beneath it. In the other corner, a compartment with a door jutted out into the cabin. Lavatory facilities?

She'd never used a weightless toilet before, and she wasn't planning on doing so on this trip.

She'd been born into a world where humanity had colonized over a hundred planets in the Milky Way. Before she was old enough to appreciate what this meant, her world had expanded to include forty galaxies inhabited by over a dozen space-faring species. But the Belascocians were like babes taking their first stumbling steps into space. The discovery of artificial gravity and superluminal travel still waited in their future. Admittedly, if they became allies of Concord, discovery would be replaced with explanation, for Concord shared its knowledge freely with peaceful civilizations deemed advanced enough to comprehend it and put it to practical use.

But any future alliance relied on the success of their mission today. So weightlessness it was.

She sat down next to Galean, watching how he fastened the harness on both sides of his hips and between his legs, then reached for hers—

"Who the *izorra* are you?"

She looked up to see Sikel glaring at her in accusation from across the cabin. "Oh!" She reached around to the small of her back and found the device, then depressed it to deactivate her disguise.

"Madari! What sorcery is this?"

"A gift from home." She reactivated the disguise and set about fastening her restraints.

"We don't need her on the mission."

Galean shot Sikel a warning look. "Yes, we do."

"But Nedeni said—"

"I know what Nedeni said, but he's not here. I'm mission leader, and I say she goes. Treat her as you would every other teammate. Am I clear?"

Sikel snarled but took his seat.

"Here. The clasp slots in this way." Galean reached over and guided her hand and the fastener it held into the slot built into the chair between her legs. The temperature of her skin vaulted at least ten degrees as she flushed hot. The feel of his fingers on hers triggered the memory of his lips on hers to flood her senses, and her mind went directly to deeply inappropriate places.

The clasp locked into a place with a solid click. "There." He shot her a quick smile, his face terribly close, and his hand lingered for an extra beat before he pulled it away.

"Thank you." She returned the smile rather sloppily, though he likely couldn't tell. The projected disguise did a decent job of mapping both facial and body motions, but human and Belascocian mouths weren't one-to-one matches, and she'd noticed while inspecting herself in the mirror that dramatic expressions displayed a touch off. If Devon had a sufficient database of Belascocian body language and movements on hand, he'd be able to sync them up to a near-perfect degree.

The last team members took their seats, and Galean signaled to the pilot that they were ready to depart. The entry ramp closed, and dim lights illuminated the cabin in a pale green glow. A rumble vibrated beneath her feet as the transport eased out of its berth and toward the launcher.

Butterflies agitated her stomach, which was ridiculous. She'd flown on hundreds of spaceships. She could fly one herself, in fact. Not particularly adroitly, but she could get from point A to point B.

But she wasn't sitting in the pilot's chair today. Instead, she was strapped into restraints worthy of a violent criminal, about to fly to space in a certified tin can. Did it even have radiation shielding? It must. What kind of propellant fueled it, and did it make the ship a bomb waiting to explode? That level of minutiae had not made it into the Consulate briefing package. Why had she gone to such lengths to get herself on the Inarska II team again?

Because she never could leave well enough alone, that's why. Because she wanted to help them have the best possible chance of succeeding, and she believed her presence increased those odds. Because they needed all the help they could get, and her help was pretty damn good.

A loud *clank* shook the walls as the launcher grabbed them, and the ship's incline shifted until it sat vertical.

The pilot's voice resounded over the loudspeaker. "We are go for liftoff in 3…2…1…."

Force shoved her back against the seat, and a giant hand pressed against her chest until she struggled to breathe. The whole ship shook amid a thunderous roar, and her teeth rattled in her head. So no inertial dampers, either.

They were through Lake Lasai in the blink of an eye, and murky clouds raced by the viewport stretching above the seats opposite her for what seemed like an eternity.

She started to grow concerned the ship was actually going to break apart. Why weren't they wearing proper environment suits? Galean had mentioned that emergency suits were stowed beneath the floor, but they were going to do them no good if half the hull suddenly ripped off the frame. The Belascocians believed they had reached a point where space travel was considered 'safe,' but she had to wonder by what fucking standards.

Finally the shaking began to ease up, and she remembered to breathe. The clouds gave way to blackness, as it took one's eyes several minutes to adapt to the vast darkness of space and begin to pick up the sea of stars. So she studied the other occupants; Txeru looked a little queasy, but everyone else acted unperturbed. Must not be their first space flight.

Galean leaned over to murmur near her ear. "We'll be about forty minutes to docking. I'm going to go check in with the pilot and see if we've had any word from Nedeni. Want me to bring you a snack?"

"Ah, no thank you. I ate before we left." Something else she was regretting at the moment.

Galean unfastened his harness and deftly maneuvered from handle to handle, floating his way to the cockpit and disappearing inside.

Deshka undid his harness halfway and shifted toward her. "It's incredible, isn't it? To be able to soar into the stars. I love it out here."

She immediately squashed all her uncharitable thoughts about the backward, barbaric nature of Belascocian spaceflight. Deshka's dreamy wonder at what his people had accomplished schooled her. It *was* an incredible accomplishment, one vanishingly few species ever achieved. And in truth, the Belascocians were only a few centuries behind humanity—a blink of cosmic time.

"It's amazing. Do you get to come to space often?"

"Only once or twice a year. But I always volunteer for those missions—usually courier jobs or recruitment meetings. One time, though, I got to go all the way out to the Ainger Habitat. The view from the observation deck was the most awe-inspiring sight I have ever experienced in my life."

She grinned, his enthusiasm smoothing the sharp edges of her queasiness. "I bet."

"If we somehow succeed today and the Tarazi are eventually disbanded, and Galean no longer needs me to watch his back every minute, the first thing I'm doing is taking a vacation to

Ainger. I heard they've added a hotel with a transparent pool that hovers above the planet's rings."

"Watch *my* back?" Galean returned to his seat, nudging Deshka out of the way then handing him a brown slab that must be food.

"Your ass, too. And your tail."

"Right." Galean lowered himself down and partially refastened his restraints, then patted Deshka's thigh. "You deserve the vacation. Let's ensure it happens."

Then his voice rose and took on a more serious tone. "Everyone, let's walk through the mission plan one more time."

Inarska II was a close analogue to the old stanford torus stations humans had built before discovering artificial gravity: a doughnut-shaped structure rotating around a central docking hub.

The hub remained nearly weightless, and they exited the ship into a circular corridor lined with handles. Nowhere to go but straight ahead.

Once they neared the exit, Marlee's legs began sinking toward the floor, until her feet hop-skipped along a tacky surface. By the time the airlock at the end of the corridor swung open, she no longer needed the handles to maneuver.

As she walked into the processing area behind Deshka, gravity welcomed her like an old friend. 0.7G, but it would do.

A security checkpoint loomed ahead to bar their entry. The officer spent about eight seconds with each traveler—more than perfunctory, but less than an inquisition.

Galean's lips hovered at her ear. "Stay calm and relaxed. Remember your cover."

"I will." She imagined her projected disguise was a coat of armor, wrapped snugly against her skin. *Become one with the armor, until you are a Belascocian. Also, a completely ordinary Belascocian that is in no way a recent convert to a revolutionary cause.* Not so hard an ask.

Three team members were ahead of her in line. The officer spent an extra five seconds with Fremen, but ultimately let him through, and the others passed through without incident. Then it was her turn.

She mimicked what the others had done, placing her aldra above a scan pad without speaking.

The officer studied his screen. "Reason for visiting Inarska II?"

"Temporary secretarial position with Osabide Logistics. The regular had to return to Ausatan to deal with an odola emergency." She'd gotten quite skilled at speaking Scocian without the help of a translator, though not without the aid of her larynx augment; if her accent was a bit odd, the security officer didn't comment on it.

"Is this your first visit?"

"No, third."

"Make certain you have housing in the next twelve hours. There's no allowance for vagrancy here."

"Yes, sir. I believe Osabide has arranged housing, but I'll confirm as soon as I get to the office."

The waist-level barrier blocking her passage slid aside. "Enjoy your stay."

She forced herself not to exhale in relief as she walked through. The officer had never even looked at her.

She kept walking, as per the plan. They would each approach the studio separately, through as many different routes as the station allowed. She'd memorized the layout before they departed, and her designated route led her through the shopping and restaurant sectors.

Despite tremendous efforts on the station designers' part, there wasn't enough light to properly brighten the interior. The dull flint walls sucked in the ambient lighting like black holes. Every span was cramped to the point of claustrophobia, every stretch of usable space at a premium. It was a far cry from the wide-open, airy, bright spaces of Concord HQ.

She'd learned in her schooling about how the early days of expansion into the Sol system had been difficult, how only the truly adventurous had given up the comforts of Earth to endure small, cramped, ugly and dangerous habitats. Life was hard in space, but humans had refused to accept that it must be. Ingenuity, invention and new discoveries had pushed their technology relentlessly onward until they were able to make space a true home.

The Belascocians still had a way to go on this front, but they, too, were trying. And even if they had never met Concord, she believed they had the spirit and determination to make it happen—assuming they got their societal house in order.

She resisted the urge to stop and do a little shopping. In her time here, she'd never had the opportunity to simply stroll the streets of Ausatan and explore its offerings. How much was universal to all civilized species—clothes, accoutrements of added flair, furniture, art—and what quirky commercial items had risen from the Belascocians' unique history? But she would not get to answer that question today.

Her route took her down a hallway connecting a series of corporate offices, including the one her cover had assigned her to. She passed the Osabide door and kept going.

The Belarria First News studio was around the curve. An atrium outside its entrance was the largest open space she'd seen since entry processing. A monument to media excess, one might presume.

She crossed the atrium and continued on into the opposite hall, then turned left, and found Galean, Deshka and all but two of the team members waiting for her.

Galean laid a hand on her shoulder. "Any trouble?"

"None. No one spoke to me."

"Good."

Deshka handed her an infragun and diamond knife; she peered into the gear bag. "Grenades?"

He shook his head. "Not on a space station."

Was the hull so paper-thin as to be blown open by a tiny handheld grenade? Her fears on the ride here tried to resurface, but she tamped them down. She was far more likely to die today from a hail of atzapar bullets than a hull breach. Yay.

Fremen arrived in an agitated state. "We've got a situation. Sikel got held back in the food court. Someone claimed to recognize him—an old coworker."

"*Madari!*" Galean cursed. "Which is a problem, since Sikel vanished without a trace from proper society four years ago and was presumed dead. Unfortunately, we can't wait. We go without him."

"I don't like it."

"I don't like it, either, but we've no choice. We stand around in this hall any longer, and we're bound to get noticed. It's time to move."

Marlee dropped the gun into one of her pockets and palmed the knife. In addition to the Shroud she now wore, Devon's bag of goodies had also included two military-grade defensive shield generators. She'd given the second one to Galean, because she could make no other choice. At first he'd rejected it, insisting his people's gear was sufficient. Then she'd reminded him what manner of wonders her people were capable of performing, and he'd dutifully latched it to his belt.

And because he'd then promptly forgotten about it, she quietly reached over and activated it for him while he checked over his weapons. The gesture earned her a tense nod before he addressed the group.

"You all know your roles. Sikel was assigned to guard the broadcast booth, so—"

Sikel came barreling around the corner, out of breath. "*Izorra!* Salbat always could talk the ear off an ardiak. Sorry I'm late."

"Glad you made it."

Fremen handed Sikel his weapons, then rolled the bag into a tiny ball and stuffed it in one of his ubiquitous pockets.

Galean splayed his palm upon Deshka's for the briefest second. "When you are ready. Arbasoak be with you."

"And with you."

Deshka strode through the front door and up to the reception counter wearing an ingratiating smile. He was a naturally affable man, as Marlee had discovered upon her arrival at the Serba, and in less than a minute he had the receptionist giggling. She motioned him behind the desk, and he leaned in beside her in interest as she showed him something on her screen.

He slapped a siliki on her neck. As she jerked in surprise, he grabbed her arm and hauled her to her feet, then wrestled her other arm behind her and bound both wrists. Though Marlee couldn't hear what was being said, his lips were moving the whole time, and she imagined he was apologizing profusely for the physical intrusion and overall inconvenience of making her a temporary hostage.

"Let's go."

They followed Galean out of the hallway and into the studio lobby.

Galean strode up to the counter. "As I'm sure my friend has informed you, if you peacefully cooperate with us, you won't be harmed in any way. We merely need to remove you from the equation for a few minutes."

"What are you? Separaxa? Tarazi?"

"What we are isn't your concern." Txeru took her from Deshka and urged her down a hallway to the left. "We're going to lock you in the supply closet until our work is concluded. Then you'll be freed."

"You won't get away with this!"

And with that outburst, Txeru slapped a strip of sticky cloth over her mouth.

Galean shook his head. "Oh, but I think we will. Deshka, keep our backs clear."

"Clear as a sunny day on the Molovo Steppes." Deshka settled into the receptionist chair and adopted an air of boredom. In theory, he'd redirect any visitors out of the lobby and waylay any employees for as long as he could.

The rest of them headed down the right hallway. In the distance around the curving corner, perfectly intonated voices chattered on about the news of the day from the broadcast floor. If all went according to plan, the news hosts would keep talking, blissfully ignorant of the fact that they'd been cut off and their signal replaced.

Fremen and Raisan took up positions at the first hallway intersection. Their clothes were (she'd been told) corporate standard, and unless challenged, they would hopefully be mistaken for employees taking a break.

The rest of them turned right, and this hallway soon led them to the broadcast booth. Galean brought a finger to his lips, the universal sign for silence. Everyone raised their weapons, and he opened the door.

"I know there's static in the transmission. I can't control solar flares, understand? I'm doing what I can to mitigate—"

In a blur of motion too rapid for her eyes to track, Galean affixed a siliki to the engineer's neck, covered his mouth with one hand, spun the chair around, yanked the man out of it and pressed him against the wall. "Tape."

Sikel handed him another strip of the cloth, and he replaced his hand with it. The engineer got out only a "Wha—?" before being silenced. Wrist restraints were next, then Galean handed him off to Sikel. "Take him to Txeru, then join Raisan and Fremen in patrolling the studio."

"Yes, sir." Sikel shoved the engineer out the door and down the hallway.

"Mattin, you're up. Make this happen."

Mattin dropped into the chair at the workstation, his gaze flying over the bank of controls and screens, muttering half-formed words under his breath.

Marlee took up her assigned position on one side of the door, and Galean joined her at the other.

"No matter what, no one gets in here until our transmission completes."

She nodded. "No matter what."

30

Nedeni waited in the shadows of the penthouse entrance. Gaining entry to the top floor was a trivial matter when one used to live in the rarified world of the highest echelons of society. He knew the security tricks utilized to keep such places safely locked away from the masses, and thanks to the Tarazi, he had the tools needed to circumvent them.

While he waited, he tracked the basic updates he was receiving. Two-thirds of the information packages had been delivered. Whether they had been opened by their intended recipients was beyond his knowledge and out of his hands. More importantly, the Inarska II team was in position and moving on the Belarria First News studio.

He drew himself to attention as the lift door opened and hesitant steps echoed softly on the floor. "Amalure? What's wrong with the lights?"

Nedeni stepped up behind President Hasane Lormain. One hand brought a blade to the man's throat, while the other gripped firmly on the man's hip. "Amalure is taking a nap for a few minutes. Let's step inside the apartment."

"Who are you?"

"A ghost. Inside, please." He emphasized the point with a nudge forward.

Lormain was no fighter; he'd been raised in the effete social circles of the elite multi-odola complexes in the Garestia District of Ausatan. His mind had been trained at the prestigious Filos Academy; no one had ever thought to train his body. So as expected, the man shuffled forward and unlocked the door to his home.

As soon as they were inside, Nedeni slapped an electronic harness on the lock that would prevent it from being easily opened again. A Kaldi squad could brute-force override it, but it would take them time, and he didn't need much of it.

The lights came on automatically upon their entry, revealing opulent but not garish decor. The space felt cold and impersonal. Not surprising, as Lormain was unbonded and lived apart from his odola. It was lonely at the top, as the truism went.

Nedeni withdrew the blade from the man's neck, but replaced it with an infragun as he stepped back. "Turn on the Belarria First News feed."

The president carefully turned around, then jerked back at the sight of the gun. "What do you want from me?"

"At the moment, I want you to turn on the news feed."

"You can take whatever you like. Jewelry, art, bonds."

"*Arimaka*, this is not a robbery. The news feed, now."

Lormain stumbled backward to his desk in the left corner of the spacious room, only glancing away from the gun long enough to press a button and activate the large screen on the wall. A visual of two co-hosts chattering about the upcoming lamrosa championship burst to life. "There. Now what?"

"You'll see soon enough."

"You look familiar to me."

"I'm impressed. We only met twice, at social occasions many years ago."

"I'm a politician, and a talented one. I remember faces. And names..." Lormain frowned "...but I must be mistaken, for the name I associate with your face belongs to a dead man."

"Your memory is undimmed, Mr. President."

"Then you're Gabirel Proml's son. Nadana...no, Nedeni. And clearly not deceased. May I ask why you would fake your death?"

"The answer will soon become evident—ah, here we go." He waved toward the screen with the gun, where the scene abruptly cut from the hosts to a visual of him standing in front of the rear wall of his office in the Serba.

"I am the leader of the group known as the Tarazi. The government and the media tell you we are terrorists, but that is only the least

of the many lies they have told you. Our mission for the last eight years has been to protect the desbida from torture and repression. Today, our mission is to expose the truth about the desbida, the Aterpe Project, and the demon's bargain made between the government and the Errigime to destroy our odolas and our society in order to hide the truth about both."

"You can turn the volume down a bit, so we can have a conversation. Take my word for it—we possess the proof we need to expose the entire conspiracy. And as of this evening, every major news-affiliate organization and research institute has it in their hands as well."

Lormain's skin blanched to a sickly gray. "Don't do this. I beg you. You have no concept of the firestorm you will set off. It will burn our world to the ground."

"I know full well what I am doing. And I am standing here in this room right now to offer you a chance to save our world from burning."

"This is madness."

"No, this is desperation. I know you didn't start the Aterpe Project. The tangle of lies and conspiracies was foisted upon you when you rose to power. I doubt you wanted it. But the fact remains that you're complicit in it now."

"I had no choice!" Lormain protested. "By the time I was told the truth, its threads wound through every aspect of government, the corporations and economy, the odolas. There was no way out. There *is* no way out."

"That's where you're wrong. The truth washes away the shadows and lets the sun bare all." He gestured to the screen.

"Are the desbida special? Yes! For them, the genetic therapy performed on an entire generation of children resulted in a mutation to their eamonals. It granted them heightened sensory capabilities, allowing them to access the emotions and even thoughts of all those around them—odola or otherwise. Is this a frightening notion? Perhaps to many of you. I say it represents the next wonderful step in our evolution.

"But regardless of how you feel about it, these abilities do not justify imprisoning the desbida behind concrete walls. They don't justify housing them in cells for their entire lives and subjecting them to barbarous experiments—experiments that have left many blind, deaf, mute, or physically debilitated in a myriad of ways."

Lormain cradled his head in his hands. "I am a dead man—and you are for the second time."

The man was practically whimpering, confirming what Nedeni had always suspected—he was a coward at heart. A consummate politician with no center, no moral compass. But this meant he could be swayed to any cause if given sufficient incentive. "Not if we play this correctly. I know you feel beholden to the Errigime. I know you fear them. But you are still our leader. The people are learning the truth as we speak. Many of the organizations I provided with corroborating evidence will not turn a blind eye and bury it. So here's my offer: I am willing to overlook the sins you have committed, so that I can try to save the best of our society. I am giving you a single opportunity to redeem yourself.

"Go on the air within the hour. Speak directly to the people. Express your outrage and horror at what you have heard. Say you've reviewed documents that corroborate my claims. Form a judiciary tribunal, right now, to investigate these allegations. Vow to improve the conditions at the camps right away and promise to, if these claims bear out, disband the camps and return the desbida to their odolas. Oh, and ensure no Kaldi squads are sent after the Tarazi. I have several thousand people who would deeply like to be able to show their faces in their pods again. To hug their loved ones.

"But—and this is crucial—don't merely say it. Do it. All of it."

Lormain shook his head and tail in unison. "They'll never allow a reckoning to occur."

"The Errigime, you mean. The Errigime is just a collection of people. Wealthy, powerful people, but they are not gods. Many of them are named in the evidence being delivered to the media as we speak. Don't be afraid to say those names on the air. We have laws. I hope we still have principles. But make no mistake: the one and only chance you have is to get in front of this. Tonight."

"Since I cannot share my eamonal with three billion people across the planet so you can know my truth, I will instead call upon a man who is respected throughout the scientific community—a man whose name and face are known to many of you. He was there at the beginning, working to help the desbida. When help was forcibly turned to harm, he spoke out against it. He was expelled from the Aterpe Project for his efforts, and since that day has lived under great threat to his life. Today, Dr. Ctaro Melar comes forward to share his story with you."

Lormain whipped his gaze from the broadcast over to Nedeni. "How?"

"He values his life, the same as you do. I offered him essentially the same opportunity I'm offering you now. Join us, and be a hero in this story. Or don't, and be left to whatever fate awaits you."

"I see." The man stroked distractedly at his sentsores. "So it's all already out there, is it?"

"It is."

"Then it seems likely I will fall no matter what—by the courts or the mobs if your maneuver succeeds, or by the assassins of the Errigime if I throw in with the Tarazi. But perhaps doing the right thing here at the end will endear me in the eyes of my arima when I go to my death."

Lormain turned and made a prayerful gesture toward the Arbasoak painting on the wall, then straightened his posture. "Very well. I will make every effort to act as you ask until such time as I am struck down for daring to do so."

Nedeni breathed out slowly. He knew the hard work was only beginning, but this felt like a vindication of every choice he had made—

Lormain abruptly rushed back to his desk and activated a small screen. "Unfortunately, we have a more immediate problem."

31

M attin growled as his fingers flew over the input pad. "Galean, I'm getting interference in the transmission. Somebody's trying to jam us."

Galean glanced at her. "If your friend is going to come through for us, now is the time."

"Right." She made sure the quantum diffuser was active, though did it really matter at this point? Then she sent a pulse.

Morgan, are you here? As expected, we're getting jammed.

Sorry, hit a little momentary snag. It's all good. Let me take care of these gnats for you.

A little snag? What did that even mean in fighter-pilot speak? Marlee wasn't certain she wanted to know. She gave Galean a confident nod. "She's moving in now."

The somewhat shrill voice of Dr. Melar replaced Nedeni's authoritative tenor on the broadcast.

"I currently run the New Horizons Institute on Veuna Atoll. It's a wonderful facility where we research and bring to market treatments and pharmaceuticals that improve the lives of millions. But it shames me to say, the Institute was my blood price—my price for silence.

"In 4837, I was the Director of Emergent Therapies at the Aterpe Project. There, I endeavored to understand the nature of the desbida mutation, so that I might help these troubled children. What I discovered shook the foundations of our world—and you were never allowed to know."

Galean snorted in disgust. "Bastard. He stood and watched while the desbida were maimed, and now he's going to take credit for saving them."

"It sucks. But his testimonial is going to convince a lot of people."

"I know. I have to remember what's important. If his defection means the end of the camps, then letting his ari stain our cause will have been worth it."

> *Marlee, you should be clear. Transmit away.*
> *You are an absolute star, Morgan.*
> *True. Good luck with your abetted revolution.*
> *Thanks.*

"Mattin, check the jamming again."

Mattin snapped his tail around the edge of the chair. "Confirmed zero interference. We are again transmitting loud and clear to all points on Belarria."

"Excellent." Galean offered her a tiny smile. "Express our heartfelt thanks to your friend."

"I will." She checked the hall again and found it empty. "If they know we've circumvented their jamming, they might send the Kaldi in now."

"Indeed."

Galean: "Deshka, Fremen, Raisan, Txeru, be on alert for possible incoming Kaldi."

Deshka: "I'll scream when they arrive, but I, uh, can't hold off a Kaldi squad on my own."

Galean: "No. If they arrive at the entrance, retreat to Fremen's location."

Deshka: "Acknowledged."

"If they breach the studio, I'll need to move as well, to try to stop them before they reach this room. Four of us will stand a chance against them. Marlee, I'll need you to stay here with Mattin. You'll be our last line of defense."

She beamed with pride. *This* was why she'd fought so hard to be here. "I won't let you down."

"I know you won't."

On the broadcast, Dr. Melar described the reaction to his discovery of the nature of the desbida mutation. He named names; she didn't recognize any of them, but judging by Galean's expression, the names mattered a great deal.

Mattin glanced back at Galean. "This is actually happening."

"It is."

She couldn't imagine what it was like, to see one's life work brought to culmination. Galean had sacrificed so much for this cause. All the Tarazi had.

Galean: "Deshka, status?"

Deshka: "All clear."

"Why aren't they hitting us?"

She shrugged. "Maybe Nedeni convinced President Lormain to cooperate, and he called off any police action—"

The walls shuddered, knocking her off-balance, as a thunderous explosion echoed down the hallway from the right. The next second, a loud thud rattled the floor.

Raisan: "Something just blew a hole in the studio! A blast door isolated the show floor, but not before...the hosts got spaced...."

Galean's hair threads stiffened, ready to go on the attack. "They're going to blow up the whole studio. They must have thought we were on the show floor. Mattin?"

"Still broadcasting. The transmitters are situated in a long array along the station hull to minimize the impact of damage to one or two by micrometeoroids. We can afford to lose a few of them."

Marlee frowned. "Surely they won't blow up the entire space station? There are, what, hundreds of people on it? A thousand?"

"At a minimum." Galean's body had joined his hair threads in vibrating tension. "And yes, they will. The Errigime will murder whomever they must in order to hold on to their power. Then they'll blame the massacre that results on the Tarazi."

She began spinning up power in the Caeles Prism. "We should go."

His gaze went to the bank of screens as, on the transmission, Dr. Melar continued his testimonial. Then he crossed to her, taking her hands in his and bringing his face close. "You go. Get to safety. You don't need to give your life for us. If we survive to the end of the transmission, you can open another portal and retrieve us."

"What? No. Absolutely not."

Morgan, are you still in the vicinity? Did you see what hit us?

A warship showed up a few seconds ago—frigate size—and fired two projectile weapons at the station. Are you inside?

Yeah. I'm with Galean and a team of Tarazi who are transmitting their message to the planet.

Bloody hells. This Ghost doesn't have shit for offensive weapons, or I'd blow this puny frigate out of the sky myself. Fuck! Okay, I've got an idea. Hopefully it won't result in my court-martial.

What—

Hang tight and try not to get blown up.

Another strike rocked the hull, closer this time, and she and Galean were knocked to the floor. Mattin's chair skidded into the wall, dumping him on the floor as well.

Marlee rubbed at her neck as she climbed to her feet. Galean crawled over to Mattin to check on him, but he waved Galean off. "I'm fine." The message continued playing as he scrambled back to the board. "Looks like we lost two more transmitters. Signal is a little degraded over Lur Menditsu, but it's getting through."

A high-pitched whine filled the air, and everyone's gaze snapped to the ceiling. At the seam of ceiling and back left wall, a crack had formed.

Galean stared at it, then at her, pleading in his eyes. "Please go."

"No. I wouldn't leave you at Seguru to die, and I'm not leaving you here, either."

He hissed through his teeth. "Stubborn Human."

"You have no idea."

Galean: "Everyone, retreat to my location at the broadcast booth. Bring the prisoners. When we leave, we're going to be doing so in a hurry."

Deshka: "Don't have to tell me twice."

Txeru: "On the way. Sikel and I have two very displeased prisoners in tow."

Galean waited.

Galean: "Fremen, Raisan, acknowledge."

Nothing.

"*Izorra!*" He placed a hand on her shoulder. "Hold this room." Then he took off down the hall.

Water rained down from the fire suppression system to stream in rivulets along the floor. Widening cracks raced down the walls on both sides, but at least these were interior walls.

Galean: "Fremen, Raisan, respond."

Still nothing.

He turned the corner and ran into a collapsed ceiling. Rubble was piled two meters high, leaving only a narrow opening at the top.

"Raisan! Fremen!"

"Ungh…. Galean?" A raspy voice cracked out from beneath the rubble. "Is that you?"

"I'm here, Raisan."

"My…my leg's trapped. I can't move."

"I'm coming for you. What about Fremen?"

"I don't know. I don't see him."

The layout of the station ran through his mind. Normally, he could reach the other side by going around and through the show floor, but the whole area was gone, and a blast door now blocked the way.

Galean: "Deshka, divert to the hallway where Fremen and Raisan were positioned."

"Already here. *Arimaka....*"

He turned around and embraced his prezia. "We need to clear a path to reach them."

Deshka nodded resolutely, walked up and dragged a jagged piece of metal away, tossing it down the hall. "Watch your hands. This stuff's sharp."

Galean sliced his palm open on the first piece of metal he grabbed; he didn't care. They didn't have time to be careful. "Just hold on, Raisan. We're coming."

"I'll wait." He sounded weak, and his eamonal was barely detectable.

Another explosion rocked the facility. The pile of rubble shifted, and he snatched Deshka by the tail and sprinted down the hallway as jagged shards of metal cascaded everywhere.

Something sharp lanced into his calf as he stumbled into the wall. When the shuddering subsided, he peered down to see an eight-centimeter length of metal jutting out of his pants. He bent down, braced himself, and yanked.

He almost collapsed to the floor from the flood of pain, his fingers clawing into the smooth metal of the wall and finding no purchase.

"Ouch." Deshka crouched beside him. "Let's get a bandage on this."

"After." He gingerly tested the weight on his leg and found it wanting, so he hobbled on one leg and six toes back to the pile of rubble. In a small blessing of arima, the strike had done half their work for them, and they could now see clearly through to the other side.

Galean: "Marlee, status?"

Marlee: "We're okay. Txeru, Sikel and the prisoners reached the broadcast booth."

Mattin: "Lost three more nodes, but we're continuing to transmit. For now."

Deshka leaned over the top of the pile. "Raisan, how are you doing?"

"I can't feel my leg and...I'm starting to get woozy."

"He's probably losing a lot of blood," Galean muttered under his breath. "We need to work faster."

32

Lormain had opened a comm link with the military commanders, and urgency lent a subtle growl to his voice. "General Orkatz, I am ordering you to stand down immediately."

A voice Nedeni didn't recognize interjected. *"Belay that order, General."*

Orkatz: *"I'm sorry, President Lormain, but I'm not able to comply at this time."*

"General, you do not report to the Errigime—you report to me. Obey my order."

No reply was forthcoming. A few agonizing seconds later, a static-filled report came in on the military's mission feed. *"Target lock on Tarazi base in thirty seconds."*

On a small screen displaying a visual from one of the pilots, the steppes surrounding Lake Lasai raced by.

Nedeni clenched and unclenched his hands in impotent fury. If the leader of the planet could not put a stop to this madness, what hope did he have?

As near as he'd been able to piece together from a series of disjointed, confusing comms Lormain had placed in the last five minutes, someone—whether an Errigime or government agent didn't matter—had implanted a tracker beneath Ctaro Melar's skin some years ago. Without the man's knowledge, one presumed, else Melar would burn in the fiery pits for eternity.

As it was, Nedeni now stood to suffer that punishment. In his slavish devotion to his mission—in his desperate gambit to win the endgame at all costs—he'd brought the key to their destruction right into their midst and sealed the Tarazi's fate.

"Everyone, gather around here. Stay together. It's going to be okay." Resamane motioned the new arrivals, a group of confused-looking mechanics and maintenance workers, into the growing circle of people sitting on the floor of the atrium. In theory, as the dead-center of the Serba, it was the safest location in which to seek shelter. In practice, this only meant that when the hull was breached, the water would take an additional few seconds to reach them.

Nedeni had messaged her moments ago to deliver the direst of warnings. The location of the Serba had been discovered, and the military was moving in.

They'd lived under the shadow of this threat every day for years. She'd long ago internalized it and packed it away with all the other concerns she lacked any way to ameliorate. But now, unless the Arbasoak intervened, their end was soon to arrive.

Several others stepped in to help corral the people streaming into the atrium, and she nodded a thanks in their direction, working to keep despair from reaching her eamonal. They could do nothing to save themselves. With the largest transport docked at Inarska II, they only had enough craft to evacuate a few dozen residents of thousands, and some enterprising people had by now absconded with all of those craft. She'd let them go without mounting a fight. Anyone who could find a way to live, should. Others were likely frantically swimming for the surface, though their chances of escaping the area before the missiles hit were far slimmer.

As for the rest of them? They would die together, wrapped in the soothing comfort of their hartua odola.

Someone wailed, and she spun to see a fellow desbida collapse to the floor in convulsions. She rushed over and knelt down, wrapping her arms around Jauri, murmuring calming words she doubted the woman could hear. She, too, felt the relentless drumbeat of everyone's terror and panic banging away in her head, trying to tear her mind to shreds. Her sanity teetered on the rickety edge and as Jauri shook against her, she felt her toehold slipping....

No. She must stay strong. For these people facing their end and helpless to prevent it. For Galean, who was fighting this moment to make this a worthwhile sacrifice. For herself, so when the missiles struck and the Serba flooded and her eyes closed, she would be proud for her soul to join with the Ozeal arima and be welcomed into its loving embrace.

Long-range proximity alarms rang through the atrium, and the cries of the crowd grew in terrible desperation. She backed away from Jauri and stood, touching trembling fingertips to her cheeks.

She said a silent goodbye to Galean, and hoped he felt it in his heart.

"The leaders of the Aterpe Project know all of this. They always have. Many of our governmental leaders know all of this. The members of the Errigime—that shadowy corporate cabal we don't speak of in polite company—know all of this. They aid, fund and even direct its continuation. They torture our children for their own benefit."

The truth was being told to the people, but the cost was going to be the lives of everyone he had devoted his life to sheltering. It was too high a price, and Nedeni's heart was shattering.

On the large screen displaying the continuing attack on Inarska II, something shifted. In the black to the starboard of the space station, a shimmering golden oval grew to light the darkness.

From it emerged a ship such as Nedeni had never seen. The hull shone a deep tungsten silver that was as smooth as glass and, to his eye, completely seamless. Scale was impossible to determine, but it seemed to stretch for as long as Inarska II was wide, which made it over a kilometer in length.

"What the *madari* is this?" Lormain began agitatedly pressing buttons and barking impotent orders.

Though weighed down by irredeemable sorrow, a little smile tickled at Nedeni's lips. *Oh, my vexatious Human, what have you done now?*

The ship did not fire any of the tremendous array of weapons lining its lower hull. Instead it hovered in space, gleaming in terrifying magnificence.

Then a message arrived across multiple channels.

"Greetings, President Lormain and the leaders of Belarria. I am Commandant Miriam Solovy, head of Concord Command and captain of the CAF Aurora. *Pardon the interruption, but I thought you should be aware of something before you continue your campaign of violence and bloodshed against your own citizens.*

"Concord prefers not to get involved in the domestic affairs of the species it encounters. But we do have high standards for those with whom we consort, and we abhor the repression and subjugation of any people. So I urge you to think very carefully about what you do next. If you have any aspirations to one day becoming our ally—if you dream of, say, sailing alongside a ship such as this one in common cause—then you will cease military action against this space station and any targets on the ground. Allow your citizens to be heard, and let truth will out."

Lormain threw his hands in the air. "How do I reply? I must make them understand how I am trying to put an end to this. They can't fire on us without giving us a chance to respond first!"

Nedeni chuckled darkly. "They're not going to fire on us. Didn't you listen to anything they said?"

"Of course I did. But you don't show up with a ship like that one unless you mean it as a threat."

"And a most clever threat at that. Respectfully, Mr. President, the message wasn't meant for you."

Errigime Member #1 followed the progress of the fighters' approach to Lake Lasai on one screen and the foreboding alien warship on another while issuing instructions to two military generals and fielding comms from half the members of the Council.

He still had the power to save them from this disaster. Kill or imprison enough people, and the Tarazi's manifesto could be labeled an elaborate deception intended to sow fear in the hearts of the people. Conflating it with the obvious alien menace should make the sale easier by muddying the waters. Paint the government as the only trustworthy institution capable of seeing Belarria through this crisis by blanketing the airwaves with soothing propaganda, while sliding fearmongering in beneath it. Lormain would need to be neutralized, but his death could be blamed on the Tarazi as well—

The door to his office slid open, and he spun to see Member #2 stride in. He cursed under his breath, for he did not need the man's meddlesome arrogance at this most crucial moment!

"Now is not the time."

"I'm afraid now is precisely the time. I had hoped this crisis would not devolve into such a dire state, but here we are, and the moment must be seized and seen through by those with the power and wherewithal to do so. I cannot let you steal our future from us."

By the time he realized an atzapar gun was leveled at his chest, the man had already fired.

The time remaining until the Serba strike ticked down in Nedeni's mind. Twelve seconds. Eleven. Everything was falling his way, save the only thing that mattered right now—the lives of the people under his care. If he had another five minutes, he could make this work, he knew it. But he only had nine seconds. And like his wife and son before them, in the end he could not protect the people of the Tarazi after all.

Unknown speaker: "General Orkatz, follow the President's order and stand down. Authorization: Izpirit Bat Etorriz."

Orkatz: "I...acknowledged." A pause followed that stretched into eternity. Nedeni held his breath, and in his mind, the world held it alongside him. *"I have ordered the fighters to disengage from their attack run and am withdrawing all warships from Inarska II."*

The ragged remains of Nedeni's heart stopped as, on the screen, a horizon filled with the still waters of Lake Lasai shifted, canting at an angle as the fighter banked away from the lake.

His hands shook; he tried to steady them at his sides. His heart sang with relief, but he must keep his wits and his honor, for the next few minutes would determine the fate of Belarria.

Lormain cleared his throat. "Thank you, General. To the other person on the line, with whom am I speaking?"

Unknown speaker: "Tell Nedeni Proml he will have his deal. It's time for us to carve a new path forward, one that will hopefully lead to a brighter future for all Belascocians. We will speak again soon, Mr. President."

Nedeni's eyes swept across the walls, then the desk. Where was the surveillance device hidden that allowed the Errigime to know everything to transpire in the president's residence?

Lormain switched comm channels, seemingly unfazed by the revelation; perhaps he'd already known. "Emergency services, initiate rescue and recovery operations at Inarska II right away."

Another switch. "Ah, Commandant Solovy, this is President Lormain. I do profusely apologize for any misunderstanding here. All military forces have been recalled and...the perpetrators of this violence will be dealt with to the fullest extent of the law. So there is no need for concern on your part. I, ah, look forward to speaking with you in the future under more favorable circumstances."

"As do I. If you don't mind, we'll remain in the area until we're certain the nearby space station is no longer in any danger. And of course, we offer our resources to aid in rescue and recovery efforts. You need simply ask."

"Thank you. Your offer is much appreciated. I believe we have matters well in hand, but if this changes, we'll be in touch. Regards."

Lormain cut the channel and dragged both hands down his face. "Arbasoak be praised. Or damned, who can tell." Abruptly his hands dropped to smooth out the wrinkles in his shirt. "Well, Nedeni. It appears you do indeed have your deal—with the government *and* the Errigime."

By the time Lormain addressed him, Nedeni thought he had his emotions back under a sliver of control, and he took care so his voice didn't quaver. "Who do you think that was on the line? The one who told Orkatz to stand down?"

"I do not know. But if I were to speculate, I'd say the Errigime has just experienced a change in leadership. A coup, if you will. Pray the new leader is a more reasonable, enlightened man than the one he replaces."

"It's more likely he's in a prime position to profit from the dismantling of the Aterpe Project, maybe even from the desbida themselves."

"That is assuredly true, else he would not have allowed your Tarazi to survive. But..." Lormain gazed at the visual of the Concord dreadnought as it floated among the stars, beautiful and deadly "...I suspect he now has his eye on a much bigger prize. This Commandant Solovy dangled the brass ring in front of the

Errigime. Let it spin and catch the light in all its brilliance. And I daresay they have fallen under its spell."

"This can be a good thing, Mr. President. From what I have been told about Concord, they will prove to be a worthwhile and positive ally, not a conquering empire."

"You have the Human, then?"

"The Human has remained with us by her own choice. In fact, despite my explicit orders to the contrary, I suspect she is on Inarska II as we speak, fighting to ensure my message reaches its audience."

"Oh?" Lormain frowned at the display of a broken and battered Inarska II as on the news feed screen, Nedeni's speech reached its rousing conclusion. "Then let's do hope we haven't killed her."

"But we are not the Errigime. Belascocians are good, soulful, loving people, and knowing this truth, we cannot allow such suffering to continue—I know this in my ari. We are also adaptable—to our environment, our nature and the progress our intellect manifests. We must welcome the desbida back into our hearts and minds, and make a new place in our world for them."

Marlee forced her eyes open. Her left cheek was smushed against a rough, grating surface. She couldn't tell what, because the room had pitched into darkness.

Everything rushed back to her in a flash. The broadcast. The attack. A shrieking roar from above them.

She got her hands underneath her and pushed up to her knees, then started feeling around. "Mattin? Where are you?"

A groan answered to her left, and she crawled that way until she bumped into a solid mass. She instructed her ocular implant to draw in as much light as it was able to find, and Mattin's shadowy form resolved against the shadows. A trickle of primrose blood stood out in the grayness, dribbling down from his temple. "Hey, can you hear me?"

His mouth moved, and he nodded weakly. "I'm here. Got to…check the transmission."

No one could ever deny a Tarazi's dedication to the cause. "It finished. You did it. You were amazing."

"Usually am." Mattin struggled up to a sitting position. "But now I just hurt."

"Me, too." The omnipresent whine that had been with them since the first strike impacted the station was growing considerably louder. Emergency lighting flickered on and off in a staccato cadence, revealing deep cracks in the walls. No further impacts shook the station, but a steady series of creaks and groans betrayed the fragility of the hull. It was hanging together by a thread. "Now we need to go. I think the station is coming apart around us."

She helped Mattin to his feet, and they both paused for a moment to recover their balance and breath. *Move, Marlee. One foot in front of the other.* Her eVi shepherded half a dozen routines to enable her to do so, and she supported Mattin as they took a step forward.

Mattin immediately stumbled with a cry of pain, and she did her best to steady him. "Listen, I'm going to send you home now. Straight to Medical for you."

"This seems a wise course. I think my leg is broken."

She opened a wormhole beside them, destination the Serba Medical wing. Then she gently urged him through. He fell to his knees on the other side, but she resisted the urge to follow and help him. More lives to save first.

She leaned out into the hall, where Txeru and Sikel braced themselves against the wall while their prisoners huddled on the floor amid a rain of dust. "You guys, too. Evacuate the prisoners to the Serba."

Sikel grunted in protest. "What about Galean and the others?"

"I will find them and get them out. You have my word."

Sikel exchanged a weighty glance with Txeru before nodding. "Galean would whip us if we let innocents die on our watch." He grabbed the arm of the receptionist and hoisted her up, while Txeru did the same with the engineer. They shoved their charges through the doorway, followed by the wormhole, amid a chorus of frightened exclamations.

Then Marlee was alone and also out of time. She closed the wormhole and left the broadcast booth behind, feeling her way along the hall to the intersection, then right.

Bright light blinded her, and she blinked away halos. "Galean?"

"Marlee? Are you all right?"

"Peachy." Deshka was holding a flashlight in one hand while Galean tossed mutilated metal sheets to the side. Shifting shadows from the light beam revealed a steady stream of blood pouring down Galean's leg.

"Galean, you need a bandage on that cut!"

Deshka shrugged. "I tried. He refused."

"It'll keep." Galean glanced over his shoulder at her as he hefted a large chunk of metal aside. "Where's Mattin?"

"I sent him to Medical. He'll be okay, but he's injured. Txeru and Sikel took the prisoners to the Serba as well. It seemed safer than keeping them here."

"Indeed. The message?"

"It's done."

She saw Galean's shoulders sag for a split second before he resumed his work. "Raisan and Fremen are trapped. We've almost reached them."

A renewed groan of metal echoed through the hall, and a rush of steam poured out from an exposed overhead pipe.

"Let me help." She hid a wince triggered by half a dozen aches—not that they could see it in the poor lighting—as she ducked under Deshka's outstretched arm. She reached through the opening and found Raisan's hand, then squeezed it. She didn't get a response.

"Assist me with this large piece."

She crawled around to the other side of Galean and took the far edge of a misshapen slab of metal almost a meter long. Together they wrenched and wiggled it out of the jumbled mess of debris until it suddenly fell away.

As she toed it down the hall with her boot, a much louder groan reverberated through the walls, and she yelped as more steam billowed out from above to scald her head. "Shit!"

Galean froze, a piece of metal clasped in both hands. "Are you injured?"

She drew in a deep breath and turned back to him. "Just a little singed. Listen, we don't have much time."

"I know."

Deshka shifted the light to reveal Raisan lying at an awkward angle. Below his hip, his right leg disappeared in a mess of bloody clothing beneath two intertwined slabs of metal.

Galean dropped to his knees. "Raisan, talk to me."

The man's lips moved, but no sounds came out. More than one reason for them to hurry.

"Deshka, move the light a little to the right. Marlee, we need to move both pieces at the same time."

She eyed the shattered pipe in the ceiling suspiciously. *Then have a wormhole ready.* She knelt beside Galean, and they both fumbled for the best grip on the slabs. Metal cut into her hands, which she ignored.

"On three. Understand?"

She nodded.

"One...two...three!"

The slabs came loose in a rush, and they both fell back on their asses.

"*Arimaka,*" Deshka let out in a horrified whisper.

She and Galean both scrambled out from under the metal to get a look at what they had revealed.

Raisan's leg was nothing but flattened, bloody clothing leading to a crushed foot. Now that the pressure was off, fresh blood gushed from his hip.

Behind him, a severed arm was all they saw of Fremen.

Galean was already crawling through to balance unevenly on the debris and somehow wrap his arms around Raisan. "Marlee!"

How to accomplish this? "Get ready. This is going to be disorienting."

"I understand. Do it."

The power spooled up in her Caeles Prism—

A high-pitched squeal erupted behind them, and she spun to see the walls of the station being ripped away into space. Perceptual time slowed down to match the hyper-speed of her cybernetic routines.

She acknowledged the encroaching pull of the vacuum by pushing all the air out of her lungs while calculating she had 2.7 seconds until it reached them. Her head turned, and she ordered the Caeles Prism to open a wormhole *beneath* Galean and Raisan.

They, together with a mass of torn metal and, unfortunately, parts of Fremen's body, fell through it and landed in a heap on the floor of Serba Medical.

"Deshka, jump!" He seemed frozen in shock, so she grabbed his arm and shoved him over the remaining debris and into the wormhole.

The vacuum tugged insistently at her back as she followed him through.

33

Nedeni's office was a morass of screens. Two separate newscasts carried on in silent glee about the events of the last day, while written headlines scrolled down two more screens:

Commission formed to investigate all aspects of the Aterpe Project.

Thirty-six dead after multiple explosions rip through Inarska II.

Desbida: tragedy of hubris or the harbinger of our future?

Bisortu Materials CEO Bentl Kaimesh killed in factory accident.

Where did the Aterpe Project go wrong, and who is to blame?

President Lormain vows to uncover the truth about the desbida and the government cover-up.

Welcoming a desbida back into your odola: a primer.

Renowned scientist Ctaro Melar exposes barbaric experiments at the heart of the Aterpe Project.

Concord: who are the aliens, and what does their arrival mean for Belarria?

The last one was a bit of a surprise. But Galean imagined too many people on Inarska II had seen the Concord warship for the government to sweep it under the rug.

Nedeni looked up from his terminal and grabbed a glass of water. "How are you feeling, Galean?"

He held up his hands and flipped them around. Two bandages remained over the deepest cuts, and jagged welts crisscrossed his palms. His left calf was held securely together with surgical tape and a skin weave, and he was doing his best not to walk with a noticeable limp. "Not quite as good as new, but I'll be fine in a few days."

"And Raisan?"

"Alive, for now. If he recovers, he'll get a prosthetic leg...but we're not there yet." Worry gnawed at him over Raisan, while sorrow swirled in his soul over the loss of Fremen. Comrade, teammate, friend. But there was much to celebrate, too.

Only after arriving back at the Serba in rather dramatic fashion had he learned that their home had come within seconds of being destroyed. Everyone here had looked death in the face...and death had blinked. If he had lost Resa, he would be a ruined soul. But he had not, and despite the losses, happiness filled his heart at how the Arbasoak had turned a kind eye toward them.

He gestured to the screens. "We've long suspected Bentl Kaimesh was a leading member of the Errigime. Who's taken his place?"

"I can't say. A man with a deep voice and a faint Emankor accent stepped in to halt the military assault at the last second. He'll be the one with the power at the Errigime table now, so perhaps he will make himself known in time."

"He did us a tremendous favor."

"And there will be a price for it. But I concede his actions demonstrated an openness to seeing reason. He realized the old power structure could not continue, and so pivoted to position himself well for the new one which will take its place."

"You sound jaded, Nedeni. We *won*. We achieved our every goal."

"We did. And I am so proud of everyone. You get to go home, all of you. No more hiding."

"So do you."

Nedeni glanced around the office a touch wryly. "This is my home. My family is gone—my true family. My wife and son are long dead, as are my parents and aitona."

"I'm sorry."

"Don't be. I get to send my hartua odola, the Tarazi, out into the world to flourish."

He hadn't expected Nedeni to sound so...wistful, nor for victory to turn out to be so bittersweet for the man. Nedeni had lost everything, so the Tarazi became his life. Galean supposed it must be a little frightening to have to contemplate starting over yet again. "What will you do now?"

"Find an apartment in Ausatan, as the Serba will soon become a lonely, quiet place. Keep the President's tail to the fire; he's a coward, and despite his public proclamation, he will not 'uncover the truth' unless he is made to do so. Reach out to those who can influence the way this plays out and try to win their backing. This is a precarious time for our people, Galean. The public now knows the desbida are not monsters, but they remain unsure exactly what they *are*. Fear will not die easily, especially when some aspects of the desbida are worth fearing."

"That's not—"

Nedeni held up a hand. "No one wants their mind read by someone they have not chosen to embrace. The web of interconnections that have defined our society for millennia is about to experience a seismic shock. We need moral, honorable, empathetic people showing us how to maneuver through the maze that awaits us. I'm going to try to find those people and give them the support they require."

"And you will. You're a wonderful leader, Nedeni, and an excellent judge of character. However little I can be of help, you need only ask."

"Thank you. But you deserve to be free of this fight and find a measure of peace with Resa. So what about you? What will you do? Follow in Vasem's footsteps and become a diplomat? You already have the inside track with the one alien species we have encountered."

Galean chuckled lightly. He doubted Nedeni knew just how close he and Marlee had grown...or maybe he did. "And I will certainly use whatever meager powers of persuasion I have with Marlee to encourage Concord to be gentle with us. We have not, I fear, made a good first impression on the intergalactic community. But, no. I'm no diplomat. I'm not even a particularly inspiring leader. If I'm anything, it's a protector, so I'll keep doing that. As you pointed out, many will continue to fear the desbida, and they'll need defenders."

He held his hands out in front of him, considering them from a new perspective. "And maybe, in time, I'll get back to building things. It will be nice to use these for creating rather than killing."

Nedeni smiled. "You know, this gives me an idea. I'll acquire the apartment in Ausatan in the short term, but now that I won't be funding this black hole of an operation, I might find myself with some disposable coins. Give me a few months, and I suspect I'll be ready for a proper residence. I'd be honored if you would agree to design and build one for me."

Galean's skin flushed with pride at the notion. "The honor would be entirely mine, sir."

Nedeni came out from around the desk and approached him. Their tails met, and they brought their hands together, fingertips touching. "Hartua odola forever, aliatua."

"Forever as we will be, aliatua."

34

"**M**arlee? Why are you wearing the glamour?"

Marlee turned to see Galean standing in the doorway to her bedroom, gazing at her with a most complicated expression. She finished folding her shirt and set it on the bed beside her open bag. "Resamane said you were on your way up. She'll be back in a few minutes."

"Yes. You haven't answered my question. You don't have to disguise yourself here among us. Surely you know this by now."

"I do. I'm wearing it for you."

"I don't understand."

"Yes, I think you do." She stepped closer, taking his hand in one of hers as she brought the other up to curve along his neck. "I'm wearing it because I want to do this one more time before I go."

She leaned in and kissed him. His lips responded immediately; his body, too. His arm wrapped around her waist and drew her tight against him. She imprinted the coolness of his touch upon her soul, the rough yet silky feel of his skin. The fluid way his lips and hands moved with hers, like a waltz performed in time to a silent rhythm they shared.

Her heart broke a little as she withdrew from the kiss and his embrace. "Thank you." She let go of his hand, then reached around to the small of her back and deactivated the Shroud. "I'm not being fair to you, teasing you with this lie that I am like you. Forgive me."

He blinked twice in rapid succession. His sentsores jerked, while conflict raged in his eyes. "Marlee, I...."

"It's okay. I know." She took a step back and tried to banish the sadness from her expression.

His face contorted further in evident frustration. "I...I wish I could see you the way your people do. I've no doubt they marvel at your incredible beauty."

"Eh, middling attractiveness at best. But you don't need to. You see the truth of me, and this is what matters."

"That I do, prezia."

The rush of emotion at his use of the endearment left her dizzy. It was the greatest compliment he could ever give her.

She blinked away brimming tears and hid them behind a brilliant smile. "You have a lot of work to do here. You have to rebuild the very underpinnings of your society. Of your odolas. I bet you'll need to reform and rebuild some government institutions, too. I've lived through a wholesale upheaval of society, and it's not easy. People will be confused. Some will be frightened.

"But you and Resamane, and Deshka, and even Nedeni, asshole though he is, can show them the way. And you will. You're going to lead your people into a better future."

His lips pursed tight, as if he wanted to say something else...but after a beat he met her smile with a rather pensive one of his own. "When you put it in such a manner, it sounds like an easy assignment."

"It is, more or less. The Belascocians are moral, honorable people with hearts as big as an ocean. You all love so strongly and so selflessly, I've no doubt you will find your way through this tumultuous time and emerge stronger for it. And you know what waits on the other side? Friendship with my people. Once things settle down a little here, I want you and Resamane to come and visit me. I can show you around Concord HQ. And I can take you to see my home, too. I'll cook you some mediocre spaghetti."

"I don't know what spaghetti is, but I would love to find out. We both would. Thank you for giving me something to look forward to when matters get difficult in the coming days."

"And they probably will." She ventured a hand out to briefly touch his cheek once more. "But have faith. Faith in your people. Show them the path and how to walk it."

"I don't know if I'm the person to do so."

"You're a builder, a creator."

"Of structures."

She shrugged playfully. "It's not so different as you think."

"Perhaps. But I'm not worried, because Resamane can inspire the people. And I shall protect her while she does."

"I know you will."

His gaze lowered to her bag with some consternation. "Must you go so soon? We can have lunch with Deshka and the others, then…." He trailed off weakly.

"I really need to get home. I have…*a lot* of explaining to do. Some apologies to hand out. Need to try to keep my job despite breaking every Consulate rule imaginable."

"If they fire you, know you have a place here with us."

"Thank you." Her expression sobered. "Listen, after I say goodbye to Resamane, I'm just going to go. No reason to make a big fanfare of it. But I will see you again."

He brought one of her hands up between them and pressed it against his chest. "Yes, I believe you will."

Resamane embraced Marlee in the most human of ways—arms wrapped around her shoulders and waist, chin curled into her neck. The woman had picked up so many human mannerisms with a natural ease; Marlee supposed it was part and parcel of her empathic nature.

She kissed Resamane on the cheek before stepping back. "I'm going to miss you so much."

"But not the Serba so much, yes?"

"I mean..." she rolled her eyes "...I'll miss the people I've met, for certain. Some more than others. But I admit I won't mind getting a touch more sunshine and fresh air."

"And home cooking."

"Your cooking is delicious!"

"You are kind, Marlee. You are fierce and indomitable and loyal, and most of all, you are kind."

Her heart pitter-pattered in her chest. Resamane was such a rare and precious individual, and she was glad she had played a small role in giving the woman a brighter future. "I'm going to tell my boss and my mother you said so."

"And tell them as a desbida, I am an authority on the subject."

"I will." She chuckled lightly. "Are you excited about returning to the world?"

"I am...but I am also apprehensive. The Serba is like a nurturing womb. It is safe and caring and...known. But it is not the real world, and if I stay shut away here, I am not genuinely living. It is time to start living."

For all that had come before—all they had suffered and built and defended—this was the beginning of a whole new journey for the Tarazi. Part of her wanted to stay and help them navigate the dangers which lay ahead. But Galean would protect Resamane's body and her soul, and she would protect her brother's heart. They would be okay.

"I wish you the best. You're going to be amazing. Now, Galean and I already talked about the two of you coming to visit me, so I'll be in touch."

"I shall look forward to it. I can't wait to see the wonders of your world—all your worlds. Can I meet Cupcake?"

"Oh! Um, sure, we can do that. From a distance. He's not too great with strangers. Though, with your abilities, you might charm him straightaway."

"And ride him?"

She held up a hand. "Let's take it one step at a time. We'll start by feeding him some roasted chicken treats and go from there."

"Yes." Resamane smiled with her whole body, and Marlee turned off the damper to bask in the overwhelming sense of warmth, comfort and well-being radiating off the woman for one last moment. It was as a soothing balm that eased the dents and dings the world inflicted, and the desire to stay cocooned within it overcame her.

But she couldn't. "And now, it is time for me to go home."

A contemplative, far-away look came over Resamane's features. "For me as well. Oh, I can't believe I nearly forgot. I have a gift for you."

Resamane hurried into her bedroom and returned a second later with a small box. "Here. For you to remember us by."

Marlee took the box and opened the lid. Inside was a necklace of beaded indigo glass draped from a woven silver chain. The glass whorled in a familiar pattern of three interlocking circles with a starburst at their center. She lifted the necklace out of the box and draped it across her hand. "It's beautiful. I've seen this pattern on the wall over there, and Galean's facial marking of course, but I've never learned what it signifies."

"It is the symbol of the Ozeal odola. My mother gave this necklace to me when I turned ten years old, and now, I am giving it to you."

Her eyes widened. "What? Resamane, I can't accept a family heirloom."

"Yes, you can. I wish nothing more than for you to have it. See, Galean, Deshka and I had a conversation before you went on the mission to Inarska II, and we all three agreed without hesitation. You are hartua odola to us. The necklace signifies this bond between us, if you accept it."

"Accept it? Yes, I accept it! I don't know what to say—" She grabbed Resamane in a bear hug and sniffled into her neck. It might have been a bit too effusive of a human gesture, for the woman let out a muffled 'oof.'

"Sorry. But not sorry." She stepped away and wiped new tears off her cheek. Oh, her heart was full. "You will always be my har-tua odola as well. Thank you so much."

"No, Marlee, thank you. You have shown us that we can free ourselves, then helped us to do so. We owe you everything."

35

The neighborhood had grown since the last time Galean had been home—since the day he'd tried and failed to convince his odola of the truth about the desbida and the therapeutics camps. A new cul-de-sac of homes had been added to the third street, and everywhere the plants were more lush and colorful. Life had continued on here without him and Resa…and he was glad for it. Glad he'd been able to shelter his odola from the messy consequences of the war he'd spent the last six years fighting.

The house at the end of Lorat Street had gained a decorative fence, and a young tree sprouted tiny leaves to the left of the entrance. He stopped where the path broke off from the sidewalk and faced Resa, his tail brushing against hers. "Are you ready?"

"I am ready, brother." Her eamonal told him she spoke sincerely and without fear.

He tried to share in the lightness of her spirit, but memories of the last time he'd come here tainted his thoughts. "If things become…if this doesn't go the way we hope, we will turn around and leave, no hesitation. We will let the past remain where it lies and start our new life together."

"It's merely a visit. And I can withstand whatever follows, good or ill."

And it *was* merely a visit. A tentative dipping of a toe in the waters of reconciliation. In fact, tomorrow, he was going to look at a prospective place for him, Resa and Deshka to stay in a suburb of Ausatan. The possibility of them ever returning to live in Maistel with the odola seemed a fantastical notion. But they could start with a visit. If things went well, a second one would come in time. "I know. But they don't get to make you suffer."

"Nor you. And we will not speak of Vasem. They do not need to know how far their eldest had fallen. Let today be a day of joy, Galean, if they can open their hearts to it."

He nodded in affirmation. One day, all the ugly truths might spill forth, and he would pay whatever price was required. But for today, their aitona need grapple with only one such truth—that they had wrongly handed over their beloved child to the state to be tortured.

"So be it. No more waiting." Together, they strode up the pathway.

The front door opened when they were three meters away. Their mother stood in the doorway, eyes wide and sentsores trembling. Age had softened her features, but she still stood tall and straight. "Galean? Resamane?"

"Hello, Mother." His voice came out unacceptably hoarse.

"Mamma." Resa took a step forward, ahead of him, and let her eamonal flare out into the world, radiating love and hope and, most of all, forgiveness.

There was motion in the doorway behind their mother—then everyone was moving toward one another, as if drawn in by the universe's gravity, and everywhere he turned, arms enveloped them.

For the first time in two weeks, Marlee donned her own clothes. An elegant pantsuit befitting a diplomat, though she slipped into flats instead of heels. After the disaster that had been trying to flee for her life and fight off an assassin while wearing dress heels, she wasn't sure she'd ever wear them again.

Lastly, she fastened the Ozeal necklace around her neck. As she did, she could swear she felt the faintest tingle along her skin where it lay, accompanied by a sensation of...well-being. Like a memory of Resamane's presence.

She'd gone directly to her mother's house on her return; it seemed the proper thing to do. It wasn't the first time she'd come home after spending some forced time in harrowing circumstances, but her mother hugged her as viciously and shed as many tears as if it was. And she found she was okay with that. The Belascocians had taught her a lot about the value of family, and she made a vow to try to spend more time with her mother going forward. And with Caleb and Alex, if they ever returned from their own excursion into the void.

But now it was time to face the music.

She tested out a wormhole and discovered her HQ pass was still active. It certainly made the trip a lot faster. She almost grabbed the Belascocian teacup she'd brought back for her aunt, but decided it would keep until after the reckoning.

Miriam and Dean Veshnael were both expecting her in Miriam's office, so she stepped into the cool, smooth, brightly lit space of the Command atrium and breathed in.

"Ms. Marano, welcome. I'll let the commandant know you're here."

She waved to the sergeant at the reception desk. "Thank you, Larissa."

"And she will see you now."

"Great." She squared her shoulders and prepared herself for the dressing-down of her life, then marched into the office.

Miriam rushed around her desk and greeted Marlee with a hug—a rarity even outside of working hours. "It is so good to have you back with us."

So much hugging! It was almost as if she'd been missed. "It's good to be back."

Her aunt held her at arm's length, critical gaze inspecting every centimeter. Her eyes lingered for a beat on the necklace, but she didn't inquire about it. "David sends his enthusiastic regards, and is insisting on a gelato date sometime in the next thirty-six hours."

"That sounds delicious. The Belascocians did not have anything approaching gelato."

Apparently satisfied Marlee had not lost any limbs or grown any new ones, Miriam released her grip and took a step back to rest lightly on the edge of her desk. "David will be horrified to learn this."

Her great-uncle adored sweets even more than she did, and she suddenly longed to see him. But first, music, consequences and so on. "Listen, I heard what you did, and I am so sorry you ended up having to get involved."

"Did you not consider that I was involved from the first minute we learned of your disappearance?"

"Right. Of course you were. I imagine a lot of things transpired here while I was gone."

Miriam smiled, a hint of amusement on her lips. "A few, yes."

"Well, know you saved thousands of lives with your masterful intervention. Thank you."

"I'm glad to hear it."

"Also, please don't be cross with Morgan for helping us. I used my most wily charms on her to get her to agree. And we desperately needed the help."

"Major Lekkas is a high-ranking AEGIS officer who is expected to be able to withstand anyone's wily charms, even yours." Miriam shook her head ruefully. "However, due to the unique circumstances, and the fact she did not fire on any Belascocian assets, I have decided not to mention her lapse in judgment to Fleet Admiral Jenner."

Marlee exhaled in relief. If she'd gotten Morgan court-martialed, the woman would never have lunch with her. "I appreciate it."

"I hope Major Lekkas does as well." Her gaze flitted past Marlee, and her demeanor subtly shifted from 'aunt' to 'commandant.' "Dean Veshnael, thank you for joining us."

Marlee schooled her expression, pivoted and greeted her boss with a full Novoloume bow. "Sir."

He acknowledged her with a graceful tilt of his head in greeting. "It is pleasing to find you again with us, Ambassador."

Her hopes lifted a bit, as him addressing her by her title just might mean she wasn't getting fired today. "Thank you, sir. I'd like to begin by apologizing for the trouble I caused—"

Miriam held up a hand to cut her off, then gestured to the small table by her viewport. "Come. Sit. Instead of leaping straight to apologies, why don't you begin at the beginning?"

"Oh. Absolutely." They all sat, and Marlee paused for half a second to drink in the view outside, where thousands of ships docked and embarked from the massive hub-and-spoke pinwheels that reached for a shining blue-white star in the distance. It was damn good to be home.

Then she clasped her hands atop the table and took a deep breath. "It all began with a murder. A murder that, though I didn't know it at the time, was not an act born of hate, but rather of love."

THE THIEF
A Cosmic Shores Novel
COMING IN 2024

The Hesgyr are thieves. "Scavengers," to hear their victims tell it; "repurposers" by their own reckoning.

As Chief of Intelligence for Non-Anaden Affairs, Eren Savitas' job is to protect the Advocacy from all manner of alien threats: sabotage, assassination, insurgency and, way down the list, theft. So when he spots a Hesgyr running off with valuable technology, he follows the alien home—and discovers a civilization unlike any he's ever encountered.

Yes, the Hesgyr are thieves. But they are also being hunted. Systematically exterminated by an enemy they can't see, touch or find. As Eren finds himself drawn ever deeper into the mystery of the attacks, he uncovers a complex web of loyalties and betrayals—and beneath it all, a secret that may hold the key to the survival of more than one civilization.

PREORDER A SIGNED COPY TODAY AT:
GSJENNSEN.COM/THE-THIEF

***

Twenty years ago, before Concord and the larger universe it revealed, humanity teetered on the brink of war with itself even as an unimaginable threat loomed in the void. Experience the epic, galaxy-spanning adventure from the beginning:

STARSHINE
AURORA RISING BOOK ONE

GSJENNSEN.COM/STARSHINE

READ ON FOR AN EXCERPT

SENECA
CAVARE, CAPITAL OF THE SENECAN FEDERATION

The kinetic blade slid into the man's throat like a knife through butter. Caleb held him securely from behind as the blood began to flow and the man jerked and spasmed.

He generally preferred clean, painless deaths. But he wanted to watch this man die, and die slowly.

When the man had lost all motor function, Caleb dumped him onto the desk and flipped him over. Eyes wide with fear, confusion and outrage met his. The man's lips contorted in a caricature of speech, though no words came out.

He had a good idea of the intended utterance. Why. It was a question easily answered. Vengeance.

"Justice."

As the pool of blood spread across the desk and formed waterfalls to the floor below, the eyes belonging to the leader of the Humans Against Artificials terrorist organization glazed over. The last spark of life within them dimmed, then went out.

One down.

Caleb Marano stepped out of the spaceport into the cyan-tinged glow of a late afternoon sun reflecting off the polished marble tiles of the plaza. The chill breeze caressing his skin felt like a welcome home. Cavare was always cool and often cold; Krysk had been a veritable oven by comparison.

He descended the first set of stairs and angled toward the corner to get clear of the bustling thoroughfare, then relaxed beside the ledge to wait for his companions.

Isabela exited the spaceport a moment later. She held a bag in one arm and a fidgeting bundle of arms, legs and long, dark curls in the other. She looked disturbingly 'momish' as she struggled to brush out Marlee's tangled hair—but he could remember when she had *been* that little girl with long, dark curls…and it wasn't so long ago.

With a groan she gave up the futile endeavor and allowed her daughter to escape her grasp and make a beeline for Caleb.

He crouched to meet Marlee at eye level. She plowed into him with almost enough force to knock him over backwards. He would've laughed but for the forlorn look in her pale turquoise eyes.

"Do you have to go away now, Uncle Caleb?"

He tousled her curls into further disarray. "Yeah, I'm afraid I have to go back to work. But it sure was great spending my vacation with you. I learned a *lot*."

She wore her best serious face as she nodded sagely. "You had a lot to learn."

He grinned and leaned in to whisper to his co-conspirator. "You remember what all we talked about, right?"

Her eyes were wide and honest. "Uh-huh."

"Good. Want one more ride before I go?"

Her head bobbed up and down with gusto, instantly that of a carefree child again.

"Okay." He scooped her up in his arms and stood, made certain he had a solid grasp of her tiny waist, and began to spin around with accelerating speed. Her arms and legs dangled free to swing through the air while she cackled in delight.

After another few spins he slowed—he had learned her limits during the last few weeks—letting her limbs fall against him before he came to a stop. He gave her a final squeeze and gently set her to the ground as her mother reached them.

Isabela wore a half-amused, half-exhausted expression as Marlee started running in dizzy circles around her legs. "Sorry about the hold up. They let us back on the transport and we found Mr. Freckles under the seat." She patted her bag in confirmation of the stuffed animal's now secure location. "Are you sure you don't want to have a quick dinner with us?"

He responded with a dubious smirk. "You can be polite if you like, but the truth is you are sick to death of me and counting the minutes until you are at last rid of me."

"Well, *yes*. But I never know when I'll get to see you again...." The twinkle faded from her eyes, replaced by something darker and heavier.

She knew he didn't work for a shuttle manufacturing company, and he knew that she knew. But they never, *ever*, talked about it. Partly for her safety and his, but partly because he preferred to continue being in her mind the strong, stalwart older brother with the easygoing demeanor and wicked sense of humor, without introducing any moral grayness to the relationship dynamic.

Because he never wanted her to look at him with caution, disillusionment...or worst of all, fear.

He merely nodded in response. "I'll come visit again soon. Promise."

She reached down to pause the cyclone at her legs. "I'll hold you to it. I'm going to take Marlee to see Mom, then we'll head back home."

He leaned over the struggling cyclone to embrace her. "Thank you for the extended hospitality. I'm glad I was able to spend so much time with you."

"Anytime, I mean it," she whispered in his ear. "Stay safe."

He kept his shrug mild as he stepped away. "Of course." Not likely.

Two insistent and tearful hugs from Marlee later, they parted ways. He watched them disappear into the throng of travelers, then headed in the direction of the parking complex.

AR

Caleb stepped in the adjoining lavatory and washed the blood off his hands and forearms. Then he returned to the office, reached under the corner of the desk and triggered the 'Alert' panic signal—the one he had never allowed the dead man to reach. There was a surveillance cam hidden in the ceiling, and he looked up at it and smiled. He had a number of smiles in his repertoire; this was not one of the more pleasant ones.

The commotion began as he exited the building. He quickened his stride to his bike, jumped on and fired the engine. Three men bolted out the door, two Daemons and a TSG swinging in his direction.

It wouldn't do to get shot. A flick of his thumb and the bike burst out of the parking slot. He laid it down as laser fire sliced barely a meter overhead, his leg hovering centimeters above the ground while he slid around the corner and onto the cross-street.

He heard them giving chase almost immediately. So late in the night the street and air traffic was sparse, which was one reason he had begun the op when he did. It reduced the chances of his pursuers taking out innocent bystanders—and gave them a clearer line of sight to him. He wanted to make certain they knew where he was going before he left them behind.

Their surface vehicles didn't stand a chance of matching his speed and it would look suspicious if he slowed...but as anticipated, they had grabbed a skycar. He kept an eye on it via the rearcam, making sure it succeeded in following him through two major direction shifts.

Satisfied, he kicked the bike into its actual highest gear and accelerated right then left, fishtailing around two street corners in rapid succession. He activated the concealment shield. It didn't render him or the bike invisible, but it did make them blend into the surroundings and virtually impossible to track from the air at night.

Then he sped toward the Bahia Mar spaceport. After all, he did need to get there ahead of them.

⟋R

Tiny flecks of light sparkled in the night-darkened waters of the Fuori River as Caleb pulled in the small surface lot. It was nearly empty, as most people took the levtrams to the entertainment district and had no need of parking.

Once the engine had purred into silence he swung a leg off the bike and glanced up. A smile ghosted across his face at the dozens of meteors streaking against the silhouette of the giant moon which dominated Seneca's sky.

He noted the time. He had a few minutes to enjoy a little stargazing, though the conditions were far from ideal here in the heart of downtown. An exanet query confirmed the meteor shower continued for eleven days. Maybe he'd have a chance to get up to the mountains before it ended.

Committed to this plan, he secured the bike in its slot. A last glance at the sky and he crossed the street and took the wide steps to the riverwalk park.

The atmosphere on the broad promenade hovered at the optimal balance between deserted and overrun by masses of people. As it was a weekend night the balance wouldn't hold for long, but for the moment it pulsed with energy while still allowing plenty of room to move about and claim your own personal space. He noted with interest the outdoor bar to the right, complete with live synth band and raised danced platform. *Not yet. Business first.*

He slipped among the milling patrons until he reached a section of railing at the edge of the promenade to the southeast of the bar. Here the crowd had thinned to a few meandering couples and the music thrummed softly in the background.

The light from the skyscrapers now drowned out the light from the meteors, but he couldn't argue with the view.

A thoroughly modern city to the core, humans having initially set foot on its soil less than a century ago, Cavare glittered and shone like a sculpture newly unveiled. The reflected halo of the moon shimmered in the tranquil water as the river rippled along the wall beneath him, winding itself through the heart of the city on its way to Lake Fuori. Far to his left he could see the gleam of the first arch which marked the dramatic entrance to the lake and the luxuries it held.

It was an inspiring yet comforting view, and one he had spent close to forty years watching develop, mature and grow increasingly more lustrous. He contented himself with enjoying it while he waited for his appointment to arrive.

The message had come in the middle of dinner at his favorite Chinasian restaurant. He hadn't even had the chance to go home yet; the entirety of the belongings he had traveled with were stowed in the rear compartment of his bike. But in truth there wasn't much of consequence waiting for him at the apartment, for it was home in only the most technical sense of the word.

Never have anything you can't walk away from. A gem of advice imparted by a friend and mentor early on in his career, and something he had found remarkably easy to adopt.

ℛ

He stowed the bike in a nearby stall he had rented in yet another assumed name and hurried to Bay F-18. He made a brief pass through the ship to make sure the contact points on the charges were solid, then sat in the pilot's chair, kicked his feet up on the dash and crossed his hands behind his head to wait.

They were hackers as much as terrorists. It wouldn't take them long to break the encryption to the bay. The encryption on the ship's airlock was stronger—for they would expect it to be—but not so difficult they couldn't crack it.

Planting enough charges at the headquarters to take it out would have involved significant risk of discovery and ultimate failure. But here, he controlled every step and every action.

The hangar bay door burst open. Three...six...eight initially. He sincerely hoped more showed up before they got into the ship.

His wish was granted when three minutes later seven additional members of the group rushed in. The surface pursuit, he imagined. The initial arrivals were still hacking the ship lock. He gave them another two minutes.

With a last gaze around he pulled his feet off the dash and stood. He headed through the primary compartment and below to the mid-

level, opened the hatch to the engineering well, and positioned himself in the shadowy corner near the stairs.

They wouldn't all come in at once, lest they end up shooting each other in the confusion. Three, maybe four to start, plus two to guard the airlock. They would fan out to run him to ground quickly.

The first man descended the stairs. As his left foot hit the deck Caleb grabbed him from behind and with a fierce wrench snapped his neck. He made a point to throw the body against the stairwell so the loud clang echoed throughout the ship.

Two down.

ℛ

Caleb looked over his shoulder to see Michael Volosk striding down the steps toward him. Right on time. Everything about the man's outward demeanor projected an image of consummate professionalism, from the simple but perfectly tailored suit to the close-cropped hair to the purposeful stride.

He extended his hand in greeting as the Director of Special Operations for the Senecan Federation Division of Intelligence approached. A mouthful worthy of the highest conceit of government; but to everyone who worked there, it was simply "Division."

Volosk grasped his hand in a firm shake and took up a position along the rail beside him. "Thanks for agreeing to meet me here. I have a syncrosse rec league game down the street in twenty minutes, and if I miss another game they'll kick me off the team." He wore a slight grimace intended to hint at the many responsibilities a high-level covert intelligence official was required to juggle...then presumably realized the impression it actually conveyed, because he shifted to a shrug. "It's the only opportunity I have to blow off steam."

Caleb smiled with studied, casual charm. "It's not a problem. I just got in anyway. And if the surroundings happen to discourage prying eyes, well, I appreciate the value of discretion."

Volosk didn't bother to deny the additional reason for the choice of meeting location. "It wouldn't hurt if your coworkers didn't know you were back on the clock yet—and that's one reason I chose you. Your reputation is impressive."

He chuckled lightly and ran a hand through disheveled hair made wild by the wind. "Perhaps I'm not discrete enough, then."

"Rest assured, it's on a need-to-know basis. I realize we haven't had many opportunities to work together yet, but Samuel always spoke of you in the highest terms."

He schooled his expression to mask the emotions the statement provoked. "I'm humbled, sir. He was a good man."

"He was." Volosk's shoulders straightened with his posture—a signal he was moving right on to business, as though it didn't *matter* how good a man Samuel had been. "What do you know about the Metis Nebula?"

Caleb's brow creased in surprise. Whatever he had been expecting, this wasn't it. *Okay. Sure.*

"Well, mostly that we don't know much about it. It's outside Federation space, but we've tried to investigate it a few times—purely scientific research of course. We know there's a pulsar at the center of it, but scans return a fuzzy mess across the spectrum. Probes sent in find nothing but ionized gases and space dust. Scientists have written it off as unworthy of further study. Why?"

"You're very well informed, Agent Marano. Do a lot of scientific reading in your spare time?"

"Something like that."

"I'm sure. The information I'm sending you is Level IV Classified. Fewer than a dozen people inside and out of the government are aware of it."

He scanned the data file. In the background the synth band shifted to a slow, rhythmic number threaded by a deep, throbbing bass line. "That's…odd."

"Quite. The Astrophysics Institute sent in a state of the art, prototype deep space probe—the most sensitive one ever built, we believe. Honestly, it was solely for testing purposes. The researchers thought Metis' flat profile offered a favorable arena to run the probe through its paces. Instead it picked up what you see there.

"Obviously we need to get a handle on what this is. It came to my desk because it may represent a hostile threat. We've put a hold on any scientific expeditions until we find out the nature of the anomaly. If it *is* hostile, the sooner we know the better we can prepare. If on the other hand it's an opportunity—perhaps a new type of exploitable energy resource—we want to bring it under our purview before the Alliance or any of the independent corporate interests learn of it."

Caleb frowned at his companion. "I understand. But to be frank, my missions are usually a bit more...physical in nature? More direct at least, and typically involving a tangible target."

"I'm aware of that. But your experience makes you one of the few people in Division both qualified to investigate this matter and carrying a security clearance high enough to allow you to do so."

It wasn't an inaccurate statement. And if he were honest with himself, it *would* probably be best if he went a little while without getting more blood on his hands.

ᴙ

He slid open the hidden compartment in the wall and climbed into the narrow passage, pushed the access closed using his foot and crawled along the sloped tunnel. When he got to the end he activated his personal concealment shield—which did very nearly make him invisible—and with a deft twist released the small hatch.

He rolled as he hit the ground to mask the sound. The lighting in the bay was purposefully dim, and he landed deep in the shadow of the hull.

As expected, there was a ring of men guarding the exterior of the ship. He waited for the closest man to turn his back, then slipped out and moved to the corner of the bay to settle behind the storage crates he had arranged to have delivered earlier in the day.

He was rewarded by the arrival at that moment of an additional six—no, seven—pursuers. A significant majority of the active members were now inside the hangar bay. Good enough.

They moved to join their brethren encircling the ship—and he sent the signal.

The walls roiled and bucked from the force of the explosion. White-hot heat blasted through his shield. The shockwave sent him to his knees even as the floor shuddered beneath him. Pieces of shrapnel speared into the wall above him and to his right. A large section of the hull shot out the open side of the bay and crashed to the street below.

One glance at the utter wreckage of his former ship confirmed they were all dead. He climbed to his feet and crossed to the door, dodging the flaming debris and burnt, dismembered limbs. The emergency responders could be heard approaching seconds after he disappeared down the corridor.

He didn't de-cloak until he reached the bike. He calmly fired it up, cruised out of the stall, and accelerated toward the exit.

Mission fucking accomplished.

◆

Caleb nodded in acceptance. "I'll need a new ship. My last one was, um, blown up."

"My understanding is that's because you blew it up." The expression on the Director's face resembled mild sardonic amusement.

He bit his lower lip in feigned chagrin, revealing what he judged to be the appropriate touch of humility. "Technically speaking."

Volosk sent another data file his way. "Regardless, it's been taken care of. Here's the file number and all the standard information, including the hangar bay of your new ship."

He ignored the mild barb and examined this data with greater scrutiny, but it appeared everything had in fact been taken care of. "Got it. This all looks fine."

"Good...there's one more thing. It's no secret with Samuel gone there's a leadership vacuum in the strategic arm of Special

Operations. He believed you were quite capable of taking on a larger role. Based on your record—a few isolated excesses aside—and what I know of you, I'm inclined to agree. So while you're out there in the void, I'd encourage you to give some thought to what you truly want from this job. We can talk further when you return."

Caleb made sure his expression displayed only genuine appreciation, carefully hiding any ambivalence or disquiet. "Thank you for the vote of confidence, sir. I'll do that."

"Glad to hear it. Now if you'll excuse me, I have to go get my ass kicked by ten other men and a cocky, VI-enhanced metal ball, after which I get to go back to the office and review the Trade Summit file for the seventeenth time this week."

He grimaced in sympathy. It was impossible to escape the growing media frenzy surrounding the conference, even with it over a week away.

Twenty-two years had passed since the end of the Crux War; it had been over and done with before he was old enough to fight. The cessation of hostilities after three years was officially called an 'armistice,' but Seneca and fourteen allied worlds had—by the only measure which mattered—won. They had their independence from the mighty Earth Alliance.

Now some politician somewhere had decided it was finally time for them to start playing nice with one another. He wished them luck, but.... "If it's all the same, I'd just as soon not be assigned to that one, sir. It's going to be a clusterfain of epic proportions."

Volosk exhaled with a weariness Caleb suspected was more real than contrived. "Don't worry, you're off the hook—wouldn't want to endanger your work by putting your face in front of so many dignitaries. *I*, however, won't get a decent night's sleep until the damn thing's finished."

Caleb sighed in commiseration, playing along with the superficial bonding moment. It seemed the higher-ups had decided he was worthy of being nurtured, at least enough to make certain he stayed in the fold. Bureaucrats. They had no clue how to manage people; if they did, they would realize he was the last person who needed *managing*.

"Well, I'm sorry I can't help you there, sir. But I will head out on this mission once I've pulled together what I need. It should be a few days at most."

Volosk nodded, transitioning smoothly to the closing portion of the meeting. "Please report in as soon as you discover anything relevant. We need to understand what we're dealing with, and quickly."

He responded with a practiced smile, one designed to convey reassurance and comfort. "Not to worry, I'll take care of it. It's what I do." He decided it was best to leave *when I'm not blowing up three million credit ships and two dozen terrorists with them* unsaid.

After all, he fully intended to *try* to return this ship in one piece.

After Volosk had departed, Caleb remained by the river for a while. His outward demeanor was relaxed, save for the rapid tap of fingertips on the railing.

He had been on leave ever since the post-op debriefs for the previous assignment had wrapped up. Whether the vacation had been a reward or a punishment he wasn't entirely sure, despite Volosk's vague hint at a promotion. Nor did he particularly care. He had accomplished what he had set out to do, justice had been served—albeit with a spicy dash of vengeance—and the bad guys were all dead. But it appeared it was time to get back to work.

The serenity of the cool night breeze and river-cleansed air juxtaposed upon the pulsing thrum of the music and swelling buzz of the crowd made for an appropriate backdrop. Time to retune himself.

He had enjoyed spending time with Isabela and her family, especially getting to play the bad uncle and fill Marlee's head with rebellious and unruly ideas sure to drive her mother crazy for months. The little girl had spunk; it was his duty to encourage it.

It had been a welcome respite. But it wasn't his life.

He pushed off the railing and strolled down the promenade to the bar area. The throbbing of the bass vibrated pleasantly on his skin as he neared. He ordered a local ale and found a small standing table which had been abandoned in favor of the dance floor. He rested his elbows on it, sipped his beer and surveyed the crowd.

It was amusing, and occasionally heartbreaking, to see how people doggedly fumbled their way through encounters. All the cybernetics in the world couldn't replace real, human connection, which was likely why physical sex was still the most popular pastime in the galaxy, despite the easy availability of objectively better-than-real *passione illusoire*. Humans were social animals, and craved—

"What are you drinking?"

He glanced at the woman who had sidled up next to him. Long, razor-straight white-blond hair framed a face sculpted to perfection beyond what genetic engineering alone could achieve. A white iridescent slip minimally covered deep golden skin. Silver glyphs wound along both arms and up the sides of her neck to disappear beneath the hairline.

He smiled coolly. "I'm fine, thanks."

She dropped a hand on the table and posed herself against it. "Yes, you are. Would you like to dance?"

He suppressed a laugh at the heavy-handed come-on. "Thank you, but..." a corner of his mouth curled up "...you're not really my type."

Her eyes shone with polished confidence. She believed she was in control. How *cute*.

"I can be any type you want me to be." The glyphs glowed briefly as her hair morphed to black, her makeup softened and her skin tone paled.

So that's what the glyphs were for. A waste of credits born of a desperate need to be wanted. He gave the woman a shrug and shook his head. "No thanks."

She scowled in frustration; it marred the perfect features into ugliness. "Why not? What the hell is your type?"

He took a last sip of his beer and dropped the empty bottle on the table. "Real."

He walked away without looking back.

STARSHINE
AURORA RISING BOOK ONE

AVAILABLE IN EBOOK, PRINT AND AUDIOBOOK AT
GSJENNSEN.COM/STARSHINE

SUBSCRIBE TO G. S. JENNSEN'S NEWSLETTER:

Get the STARSHINE, VERTIGO *and* SHORT STORIES OF AURORA RHAPSODY *ebooks for free, be the first to hear about new book announcements and more*

GSJENNSEN.COM/SUBSCRIBE

Author's Note

I published my first novel, *Starshine*, in 2014. In the back of the book I put a short note asking readers to consider leaving a review or talking about the book with their friends. Watching my readers do that and so much more has been the most rewarding and humbling experience in my life.

So if you loved **MEDUSA FALLING**, tell someone. Leave a review, share your thoughts on social media, annoy your coworkers in the break room by talking about your favorite characters. Reviews are the backbone of a book's success, but there is no single act that will sell a book better than word-of-mouth.

My part of this deal is to write a book worth talking about—your part of the deal is to do the talking. If you keep doing your bit, I get to write a lot more books for you.

Lastly, I want to hear from my readers. If you loved the book—or if you didn't—let me know. The beauty of independent publishing is its simplicity: there's the writer and the readers. Without any overhead, I can find out what I'm doing right and wrong directly from you, which is invaluable in making the next book better than this one. And the one after that. And the twenty after that.

Website: gsjennsen.com
Wiki: gsj.space/wiki

Email: gs@gsjennsen.com
Twitter: @GSJennsen
Facebook: gsjennsen.author

Goodreads: G.S. Jennsen
Pinterest: gsjennsen
Instagram: gsjennsen

Find my books at a variety of retailers:
gsjennsen.com/retailers

AMARANTHE UNIVERSE

AURORA RHAPSODY

AURORA RISING
STARSHINE
VERTIGO
TRANSCENDENCE

AURORA RENEGADES
SIDESPACE
DISSONANCE
ABYSM

AURORA RESONANT
RELATIVITY
RUBICON
REQUIEM

ASTERION NOIR

EXIN EX MACHINA

OF A DARKER VOID

THE STARS LIKE GODS

RIVEN WORLDS
CONTINUUM
INVERSION
ECHO RIFT
ALL OUR TOMORROWS
CHAOTICA
DUALITY

COSMIC SHORES
MEDUSA FALLING
THE THIEF (2024)

SHORT STORIES

Restless, Vol. I • *Restless, Vol. II* • *Apogee* • *Solatium* • *Venatoris*
Re/Genesis • *Meridian* • *Fractals* • *Chrysalis* • *Starlight Express*

Learn more at gsjennsen.com/books or visit the
Amaranthe Wiki: gsj.space/wiki

Acknowledgements

Many thanks to my beta readers, editors and artists, who made everything about this book better, and to my family, who continue to put up with an egregious level of obsessive focus on my part for months at a time.

I also want to add a personal note of thanks to everyone who has read my books, left a review at a retailer, Goodreads or other sites, sent me a personal email expressing how the books have impacted you, or posted on social media to share how much you enjoyed them. You make this all worthwhile, every day.

About the Author

G. S. JENNSEN lives in Montana with her husband and two dogs. She has become an internationally bestselling author since her first novel, *Starshine*, was published in 2014. She has chosen to continue writing under an independent publishing model to ensure the integrity of her stories and her ability to execute on the vision she has for their telling.

While she has been a lawyer, a software engineer and an editor, she's found the life of a full-time author preferable by several orders of magnitude. When she isn't writing, she's gaming or working out or getting lost in the mountains that loom large outside the windows in her home. Or she's dealing with a flooded basement, or standing in a line at Walmart reading the tabloid headlines and wondering who all of those people are. Or sitting on her back porch with a glass of wine, looking up at the stars, trying to figure out what could be up there.

Printed in Great Britain
by Amazon